"A captivating look at the intriguing figures
in King Arthur's golden realm."

Kirkus

"A layered, engaging retelling,
sure to please fans of the Arthurian tales."

Publishers Weekly

"Readers feel as though they could slip from the
mundane to the fantastical at any moment…"

Library Journal

"Barron's take will leave readers with
entirely new insights into Arthurian legend."

Booklist

"A brilliant reimagining of the Arthurian canon,
Queen of None balances pulse-pounding action
with Byzantine intrigue."

S. A. Cosby

"A tale of love, magic, triumph,
and heartbreak, all set against a rich and
beautifully-described background."

A. C. Wise

"A unique and amazingly vivid
perspective on Arthuriana."

Nerds of a Feather, Flock Together

QUEEN
OF FURY

ALSO BY NATANIA BARRON

The Godlings Saga
Pilgrim of the Sky
Gods of Londinium

These Marvelous Beasts
Frost & Filigree
Masks & Malevolence
Time & Temper

Rock Revival

QUEEN
OF FURY

NATANIA BARRON

SOLARIS

First published 2024 by Solaris
an imprint of Rebellion Publishing Ltd,
Riverside House, Osney Mead,
Oxford, OX2 0ES, UK

www.solarisbooks.com

ISBN: 978-1-83786-063-0

10 9 8 7 6 5 4 3 2 1

A CIP catalogue record for this book is available from
the British Library.

Designed & typeset by Rebellion Publishing

Printed in Denmark

For Michael, my carioz.
To E.J., who believed.

"I do understand that you can look into someone's eyes," I heard myself saying, "and suddenly know that life will be impossible without them. Know that their voice can make your heart miss a beat and that their company is all your happiness can ever desire and that their absence will leave your soul alone, bereft and lost."

Bernard Cornwell, *The Winter King*

And these are love's records; a vow and a dream,
And the sweet shadow passes away from life's stream:
Too late we awake to regret—but what tears
Can bring back the waste to our hearts and our years?

Leticia Elizabeth Landon,
"A Legend of Tintagel Castle" (1833)

But do as ye list now, my lady gaye.
The choise I put in your fist.
Even as ye woll, I put it in your hand,
Lose me when ye list, for I am bond.
I put the choise in you.

"The Wedding of Sir Gawain
and Dame Ragnell" (c. 1450)

Gawain bent low for courtesie,
    And thanked her for her grace;
He laid his hand upon her knee
    And looked into her face,
And wondered if he did not see
    The dragon in her place.

Bernard George Augustus Simcox,
"Gawain and the Lady of Avalon" (1869)

CHAPTER ONE

HWYFAR

"HARLOT! MENACE! DISGRACE! You bring the doom of Avillion!"

King Leodegraunce, my father, roared, then spat at me, flecks of mucus landing on my face and neck, as he shrieked each and every curse in my direction.

"Father, it's time for your draught." I kept my voice calm, trying again, attempting to approach the bed as I felt spittle slip down the front of my shift.

My father had been a proud, brawny man when I'd left for Carelon nearly a decade before. As Avillion's king, the task of raising my sisters and me had fallen to him after our mother's bitter departure to Lyonesse, when I was scarcely five years old. Though I would never call him a doting father, he'd been a good king and a strong man, in mind and body.

This was not the man I knew.

This King Leodegraunce was a wraith, tendons along his body straining against the leather straps keeping him tied to the very bed in which I was born, wiry muscles pulled too taut over long bones. His eyes burned with hatred, fathomless black marbles in his pale face, his uneven teeth bared behind chapped, flaking lips.

How do you mourn someone who is not yet dead? My eyes burned with tears, throat thick as I watched him struggle uselessly.

I had only been in Avillion a scant few weeks, and each time I visited him, these interactions worsened, taking a little more of my own strength and resolve. Neither the Skourr Council nor the Knights of the Body thought it prudent to alert anyone outside the Isle, even King Arthur, to the state of our king. Avillion was yet a free kingdom, and at peace for a thousand years; we could not display such weakness.

He had nearly killed one of the Skourr priestesses when she had tried to give him his food just a few days before. King Leodegraunce suffered no small sickness, and every day I lost more hope that I would ever speak with him again without fearing for my own life.

"Princess Hwyfar, we must speak," said Kian, our *goursez*, my father's oldest friend and chief advisor. The old bard was my childhood confidant and Gweyn's favorite person in all of Withiel. "This is just too painful to bear, and he—"

"Vile whore!" King Leodgraunce's threats went on. "Foul temptress!"

I watched my father struggle in vain as I grasped the wooden bedframe, my own breath uneven, chest constricting. From Kian's briefings, it seemed the king had been deteriorating for some time, but his descent the last two months before my arrival was precipitous. To say nothing of the blighted apple orchards and the plagues among the livestock; in ancient times, they said the land suffered when the king suffered, and I saw it now with my own eyes. I may not have had the power of the Isle in my blood any longer, but I knew magic when I saw it.

The once great King Leodegraunce let out a high, mad scream that shook the rafters of his royal bedroom, body sinking into elegantly embroidered green silks and thick golden velvets now stinking of piss and feces, while hollow-eyed servants watched in horror.

Then: he calmed. The lines in his face smoothed, his lips slipped down over his teeth, his eyes closed.

His voice came in a whisper now. "The brooms. The brooms. It's nestled amidst the brooms!" His favorite refrain.

Just as his fit fled, my own emotions spilled over. I could

weather the storm, but the moment he stilled I lost my resolve. Years, I'd lived behind a mask of composure, ribaldry, and indulgence. I was infamous, unrivaled, a woman of reputation—and, I thought, freedom.

Yet now, here, among the stones of Avillion, I was run ragged and raw, the memories of my childhood—raised among the Skourr priestesses—rising like a plague of locusts from the depths of the earth.

I had no intention of finding out what Kian wanted to discuss. It was time to hide, to lick my wounds and gather what strength I had left.

I was once betrothed to King Arthur Pendragon.

Upon my arrival in Carelon, however, Arthur took one glance at my younger sister Gweynevere, who'd attended me on the journey, and decided, as powerful men often do, that he desired her above all else. Above me. And as Arthur takes what he wants without question, Gweyn went with him, weeping and shaking. She was younger than I was, only fourteen. She did not have a choice, and yet she devoted herself to him. For Avillion. For our family. For the stability of the realm.

In recompense, Arthur built me a grand apartment and dominion over a tiny kingdom of pleasure. I spent my days entertaining minstrels, troubadours, and errant knights, taking every lover I wished, and—when I emerged from whatever drinks and powders I'd been consuming—occasionally attending royal events. To the world, no doubt, I seemed a most enviable libertine, indulging in decadent food and expensive drinks and bedding renowned men and women at court; but it was a trap. I could not leave, not while Gweyn was queen. And even as those pleasures began to pall on me, ceasing to be a comfort, I lingered in those golden halls, chasing a feeling I could never quite reach.

Gweyn's death opened a chasm in me, cracked me open, changed me. I left so many words unsaid between us and was unsupportive of her new faith. I called her a coward and toyed with her servants to get information about her. In the end, I did not deserve her as a sister any more than Arthur deserved her as a wife.

Bur Arthur, not satisfied with just one of my sisters, then married my middle sister, Mawra. Now she is Queen of all Braetan, while I attend to my raving father, the King of Avillion, and this ancient land slips away beneath my grasp. I have never wanted to rule—I gave up any hope of queendom when Arthur's gaze slid off my face and beheld Gweyn. I came to Avillion for her, to help our father, because it was the right thing to do. It was what Gweyn did. But I vastly miscalculated my own abilities. I was no nurturer, no patient attendant. I resented every moment I walked the craggy passageways of the keep.

The keep is called Withiel. Once a temple city atop the long cliffs on a sizable cove, it is now little more than a charming ruin inhabited by priestesses, apple orchards encroaching on the streets, rotting fruit clogging the drains in the late fall.

I still remembered every corridor, secret passage, strange alleyway, and hidden corner in Withiel from my childhood explorations, but Kian found me anyway, drunk and sulking in my favorite alcove. I barely fit in the hollow above the throne room, being most unusually tall, but I reveled in the cool stone on my hot face and arms, the wintry draft across my ankles, the utter silence.

Until Kian peered in.

He had been chasing after me since I was seven, and I was foolish to think he would not find me now, though I was a head taller and ages older now.

I had a platter full of cheese by my side and the remnants of two very large flagons of apple mead—that was the one thing I had truly missed living in Carelon. Something about the sea journey spoiled the sweet liquor. I'd had to suffer through ale and fortified wine for far too long.

"You're already drunk." Kian frowned at me, tufty brows furrowing.

I have always been very good at getting drunk quickly.

"I am fortified." I tried not to slur my words, but my tongue felt too big for my mouth.

Kian's sigh was both familiar and effective, leaving me to ponder the dregs in the bottom of my cup. Drink was never the best solution—even I knew that—but so frequently the easiest. Sweet, dependable oblivion.

Yet even I had to admit that doing so alone and in the dark was troubling. For years my drunkenness had grown out of merriment and been enjoyed in the company of other revelers; here, it was fueled by misery and guilt.

"You're quite mistaken if you think courage is found in the bottom of that cup." Kian squatted down to look at my face. "But I think you know that."

I turned my tear-streaked face away, sniffing piteously.

"It isn't fair."

"Ah, well, my dear, fairness doesn't generally come into the tales as much as we think," he continued, nudging me to make room for him to sit. I'd lost count of how many times we'd done this when I was a child. "There are a lot more warriors and kings who die of unseen or simple matters than any kind of poetic truth. Ruptured bladders. Infections. Bad falls."

"He was a decent king," I said, jostling the flagon at him. My dress was half off my shoulder, but I did not care. Kian preferred books to people, and I had no doubt my disarray inspired nothing more than pity. I hated when people pitied me. "He was a *strong* king. And now he doesn't even know his own reflection, let alone his firstborn daughter."

Kian dropped his head into his knobby hands, and rubbed at his sandy locks—now quite grey about the temples—and down his short beard. Unlike so much in Avillion, he was almost unchanged by time; he'd always had a boyish face and a compact, strong build. His robes of green and striped blue were a bit faded with time, but he still wore the vestments of his duty with ease.

"He was all those things, but he is a mortal man, and some afflictions have no true explanation. They strike without warning."

"The King of Avillion should be better than this, should live longer and without affliction," I snapped at him. "I may be a drunk but I know our histories. And I know Gweyn shouldn't have died in childbirth so easily, either. Our line is failing. Putting your faith in me, in any capacity, is folly."

The *goursez* took my free hand in his and squeezed, falling silent. When he spoke again his voice was kind, but sad. "I know. And I do not understand what is happening to the Isle, nor do I know what to do. The last two years have been half in a mist. The decline was subtle at first, but even just in the weeks since you've been here, the change has grown more pronounced."

"Is there nothing we can do?" Reluctantly, I squeezed his hand back. Weeks ago, I could barely look at him, and now I was desperate for his comfort.

"We are keeping vigil at the temples and shrines, but I must confess to you, princess, a selfish part of me just prays he will let go. The pain he endures daily must be beyond torture."

From below, I could hear the scraping of chairs in the hall, the murmur of the Skourr Council priestesses and castle servants. Tonight was another feast day—I had forgotten just how many forsaken feast days there *were* in Avillion—and I had no desire to partake in the festivities.

Yet I was the only member of my family left to attend them. I had spent the majority of banquets since my return solidly drunk and making enough of a fool of myself—by singing bawdy songs and telling obscene jokes about Arthur and his horse—that Kian had to intervene on my behalf.

It was not a tactic I could employ forever. Not just because it lacked elegance, but for its toll on my body. Waking up in my tower bedroom, my mouth desiccated and sour, my skin sore and aching, Laustic cleaning up the night's sick from the floor. I had little dignity left, it was true, but even I was tiring of myself.

But my father's illness was not the only reason I drank. I drank out of guilt, for having failed to avert my sister Gweyn's death. For not having had the courage to linger in Carelon the spring I fell in love with a woman named Nimue—only to return to find her dead, and Merlin with her. For every lover I'd had who fell in love with someone else and lived happily together. For every whispered rumor in Court I'd pretended to ignore.

Pushing aside those thoughts, I swallowed down what was left of my mead and wiped at my face with the hem of my gown.

I snorted. "I know. I am every inch a princess. But nothing more."

I did not know if Kian understood where my drunken mind twisted. Before I was brought to Carelon, the Scourr priestesses severed my magic. They called the practice Sundering, and it was done without my consent, to prevent me from heeding the call of Avillion. They claimed that the call was what made Queen Igraine mad: she had not been able to return to Avillion, and her body, and its magic, had withered. They hoped, without access to magic, I would be a docile queen and pose no threat to Merlin, Morgen, and their ilk. Except Arthur never married me, Gweyn was Sundered as well, and I remained bereft of power; and always, always alone.

Kian's expression softened. "Well, you are many inches. In spite of your attempts to the contrary, you look like a warrior giantess of old."

"Or perhaps you are shrinking, old man," I said, jostling him in the ribs.

"Hwyfar..."

"Yes, Revered Elder." I felt some giggles coming on.

"The Feast of Fire begins tonight. You will be expected—"

"I am aware. The Skourr Council will be there, as well. You reminded me six times since breakfast."

Clearing his throat, Kian continued. "Well, you must forgive me, but the way you drink, it is often difficult to know whether or not my messages are received. You have missed out on quite a few important events."

"The Skourr Council is a flock of boring old women who exhaust me by simply existing," I said, petulant as a child.

"They sit and blather for hours and hours, and I can feel my hair graying and my skin sagging just listening to them."

"Your fate is tied to their opinions of you," Kian reminded me, not for the first time. I was lucky, I knew. Many princesses did not have a living embodiment of their conscience attending on them, as I had in Kian. I was certain he'd wished it was any of my sisters in this situation, and yet he was left with the eldest drunk, who had more lovers than Avillion had apples.

If Gweyn hadn't died—and she should not have died—Mawra would have been here, and not married to Arthur. If she had not married Arthur, she would never have fallen in with the Christian priests, and with Lanceloch du Lac and his tiresome sermons on penitence and absolution and piety.

Every time I thought of Mawra sitting in black silks, stripped of the colors of Avillion, poring over texts advising women to be chaste and silent, my blood boiled.

I slurred a curt reply before crawling out of the alcove. "My fate is my own."

"Princess Hwyfar, I have told you this before: if you would like to leave Avillion, you may. The Skourr Council already has lists of claims to the succession, but yours is the strongest. If you do not, the safest course of action will be turning the crown over to King Arthur. We have limited forces, and if word of King Leodegraunce's illness spreads, we will be ripe for the picking." Kian was trying to get me to look him straight in the eye. But I, though well into my twenties, still found myself acting like a spoiled child around him. I pointedly looked away.

Except those last few words were more of a threat.

I heaved a petulant sigh. "Avillion will remain sovereign. Arthur can rot." Gweyn had not surrendered the crown, and nor would I.

"And there's that furious child I remember," said the *goursez*. "Now. You've a bell or two before you are expected downstairs. I would suggest a cold bath, some milk, and some attentions from your attendants. Then we can speak again of Avillion's fate and your role in it."

18

CHAPTER TWO

GAWAIN

I MADE IT a habit, every winter, to visit Queen Gweynevere's grave in the royal mausoleum at Carelon, on the anniversary of her death. Though there were plenty of mourners in the early hours, mostly the sort paid for by the Court and dressed in garish attire, by evening all that was left were low-burning candles and broken hellebores scattered about the gravesite.

Most people did not remember that we'd been almost of an age when she'd come to Carelon, an unexpected bride.

My mother, Anna, often reminded me that Merlin had been against that union, that he'd foreseen an uncomfortable future for Arthur. But Merlin surely had not seen his own death, and neither, it seems, had he seen Gwyen's. For by twenty-three she'd been gone. So I did not hold much faith in the old mage's warnings.

I'd been a new squire, sent from Orkney alone, a stranger to Carelon; she, Arthur's new wife, barely fifteen, unfamiliar with the Court and raised as a priestess on the far away Isle of Avillion. Together, we'd learned to navigate politics, weather Arthur's moods, evade him when necessary, and keep each other occupied. We'd become the best of friends.

"It's much colder this year than last year, Gweyn," I said, pulling the bearskin cloak tight around me. I had just a small oil lamp; knowing how easy it was to see me, I did not wish to draw much attention. Such is the curse of being the tallest knight among Arthur's ranks. If the gravediggers knew of my patterns, they never mentioned it. "Either that, or I'm just getting older. The knee hurts more this year, too. It's a good thing I like you so much, because I don't think I'd do this for anyone else."

No, I did not expect answers from a ghost. I might have a reputation for dimness, but I've also been waist-deep in dead bodies enough times to know that once a body's dead, there's no coming back from it.

Gweyn had been a truly good person, as pure and joyous as anyone I had ever met, and utterly unlike her sisters. But, I suppose, I could understand. For I, too, had two siblings, and we were each so very different. I could not judge Hwyfar and Mawra by Gweyn's standards, just as I hoped people would not judge Gareth and Gaheris by my idiotic actions over the years. Gweyn was singular.

Our friendship had been as strong as any I'd had in my life, and we'd protected each other fiercely in what ways we could… until I was sent to war, and Gweyn was sent to childbed, and the complications of adult life meant that the bond of friendship could no longer stretch so far.

After she died, I'd lost a part of myself for a time, to drink, to violence, to rage. I was not proud of the man I'd become. She had been a conscience, a kindness, when I had so little. And it took me much suffering to find my way back to it again. I nearly lost the trust of my brother Gareth in that time.

Every year since her death, I would come out to the mausoleum and sit under the apple tree that hung bare over her grave and talk with her in the setting sun.

It just made me feel better, because I had never once seen Arthur visit the grave since Gweyn's death, let alone Queen Mawra. And her other sister, Hwyfar, once a weekly attendant, had left Court weeks before. Not that we had crossed paths much. That woman was a living tempest, surrounded by a constant stream of drunken minstrels, artists, and layabouts.

I had never been able to shake the feeling that Gweyn was lonely, even with her sisters at court.

What brings you joy, Gawain?

"If I told you that nothing brought me joy right now, you would remind me that the whelps in the kennels had pink little tongues that curled when they yawned, and I would have to agree. Because even though I can be a sulky bastard, I cannot argue with that. Gringolet always brings me joy, even if I can't ride him some days, since my knee feels like woodworms have bored into half the bones."

I kneaded at the muscles around my doomed knee, stretching my calf, the stretch making pain lance down to my toes. Oh, there were plenty of tonics and tinctures I could take, but they made me groggy and angry, and I could not live with the sort of man they made me into. Not after everything our family had been through.

What gives you peace, Gawain?

"Coming to see you gives me peace. Especially when no one else is around. I would never admit it in a thousand ages, but listening to Palomydes sing gives me peace, too, especially because I don't know the words to most of his songs. I can just focus on the melodies. Not sure if he realizes it, but he sings loud enough that half the barracks can hear him at night. I don't have the heart to tell him, for fear that he would stop. When we were in the field, listening to those songs kept me from the brink some nights."

Sighing, I swallowed back the sharp fear that came with memories of fighting the Ascomanni, errant kings and lords, Sachsen overlords, and worse, the sea of corpses, unable to recognize bodies of those I loved from those I was wont to kill. And sometimes, not knowing if I *had* confused them, in the heat of battle.

Breathe, Gawain. The first gift of Avillion is our breath, the breath of life. You may not be an acolyte of the Isle, but you are born of the same line, and you can follow your breath to stillness when you find yourself near the point of breaking.

She used to hold my hands when I was swallowed up by the old memories. The first few years were the hardest, when I was barely more than a child, sent to the front. Arthur was hungry for me to make my name—beloved of Uther, he called me, the Pendragon legacy: a giant among men.

Yet I wept and shook in the dark the night I killed my first man. And many times, after. And I, like many of my men, came through the war broken, changed, confused... and those were not tales welcome at Court.

Gweyn, though, would always listen. She told me that some priestesses of Avillion experienced similar afflictions, and though few were ever cured, it was important to speak one's fears and bring the body and the mind together. Later, when she became a Christian, she said the principles were much the same: joy, peace, and pain.

I think that's where her questions came from. She got me talking like no one else ever could.

What brings you pain, Gawain?

"I used to fear being forgotten. I realize now, there's a fate worse than that. It's the look on people's faces when they see you failing, when you're no longer useful as you used to be." I groaned, moving a bit because my right leg was starting to bark in anguish. "I can see them work through it in their heads—what good is Gawain of Orkney if he can no longer fight? What can a giant of a man do, if not frighten enemies and crush skulls and spin legends? Marry, move on, go to pasture like a spent bull, I suppose. Once, maybe, I had pity for myself. But it's seeing their pity that gives me the most pain now."

I don't know what she would say to that. Gweyn was so young when she died.

I was growing past her memory, even in my fantasies. Carelon no longer seemed like a place she just left, hints of her still on the wind. I no longer expected to see her face in the halls; all hints of her had nearly faded. And I, too, felt like a ghost of its past, a relic waiting for replacement in a new and uncertain future.

* * *

IT RAINED SO hard in the weeks after I visited Gweyn's grave that the gutters fell from the eaves on the west wing, killing a man fixing the shoes on his donkey below. And one of the gargoyle's heads ruptured in the middle of Mass. Arthur thought it was a sign from God. I said it was bad craftsmanship.

There were more Christian priests in the halls every day, the Masses ran longer, and more wars were ended by diplomats rather than soldiers.

And what was I, without a sword in my hands? A knight of missed opportunities. A knight of proximity, favor, but no longer of renown.

Nephew to Arthur. Once a prince, now simply *Sir* Gawain. One among many, and no longer celebrated as were my younger brothers, Gareth and Gaheris. They moved through court intrigues and alliances with ease while I retreated to my rooms more and more, diminished by time and injury and grief.

With Merlin no longer present to hold back the tide of this new religion, King Arthur and Queen Mawra were now its most welcoming hosts—though the king had not yet entirely converted. Du Lac, of course, ever the flagellating hermit, was among the first to heed their call of purity, piety, and prayer. My mother, his second wife, sneered in private, but outwardly stood by his decisions with a placid, resolute endurance I could never understand.

It was she who surprised me in my chambers on a rain-streaked night, as I arrived after spending hours going over rosters of new squires with Bedevere—just busywork.

Anna Pendragon, Lady du Lac, was sitting in my small parlor, a book in her lap, reading, her greying hair braided into pale loops like the reins of a horse on each side of her angular face. Since her sickness a few years ago, she looked healthier, but the fire carved shadows into her face I had not noticed the last time we had spoken. My mother was there too, ever floating in and out of my life like an unexpected ship in harbor.

She was only thirteen when I was born, and I suppose we were children together, in some ways. Though it was not unusual for a noble-born princess to be wedded so young, to give birth at such an age, that was just another sign of my father's cruelty. Lot of Orkney's first language was violence.

I learned my father's patterns when I was not yet six years of age. If I could misbehave in front of him, after he drank enough wine at dinner and before he went to my mother's chambers, he would hit me instead of her. Most of the time. If I could withstand it, he would spare her altogether.

Though I never told her, I think she knew.

"I do not recall giving you a key to the chambers," I said, as my mother rose.

She was tall, my mother, though still rising only to my shoulder. I leaned down to kiss her cheek, and she beamed up at me, eyes dry but shining with a mix of pride and scrutiny. I always had the sensation that my mother saw everything, every change in me, when she looked into my face.

"You are limping more than usual," she said, as she reclaimed her seat, avoiding my observation. "Have you been taking your Aunt Morgen's potions?"

I sunk down into my favorite chair, breathing a sigh of relief. On campaign, and visiting other fortresses, chairs rarely could accommodate me. Here, in my room, the furniture had been made to my specifications, and my body did not scream in protest.

"Sometimes," I said, trying to hide the grimace as my knee spasmed when I turned. "When I remember."

The first injury to my left knee had been courtesy of my mother's second husband, Lanceloch du Lac, when I was but twenty, during a tournament. The second, and more grievous, had been gained upon the field of battle, and nearly took my whole leg—and my life with it—but for the intervention of skilled bards. I am not certain I would have survived it if Palomydes and Bors had not been by my side.

The bards saved my leg, but the pain never really left.

"If the draught makes you too drowsy, I can ask her to adjust the components," my mother said. "And she could always try a spell."

I hated the taste of Morgen's concoctions, and they made my brain feel slow. Gods knew I was slow enough as it was. Magic was out of the question.

"Aunt Morgen can experiment all she likes with potions," I said, as a servant approached me with a warm flagon of tea. I rarely drank these days—it had brought me far too close to the kind of man I most feared becoming: my father. "But I would prefer eschewing spellwork as long as possible."

The skeptical look she gave me was so like Gareth's own expression I almost laughed. He had been a good companion on our last campaign, and I was glad for my little brother's company, while Gaheris served Lanceloch as his squire. How he could stomach breathing the same air as our stepfather, I could not fathom.

"I will not waste your time, Gawain. You have been avoiding me. And everyone. So I came to you. Your uncle wishes to speak to you. Of marriage."

I glanced down into my flagon. The tea was bitter, the buds of chamomile steeped too long. "So we come to that again."

"It is well past time, and no one doubts your commitment to the cause, or your sacrifice to the Crown." To her credit, there was true pity in her voice, even if I knew it came with a measure of relief. What mother dreams of her child covered in gore on the field of battle, bleeding out in glory?

"A marriage seems both late and excessive. Besides, I have no desire for such things." I had used this argument before, but to no avail.

"It is strategic, not for desire's sake. You know this." Her gaze was unyielding. "It is your duty."

So many unspoken words between us. I could not balk at this, could not say no to her face. What monster would I be to do this? She had been *twelve* when wed, and Arthur well past twenty. My father raped her into childbed—Uther Pendragon, my grandfather, brokered their marriage with Merlin's blessing. I had heard the phrase before: bled, wed, and bred.

I groaned, rubbing my forehead. "What kind of husband would I be?"

"A good one."

"As my mother, you know my faults better than anyone."

Her smile was sad, but her voice warmer than I expected. "Yes, and you do, too. Which means you will be a far better husband than most. You have done what few men have managed in a lifetime, Gawain: you have chosen the harder path of contrition and redemption."

She meant Gareth. Once, I never could have imagined we would sit across from each other in the same room. After Gweyn's death, rage consumed me, fueled by drink and a thirst for violence: it nearly cost us our relationship. After, Mother nearly died. I saw the ruin of my life, the ruin of my family. I could not live that way, as my father had.

Duty. Redemption. Contrition.

I could not fight my way out of this.

Clenching my fists, I acknowledged my defeat. "I will speak to Uncle."

"*And* be open to his suggestions?"

"Of course, Mother."

"Marriage is not a recipe for monogamy, Gawain. Do not let the Christians and their long sermons on purity fool you."

I laughed, and the fire crackled along with me. "Oh, you have no worry on that count. I hold no court with the Christian priests. But I have also lived half like a monk these last years."

She relaxed perceptibly.

"Then, let us detail the responsibilities of what you shall do when you have your own castle and lands, and can be rid of these priests and rules. For remember, you will not just own whatever Arthur gives you, but Orkney Castle as well. You may no longer be prince in title, but you will always be a prince by blood."

26

CHAPTER THREE

HWYFAR

FOR TRADITION'S SAKE, I sat in the middle of the Great Hall, at midnight, as the ruling noble of Avillion, to welcome the flame, a practice going back thousands of years. The idea was an ancient one: that in the wintertime, the king—or lord; this was once performed in every Avillionian village across the island— would have to face the Lady of Night alone and welcome in the Daughter of Light. Mostly, I found the ritual tiresome, though marginally better than Christian mass.

My mother told me fire would arrive of its own volition, kindling in the hearth by magical means, when the Isle was stronger. And as a young child, I believed it until I noticed the "floating flame" was just a child bringing forth a sparkling candle, dressed all in black. Like most of my memories of Queen Tregerna of Lyonesse, it is a murky one.

We all supposed she was dead, but of her, and the two hundred members of court who had gone with her to reclaim her throne—and reject us—no sign had ever been found.

Dressed in velvet from neck to ankle, I squirmed in my seat. The material was shot with long strands of silver silk, imported with much ado from the south of Mediz; the silver gleamed like raindrops frozen on the fine cloth. The loom-maidens had praised my body and form, my proportions, and my hips, of all things.

I looked like a giant black candlestick.

My stomach rumbled at the smell of the awaiting feast as I shuffled again in my heavy dress. I was sweating, and was supposed to be the picture of calm, but I hated sitting still.

Willing my body to the picture of poise, I focused on the eventual obliteration of feeling to come. There would be drink and merriment and, perhaps, for a few hours, I could lose myself to all the pain around me and within me.

In the distance, the bell towers began ringing. The sound reverberated through the Great Hall, causing the windows to rattle, setting crockery trembling, and making my teeth hurt. They never rang so loudly and with such little restraint on any other day of the year, but the old stories went that the sound frightened away the ghasts and wraiths intent on stealing away the sun.

I shivered against an unexpected chill, lost in the abrupt silence as the bells ceased their clamor. Gazing up, I beheld just the outlines of the high, narrow windows arcing over my head. Between those timbers, if I squinted, I could glimpse frescoes of my father's exploits, my parents' love story, the birth of my sisters. Once King Leodegraunce was dead, the painters would begin a new fresco.

Unless, I reminded myself, I simply threw Avillion at Arthur's feet. I could be rid of this, my duty to the family, in one simple act. Never in my life had I held such power in my hands. The irony, of course, that the power was in surrender.

Sister.

Heart in my throat, I turned slowly in my chair. The air felt heavier, then, with no explanation. I gripped the heavy lengths of my velvet skirt, feeling the silk crunch against my palms.

Then again: *Sister. What brings you pain?*

I did not have to guess at the voice; I had missed it, its softness and its roundness, its familiarity, every single day since she had died.

Sometimes, the king can see across time on his throne on the Night of Fire. And sometimes, they say, the veil is the thinnest when the heart is the weakest.

28

I bit down on my lips, jaw trembling. Could anyone else hear her? From the corner of my eye, if I didn't look straight at it, I could see an impression in the dark, a wavering form.

Almost all of me is gone yet from this earth, said my dead sister. *Do not squander your time here. Do not forget your connection to the Isle.*

There were so many things I wanted to ask her—but above all I wanted to beg her forgiveness. I had let my anger at her newfound faith put a wedge between us, and I did not tend to her as I ought to have upon her deathbed. I resented her happiness, even in her farce of a marriage.

You will need the spear, the cup, and the shield. You will become a mother of joy, a harbinger of peace, a queen of fury; or else the blight will devour this Isle, and the mists will take it forever. Find what belongs to us and make the fields blossom silver and blue. With the graal *begins your inheritance, the bridge of all faiths.*

"Gweyn, please, I…"

Do not forget yourself, Hwyfar of Avillion. You have done so for too long.

I gasped as the brazier roared to life, but my pitiful sound was swallowed up as the doors burst open in all directions, and people—*my* people—spilled into the room, masks on their faces in fanciful imitations of animals, spirits, wood gods, and flowers. The music struck up around me, harps and lyres, woeful pipes, and clanging cymbals. In that moment I could feel the music, each sound and vibration shivering down my skin.

No one noticed my ethereal visitor. Had I dreamed it? Was I mad?

Hands still trembling, a wavering smile painted on my lips, I put my efforts into draining my father's honeywine reserves as best I could, allowing that weighty numbness to take me over and eradicate the memory of what had happened in the dark. I welcomed the blurry oblivion, the velvet softness sinking into my brain.

"This one is a particularly good batch of honey wine," said a voice to my right. "My foster mother arranged for the shipment, if I recall, as part of my initiation into the Skourr Council. Did you know that we all have a price, a dowry, to enter? Though we may not marry, in some ways we are still bound by the same rules."

Blinking through my drunken haze, I recognized the blue robe and silver circlet of a veiled Skourr woman beside me, her long black braid curling at the end and down her narrow shoulder.

The Skourr Council were seers, all. But unlike my sister Gweyn, or the prophets of Carelon like Vyvian and Merlin, they worked together to build a vision, and a vision of Avillion alone. The old story goes—and there are always old stories for everything in Avillion—that as young girls, the Skourr women have dreams of blooming apple trees right before their first bleeding. If they reported such a dream to their mothers, they would be brought to the local Skourr emissary or some nonsense. There was a ritual involving water, a log, and a sprig of holly, but from my understanding one could very easily buy one's way onto the Skourr Council if the price was high enough.

"Rutting divine," I replied, tipping the flagon toward her and then taking another deep draught.

Truth be told, however, in that state, I could not taste the difference between horse piss and the vintage I was drinking if my life depended on it.

"You did well this evening," said the Skourr woman, flexing her long, many-ringed fingers. "But I wanted to ask after you. You were quite pale when the lights came on."

"I do not recall asking for your opinion on my performance. And I can't tell any of you apart with those dreadful robes."

"I am Skourr Ahès." She bobbed her head.

I snorted, thumping on the table to get the wine girl's attention. "Tell me, then, O wise priestess. Our king lays dying, and his closest of kin and eldest child is an embarrassing giantess who avoids responsibilities at all costs, only performing her duties out of longstanding guilt over her sister's death." My mouth went dry at the thought of that vision, or my madness. "What does it matter how I fare?"

"I know you have had an unusual past, princess, but I do not see such an unflattering portrait," said Ahès, after a moment's contemplation. Like the rest of the Skourr women, her face was covered save for her eyes. In the light, as it was, I could see nothing but the bright intelligence there.

"I care nothing for the whisperings of political witches, let alone their opinions of me. You know very well why."

"I was not a Skourr priestess then." Ahès gave me a direct look. "But unlike the other members of the council, I do not underestimate you. Even in your present state. Which, I admit, is pitiable."

"You are truly winning me over with your flattery."

"I do not believe in coddling nobility. I was raised among them."

The wine was bitter. I put it down. "Ah, then you are an expert."

"Merely practiced. One learns the patterns at court after a time."

"I have always gone out of my way to avoid such pursuits. The moment I am aware of court patterns and politics is the moment that I have been there too long."

"Is that why you lingered so long in Carelon, then? Was it too great a challenge to untangle?"

I bit down on my teeth hard. Were I a man, no one would have dared speak to me like that, least of all a Skourr woman. But I was too inebriated for barbs. "And I suppose you have always spoken to King Leodegraunce in such an insolent manner?"

Unbothered, Ahès leaned back a little in her chair as a pack of minstrels passed behind us jangling their bells and trying to get my attention. I shooed them off with a scowl and a hiss.

"In truth, I have not had much of a chance to speak to King Leodegraunce at all." Skourr Ahès sighed. "I was raised to my position only a few months ago, just as he began to spiral into the worst of his illness. Still, I can recognize a disaster about to happen when I see it."

"I need not heed your advice." I turned to face her fully. "I answer to no one by myself."

"Perhaps. But you *should* listen to me," said Ahès. "You have few friends here at court, and much work to do."

The music rose again, and the Skourr woman rose and blended in with the crowd. I made a childish face at her back and did not care if our guests saw.

I forced some bread down my throat, our famed Braids of Una, to push down a wave of nausea. Vomiting profusely before the court was perhaps beyond even my capacity for personal self-destruction and public embarrassment.

The plentiful bread aided me toward sobriety, and though my head began to ache in earnest, I ate a little more and endured some small chat with a few eager members of court asking after my father's health.

Then came the dancing. I am not, nor have I ever been, a dancer. I do, however, find myself an avid appreciator of court dance, especially when the players present with as little clothing as possible. I have employed many in my service over the years.

Fire Feast dancing was not, however, to my taste. Unlike the majority of dances on Avillion, it was structured and rigid. That was intentional; I remember learning as a child that the idea was to perform a dance of discipline for the Fire Gods and spirits, to show restraint and respect in the face of such chaos, and that would somehow prevent them from striking us down with lightning or burning us in our beds.

Alas, no matter how many times the dance was done, those atrocities still happened all over the realm. And in Arthur's, too, though they did not perform such ridiculous dances there.

I was growing bored and looking for Kian, who always had a good way to sneak me from the events I was loath to participate in, when I heard a shout from the dancers. For a moment, I thought they had perhaps found a little more mirth in the movement than expected.

Shrieks followed, and even though the haze of drink was still lingering around the edges of my mind, I knew the sound of agony when I heard it.

The dancers parted, multicolored patchwork gowns and masks catching the light and slinking into the darker corners of the hall in clusters.

I saw the black pool of blood growing beneath the man at the center of my hall and stood up as the Knights of the Body took formation around me.

Avillion had been at peace for a thousand years.

"Where is Kian?" My voice was drowned out.

But Kian ran by me, kneeling over the prone man's form. Six guards were by his side now, clumsily reaching for their weapons as if the man's assassin was willing to show themselves after this treachery.

I looked around for the Skourr woman I'd seen earlier, but did not see her—nor any of her sisters—among the crowd.

"Silence!" Kian's shout did much more to stun the audience. "Give the man some air!"

"Princess... Hwyfar..." the man gurgled. "I must... tell the princess..."

I walked steadily toward the prone figure of the bleeding man. The tile steps down from the dais were gritty with dirt and straw, my skirts rattled with their black beads and silver bells; I was well aware I drew every eye. In most circumstances, that was something I relished. Not so here.

The fire still crackled and smoked, just a few paces from where the man was, and the flames flickered in the reflections of his watery eyes.

I knew the man. One of the Knights of the Body.

Sir Bruin. He was one of the queen's guard, back when there was a queen in Avillion, and he had been my royal escort before I left for Carelon. I had not seen him since my return, and though he had aged and changed in the intervening years, I recognized his thick mustache and scarred chin well.

I leaned down next to him.

"You have served Avillion well, Sir Bruin," I said to him, half surprised that the words came out so clear and appropriate. Rage welled up in me as I took in his wound: a dart to the chest. He was here to deliver a message, bleeding out in a way that would give him time before falling into the abyss. "I am here."

He turned his wet eyes to me, the muscles on his neck working as he tried to speak again, tendons straining against his collar. "The prince comes," said Sir Bruin, reaching out to grasp my fingers. A meeker soul might have flinched, but I squeezed back, blood slick and sticky against my palm. I could feel his warmth oozing into my silk slippers, hot and fresh.

"The prince?" I had no brothers.

Looking across to Kian, I saw a look of understanding. The *goursez* began unbuttoning Sir Bruin's jerkin, pulling the leather and cloth aside gently to reveal a mark on the knight's chest.

It looked, at first glance, like any entrance wound. But then I noted how it splayed out, the edges blurring into Sir Bruin's sweat and blood-matted hair. A chevron upon a scarlet field.

The symbols were plain enough, and in Carelon dozens of knights had similar blazons. But I knew this one well, for it was Avillion's ancient foe: the shield of Ys. The lost Isle.

"Prince Ryence," I said. Reflexively, whether to blot out the sight or to help the man with the pain, I had put my palm over the wound. I stared down Sir Bruin. "Am I right? Is this a message from Prince Ryence, my father's half-brother?"

Ryence was my father's younger brother from his mother's second marriage. I had met him once or twice as a child, and though there had been rumblings at court for ages that he saw himself as the rightful ruler of Avillion, I had not given credence to the rumors. And judging by Kian's face, neither had my father.

Sir Bruin trembled, tears now coursing down his cheeks. "Forgive me, princess. I made a pact, and swore my life. Then I—" He coughed, spit and pink froth flecking his lips. "Last night, I assisted Prince Ryence's forces to land on Avillion and when I had a change of heart, then he sent me here—as punishment."

With an immense effort, Sir Bruin dragged his hand over to the other side of his chest and tapped at his shoulder.

Kian, lips trembling against angry tears, retrieved a small scroll there. He frowned over at me. I could see the pain in his face, the shock. Even I, an Avillionian of most dubious devotion, felt the violation. This act, timed to disrupt one of our most beloved celebrations, was nothing short of blasphemous. "Traitorous fool."

"And little protection against it," I said, snatching the scroll from Kian.

I stood and looked around the frightened folk gathered, all clutching to one another, children crying. "Go home," I told them. "Lock your doors, pray to the gods and spirits of this island that we have not tended these groves for these long ages in vain. Guards, search the premises for any other disturbances."

My knights did as they were asked, a few remaining behind, while I listened to Kian helping the man to the next life. Sir Bruin was in pain, his life blood not fast enough to deal a swift, merciful death.

I heard Kian uncork the poison and then forced myself to look as he poured it down Sir Bruin's throat. It was both a mercy and a punishment to be given this swift death, for a knight who had lived boldly and brightly.

The scroll was small, but the writing pristine. It was in the dialect I spoke at home, in Avillion, an ancient language both familiar and sacred. To see the words written in such a confident script by a usurper spoke of deep insurrection within the court and among the priestesses and Skourr council. My face flushed in anger, stomach twisting at the very real invasion of privacy and peace, legs heavy with dread.

"What does it say?" Kian looked up at me, having just closed Sir Bruin's eyes and laid a blessing on him. "Princess?"

I took a deep breath: "It says, 'Behold: your ruin, written in blood and flame. Ys lays claim once again to the golden grove.'"

CHAPTER FOUR

HWYFAR

I DID NOT want this burden.

Yet, no matter how many times I tried to convince myself out
of it, I could not yield Avillion to Arthur. Of all the answers
to the immediate problem, it was the simplest. A mad king, a
blighted grove: I could simply raise consensus among the Skourr
priestesses and the Knights of the Body, and Arthur would crush
Prince Ryence's forces.

Gweyn. She had seen into my soul. Even if I did not believe
her vision real, I knew the power of dreams, of portents. Her
spirit lingered in my grief, and if I let Avillion go, I would have
to let her go. It was unthinkable.

Which left my other sister. I did not consider her an ally. When
we both lived in Carelon, she openly conspired against my way
of life, threatening to close my wing of the castle due to "disease
and misuse." If knights were found in my quarters, they were
quickly assigned to the front. Some even died that way.

No, Queen Mawra was not my ally.

Kian and a handful of remaining knights shuffled me off to
one of my father's old war rooms. Strictly speaking, I had never
been allowed in the place, but that simply meant I had found
my own way in, many times before. This particular room was
called the Boar Room, as it was trimmed in a wide assortment
of boar trophies, ranging from a small piglet with white eyes to

an immense full-sized stuffed sow with gilded horns who stood sentinel beside the roaring hearth.

The Boar Room stretched before me. After the splendor of Carelon, I expected it to feel diminished. It did not. I felt the gravity of the place, the weight of so many decisions, in the very air.

Unlike much of Withiel, the Boar Room was well-swept, clean, and showed all the signs of frequent use. In the middle of the narrow chamber rested a long oak table etched with thousands of runes. I had traced my fingers along them as a child, trying to sound out the spells, but both too impatient and too young to manage it. In the ensuing years, the runes had become somewhat worn, but their spiraling designs still dazzled the eye.

The Skourr priestess I'd met before, Ahès, sat along with her fellow Skourr Sisters, veils removed before me. She had broad lips and sharp cheekbones, handsome in that Welsh way I knew and so admired. I thought I might recognize a handful of the other priestesses from my youth, but I could not be certain.

"Your highness," said the older woman to Ahès' right. "As Skourr protocol dictates, we are gathering to address the very real threat at our door, breaching our defenses, infiltrating our sacred celebration—and turning one of our own against us."

"I had thought with an island full of priestesses, breaching those walls should be rather difficult," I said, moving across the room and running my fingers across the table. My father's chair stood empty at the head, and I picked the nearest one, swallowing back the bile that kept threatening to rise in response to both my anxiety and the truly shocking amount of strong drink I'd downed earlier in the evening.

Ahès leaned forward, her glittering rings catching in the nearby candles and her eyes flashing. "You may have been gone a long time, Your Highness, but I cannot believe for one moment you have somehow missed the deterioration we have suffered in this place. Withiel is in decay, and Avillion along with it. It does not matter how much work the priestesses do—if the king is ill, and if the land is dying, our powers diminish along with it."

"I have been occupied," I replied, as casually as I could. But judging by the looks the Skourr Council gave me, I looked about as terrible as I felt. To say nothing for the state of my gown. I had taken off my bloody shoes, at least. "Can someone bring me some water and a cloth? I am still covered in that traitor's blood."

I could not decide if I was angry or terribly sad. I could only think of my father's response to Sir Bruin's betrayal and death. He cared deeply for each and every one of his lords, treating them as equals regardless of their wealth. In one thousand years, their brotherhood had been a mirror of the Skourr Council, and an unbreakable bond. And now, it had ended, bleeding out in my hands.

A maiden appeared, carrying hot steaming cloths on a golden platter and, behind her, one of my loom maidens stood with my warmest cloak. There was fruit and more Braids of Una, as well. And wine.

But after Sir Bruin's treachery and my clearly diminishing mental state, I could not bring myself to reach for it, and instead took some cider.

Once I was at least visibly clean and warming myself a little more—I had chosen the chair closest to the hearth—I was ready to begin conversations again.

I leaned back in my chair to better observe the room. Seven knights, plus Kian; seven members of the Skourr Council. I looked each of them in the eye, as my father used to do. "So, in blood and fire, Avillion cries out."

"Somber words for a somber day." Kian dragged his hands through his hair, misery in the drawn lines around his mouth.

"You must forgive me," I said, desperate to make light of the situation, but still feeling as if I was slowly drowning in despair and grief. The shock of Sir Bruin's body bleeding out and realizing his treachery had shaken me. To say nothing of the vision of my dead sister foretelling said event.

Ahès leveled me with a searing stare. "It is time, Princess Hwyfar, for us to have a very serious conversation."

"You sound like Sir Cador used to when he was scolding me as a child."

And as if I had conjured him myself, I heard Sir Cador's voice from behind me:

"Sometimes you need that sort of tone, Your Highness."

I turned slowly. One of the six knights was indeed my dear Sir Cador, the man who had raised me alongside my father—the man who had done all the things a father ought to while King Leodegraunce was preoccupied running his island nation.

He'd been fully suited in his armor, but with a click and a snap, the smooth slink of scale and chain, he removed his helmet. Were I like Gweyn, I would have surely run into his arms and embraced him, and likely wept until I was raw. He had been away for months on some covert business for my father, or for the Skourr Council, and weathering the king's illness alone had been a burden I felt in my marrow.

Sir Cador—the man who had taken me out on adventures in the Mere Wood, who had taught me to ride and fletch my own arrows, who had showed me how to sew my own wounds in the field and feel at home in the forge—stood before me now, broader and grayer than I remembered him, but still very much the same man. The same kind eyes, the same thick mustaches and close-cut beard. Time had marked his skin, but he was the man I had trusted.

I stared Sir Cador down, however, with all the coolness of an unaffected princess, and nodded. "Well met, Sir Cador. Perhaps I have spent too much time among the minstrels."

Sir Cador came to sit beside me, and once situated, motioned the rest of the knights to do the same. The jangle of armor and the scraping of adjusted swords settled into an uneasy silence.

Sir Cador looked down the table, lingering a moment at each of the attendants. Then he said: "Skourr Council, the King's Body wish to invoke the Wrote of Thiton."

Thiton was one of the nine founding mothers of Avillion, and one of its first queens, but her significance in this moment was unclear to me.

"We will hear your case," said the tallest of the Skourr priestesses. She had a single eye, fogged by age, set in a sharp face cloven with scars that looked like she'd survived a mace attack. "But first, we must make account of ourselves for the record."

Relief flooded me, as I had been worried I would have to identify all the attendants myself, as my father so often did.

Another priestess—short, with curly black hair and deep brown eyes—produced a scroll, an ink pot, and a quill.

Sir Cador nodded and gestured to himself. "Sir Cador, Duke of Cornwall." I had forgotten he had that lofty title. That castle had once been Gorlois', and by rights was—according to some—owed to Morgen the Enchantress.

The knights all began removing their helmets and I was surprised to recognize more than a few of them. They had been childhood friends, or young knights when I was a girl. I suppose, in my own distress, I had marked them for strangers. Something tense and coiled unspooled in me, and I allowed myself to relax a bit.

"Sir Erec, son of King Llych." He was a lithe man, strong and comfortable in his armor. His wideset grey eyes were thoughtful, but made fierce by his thick, bushy brows. Yes, I recalled he lived here with his wife, Enide. They had been married years before, barely more than children, and she was known about court—and was a decent archer, from what I remembered. He was a second son, and his father had pledged allegiance to Arthur, so he was no prince.

"Sir Yvain." The next knight was my dear childhood friend. A bastard by birth, he looked much like his father King Uriens, but with soft, black hair, and a smattering of freckles. His mother was the famed witch Modrun. The years had served him well, and he clearly still trained, for his neck was wide and his jaw cut with gemstone precision.

"Sir Branor," said another, making the count to four. Swarthy and close to Cador's age, he bore many scars of battle, including a ruddy line that went from his temple down beneath his breast plate. And he was missing an ear. Rather than hide from these features, however, he shaved his head completely. He may not have been particularly tall, but he held himself with poise.

The next was Sir Safir, brother to my old friend Sir Palomydes at Carelon. Together, they had come from the East, dispossessed sons of a wealthy king called Esclabor. He wore his long hair in tight braids, a symbol of his unusual faith, each clasped with silver and gold at the ends. Swarthy and handsome, his deep brown eyes shone bright in his young face.

"Sir Safir of Albracca," he said, making eye contact with me and nodding. I liked that very much. Bold, handsome, and unafraid.

"Sir Lanval," said a devastatingly handsome knight who reminded me of Lanceloch du Lac: he had a bone-deep intensity, as if his whole body were poised for action, or lovemaking, or violence. His eyes were dark, his hair an auburn hue, and his lips full and ripe for passion.

And lastly, a face I knew without introduction: Sir Kahedin. He was the son of King Hoel of Brittany, and their kingdom was the closest to Avillion. Like many foster children, he grew up among the three daughters of Leodegraunce as almost a brother. A few years my senior, he had been my first conquest. He remained unchanged, save for a few wrinkles around his mouth: he was still pale-eyed and dark-haired, gentle-featured, and his voice was sweet and low.

"And Sir Kahedin," he said, clearly trying to suppress a smile.

I knew Ahès already. The woman with the single eye and scar introduced herself as Gliten. The scribe was called Mazoe.

"Larenne," said the woman to Mazoe's left. She looked hewn from the same stone as me: tall, broad, with red hair and lashes and a dimpled chin, no doubt a daughter of Avillion through and through. I wondered, briefly, if she could be a bastard sister or unknown cousin.

In contrast, Sewena was plump and small, her hands birdlike, and her features pinched and pretty. She had a tattoo under one of her blue eyes, which marked her as a Farseer. Her countenance was more suited to laughter and merriment, however, and she looked genuinely pleased to see me, which was a marked difference.

The last two were twins: Elowyn and Wenna. They were twin flames of ire and scathing judgement. Tall, reedy, narrow, they looked more like planted willows draped in cloth, their long black hair waving down in mirroring cascades over their shoulders. Wenna was blue-eyed, but Elowyn had one blue and one brown eye. I wished to examine it closer, and not just because it was unusual. They were both beautiful, but Elowyn was fierce, her lips pressed together to the point of bloodlessness.

The room went quiet, and I understood with a start they were waiting for me to introduce myself.

"Hwyfar Adwenna, Princess of Avillion," I said in my most grandiose accent and sweeping affect. "Though my title means little at present, I suspect."

"Be that as it may, we are in crisis, princess," said Skourr Gliten. "And I understand you find this pageantry both unnecessary and boring, but I assure you protocols must be followed in times of insurrection, even though it has been a thousand years since it has been required of us."

I nodded to her. "Like the rest of you, I imagined that the long-lived line of Leodegraunce and his father before him would mean I had many years of willful ignorance before being thrust into such dire situations. I apologize if you came seeking a measured, dedicated princess—I was groomed once, and we are all aware of how that story ended."

The Knights of the King's Body exchanged glances I could not interpret. It was Sir Cador who spoke for them: "You do not seem to quite understand your unique position, Your Highness."

Fatigue and frustration vied for attention in my head, and I truly wished for sleep, or better powders, or a clever escape. Since none of these were an option, I relied upon performance instead.

"Though I am, perhaps, long absent from these halls, I am well aware of my circumstances. I am the only heir to Avillion not only both alive and sane, but entirely unencumbered by the bonds of marriage," I said, looking Skourr Gliten in the eyes. "My only living sister is Queen of all Braetan and has proved herself a somewhat unreliable ally of Avillion, now being a most dedicated follower of the Christian faith."

I had only begged Mawra once in my life, and it was to come with me to see our father. It was not, I assure you, out of the kindness of my heart, but rather of cowardice. I had no appetite for returning alone to the land of my birth, where I had once ridden out as future Queen of Braetan, Arthur's promised, and facing my father alone. But no matter what arguments I made, no matter how many times I read the letter from Kian, she insisted that her business, and her heart, lay in Carelon, and that her faith prevented her from returning to the Isle.

Which was a great irony. For I knew Mawra was bedding Lanceloch du Lac now that Arthur was done with him. And du Lac was still married to Arthur's own sister, Anna. Though I held no true value to marriage and its insufferable bonds, I did think it quite odd that Mawra had so asserted herself into her new pious church that she could not visit Avillion, yet also lived in so-called sin against it.

Skourr Gliten frowned into her chins. "We hear rumors that your sister has converted to the Faith of the Christ and the Body Broken," she said. "That she has shunned the prayers of her birth, abandoning the Skourr and the Vine and the Fruit."

"So it seems, but that is altogether her concern," I said, making my best effort to remain relatively neutral. It was clear that information flowed freely from Carelon to Avillion. "I have never been a staunch woman of worship at the Altar of Avillion, of which I am certain you are all quite aware. If you see me as a foil to the growing threat of the Christ's men, well, I'm afraid you are mistaken. My sister Gweynevere was also a convert, but she found a balance between the two beliefs."

Balance, even though I scorned her for it.

Even though she died thinking I was angry with her.

The clawing feeling in my chest deepened, and I reached for more bread. The salty crust helped me from twisting down into the depths of grief. Not here, not now. I could not risk it.

Ahès who spoke next, her rough edges slightly softened. "We appreciate your candor, Your Highness. Which is why we are asking of you an unusual request. Avillion is directly tied to the strength of its ruler; it has remained, unified and unconquered, for over a thousand years. Our kings and queens are long-lived, our orchards sacred and flourishing, but now King Leodegraunce's mind is broken, and a blight is on the land. We see our borders crumbling, and the threat of Prince Ryence breaching our own defenses."

"And the only heir you have is an indolent, spoiled woman with more inconstancy than May in Carelon," I finished for her.

Sir Kahedin snorted. At least I was entertaining to someone.

"We are asking, formally," said Sir Cador, "that you consider declaring yourself regent."

That I had not expected. There was no precedent for such a situation in Avillion. Their circumstances must be more dire than I knew. It was very clear a whole world existed in Avillion that I had willfully ignored, or else it had been kept secret from me. And why would it have been otherwise? I should have been Arthur's wife. I was a borrowed child, coddled by Cador and loved by my sisters, but I had not been destined to stay in Avillion.

"Regent," I replied, dragging out the word. "But not declare myself queen."

"Our laws are old, and strict. The king has not named you, nor has he died. If he has promised anything to Arthur, we have no record of it. Until that time, we can do nothing. Upon his death, as there is no writ of succession, the Skourr Council and the Knights of the Body would declare the next monarch," said Skourr Gliten. "But we believe, should you accept the title for now, this will show strength to our enemies."

"I imagine that Arthur would prefer we unify," I said, trying to pull the threads together. There was more in what they were implying, and the creeping knowledge of their intent settled on my chest. "Unless you feel that my marriage is a bargaining chip in our relations with Carelon."

Sir Branor cleared his throat. He was the Marshall of the King's Guard, overseeing all the fighting men and our soldiers. "We need more soldiers. Carelon has taken so many pledges but returned none. Now, with this threat at our borders, we need a way to convince King Arthur to send a legion our way, to send a message to Ryence the Pretender."

"Oh, he has a fancy name now, does he?" I asked. "I prefer Ryence the Sniveling Murderer, Officious Prick, and General Maggot-Face. But you may call him what you like."

"You see, Your Highness—" Sir Branor tried, but I interrupted him.

"No, I understand what you are asking me. You would like me to bargain my life and my body for Arthur's favor and troops. Until such a time as you can decide on someone more qualified, or at last cave to Arthur's grand vision to make Avillion another jewel in the crown of Braetan."

"You are very direct," said Skourr Gliten.

"She is that," Sir Cador replied, wiping his sweaty brow with a handkerchief. "But I would expect no less. You have always been without pretense, Your Highness, and it is appreciated in this hour."

All those expectant eyes. It was a bit like being on stage, I knew, from my forays with the minstrels. There was a power in it I did not altogether dislike, a strength of attention I had never quite commanded in Carelon as the remnant of Arthur's mistakes, nor at any other court I had attended, whether Lyonesse or otherwise.

I did not relish the idea of marriage, but neither did I believe that I had to bow to its limitations. I had seen what Arthur and his knights were capable of, fretting about the margins of their marriage contracts. Perhaps I was untested, perhaps I was indulgent... perhaps I was both.

"Very well," I said, looking from Sir Cador to Skourr Gliten, and then to Skourr Ahès for good measure. "I will do as you ask."

They did not know I did this for my sister, who had returned from the grave to frighten me half to death. Or that I was terrified. Or that, as soon as the war was won, I planned to leave before any marriage contract could be sworn: I knew how to get in and out of Withiel better than any living person.

The relief on their faces was tangible.

"I will position myself as regent, until the time that you can make a better decision, and in doing so I will petition Arthur for troops and assistance in hope of a suitable alliance. Sir Cador, I leave it to you to flush out the castle for any signs of other infiltration."

Sir Cador bowed, falling to one knee. "We have already commenced, Your Majesty."

Majesty.

"That will take some time to get used to," I said, as he took my hand and kissed it.

It was Skourr Ahès who gave me a knowing grin. "There are a great many things you are about to learn, Your Majesty. But before we begin, there is one more person you must speak to. And she awaits you in the Queen's Tier."

CHAPTER FIVE

HWYFAR

No MATTER HOW many times I asked Sir Kahedin and Sir Safir who exactly it was waiting for me in the Queen's Tier, they would not answer me. I had not visited my mother's chambers since I was a child, fearing it haunted. We were not close, she and I, and I do not think she wanted one child, let alone three. We had that in common. I never dreamed of daughters or sons. I only dreamed of the next pleasure to experience, the next sweet plum to pick, the next soft silk to touch. Raising children seemed a sentence of pain and a sincere lack of pleasure.

The Queen's Tier was a horseshoe-shaped level on the east wing of Withiel, a palisaded garden with a tiled interior. I remember my father telling me it was the fashion in Lyonesse for such things, to build rooms open to a central, open-air courtyard, and it had been made for her specifically.

I was surprised to find, however, that it felt as old as the rest of Withiel. Unlike Carelon, which constantly shifted between marble and brick and granite to reflect the different ages in which it had been made—from Uther to Arthur and beyond—the Queen's Tier was the same dark stone as the rest of Withiel. I wondered if they had simply removed part of the east wing to make the courtyard. If I were the sort of woman who enjoyed researching in dark libraries, I would have considered doing just that. But, I realized, should I become Regent, I could order another to research on my behalf.

The Queen's Tier was in a state of disarray, which surprised me, even knowing my father had never recovered from my mother's departure. It was swept clean, mind you, and no-one could say it had not been maintained, yet it had an empty, abandoned feeling. As we passed the rooms, the deep crimsons and jewel greens of Lyonesse decor felt out of place and frozen in time. Unlike Avillionian fashions, which favored a riot of colors and a profusion of chartreuse, Lyonesse was a culture steeped in a tradition of silk brocade and sultry damasks, wonderfully made but subtle in contrast. The furniture was stark, fastened with hand-hewn iron and dark wood, the tapestries geometric and sparse.

"Did you know," I said, by way of conversation and hating silence, "that in Lyonesse, young girls are raised alongside boys with absolutely no distinction made? They dress in breeches."

"That explains your particular quirk, Your Majesty, for it is not the custom here in Avillion," said Sir Kahedin, not bothering to look at me. I wondered if I was going to be affixed to these two from now on. It could be worse. They were both more than adequately handsome. Although I had yet to hear Sir Safir say more than a few words.

"It isn't a quirk," I said, brushing invisible lint from my shoulder. "It's my heritage. Perhaps the only sensible thing I've kept from my mother." I pulled up my skirts to display the leather breeches I always wore. Far more comfortable, easier to navigate in, and proof against chafing.

Sir Kahedin snorted but Sir Safir continued forward until we reached a narrow door. He swung it open, revealing a narrow staircase.

"It's this way, Your Highness," Sir Safir said. He had no hint of an accent to speak of, though I had expected it—Sir Palomydes, his brother, had a lilting accent that warmed me like fresh tea after a cold afternoon. "You will need to make the ascent alone, according to the Skourr Council."

Ah, a mystery. Or perhaps women's things. I had no idea. "No warning?" I asked. "Should I bring a dagger or two?"

Sir Kahedin shook his head. "Not that I am aware of. I'm afraid I do not know what you will expect, only that the Skourr gave us clear directions."

The stairs were worn so smooth they dipped in the center, which dated them far beyond many of the other stairways in the castle. Yet clearly avoided for decades: the railings and window ledges lay thick with dust.

Perhaps the stairway was older even than my mother's arrival. Perhaps, when she and my father were young, they had trodden this way night after night. Or, yet again, there may have been another king and queen, centuries before, or priestesses…

That feeling rose again: a strangling, tickling in my throat. The uncanny sensation I experienced when I saw Gweyn, and when I began to fall apart. For a moment I forgot how to breathe.

The walls were dry, crumbling to touch as I steadied myself. I typically scaled more than one step at a time, with my long gait, but in this case, I knew not to waste my energy. Even I have moments of solid reason.

Once I finished the spiral ascent, removing my hood as the air grew hotter, I saw a flush of orange tinting the rough-hewn walls, showing every pit and imperfection, each chisel scrape: a fire ahead of me.

It took a moment for my eyes to adjust to the light, but at last I beheld a round, bare room, carpeted with ancient textiles and strewn with square pillows. In the very middle was a mirror, tall as I was and trimmed in copper. The fire roared into the reflection, shimmering on the perfect surface.

Drawn to it, I took a few soft steps forward, searching for a sign of anyone else. Priestesses had a habit of lurking in all the corners of Avillion, as I had learned through unfortunate experience in childhood. It appeared, however, that I was alone.

The room had no windows, and the hearth against the far wall was barely more than a gaping stone maw, unlike any other I had seen at Withiel.

"There you are," said a voice. "I am glad to see you have listened to the Skourr Council, Your Highness."

I turned slowly toward the mirror to see a figure standing where my reflection should have been. Morgen le Fay wore robes of state, the same brown Merlin had once donned, but with ornate embroidery on her shoulders and her long braids tied with silver and gold floss. She did not carry a staff, but she did not require such outward declarations of her power.

Unlike her half-siblings Arthur and Anna Pendragon, who had bright blue eyes and golden hair and a height and build more akin to my own, Morgen was small and earthy, but still composed of sharp angles and an unusual beauty I had rarely encountered in other women. Her lips always surprised me, redder than spring berries and wide, luscious, their curves accenting her dark, feline eyes and bold brows. She still possessed a sprightliness and power to her gait that belied her small stature.

"Morgen," I said, trying not to look impressed by the mirror's power. In truth, I had never seen such a wondrous item. Though magic existed around me in all forms in Avillion, it was rarely presented in such close quarters, nor so flagrantly. I stepped closer and the image shimmered slightly as I stirred the air. "I cannot say that I was expecting *you*. The Skourr Council was, expectedly, rather cryptic."

"They must be," said Morgen, gesturing at the edges of the mirror from her side. "This kind of magic only works with the right kind of individual, and I had every hope you might fulfill that requirement, given your parentage." She paused, a frown furrowing her wide brow. "My condolences over your father's illness. I have sent some of my best healers to aid in whatever way we can, but I fear the situation is dire."

"I appreciate your kindness, but I am afraid we must speak of even bleaker news: we are on the cusp of invasion, and a member of my guard was murdered in cold blood at the Feast of Fire."

Morgan did not look surprised, but instead shook her head. "Ah. Prince Ryence, I presume."

"If such a bastard can be called a prince." I did not tell her my preferred moniker, deciding wisely that humor would not endear her to me.

"He has formidable sources. And allies."

"I am aware. In the meantime, I am to be named Regent."

Morgen nodded. "Then I suppose you are not aware that King Leodegraunce promised Avillion to Arthur upon his death."

A sinking, plunging feeling in my chest stole my breath for a moment. Avillion had always been free. If my father had made such a promise, it was clear that the Skourr Council had no knowledge of it, and they expected me to take up duties as monarch should he die, even if I was not named as heir.

I kept my composure. "I have been away from Avillion a great many years, my lady. I am afraid I was not informed."

Morgen's image wavered slightly, rippling like water. I thought I could see long threads behind her for a moment, glowing and trailing in an invisible wind. "It was a verbal contract, upon your sister Gweynevere's wedding, a foundational promise— initially a part of your own marriage agreement."

Ah, we were already at the game. Bargains, veiled threats, the dance of politics. It was ever a skill I could summon, but never one I truly enjoyed; best leave dealings to the bed chamber. Alas, not possible with Morgen.

"Regardless of promises, Avillion has sent knights to the shores of Braetan for decades, now. Hundreds have trained and died for Arthur's endless wars. Now we find ourselves incapable of fending off this foe, even with our priestesses and mages. We do not have the numbers. And if Avillion falls to Ryence, there is no saying where he will turn next."

"Even without allies, Avillion would not fall lightly."

I still had another thread to pull tighter. Taking a deep breath, summoning my most sober tone, I said, "Morgen, the orchards are dying."

"I see."

I nodded, hoping she did not notice my trembling hands.

"Avillion is weaker than it has been in three generations. And Ryence has already proven himself craven. We need knights, my lady. We need war leaders. We need commanders."

"According to the High King, you need a husband."

If I flinched, I could not be blamed. "I do not see the significance of that in our conversation."

"You hold more power than you believe. As heir, you must officially renounce the throne, should you hold to the terms of your sister's marriage contract. Perhaps there is a way we can come to a mutual agreement—one would assume you would want the protection of your own assets through a long-due match, for whatever happens after Avillion is saved."

Talk of marriage always stoked the flames of my own anger. I did not need *tethering* to anyone. "Then tell me, Morgen. I was meant to live as Arthur's queen, and I followed every last rule. Yet, here I stand, unmarried and poised at the precipice of queenhood. Do the scrolls not tell you my fate?"

She stilled, her image blurring a moment. Her voice was softer when she spoke again. "You do not appear in the scrolls. Nor do your sisters. You are simply listed as the daughters of Leodegraunce. Or, should I say, the *wives* of Pendragon."

This idea that my sisters and I had been accounted for in the scrolls as some monolith of bonded womanhood made me want shatter the mirror with my bare fists. I tamped down my own fury until later, when I was no longer within earshot.

"I did not marry Arthur," I pointed out, as if that detail needed any more elaboration. "I am no wife."

"I suppose. But you were betrothed. Documents written and sealed; rituals performed. Scrolls of prophecy do not always distinguish themselves so clearly."

I laughed. "And yet we are closest to Arthur. How strange."

"Indeed, there is a mist about you and your sisters, likely from the line of Lyonesse, and your mother's protection. Though Queen Tergerna left you when she was young, her powers were great. You are formidable, too, even if unconventional."

Formidable? Had Morgen the Enchantress called me *formidable*? I could think of many descriptions worthy of my reputation, but that was not one of them.

"Regardless of scrolls and mists, I need soldiers, and soon. We expect Ryence and his forces within the month, if not sooner. There could be more traitors in our midst, and Ryence is far from our only threat. If we appear weak, Avillion will become a target of more errant kingdoms."

Morgen nodded, and I saw a flicker of weariness in her expression. "Indeed. The schemes of men are all too predictable."

I pressed my advantage. "I know the knights are restless in Carelon now that the fighting with the Ascomanni has come to an end. Surely you can spare some."

"Yes," said Morgen. A dark spot shifted at the edge of her robes, and I noticed the outline of a cat in the mirror, striped and alert, with amber eyes. "And among them will be your choice of suitors."

My skin prickled. "Arthur wants to see me chained."

"Arthur wants to see you take your responsibility to Avillion seriously."

Would that I could have snarled. Instead, I said evenly, "We all become Arthur's pawns in the end, I suppose. One way or another."

Morgen stiffened. "We will expect your decision once Ryence has been dealt with. Do I have your word?"

I swallowed back on the choice words that resonated in my head. *Choice of suitors,* indeed. In my mind, I expected I could worm my way out of the situation once Avillion was secured. Perhaps Cador or Kian would take over the regency. For now, I needed more knights, and knights I would have.

"Hwyfar."

"You have my word," I said, not keeping the contempt from my voice. "How soon do you think they will arrive?"

Morgen shrugged, giving a little tenuous sigh. "We will dispense the knights as soon as we are able. We have six new ships, and if the weather holds, it should be no more than a fortnight. Less, if the decisions are made more swiftly than as of late."

The mirror shifted and I felt a sense of dread crawling over me. Not only at the prospect of marriage, but again for this back-and-forth bartering, this sense that Morgen and the High Priestess Vyvian—and most of all Arthur—had hidden agendas and circumstances beyond my reach. To them, I was a political interloper, a branch of Igraine's line long thinned by politics and indulgence. I used their ties to Avillion to get what I needed.

Morgen forgot that I, too, was once a child of this isle, wedded to the earth and waters, with magic at my command. Until that connection was forcefully taken from me.

Before I was sent to Arthur as his betrothed, I was Sundered from my ties to the power of Avillion. I could never be a priestess; I would never hold magic in my hands, never shape the world through visions or healing. My sisters had done the same, though with Gweyn, it was more traumatic—she had already begun some of her training, promised to the Temple, when Arthur chose her. A knife, a priestess, and a dark night broke the threads that bound my sisters and I to Avillion in power, but never in spirit.

I could still feel magic. I could see it, sometimes. There were minor charms available to me, small spells of protection that every child on Avillion knows. But the true power of Avillion was forever lost to my blood, taken from me the day before I left for Carelon, only to be rejected by Arthur. For nothing.

I would be no threat to Morgen or Vyvian, at least not in the way my mother could have been. Whether any of my mother's gifts had passed to me was up for debate, but Morgen knew well I could do very little personally.

"How is my sister?" I asked, knowing that our discussion was coming to an end. This kind of magic was precious, powerful, and spare. I knew enough about such items to recognize the effort that had gone into this meeting.

"Your sister needs to be careful," said Morgen.

CHAPTER SIX

GAWAIN

"GAWAIN, HAVE YOU ever considered that, inverted, the sword is very much like the cross of the Christ?"

This is what Arthur asked me when he at last called me to his privy chambers to discuss my imminent and doleful future. It was late morning, and the crows had gathered on the parapets outside the window of his chambers. Mawra sat with him, dressed in black and hooded—some significance lost upon me pertaining to their learning of the Christian faith—poring through one of the gilded silver books the priests brought in offensively large numbers to Carelon every day.

I had also seen bear scat in the shape of a cross during a hunting trip once, but I did not tell Arthur that. I knew my uncle well enough not to resort to jesting during his thoughtful moods.

"I had not," I said, taking the proffered seat at his long table. He had set large platters of food out for me—a practice I found people often performed, assuming that, as a person of significant stature, I required sustenance at every possible turn. I had already broken my fast, however, and had no appetite.

"Something Brother Hadinus told me this morning," Arthur said, looking up at me as if for the first time across the table. "I just keep thinking on it, how one instrument can be of peace and forgiveness, and another of death—yet both also represent suffering."

Arthur was unchanged since our last meeting, though dressed

for the quiet of his personal chamber and not the glamor of court. He displayed fewer rings on his long-fingered hands, less embroidery on his cloak. Well into his forties, he still had a youthful face with a short, blond beard, and the same keen blue eyes and high brow as my mother. I am told they both took after Uther in their coloring and bearing: angular, broad, imposing. I supposed I did, too. Just as well. I already had enough of my abhorrent father in me without looking like him in addition.

But where my mother had a shrewdness about her, Arthur did not. To put it kindly, he was a perpetual learner. He was unusually innocent in some things, I suppose; fastidious too, and strict in his adherence to the rules. The Pendragon dream, after all, rested upon him. He had seen this dynasty through and sired another generation after the turmoil of Uther's reign.

And he showed me kindness when I'd known nothing but pain, been a foster father and given me purpose. But I could not follow him into his new religion any more than I could stand seeing Mawra at his side instead of Gweyn.

My reply was noncommittal. "Ah."

"Ah, indeed. Ah! Gawain. It is good to see you." Arthur reached over and clapped me on the shoulder. "Good, solid, steadfast Gawain. I always forget how enormous you are! Every time you are away it surprises me again. How the chairs groan!"

Though I doubted I had grown much since the age of twenty, my size and stature remained a constant point of commentary at court, years later.

I raised my cup to him. Morning ale, watered down and flavored with clove. "Mother sends her best wishes."

"My good sister, mother to my favorite nephews." Arthur raised his glass to me. "Now! We must discuss a very important matter. Well, *two* important matters."

"Two?" I had prepared myself for discussion of marriage. But beyond that, I could conceive of no other topic.

He leaned over to the queen. "Mawra, tell him what you have been reading about."

Queen Mawra looked up at me, her dark eyes piercing, bright. She was so unlike her sisters: petite, raven-haired, clever. I had never seen affection between her and Arthur, not once. And she was certainly not with child—not that such a thing was needed with Mordred healthy and thriving. Mawra's late younger sister Gweynevere had been Arthur's first wife, and the eldest, Hwyfar, had been his first betrothed. Gweyn had been a gentle, nurturing soul, a friend; Hwyfar a tempest in human form.

"Have you ever heard of the *graal*, Sir Gawain?" Queen Mawra asked me.

"The what?" I asked.

"I shall assume that means 'no,'" the Queen replied in her imperious tone.

"My pardon, Your Majesty, but I find little time for reading while campaigning at the borders and preserving the peace of the realm," I said.

Arthur interrupted before she could contradict me. "The *graal* is a collection of relics. Well, the Christians call them relics—Merlin referred to them as objects of great power. They were once kept in the Holy Land, but were spread through the known kingdoms by a wayward priestess ages ago. Or so we thought."

"Great power?" I asked. "I should think Carelon has enough power these days that we are in no need of magic implements."

"Merlin was convinced they could aid Carelon." Arthur was all seriousness. "Toward the end of his life, he insisted that if I should find myself in a place of confusion, of difficulty, that I ought to seek them out. Claim them. And Brother Hadinus tells me, this very month, that there are writings in their scriptures of these very implements! It may be that our *graal* contains the very same cup by which the Christ drank, the lance by which he was pierced, and the shield—well, I am unsure what the shield was, but it is undoubtedly important."

"We believe," the Queen said, with a smooth patience I had to credit her for, "that one lies in Avillion. But very well hidden. And until now, we did not have a way in to retrieve it."

I gave her a curious look. "Is Your Majesty not from Avillion?"

"As a Christian, I am no longer welcome in Avillion," she said flatly. "But my sister Hwyfar has returned and has the ear of my father—and many of the inhabitants there. And, we have learned, she is in dire need of our assistance."

"Prince Ryence, the half-brother of King Leodegraunce, is preparing war upon Avillion," said Arthur. "Morgen has informed me of this, and Hwyfar has sent for aid. My pardon. *Queen Regent* Hwyfar."

The king and queen exchanged amused glances. Clearly, they had the same impression of Hwyfar as most of the court did. It was difficult to forget a woman who had caroused with half the court and lived with an entire troop of minstrels in her apartment for seven years.

The Queen leaned forward, her cross glinting in the light. "Hwyfar will be in far above her head. We would like you to take a small group of knights to her assistance, and while you are there, question her—delicately—about the location of the *graal*. She may know more than she indicates. I suspect our mother may have been involved, and Hwyfar remembers more of the lost Queen of Lyonesse than anyone else."

"Am I to suppose Ryence is not as much of a threat, then, given you appear more focused on the *graal*?" I asked.

"Think of it as a last campaign," Arthur said, smiling broadly. "Avillion has been at peace for a thousand years, and while Ryence is indeed a bit of a gnat, I doubt he will be difficult for you to subdue. He's an old traditionalist who loves nothing better than a duel. But you can be a soldier of diplomacy, rather than a warrior of bluster."

"You want me to play diplomat?" I asked, looking from king and queen then back again. I laughed at their mirrored expressions of sobriety. "You'd best find someone better suited. My justice is served on the end of a sword, not with delicate debate."

This whole business made me uncomfortable. It sounded as if Hwyfar and the rest of Avillion were truly upset over their circumstances, and Arthur and Mawra saw it merely as an opportunity for their own gain.

"You grew up at court," said Arthur, waving a dismissing hand. "You are my nephew. And we all know your days behind the shield are limited, Gawain. It is time you built yourself new skills, more refined skills."

"We all must be reasonable," said Queen Mawra. "You cannot brawl your way through every problem forever, Gawain."

I felt the growing cinder of my temper rise, but I pushed it down and did what Gweyn always taught me: I thought my way through it.

Arthur, who had never seen death on the battlefield—Arthur, who had commanded from inside these walls only—had no idea what I had endured, what my body had endured, these past years. Time and again, from the age of sixteen onward, I had killed—murdered—in his name. He had never seen bodies flayed open, guts upon the bloody fields; comrades in arms leaking their last, calling the names of their mothers, lovers.

And in times of peace, I had played the peacock on his tournament stage, battling against my own brothers, as if the games did not bring back memories of those haunted fields every time.

No, Arthur and Mawra would never understand. And yet presumed to tell me how I ought to spend my remaining years.

In my younger days, I would have thrown a chair, bellowed like a giant who'd stubbed his toe on a great boulder. Yes, even in front of Arthur. He had seen me behave thus dozens of times; but he had also helped teach me temperance. Along with my mother, and with Gweyn, when she was alive.

I chose not to be that man. Not today.

I clenched my jaw, I breathed through my nose, and I settled back into my chair, focusing on the feeling of the cold marble table beneath my hands and the soft leather of my boots. I felt the calming memory of Gweyn, like a spirit on my shoulder, and I kept my composure.

"Whatever you do, do not underestimate Hwyfar," said

Queen Mawra, leaning forward. "Untested though you may be in the ways of court politics, she is chaos embodied and does not play by the rules."

"So, you wish me to play a game you know I've no tact for, with a woman who abides by none of the rules?" I asked, even more confused.

"We are offering her assistance in exchange for her consent to marriage, finally," said Arthur smoothly. "And by doing so, we can finally secure the crown of Avillion. As Leodegraunce's heir, she must consent. So, we are asking her to pick from among the knights we are sending, and if she does not, we will choose for her."

"I hope you don't mean—" I began.

Arthur chuckled. "Not you, of course. You deserve a far more pristine prize." He laughed; I must have made an expression. I'd tried not to, but often my emotions got the better of me. As my mother often told me, my face could be read as clearly as the weather.

Queen Mawra muttered into her drink. "I fear for the poor man she does choose. Though by sheer odds, she's bedded half of the Table at this point, so they should be familiar to her."

Arthur winced at the jibe, and even I felt it was a bit harsh. Hwyfar's reputation was certainly notorious, but I remembered her when she first came to Carelon as Arthur's betrothed: intelligent, stunning, outgoing. What and who she had become, was far from her doing alone.

Arthur considered me a moment. "If she proves too headstrong, determine if she is worth the effort of a peaceful handoff; then either do away with her or marry her off to someone who can cow her. But your first mission is to learn her proximity to this *graal*. Carelon needs it. It is only a part of our greater mission, but it will help us toward our final supremacy."

"I doubt anyone on earth can cow *her*," Queen Mawra said with annoyance. "But she will be too bored for court intrigue—I suspect she will do whatever she can to seduce you and your men, let you have your way and be on."

The king laughed. "Darling, you do have a way. But fret not. I do not have to worry about my nephew. He would never pursue a woman of such ill repute." He turned to me. "Am I right, Gawain?"

I cleared my throat, suppressing memories of Hwyfar's glorious form. Though we were not close in any sense, I, like many of those at court, was not immune to her beauty and presence. "Of course not, my lord."

Arthur nodded with a smile. "Good. We will make you the best match imaginable when you return. But until then, you must keep your wits about you and remain pure and focused."

At that moment, the door to the privy chamber opened and Lanceloch du Lac entered, dressed in charcoal grey and silver. He, like Mawra, had taken Christian vows and adopted sober dress, and wore a garish pewter cross at his chest. He saw me and his expression went from mild interest to a kind of cautious fear.

We never got along well. And perhaps my stomach had been trying to warn me. For weeks it had been like this, a constant unsettled feeling in the pit of my stomach. I remembered feeling such a way as a child in Orkney, but never since arriving in Carelon. It disturbed me.

I no longer blamed Lanceloch for my fall from grace as Arthur's favored knight, but the toll of our strained relationship would never mend. I despised the man, and his obsession with purity and penance made him all the more insufferable. His marriage to my mother was a hollow sham, a bitter, strange pageantry, and whenever I saw his face I played out elaborate fantasies of my gauntleted fist making contact with it: how his nose would crack and splatter, the cheekbone collapse, the lip split, and teeth give way, clinking to the ground one by one.

"Ah, Lanceloch, we were just discussing the *graal* campaign with Gawain here," said Queen Mawra, her face brightening beyond what I would think appropriate. Rumors had even made it to the field about their purported affairs, right under Arthur's nose.

If Arthur cared, he made no indication.

Lanceloch came to stand a bit behind the king, bowing in deference, before addressing me. "Sir Gawain."

"Lance," I said, not looking at him. "I was just leaving, I believe, as His Majesty was preparing my final orders."

I could feel the awkward look between him and the king, and I did not give an aurochs' arse. Lanceloch could drown in a bog for all I cared.

Arthur sighed, but I knew he would say nothing. This was the one advantage I had over Lanceloch: I had known Arthur far longer than he. I understood the way his mind worked, and had the ties of blood.

"We will send twenty-four knights, with ten to each command," said the king, handing me a small scroll. "And upon your successful return, my boy, we will finalize your marriage. And your lands. You shall have a splendid new beginning. Think on it while you are away, but keep your eyes open."

New beginning, indeed. After he indulged me with this final mission, I would no longer gather pitiful glances at court or remind him how much damage I had taken in his name.

"Of course, Your Majesty," I said.

I took the scroll, and cracked the seal. A ship to Avillion, a smattering of signatures—decided long before my own consent. Half the knights listed I would have asked along, anyway, including my brother Gareth and my dearest friend Palomydes. Arthur knew me well enough, at least, and that was some comfort.

"Remember, Gawain," said Arthur, as I read the summons. "When this is over, a wife is what you need, even for show. Just a decent mark in the books, good lands and good connections; I prefer a marriage of convenience, so you need not worry about progeny. I have Mordred for that. Given your proximity to the throne, it would be good for the Table to see you as neutralized."

Neutralized. Retired. *Hidden.* I was too tired, and too outmatched, to fight back. So I agreed, and began my preparations for Avillion.

CHAPTER SEVEN

GAWAIN

WE SET SAIL four days later. I enjoyed sailing, but Gareth had never endured a long journey on the sea, let alone the choppy waters toward Avillion.

"Be careful," I warned Gareth as we disembarked from *The Queen's Raiment*. We had spent the better part of the last two days doing everything possible to assuage his profuse vomiting, but to no avail. The poor oaf was unable to keep even gruel down, and so dizzy he hardly made any sense.

"Let me be," Gareth said, voice weak, "I'm fine." His legs trembled on the planks as we made perilously slow progress toward the ground. "And I would be even better if you didn't coddle me like a child."

"Coddle? No child of Orkney has ever been *coddled*," I said with a laugh. "Have you met our mother?"

Gareth almost laughed, but it turned into a stifled gag.

The wind whipped across our faces, tossing our hair and heavy cloaks, and I had to squint through the bright morning light across the pier to the other ships to make out the rest of my companions. I watched Palomydes and Bors debarking, deep in conversation and laughing. Lanval was already ashore, embracing one of the emissaries from Withiel Castle like an old friend. Had he mentioned a brother? Probably. I was terrible at remembering the detail of other people's families. Mine was already quite confusing enough. I even had a brother I'd never met who was just a child, being raised in Gaul.

Most of the sweeping green countryside was covered in a fine dusting of snow, a heavy mist hovering just above the surface, portions of it burning away in the morning sunlight. It smelled sweet and loamy, and I was surprised how much the earth gave way beneath my boots when I at last reached the ground.

"I have never been so happy to see snow in my life," said Gareth. I still had to help him stand and could feel my brother's body trembling under the weight of the seasickness. He was not alone, at least. Sir Lionel was bent over on the edge of his ship, *The King's Pride,* voiding the contents of his stomach with exceptional velocity.

"It's a fresh fall," I said. The weather seemed a much better topic of conversation. "I never considered snow here in Avillion, I have to admit. Always thought it was the kind of place that was in perpetual springtime."

"I suppose even the witches of Avillion are helpless against the seasons," Gareth replied, falling to one knee. He put his hand flat on the earth, snow melting around his fingers, and sighed deeply.

"Remember they call them Skourr priestesses here, brother," I said, lowering my voice.

"Skourr Priestesses," whispered Gareth, almost reverently. "I forget. But it also could be on account of how little I've had to eat."

"Oh, you've had plenty to eat," I said with another laugh. "I know, because I personally helped swab it from the deck."

THANKFULLY, UNLIKE SOME of the ports I had seen in my life, the trek from the ship to the castle was not a long one, nor was it fraught with strange creatures or marauding enemies. At least not yet. Arthur had told me that the Isle was relatively defenseless, and although Withiel Castle had significant fortifications, should there be an unexpected assault they would be ill-prepared. But the skies did darken, and we were chilled down to our bones.

The snow could not cover the sad state of the trees, though. Far from a farmer, I still noted the protruding growths on the sides of the apple trees and how the willows withered at the ends, dry and brown.

"It feels eerily quiet here, does it not?" It was Palomydes who asked the question, checking his horse beside my own charger.

"It does," I said, taking a glance over his shoulder. The men were restless. Many of them had other plans for their winters and springs, and the idea of a sea journey to help thwart an invasion on an island full of witches was not ideal. Palomydes, however, was never concerned in the least about such things. "Some folk believe that the land itself reflects the health of the king. And given the rumors of Leodegraunce's state…"

"Have you met the man?" Palomydes asked, batting away the pelting ice coming off his helmet. "The King, I mean."

"Leodegraunce? Yes, a few times. But that was ages ago. I'd barely come to Carelon when they arrived with Hwyfar and Gweyn. It was quite the retinue. And as you know, it did not precisely go to plan."

"There are some that say the Isle weeps for Gweyn," Palomydes said, his low, musical voice breaking slightly. "Do you think that's true?"

I still wept for Gweyn. But all I could say was, "There was no other like her."

"I do miss Lady Hwyfar—my pardon, *Queen Regent* Hwyfar—around the castle. She always made me laugh." Palomydes' smile was wistful. "She also played a most impressive harp. But I do not recall you spending much time with her, Gawain. I'd have thought you would notice a woman you didn't have to bend in half to look at in the face."

Oh, I'd noticed Hwyfar of Avillion. The woman was practically etched into my memory, from the first day I saw her. She was passion embodied, and the subject of many of my young fantasies. But though I shared a deep friendship with her sister, we had never spoken more than a few words since our youth.

"Alas, life on the front gave me little taste for idleness and harp music, what with all the corpses and trying to prevent my knights from becoming them."

"Ah, such woeful conversation," came Bors' booming voice. Unlike the rest of the knights, he seemed made for this weather: his dark beard and great, white teeth glittered in a broad smile as he cantered his sorrel charger around, patting the beast on the neck affectionately. "We are free from the daily drudgery of court, my lads. No state dinners. No morning drills with Cai. And no lectures from Sir Ectyr, either. Gods above and below, look at this place."

"I see crusting snow and withering trees," said Gareth. He'd disembarked his horse as we neared, and the rest of the knights began to do the same. Withiel rose before us, towers of striped stone and moss, a crumbling city, built half into the cliff face. "A bit sad, really."

"Ah, lad," said Bors, shaking his shaggy head. "You've got to learn to stop looking with your eyes. Can you not feel the difference?"

"I'm with the boy," said Palomydes, pulling down his head wrap so it might cover his ears a little more. "This weather is chilling me to my bones, and it's quite a challenge to think of anything other than a warm fire when my toes are numb. Where's Lionel? He said he had an extra cloak."

But before Lionel was located, I turned at the sound of trumpets—high, silvery notes—coming from the castle walls themselves. Squinting, for my eyesight was going the way of my knee, I spotted a half dozen heralds in thick, blue robes.

"Looks like that fire is within reach for you, Palomydes," I said, slapping my friend on the back. "Surely we've taken more perilous journeys before."

* * *

I COULD NOT help but wonder what the Grand Hall at Withiel had been like in its heyday, for even in disrepair it was a wonder to behold. The frescoes, alone, inspired a sense of awe and wonder, regardless of the crumbling plaster and the bare beams pressing on the wavering surfaces. I had never seen such vibrant colors before, nor such realistic depictions of faces. Like parts of Carelon, Withiel was draped in miles of velvet cloth, cloth of gold, damask, and sturdy wools. And when Gweynevere was queen, I remembered some of the patterns and colors I now beheld: deep greens, pale crimsons, rich violets. I was in awe.

But the carpets were threadbare, the furniture worn of its gilding, the marble tiles at my feet chipped on the edges. The bones of the place were still intact, but I had a sneaking suspicion that the body was withering.

Hwyfar, the new Queen Regent, was keeping us waiting. We had met the Knights of the Body emissaries at the stables and exchanged good words. Palomydes and his brother Safir wept to see one another again, speaking hastily and clasping each other's faces. Sir Morien, who had briefly trained under me as a squire, was now a full-grown man, though he retained the serious manner he'd had as a child. Once our greetings were made, we were guided through the winding walkways and open-air gardens through to the Great Hall.

The Skourr Council stood, their heads veiled with opaque black silk, unmoving before the Queen Regent's dais. Someone was playing a harp behind us somewhere, and it smelled of sweat and stale wine and old apples. I felt a deep unease at their presence I could not explain.

Palomydes leaned over to me, whispering. "These are the priestesses, no? Like our own Morgen and Vyvian?"

All the mounting, dismounting and genuflecting had left my knee barking in pain, so I shifted with a grunt. "Of a kind. Yes, they train in the same ways. But the Skourr Council are bound to Avillion. They never leave the Isle. Morgen and Vyvian, and their sisters before them, are a different sort."

"They are beautiful. In a somber kind of way," remarked Palomydes.

"You always find such things beautiful. They look like they're on their way to a funeral pyre. Or lighting one. Hopefully not yours."

"I see less mourning in them than I do power," said Palomydes, voice soft, almost dreamy. "What would they think of a man like me? You know, in my homeland, we had similar priestesses, but they were promised to a single goddess. I should like to know more of their power and understand if there are similarities."

"Well, I sincerely advise against seeking out their 'powers' or looking under their veils. I have heard stories of them turning men's pricks to stone—or worse."

I had not actually heard such perfidious rumors, but Palomydes' look of shock and scandal was so utterly perfect that I had to summon all my composure not to break into peals of laughter.

The smell of fresh baking bread filled the Great Hall and with it, the clanking of metal in the distance. My stomach lurched, spun, and I felt a mix of elation and anticipation, utterly baffling to me. Glancing over at Gareth, I noticed my brother going a little pale about the cheeks. Still nauseated. This tardiness did not bode well for any of us.

Least of all for me.

Still, I was not prepared for the next moment.

Hwyfar, the Queen Regent of Avillion, strode into the Great Hall. My mother, Anna, had always said that Hwyfar owned every room she occupied, and I supposed it was even truer here in Withiel Castle. There were no cupbearers, no ladies in waiting, but she did not need such things.

For one bright moment, Hwyfar stood at the entrance to her own hall and stared down the greatest knights Arthur had to offer, and we were all wanting in her presence.

Hwyfar was dressed in trousers made of thick, stitched leather, and boots that rose to her ankles. Over them she wore ceremonial greaves, etched with the knotwork designs for which the Isle was famed. Instead of a gown, or a man's tunic, she preferred a strange conglomeration of both: her heavy bosom was well-shaped by a bodice of stitched gold, but she wore over it a long kind of robe akin to the sort Palomydes sometimes favored. It was green as moss and textured in velvet to further mimic nature. She wore three torcs of gold on her neck and a simple circlet on her brow.

And gods, her hair. Hwyfar's copper fall of hair was a similar hue to my own, but I so rarely saw it in Carelon that I could not help but stare. Her hair was worn long, and fell past her waist, like a maiden's, with twisting braids at the top studded with pearls. It framed her fierce features—those deep amber eyes, the high brow, the wide lips—and lit from behind as she entered, kindling her with an unearthly glow.

To make matters worse, she carried a sword slung across her back. Gods, but she set my teeth on edge. And not in an unpleasant way.

"When you are in my hall," said Hwyfar, the Queen Regent of Avillion, "you take the knee."

Her low voice resonated through the hall, and I found myself starting to obey without question. I felt my throat constrict, my hands clench, as all the knights clattered to their knees. She was no enchantress, but she would have given Arthur a run for his life if she'd been queen instead of Gweynevere. None of Gweyn's softness, none of her sweetness, was in Hwyfar. If it had ever been there before, it had been burned away by her fury.

By the sound of more armor, I supposed the rest of her retinue was filing in. They were sparse, but strong.

I was a prince by birth, by the gods. I did not need to bow to her. And yet Arthur had given us explicit instructions to indulge her as needed. She would not be queen long. Soon, the High King would be lord of Avillion, Lyonesse, and beyond. We need only be patient.

So, despite the pain in my knee, I bowed, knelt, and breathed.

I felt a strange feeling uncoiling in my chest, a need and a desire that I did not know what to do with. How long had it been since I had bedded a woman—since I'd even *considered* it? Too long. The tension was sudden, overwhelming, my throat dry. I tightened my fists around my drawn and proffered sword.

"Gawain of Orkney, is it?" Hwyfar's voice drew nearer. She had walked straight over to me, speaking my name with that same slight accent Gweyn had, drawing out the first syllable of my name.

"Yes, Your Majesty," I replied. "We come at the command of Arthur, High King of Braetan."

"Indeed, the king sends me his most decorated war captain and firstborn nephew." Her tone was amused. "He must truly care for the plight of Avillion."

I looked up to see her towering over me, a crooked smile on her face, arms crossed before her. Her gaze held me down with the weight of an anvil, unblinking, and for a brief moment, I considered she might be a witch, about to turn us all to pigs. But then Queen Regent Hwyfar laughed through her nose, and began walking down the line of knights, examining each in turn.

"You may rise," said the Queen Regent. "All of you. Unless you enjoy looking at the ground. And in that case, I could use some opinions on the tiles. I have been considering a renovation."

The spell broke, just as abruptly as a summer shower. I rose and looked around, blinking, unsure what had just occurred. Hwyfar was no goddess. But she was mighty, and clever. I recalled her having spent a great deal of time around minstrels and troubadours. No doubt she had learned to incorporate some of their theatrics into her own conduct.

I needed to be careful.

So I tried to train my eyes from her face, but, but gods, I did not *want* to stop looking at her. I wanted her to look me in the face, again, to dare to see me. What was wrong with me? I felt drunk.

"No doubt you are all tired and hungry. We have prepared a welcome meal for you," said the Queen Regent, clapping her hands three times.

The tapestries to the right and left of us fluttered open, and a small army of servants appeared, all carrying trays of food or else tables and chairs for sitting. There were huge ewers full of cider, by the smell, and long, twisting loaves of bread, too, still steaming hot from the ovens, plus ceramic pots of butter and long loaves of cheese.

Sir Cador, the captain of the Knights of the Body, swept by, hastily introducing his knights to my own, while we all sought our seats amidst the tumult. We were to eat together, then, at long tables, before any kind of discussion began. I supposed, here in Avillion, we were to abide by their rules, however odd they might seem. Besides, I was famished as I had not been in ages.

We ate, and I tried to focus on the conversations at hand, but I was ever distracted by Hwyfar's presence, though I sat as far away from her as politely possible. She sat on the throne, indolent and lazy, leaning to one side and twirling a string of pearls. Those long, pale fingers reached up into her hair now and again to drag down her unruly locks.

Even when I wasn't looking at her, I could *feel* her. And the more I tried to avoid looking at her, the more I wanted to look at her. I felt giddy. Happy. Like I'd been sitting in the sunshine all afternoon, and had just cooled my throat with restoring spring water.

"Well, looks like Gareth finally has his appetite back," said Lionel, elbowing me in the arm. "I think you nursed him back to health pretty well. Can't say I thought you were the nurturing type, Gawain, given what I've seen you do on the battlefield, but I am always willing to be surprised."

I picked at the bread before me. It was fragrant, seasoned with a flavor I could not place. "I take no credit for his healing. I think it was just a matter of planting his feet on the ground long enough to settle his stomach."

Lionel glanced over to where Hwyfar sat, leaning over to one of her priestesses to whisper something. His pale brows knit together. "I swear she was not so tall when she was in Carelon. Is it possible for a woman to grow years past her bleeding?

Perhaps she has some potion. Which, in my case, I should look into. I never did grow to my full potential."

"Height is no great blessing, Lionel," I said, stretching out my legs to demonstrate just how compact I had to be to sit at the long table. The chair groaned in reply.

"Well, it has some advantages." Lionel grabbed another loaf of the long, braided bread. He turned it in his hands before taking a giant bite, leaving crumbs in his beard. "You should see the way folks watch you when you walk in. Anyone would be glad of such a lover. How can the rest of us measure up?"

"My brother is aware of his power," Gareth said, grabbing some cheese. "But alas, it is wasted on him. He much prefers the comfort of war strategy, detailing rosters, and polishing his collection of swords to the complications of relationships, these days."

That was not an unfair assessment. Grief had worn me away in some aspects. Lovers had come and gone, but few had lived long enough or connected deeply enough to leave a lasting impression, save Drian, and he had been a love on the field, fleeting and fast—then dead. I desired friendship and love, and that was difficult to come by, and I was ashamed to admit it to my comrades.

"Haven't you heard, Lionel? I'm to be married when I return to Carelon." I took a deep draught of my cider, the tartness quenching and fresh. "So, your ruminations mean little."

Lionel made a gagging sound. "All the more reason for us to find you a comfortable bit of flesh for the—"

"What do you think is in this bread?" This came from Lanval, who was examining one of the chunks, picking out the little bits I could not identify by taste.

"Flour," I said, glad for the interruption. "And something that tastes like grass."

"Marriage or not," said Gareth. He leaned over to me, dropping his voice low enough only I could hear. "You might want to stop staring at the Queen Regent, brother. You look like a forlorn whelp."

"I look like no such thing," I said.

Gareth snorted into his drink. He knew me better than I would like to admit.

"Just watch yourself," said Gareth, as if he were some storied expert in matters of the heart. "I know just as well as you do that Uncle Arthur gave you explicit instructions to keep well away."

"Of course," I said, laughing. I hoped it sounded genuine. "I'd be mad to think anything otherwise."

CHAPTER EIGHT

HWYFAR

When I awoke the next morning, I smelled bread baking from floors below me and heard the shuffling of servants and the rattling of armor.

We would be meeting with Arthur's knights, and so I must look the part of the queen, especially for the haughty princes of Orkney. And the idea of beautiful raiment put me in a better mood. I wore no armor, but instead a gown of thick wool-of-gold. This particular fabric was known only to Avillion, and we did not export it. Those who have tried, so the story goes, reached their destinations with nothing but empty coffers full of ash. The wool itself did not come from sheep, but rather small goats that grazed the mountainsides. Their fur was delightfully soft and warm, with a smooth, almost shimmering texture. But only one kid in thirteen was born with the right color coat, and so the material was saved for royalty alone.

The dress had been re-cut, likely by a most terrified tailor, from one of my mother's old gowns. She had fancied the boxy shapes of Lyonesse, along with the fringe and beaded borders. I kept the fullness of the skirts, but instructed the seamstresses to add wrapped silk sleeves to it, embroidered with the double-swans of my father's crest. As Queen Regent, I did not have the right to my mother's crown, but I was granted access to the treasury and had set aside several sets of jewelry made to appear as regal as possible. My mother's hoard of amber was immense, from the palest of yellows so faint they were nearly translucent, to deep emerald greens and fiery reds. I wore my favorite that day: a gigantic sphere streaked in both opaque and transparent deep yellow, set among tiny green amber chips placed to look like leaves.

I had to wear a long cloak in the cold, a rabbit-fur-lined affair I had found in my father's things that fit my own broad shoulders, but it was heavy and cumbersome. I would have to go back to doing some sort of training, I realized as I met one of my handmaids at the door. I only knew how to use a staff, and it had been years since I practiced. My body had gone soft— something I, and my lovers, quite enjoyed—but the muscle beneath was not as reliable as it had once been. So the immense sword was for show more than anything.

The Orkney princes. I remembered them only scarcely, having spent the majority of my time in Carelon avoiding their kind of company, but I was surprised at how well they had come prepared to meet me that morning. The day before, in the Grand Hall, I watched them both in their armor and regalia, travel-worn and exhausted. I only knew Gawain by his unmistakable breadth and by his red beard and mustache. I thought I caught a glimpse of warmth in his eyes as he watched me.

"Her Majesty, Hwyfar, Queen Regent of Avillion," came my announcement as I entered the private dining quarters on the third-floor terrace

Sir Gawain stood, Sir Gareth by his side, and I took in their faces, their clothing. They dressed as princes ought, tunics clean and pressed and of fine silks; their belts shone in brass and silver, the rough design familiar to me as the style of the Orkneys and not Carelon. Both had blessedly bathed, and stood together, mountains of muscle and manhood. Quaint, and likely just as Arthur had asked.

For their part, I could see only the vaguest similarities between brothers. Since the last time I had seen Sir Gawain, he had aged well; he was still fair, freckled, and green-eyed, but his bearing was broader, his face more rugged. The beard suited him well, in addition to the longer hair—he wore it pulled back into a queue now, rather than cropped short as I recalled. His brows were darker than his hair, and he had high cheekbones and a nose shaped by many a break, as well as a scar through one brow. Handsome, uniquely so—though scowling at the moment.

Sir Gareth, on the other hand, was the sort of man made for songs, his dark hair silky and long, tied back in a gold lace. He seemed more at home in his own skin than Sir Gawain, who shifted a little on his legs even as I watched. Sir Gareth's face married the severity of male virility with the softness of a woman's touch—his mother's lips, I realized. And his eyes, though a simple pale grey, had a vibrant intensity about them. Yet he reminded me of someone else, and I could not recall precisely who.

"Sir Gawain and Sir Gareth, Princes of Orkney," said the page, unnecessarily. So was the shape of my life, a new and constant string of unimportant and yet essential pageantry.

They both bowed, and rather well, even if Sir Gawain had a hitch in his step. An old injury, I suspected. When I bade them sit with a flap of my hand, I saw the wince he tried to hide.

When Gawain stood again, our eyes met a second time. For a brief, breath-taking moment, I saw myself entwined with the eldest prince of Orkney, our bodies flushed with arousal, my lips trembling like some newly deflowered maiden. I could smell his sweat, sense his own burning desire. My body simmered to life, a tingling in my loins, the likes of which I had not experienced in months.

I quickly quashed the fluttering in my stomach, though a lingering dampness remined about my person. I never had been with a man so mighty of body, so solid and strong.

No, *no*. I was most certainly cracking under stress. I had to calm myself.

Sir Cador came in behind me, followed by Sir Safir and both Skourr Gliten and Skourr Ahès. Kian was the last to enter, dragging shut the large doors behind him and giving me a knowing look. There were more announcements, and at last everyone took their seats, and I arrayed myself in the enormous chair at the head of the table. I had to admit, I liked the sense of control it gave me, even if it was an illusion. This chair had been part of a set gifted to my parents on their wedding—the other had been lost, perhaps burned, after my mother's departure. It was made of carved oak, but looked like a pile of antlers, enveloping me.

"At last, we are gathered," said Sir Cador. He gestured to the food on the table. "I realize that to our guests from Braetan, this practice is strange, but we dine and discuss here in Avillion. We believe in the sacred connection arising from eating together as equals."

Sir Gareth bobbed his head. "I could grow accustomed to such a concept. I have had to endure many long, thankless discussions with an empty stomach and a darkening mood. A welcome departure, I say. And the bread is the best I've ever tasted."

"These are called the Braids of Una," I said, picking up one of our prized loaves and holding it up to our guests. "You may have already noticed we enjoy decorating our bread, and braids are sacred here on Avillion. Una was a priestess who became a saint for her contributions to bread-making, bringing to us our recipe for sourdough. The honey is from the same hives she began over a thousand years ago."

"It tastes marvelous, Your Majesty—I cannot stop eating them," said Sir Gareth, already beginning on a second braid. "I am in awe, indeed."

"Try it with the spiced honey," I offered, giving him an indulgent smile. "I promise you will be surprised how the addition complements the sour-sweet bread."

"You seem quite the culinary historian, Your Majesty," said Sir Gawain, while his brother closed his eyes, indulging in the flavors.

He was not exactly giving me a compliment, but as regent I could choose how to interpret the conversation as I wanted. "Why yes, I am. You, no doubt, are aware of my reputation at Carelon," I said, not waiting for him to answer. "And you will have learned that I value the experience of the senses above politics and war games. But do not mistake my understanding of one game for a lack of the other."

"Clearly that is not the case, Your Majesty," said Sir Gawain, one scarred brow raised just a bit above the other. He had an oddly expressive face for one with such a brutish countenance, and I watched as he only picked at the fruit on his plate, far less enthusiastically than his younger brother. They were so very unalike. "But not all of us can live such indulgent lives, or avoid politics and war games."

Sir Cador bristled, but I held up my hand. I felt a thrill in my chest at this lively discussion, and I was not afraid of Sir Gawain.

"The people of Avillion have lived a thousand years of peace, until quite recently, and we do not see war as the natural enemy of pleasure. For we understand there is far more to gain from pleasure than from conflict," I continued. "It's been how many weeks since the last war, now, in Carelon? Six?"

That struck a nerve. Sir Gawain glared at me. I could swear I felt the air sizzle between us, hot as fresh ash. "I doubt I can count more years than you do, Queen Regent," he said, words clipped and precise. "But I have fought more battles, upon more fields, and looked into the eyes of more dying soldiers than you can fathom. So do not presume to lecture me on war while you dine on your precious braided bread."

"Do please excuse my brother," said Sir Gareth, snatching another Braid of Una from Sir Gawain's plate. "He has not had enough sleep."

"I slept perfectly fine, thank you, my brother prince," said Sir Gawain, visibly biting back other words. "I did not come all this way to be tutored on Carelon's moral shortcomings by an indolent princess."

"Sir Gawain," Sir Cador said, but I hushed him with my hand.

I was quite wonderfully entertained. Having grown up with sisters, and with a very strict leash at court, we never were allowed to tussle in public in such a manner. I wondered if Arthur's knights were all at one another in such a way. If they were, I might be enticed to pay more attention to politics.

"Sir Cador, please do not upset yourself on my count. Sir Gawain's opinion of me is no different than any of the other knights of Arthur's table." I waited for his response, and when none came, I continued. "Of course, when I arrived in Carelon, I was the king's intended—when his interest moved on, I had to find my entertainment elsewhere. Certainly no knight among you would have done otherwise, and yet I am judged by different standards. Though I kept myself quite occupied at Carelon, I was not immune to the rumors and scandalized whispers. I understand seeing me now as Queen Regent invites a new interpretation of my person."

"Indeed. Which means we must put aside quarrels and previous perceptions and discuss the matter at hand. For regardless of your opinions on war, it has come to you," said Skourr Ahès, her voice resonant and bright. "Prince Ryence the Pretender and his large force are approaching. Treachery and murder in our own halls. As the Queen Regent mentioned, until quite recently, Avillion has been at peace. And we wish to keep it that way through whatever means possible."

CHAPTER NINE

GAWAIN

GARETH'S WARNING HELPED me see Queen Regent Hwyfar more clearly for what she was the next morning: I knew she was playing a game. She had to be. As powerful as she was, as beautiful and as clever, her time was limited, and she was mightily out of her depth. She knew nothing of war, nothing of sacrifice. This mantle of regent was a performance, nothing more.

She dared to mock politics and *war games*? As if my men had lived, fought, and died upon bloody battle fields as entertainment? As she played the libertine and rolled about with half the court?

My blood boiled.

So we ate, and argued, and the Queen Regent pressed her lips together and stared me down, but when the Skourr priestess demanded we speak of war and the issue of Prince Ryence, I did pay attention.

It's true, I have never been a man of politics and intrigue. It bores me. But show me what I can separate with a sword or bash with a shield, and I will ensure the job gets done.

I was not, however, prepared for the what followed.

The older Skourr priestess pulled out a long scroll from some unseen pocket in her robes and flung it upon the table, unfurling with a rustle and a hush of parchment against woodgrain. Then she passed her hand over it, sprinkling red dust.

The dust did not rest upon the parchment, but instead hovered in mid-air, clinging to invisible earthworks and terrain, solidifying before my eyes. I looked over at my brother, and his expression likely mirrored the awe in my own.

"I believe you are not used to such displays of magic," said the Queen Regent, the note of satisfaction in her voice clear.

"The arts of Carelon, as you are aware, are far more subtle," I replied, moving my head to change my vantage point. Merlin, I was certain, had such capabilities during his lifetime, but he saved them for Arthur. The map before me was stunning, and the near-transparent red terrain remained, and now I could see the imprints of little roads, clusters of buildings and tents.

It was Avillion, rendered in perfect detail. And just to the west, I could make out the edge of another landmass, and a fleet of tiny red ships.

The air in the room smelled sharp, like tanning leather and copper. I did not want to think what the powder and magic were made of. My mother, ever wary of magic, often told me to stay well away from such power. It was one of the reasons we had never been given prophecies—or if we had, she had never told us. She did not trust Merlin, most especially. And though there were many circumstances in which I did not heed my mother, the way her eyes had looked when she had warned me chilled me to my soul. So, reluctantly, I had listened.

Swallowing down my awe, I moved around the table to where the ships were. "This represents where the fleet is now?"

Sir Cador nodded. "As far as we are aware. We have impressions of the surrounding seas, and our priestesses can help delay the inevitable. But we do not have the power needed to prevent the fleet from landing altogether. We suspect they will make landfall within the next two weeks, here."

The old knight, who had the face and build of a war general but the demeanor of a kindly uncle, gestured to a small cove on the far side of the isle from Withiel. The town nearest the cove could not have housed more than a hundred souls, judging by its size: a temple, a scattering of houses, a field. But the fleet, yellow-sailed, angled ships with boar's-head prows, easily carried a thousand men.

A thousand men.

Looking around the table, even taking our knights into consideration, I could not imagine our numbers would even begin to serve against them. We had brought twenty-four men.

Gareth gave me a doubtful look, but I had no intention of alarming my hosts. They, too, understood the situation, and they faced it head-on. Not to mention, if they could perform such magic as what I beheld in that moment on a larger scale, perhaps my assessment was in error. I had no idea what they were truly capable of.

I had underestimated a woman of magical prowess once, and she had killed the most powerful enchanter Braetan had ever seen.

"We intend to meet them before they are able to churn through the island," said Queen Regent Hwyfar. She pressed her hands onto the table, and her knuckles were white. "If they make landfall where we suspect—and given the winds and the currents, it is unlikely they will manage anywhere else without risking their fleet, especially giving our coaxing—we do not want them ruining the western slopes and haranguing our people."

"So, you want to ride out to meet them," I said to her, meeting her amber stare.

She did not look away. "I intend to, yes. We must prepare for war, but first we must ensure it is the right course of action. I do not wish to sacrifice the lives of my people acting on impulse and fear. We will send word ahead, and when we receive their promise of goodwill, we will meet under a banner of peace to treat with them."

If only Arthur had listened to reasoning like she did. My knee twinged as I took the corner of the table, and I had to bite back on my tongue to stop from shouting. The trip had made it worse, and sitting this long was aggravating.

"It cannot be a large party," said Sir Cador. "But we will need to send our best."

"I do not know Prince Ryence well." The Queen Regent was staring now at the yellow ships on the map. "But we know he has gone to great lengths to poison our court from within, and we must be cautious."

"Yes," I said. "The messy affair on the Feast of Fire night. We heard. Have there been any incidents since?"

Sir Cador frowned. "Not that we have seen. Sir Bruin was a widower, and his sons are in Carelon. I sent word to King Arthur, of course."

"It is tempting to think that our troubles are over, but I believe that is Ryence's intent," said Kian, the court bard. "Not the most elegant of intrigues. But it may be we are expected to underestimate them. Sir Bruin was a good man, or so we thought. He perished before we could speak to him further on the subject."

"Have you any suspected parties?" Gareth still gazed at the magical terrain before us now and again, as if he could not convince himself of its existence. "Observed any strange behavior?"

The bard was the one to answer again. "We have a few, but the trail is tenuous. We were hoping that might be a task you could aid us in, while we prepare. It may be that those in court would be more willing to loose their tongues to famed knights."

I laughed. Couldn't help myself. "*Famed* is a generous word. Especially in a place like this, where legend walks the hills."

"Legend walks in Avillion, yes—but it also shits, ruts, and dies," Queen Regent Hwyfar said, her eyes cutting across the table toward me. "I did not consider you so whimsical, Prince Gawain."

"Far from that, perhaps just tired. Your apple mead lingers well past dawn," I admitted. It was not altogether dishonest, though I had not partaken in it. Gareth, on the other hand, had imbibed far more than he was prepared for. "But in terms of our aid to you—I am happy to go with you to treat with the enemy, if that is what you wish. We could propose a mutual location under the banner of peace, bring a small force, and under the rules of chivalry, conduct discussions. Meanwhile, Gareth can continue here—he is known for his circumspection, though you would never guess by his size."

Gareth grinned at me, and for a moment I saw the little boy I remembered, happy to have skewered a fish on the riverbank in Orkney. "I would be most honored to do so. Perhaps, Bard Kian, I can work directly with you on the matter. We can discuss together."

"I will also need an assessment of our garrison," said the Queen Regent. She gestured to the Skourr priestesses, and the younger one sprinkled a bit of blue dust on the map this time. Now, we saw Withiel castle rendered in perfect verisimilitude, down to roaming cattle and a pair of children playing hoops and sticks in the courtyard. "I do not wish to leave my castle untended and vulnerable."

"We will need to discuss your capabilities, then," I said. "Points of vulnerability, areas that need reinforcement—stores of weapons, food, and how many hands you might have. Of course, there are considerations for capacity, as well. Withiel is an ancient structure, built as a defensive fort, so with a little work, we could house a few hundred civilians if needed. And, if possible, a brief understanding of how priestesses might be able to assist in defense."

The Queen Regent looked at me again, but there was no defiance in her expression. Instead, I saw a glimmer of curiosity. "Yes. Very well. Sir Cador, please work with the princes and ensure they have access to our garrison, and I expect Sir Morien will be a most helpful guide in these matters. Skourr Ahès and Gliten can answer their questions about priestesses, and you and Kian can give them access to the castle."

I was pleased at the outcome, in spite of the bickering. The Queen Regent had certainly grown into her responsibility—far more than I would have imagined.

Standing from the table, the deep folds of her luxurious gown rustling as she did so, Queen Regent Hwyfar looked around us all. "This is a desperate hour for Avillion. We have not had war on our shores for a thousand years. There are dark days ahead of us, but I will not have it be known that the Isle went down without a fight."

We all rose and bowed. Even I, who wanted nothing more than to avoid such feelings of fealty toward a woman who had been queen only in name and for less than a season.

I was about to leave, waiting for the rest of our small council to depart, when I felt someone tap my shoulder.

"Prince Gawain, a word."

I turned to see Queen Regent Hwyfar right behind me, and barely had to look down into her intense gaze. I took a step back, not because instinct told me, but because I had been taught well.

"Your Majesty," I said, barely missing twisting my knee to give her a wider berth.

She must have seen my pained expression, for her brows knit together and she said, "I think you might benefit from one of our healers. They are well-versed in matters of the body, and may be able to give you some respite from the pain. You are yet young, but you have fought many battles. We are far from the age of immortality."

"No need," I said, which was not the truth. Of course, she was right. But I did not want to let her see my weakness. Which made no sense. I hated myself enough for the injuries I'd been given, and those I had inflicted, but I did not need to add her pity to it.

"Prince Gawain, if you are to help defend this isle, I need you at your best. Please do not let pride get the best of you."

"A little rest is all I require, I assure you." A lie, and she knew it, too.

"Then you are indeed blessed among all people," she said, brushing past me in a whirl of skirts, a curl to her lip. "Either way. I am expecting arms training by either you or one of your companions in the morning. I hit very hard, but I need practice. One among your retinue will meet me at first light tomorrow morning, in the training ring by the garrison."

"Surely Her Majesty has plenty of willing knights among her own ranks," I said.

I did not expect her reply.

"I have already mastered the arts of Avillionian hand-to-hand combat, Prince Gawain. We use spears and lances, bows and arrows. But we have never been much for large swords. And it is against their sworn oaths to teach the rule of steel to any daughters of Leodegraunce. So, I seek your expertise in this matter, as you would not be beholden to those strictures."

"Ah," I said.

She was just at the door, her guards falling in line, when she gave me another appraising look. "And if you change your mind about the problem you *certainly do not have*, I would suggest calling for Kian first."

Were she a man, the scene might have ended very differently. Only Arthur had ever spoken to me in such an imperious tone, and I only allowed it because he was both my uncle and my king. Yet, once again, though anger blazed through my body and my face flushed, I could do nothing but watch after Hwyfar as she left the room, the immense oakwood doors shuddering in her wake.

I had not realized Gareth was still in the room until he spoke from behind me. "She knows your weak spots, brother."

I knew he did not just mean my knee.

CHAPTER TEN

HWYFAR

I REGRETTED, GRAVELY, my insistence to Gawain that we begin training the next morning. It was a bit of posturing on my side, a trick I had seen at court many a time: show that you are dedicated and strong, and make others rise to your standards. Gawain had not flinched, but as priestesses stoked the morning fire in my room, I had a dire headache and I felt raw from the inside out from my evening of drinking, not to mention feeling as if I had been boiled in my own skin.

All I remembered from the night before was arriving alone in my room, the overwhelming emptiness swallowing me whole. I had tried to conduct myself in a queenly manner, but the more time passed, the darker my thoughts wound, until I found some of the fortified apple mead and drank myself into a stupor. In the night I'd half fallen out of bed and was sick on the floor beside me. I vaguely remembered a handful of faces around me at some point, bringing me back into my covers and washing me up, but none familiar to me. I must have had the presence of mind to ask about the morning training, though.

Upon waking, the chasm of loneliness inside of me opened up again, and I remembered Nimue's face from my dreams: her deep eyes, her curving lips, the traces of dark hair at her brow and temples, the smell of her musk, and the way she kissed me as if she would drink me dry. No one had loved me as she had.

And I had left her. In my grief over Gweyn's death, I had left Nimue alone, and returned to find her dead. Did death and loss follow me everywhere?

When the shadows passed, and I was done vomiting, I began preparing for training. I did not have a complete set of training leathers, but I had adopted trousers for many years, and so I was able to assemble a passible outfit for training before making my way down to the garrison training grounds. It was snowing, and I found some of my father's old furs and a leather doublet that would suffice for the occasion. The result was not anywhere near as impressive as my previous day's ensemble, but it would do.

It was not, however, Gawain who met me at the garrison training grounds, but my old friend, Sir Palomydes.

Sir Palomydes was dressed in dark leathers and thick, green wool, trimmed with white ermine. His long, curly black hair was pulled back into a neat plait behind his head, and his face more cleanshaven than I remembered. I suppose he was one of those kinds of men who could never look *wholly* cleanshaven, given the thickness and darkness of his hair.

He was shorter, too, than I recalled, though every inch of him was honed: narrow, lithe, strong. And he smiled at me warmly, his eyes glinting.

"Good morning, Your Majesty. It does my heart good to see you again," he said, falling into a smooth bow. "I am impressed by your dedication to this early hour."

"I am told that discipline helps shape a good warrior," I said, giving him my hand. He took it, lingering for a moment before kissing my fingers. I did not wear my rings, knowing they would interfere with the work, and the feeling of his warm, soft lips on my knuckles gave me a momentary shiver that had nothing to do with the cold.

"Ah, well, perhaps we put too much esteem upon discipline," said Palomydes, chuckling. He unsheathed one of his curving swords and held it out, the blade catching in the cold morning light. "It certainly has its place. But it is only the foundation.

I have fought my whole life, you know, from the shores of my homeland to this strange isle. And I have learned that honing instinct and intuition are just as essential to remaining alive as learning poses and maneuvers."

"Well, I had minimal training," I said. "And my intuition is hardly lauded across the lands. So, I am relying on someone with more experience to help guide my hand."

He gave me a grin, with just a hint of shyness. "Ah, well, I would not presume my abilities keen enough to guide the hand of a queen—"

"Queen Regent," I corrected.

Palomydes shrugged. "You are a formidable student, I must admit, regardless of the title. I am told you were taught your way around a spear and a staff at a young age."

"I mostly used them for chasing off cats," I admitted. "Though I was rather good at it. The daughters of the king were never permitted steel."

Palomydes' eyes darkened for just a moment before he said: "Gawain indicated you wanted to learn how to use a sword."

"I do," I replied. "I have never been one much for rules. And my father, though still alive, has not the capacity to prevent me from breaking this law."

"And the Skourr Council?"

I looked around. "I see no one here, Sir Palomydes. And I do not think we will disturb the Skourr priestesses, for they are deep in their morning prayers and shall not join the mortal world for another few hours."

"Very well," said Palomydes. "First, we will need to select a sword for you. I am told you have a key to the cache."

Though I could not say why, exactly, I was very pleased with myself on that particular matter. Sir Cador would not budge in terms of giving me access, but it was through Kian I found my way. And through Gweyn, partially. I remembered she had told me about an old key that lay on one of father's shrines in his personal temple, one she remembered for its intricacies, that matched the lock on the garrison cache. I asked Kian a few nights before if I might visit the temple, to pray for father, and as Queen Regent, he could not refuse me. Though he followed me in, he had no idea of my capabilities with sleight of hand.

"It's my mother's cache," I said proudly. "And it lies inside the garrison; no one has been able to get to it for years. But my sisters and I have our ways."

I had not forgotten Gweyn's warning, but my mind was a mire: I needed to think beyond Avillion, to her portents. Perhaps this was the first step toward untangling that web.

I held the key out to Sir Palomydes, and we walked together into the garrison cache, a small stone room just to the west of the sparring ring. The key itself was hammered iron, twisted into the shape of acanthus leaves and shaved along the edges to expose a brighter metal beneath. It almost looked like a little axe.

Holding back my own sense of wonder, I gave only a casual glance behind me before I turned the key in the ancient lock and felt the mechanism give way. The door, strapped with more iron than fortified with wood, groaned as I pushed it in, and indeed it took Palomydes' help for me to get it all the way open.

The morning light shone into the small room by way of a narrow, high window, streaked with particles of dust.

Thankfully, I had brought a lamp for just such circumstances, and after fumbling to light it, I was able to bring the rest of the room into focus.

Both of us let out gasps of wonder at the sight before us, and Palomydes said something in a language I did not know.

The cache room displayed weapons of every style and shape, beautifully wrought by artisans of Avillion and imported from near and far. There were bucklers and shields, fine chain shirts, pole-arms—enough for an impressive retinue.

At the very end were three suits of plate, dust-covered but glinting, still. One was covered in rust, but I could see the roses on the etching, the delicate cloisonné, and it had a blue sash around the middle emphasizing the waist—a woman's shape. To its right was a darker suit, shaped much the same, but chiseled with dragon scales and painted in red and copper the emphasize the design. It was an armor for movement, for flexibility, and it had a deep green sash across the shoulders.

The last was gold armor, taller and broader than the other two. The chest was a crisscross of knot work portraying two lions nose-to-nose. It had fine, pointed shoulders, a narrow waste of articulated steel, and a crowned helmet with the yawning mouth of a vicious lioness.

"By the heavens," said Palomydes, and I could hear the reverence in his voice. "What did you just say about women and steel?"

"These were for us," I said, knowing it true, but not understanding how it could be. There was no doubt that someone had commissioned these for us—our personalities were written in the lines each of them, as plain as our own fingerprints. "I think my mother... I think she planned to give them to us, when we were grown. But she never stayed. And my father never spoke of them."

"These are more than beautiful," Palomydes said, giving me a hesitating look. "Do you mind if I look closer?"

"Of course," I said, choking back tears. I did not want to seem vulnerable, but no matter what I did, the beauty and the meaning of these suits of armor kept rising up to swallow me.

Palomydes moved aside some of the fallen polearms and staves, reverently replacing them, before moving closer to the armor. I held out the lamp, trying not to let it shake as hot tears flooded my cheeks.

"You said, 'us,'" he said, not looking at me, but instead taking the golden sash from the lion suit between his fingers. "Your sisters, I presume."

"Gweyn and Mawra," I said, barely able to get their names out of my mouth. "The wives of Arthur."

"This is silk," he said, a note of surprise in his voice. "And not just any silk. Come, touch it."

I walked carefully to him, and he lay the swatch of cloth in my palm, patting it with his warm hands.

The silk was not as smooth as the sorts we had imported from the Kingdoms Beyond, secured though trade established in Uther's day, but it had a softness and depth I had never seen before. As I moved the fabric across my fingers it caught in the dim light, glistening.

"I did not expect you to be an expert on fabrics, Sir Palomydes," I said.

He gave me that shy grin again, his full lips moving over his lovely teeth.

"Well, there is a great deal you do not know about me, Queen Hwyfar," he said. "My mother was a merchant queen, you know. She married my father not because of her birthright, but because of money. And her family came by that fortune with the trade of silks, velvets, and the finest cotton you ever touched. Her kingdom was a chain of islands—neighboring my father's larger island of Uhr—and her family created a gateway from the Golden Kingdom of Sivhana. This silk," he continued, gesturing to my hand, "is only found in one place. That gold is natural, and is on account of it being wild silk, collected from the trees of a very specific caterpillar. It is not boiled or farmed as much of the silk we see now. I am told it has healing capabilities, besides being so beautiful. It is the silk of queens, empresses, and goddesses."

"Wild silk?" I had never heard such a thing. Nor had I contemplated the secrets of cloth as Palomydes certainly had.

"Indeed," he said. "But I can tell that I have already enthralled you. Perhaps we should leave the mystery of the silk and the armor for another day and enjoy some sparring out in the training yard."

I could not stop staring at the silk, as the interlacing red patterns embroidered: the lions, reared up and facing one another. I had seen this pattern before, but I could not recall where. Touching the silk made me feel warm, welcome, comfortable. My lips tingled, my heartbeat slowed. I closed my eyes, breathed deeply. It felt like a memory, a reminder of someone... a reminder of myself.

Just as I was about to pull my hand back from the cloth, Palomydes let out a strangled gasp and took my wrist.

"What are you doing?" My fury rose, thick in my throat, that he would dare touch me in such a way without my permission.

"Your Majesty," said Palomydes, eyes wide and staring at my forearm. "You're bleeding."

"Don't be absurd," I said, but then, as if a fog lifted from my mind, I *felt* that he was right before I *saw*.

Upon the inside of my arm appeared a stitched wound the length of one of my fingers.

Dread uncoiled inside of me, and with it, a sense of utter violation. Betrayal. I felt the bitter tang of magic in my mouth, and with it the memories of my Sundering rushed in: strapped to the table, a knife over my head, faces I could not see. Hands over my mouth, pressing down against my stomach, my lips splitting and bleeding—screaming in silence—my Sundering.

Palomydes pulled a length of cloth from his own tunic, ripping it quickly and efficiently, and began wrapping it.

I could not remember how to swallow. I felt sick, confused. I had been spelled before, as a child, more than once, and was familiar with these sensations—but there was more of me, now, and I had not lived alongside magic for a long time. My vision prickled with dark blossoms at the edges.

"I do not mean to pry," said Palomydes, "but I am concerned for your wellbeing. Your Majesty, are you safe? Can you hear me, Hwyfar?"

My voice was thin, my ears ringing: "I need Skourr Ahès at once."

I DO NOT recall how I got back to my quarters, precisely. In my distress, the castle did not lead me astray, and as I wound my way through the rough-hewn hallways, clasping my wounded forearm to my chest, I could only scold myself for being so naive.

It was instinct that had me call Ahès to my chambers.

I waited, trembling, understanding that I had been violated once again, by magic I did not understand, and my fragile exterior was crumbling quickly.

Ahès arrived, escorted by Sir Morien, looking bright-eyed but a bit disheveled. Though the guards had informed me that the Skourr priestesses were praying, I indicated that if they did not follow my directions I would likely have one of their heads on a pike. Or, at least, one of their members.

Unkempt though she might have been, her eyes still shone with irritation, as she dismissed Sir Morien.

"Well. I am here," said Skourr Ahès. She added after a pause: "Your Majesty."

I held out my arm. "Most of me. Less a bit of blood. Tell me, how did you do it?"

"Do what?" She narrowed her eyes at my arm. "That was not stitched terribly well. I suppose you want me to look at it."

"I know what this means," I said. "Don't look at me like a puzzled cow. This is Skourr magic."

"It most certainly is not," Ahès said, and I could tell I had offended her. She tore off her veil and tucked it into her robes, then rubbed at her eyes and face. "We do not butcher our queens. Especially without their consent."

The way she said it did nothing to alleviate my concern. "For your sake I will not immediately argue. If you value your life, you should explain yourself now." There was a note of desperation in my voice even I could hear. It made me even more angry.

"You are known for your bouts of inebriation, Your Majesty," said the priestess, haughty and judgmental. "It is very likely you fell last night, and one of the medics came and—"

"Do not take that tone with me, Skourr Ahès," I snarled. I towered over her, head and shoulders, but to her credit she did not shrink under my glower. She squared her shoulders, tilted her jaw up at me, and glared right back.

I continued. "I know I am only a temporary queen. I know, very well, that there are machinations in this castle far beyond my understanding. But I cannot, and will not, allow this kind of treachery. I know this is magic. I tasted it. It was the same magic that Sundered me."

The Skourr priestess's nostrils flared, her lips parting slightly. She took a deep breath, then spoke softly but firmly: "Sundered you?"

"The Sundering. When I was sent to Carelon. They—they took—" I was shaking, now, gasping for air between words. I wanted to choke, to gag. I barely managed to calm myself to continue. "There was a Skourr priestess, and she cut out my connection to Avillion. They did the same to my sisters, to prevent us from being threats to our future husbands."

I searched her eyes, red-rimmed and weary, and I saw no trace of deceit. Just shock.

"I knew it was possible." Ahès' voice was barely audible. "I had no idea it was done."

Holding up my arm, I showed her the wound. "This was concealed. But I went to my mother's cache in the garrison, where there was armor meant for me—armor perhaps made by her, I think, I remember she was a smith. I touched the armor, and it broke the illusion. And I could taste the magic on my tongue. It was the same power from the Sundering."

"May I look more closely?"

Gingerly, I held out my arm.

Ahès' fingers were gentle and breathed in sharply when she reached the top of the wound.

"What is it?" I asked.

"This is strong, strange magic. But is not the magic of Avillion."

"I am certain it is the magic of the Sundering."

Ahès eyes were full of pity. "Then I do not believe Sundering is the magic of Avillion. Here on the Isle, we possess power mostly in the realm of prophecy, illusion, and the magic of the earth. Elemental magic. I do not know what they sought in you, or what they did, but I recognize that such power comes from one place alone. The Island of Ys. This spell was used to mark you."

I felt my skin prickle with foreboding. "Ys has allied with Ryence. How do you know all this?"

"And I am afraid to tell you how." She trembled, dread creeping into my chest at that. "But I think it will help if I share, though you may not see me in the same way again."

"I see you as a nuisance and a haughty priestess," I said. "I do not think my esteem can tumble much further."

Skourr Ahès nodded, then went to the door and pressed her hand to it, then listened before whispering words too low for me to hear. Then the door creaked, a high, strange sound like boughs overhead, and she at last seemed content.

With a deep sigh, the Skourr priestesses turned toward me. "I know the magic of Ys better than anyone. My father is King Gralon, the priest-king of the isle, who has given Prince Ryence harbor these years."

That did indeed make me doubt her allegiance even more. "Then, surely, I should suspect you in all of this," I said.

She shivered again, and I realized that it was in pain. "It is true, except you must know the rest. I know some of these spells, but only because they were given to me, and only in small amounts, before."

"Before what?"

Ahès looked up at me with an expression of such deep sorrow that it took my breath away. She pulled the thick wool sleeve of her robe aside, and then ran her hand over the skin there. Just as I had seen upon my hand, the skin shifted and changed, revealing mottled scars that could only have been brought by fire.

I gasped, and she reached up to her face to reveal half her skin matching—her brilliant blue eyes were a frosty blue, the edge of her lids melted into the skin.

In an instant it was gone again.

"I was born to a Skourr priestess, and King Gralon. An experiment. But I did not possess enough power from Ys as was hoped. My father had me burned and thrown into the sea when I was six. I was found by Meliadus of Lyonesse, your uncle, who was sailing by on a mission, and sensed the power of Avillion in me; he helped me heal.

"I was sick for weeks, tossing and turning in agony, and he heard my story through my fever. But he kept me safe and nursed me back with the help of his healers. When I showed promise in enchantment, he sent me here."

I was quite certain there was more to the priestess's story, omitted for her own protection. "So you knew of Lindesoires, the vanished castle."

"In my youth, and only briefly."

"Then you knew more than I ever did. Before it was lost, it was lost to me." I sighed, weariness settling on my shoulders. "You should not have to hide so—not from me, not from the sisters of the council."

"I am not ashamed of my scars. The concealment is for my protection—now more than ever. My father can never know I am alive. I know too much. He has sought Avillion for ages, sought to drain its magic. Ys was not always so, but now it is a parasite, a corrupt power."

"Do you believe there are agents of Ys now, in court?"

"If the Sundering happened as you say, they must have been for a while now. Any of the Skourr priestesses could be." Ahès pressed her hand to her cheek, gazing into the fire. "I know not who to trust—anyone in the room after Sir Bruin's treachery is a suspect. Your Majesty, I am concerned for you."

"Isn't that your regular occupation?"

The humor did not sway her. "Queen Hwyfar."

"I am not a queen, not really."

"You should be," said Ahès, and there was real anger in her countenance. We had to have been around the same age, but I had not marked her for a woman of ambition.

97

"I have never wanted to be queen, not really—but now I find myself protective of the title, and this land, in a way I never anticipated," I said, lowering my voice. "Skourr Ahès, you know I am only doing this so we do not appear weak, so that Avillion can stay strong before we are absorbed into the greater of Braetan."

"Is that truly what you want?"

"I want many things, but a queenship and the responsibilities that go along with it were never a consideration. I was too young to even know what Arthur would have wanted of me, and when I saw what happened with Gweyn…"

Speaking her name felt like a betrayal, somehow. I had not done so in unfamiliar company. The pain of her loss stuck in my chest, and I had to move to the window, to turn my face away.

"I knew Gweyn," said Ahès, very softly. "We were novitiates together, you know. When your father asked her to go to Carelon with your bridal party, she was torn between her duty to the Skourr and her duty to you and your family. No one could have foreseen what happened, but… but I think she did."

"She always had a window into the unseen world," I murmured, thinking again of her warning—wondering, not for the first time, if I had summoned her ghost with my drunkenness. I wondered if she could only reach me when my own guard was lowered by drink. "And I think for that, she was always alone."

"A daughter of the Skourr is never alone," said Ahès.

"But she, like me, was a daughter of the crown. And our claims, heirs, and wombs, are worth more than any sisterhood. No matter what you taught her, what good did it do in the end? She died alone. And here I remain, among her ashes."

The Skourr priestess gave me a sad look, but nodded. "Fate is cruel, oftentimes to the sweetest and softest among us. I mourn her, too."

"Gweyn would never have allowed for any of this." I held up my arm again, anger making my voice shake. "If I am to be its last regent, I will not allow us to fall prey to corrupt magic. For the preservation of Avillion, for my sister's legacy, I will not hand over a broken country."

Ahès bowed. "I will make some discreet inquiries among the Skourr and try and discover what has occurred. Meanwhile, we will need to discuss your protection. I suggest you continue your training with Palomydes."

I had not told her as much, but decided it was best not to play the innocent. "It is somewhat unconventional for a daughter of Leodegraunce to be trained in steel."

The priestess only nodded. "You are an unconventional daughter. And when, and if, you are ready, there are some services I may be able to give you in more unconventional ways of magic."

"I will be leaving the castle soon," I said, trying to fight against the glimmer of hope I felt when she spoke of magic. "To treat with Prince Ryence. I expect that should give you some time to question."

Ahès considered a moment. "I will send the twins with you—they were raised along with me, with Gweyn. I wish I could come with you."

"Perhaps you could."

"I know the magic of Ys, Your Majesty. I may be the only person here who does. But I must tread very carefully, and I cannot do so from a distance."

I would have to trust her, or make the appearance of it, for now. So far, I had no other hope aside in myself, and that could not endure forever. Alone, I would fall, just as Gweyn had.

CHAPTER ELEVEN

GAWAIN

"How much do you know of smithing?"

The question came after noon prayers—which I'd attended in spite of my better judgement—from none other than Palomydes. He did not join me in the temple to Ayr, but was waiting politely, leaning against one of the trees that made up the structure's walls and beams.

"Next to nothing," I replied, head still buzzing from the interminable singing. "I'm a prince, remember. I didn't exactly grow up among the crafters. I learned how to swing steel, not work it."

Palomydes chuckled. "I thought that might be your answer."

"Taking up blacksmithing in your old age?" I asked.

"I'm younger than you are, you twit." Palomydes batted my shoulder, and we fell into a comfortable rhythm down the winding stairs toward the castle proper.

"Spiritually you will always be my elder. And morally, I suspect," I said.

"I cannot argue there. But no, I am not planning any deviation from my sworn oath to Arthur. I have, however, discovered a rather inexplicable artifact—or rather, artifacts—that need the utmost care."

We had an agreement, the two of us, forged during long campaigns in the field. It was an oath of secrecy, when we stumbled upon matters too complex for one of us to figure out, with the potential to break or disrupt the status quo. I have never been a man of politics or the machinations of court, but I learned quickly that information was just as dangerous as a festering wound if you waited to treat it. Besides, I am not a clever man, and having the aid of someone like Palomydes results in far better outcomes.

Utmost care was the phrase with which we invoked this secrecy.

"Understood," I said, already curious but cautious. Withiel and Avillion were full of crevasses I had no intention of delving... well, at least not those made of stone. "Should we find a better place to speak?"

I prayed he had not accidentally stumbled upon the *graal*.

Palomydes nodded and we found our way to a small orchard, trees still thick with snow, looking for a denser area we might be concealed but have a decent view of where to see any potential eavesdroppers.

It was cold, but not nearly the kind of chill I had endured in Orkney, so I was untroubled by the bitter wind. The furs, white fox from the Queen Regent's own stores, tickled my neck. Meanwhile, Palomydes' teeth were chattering.

"You could have picked somewhere near a fire," I pointed out as he clapped his arms and shivered.

"Halls echo," he replied.

"True. But I may not understand you with the clatter from your teeth."

He glared at me. "I went training with the Queen Regent this morning."

"Yes, I asked you to. Did she embarrass you?"

"No, that is far from the source of my troubles. We did not get far in training before we stumbled upon an alcove in the armory."

I raised my eyebrows in silent teasing, but my painfully chaste friend scowled back. I gestured for him to continue.

"We found armor there, of a kind I have never seen. With silk and fabrics I recognized from my homeland. Which means they could have only come from Lyonesse, given their age, because that is the only place we would have traded with. They hummed with power. And the Queen Regent... She was surprised. And then she began bleeding."

"You said you were not fighting." Good, not a *graal*. But still strange.

"Indeed. Touching the armor broke a spell, I think—she had been injured, and it came to light. She was very upset."

Magic such as this made me uncomfortable. It was one thing to think of the old magic of Avillion, the tree-magic and the illusion—but any power that required blood and deception... Palomydes had a bit more exposure to spells and enchantments than I did, and I trusted him on the subject.

I tried not to look as concerned as I felt, a crawling sensation slinking down my spine. "I can see why you would be concerned. Hwyfar is not a woman to express surprise in anything. It is not in her nature."

"Gawain, she is only human, and she is in a desperate situation. You are not the only one who lost Gweyn."

I cleared my throat. "I know that."

"Oh? And what gives you such insight, Gawain?"

"She reminds me of me," I said. "Hard skull, soft center." I knocked my head with my glove. "Can be fragile, sometimes. Especially when out of our element."

Palomydes looked grave. Or concerned. Or both. He knew me better than anyone, and his pause made me concerned. Was he in love with Hwyfar? Could I bear such a thing? No, that was a mad thought. She was no one's, least of all mine. And soon she would be married, likely to a member of my own brotherhood.

"Oh dear," I said, when he said nothing. "You have not fallen prey to her curves and wiles, have you?"

"Of course not," said Palomydes. "I prefer my field *lemmans*, as you well know. I have no heart for commitment." He meant it. But I did believe he cared for her and retained some sense of loyalty to her, somehow. Hwyfar had that effect on people.

"Be careful. We are not here to make friends, but to secure alliances," I cautioned.

"You are still planning on going with her to bargain with Ryence."

"I am. We received confirmation Prince Ryence will meet under the code. Gareth will stay here, but Ryence will need to see someone—"

"If you say *impressive*, I will expire here and now."

"Someone close to Arthur." I paused, running over his last words more fully. "And I *am* impressive."

"You are tall. And wide. That is not the same thing."

"You speak true, my friend."

Palomydes held out his hand. "Then I would like permission to learn what I can about the armor, and who may be plotting against the Queen Regent. I sense there is more than we know about her, about this place, perhaps about this entire situation. And I would not forgive myself if I did nothing but grow soft on bread and honey while you put yourself in harm's way."

"Ryence is no true harm. He will piss himself as soon as he sees us."

My wary friend was not convinced, but he forced a smile for me anyway. "All the better. Let it never be said Arthur's knights are not thorough in their duties."

I breathed a long sigh. Everything about Palomydes' discovery reeked of danger, and the kind of danger I wanted nothing to do with. He was looking for my approval, which I could not give him—not as his captain, not as his superior, and not as Arthur's representative. He knew that.

"If the Queen Regent's life is threatened," I said, choosing my words carefully, "you may, of course, discover what you may. But our primary focus is fortifying the castle. There is much work to be done." There was the matter of the *graal*, but that was my burden, not Palomydes'. Part of me wanted to ask him to look for clues I might submit to Arthur, but the idea of transferring that responsibility did not sit well with me. Damn my honor.

This appeared to appease him, and he nodded, shivering again into his dark furs. "Good."

"Gareth will remain here with you to assist in your personal machinations," I said. "You'll need to come up with some kind of excuse for him sneaking around. Wily fellow, my little brother, and surprisingly stealthy in spite of his stature."

Palomydes gave me a whisper of a smile. "Ah, well, there are plenty of diversions for him at Withiel—I've already seen his eyes wandering. If not after a sweet priestess, then certainly for some more sweet bread. I would not worry on that account."

CHAPTER TWELVE

HWYFAR

EVEN WITH THE distraction of packing for the journey—my legs itched to get on a horse and do something with myself other than mope about the castle like some forlorn ghost—my mind kept going back to the memories of my past, and to the look on Ahès' face when I'd mentioned the Sundering: the priestess had said it was not the magic of Avillion. My sisters and I were parted from our magic, our inheritance, put through immeasurable pain and violation. It had altered us forever, perhaps opened up a pathway for Gweyn's death. Had Father known?

I would have to stop drinking. Stop my powders. My tinctures. My only other option was to hire a taster, and no queen or king of Avillion had ever had to do such a thing. More steel was one thing; there had been a murder in my hall, after all. But outward mistrust of my own staff? My own Skourr council? My Knights of the Body? If there were traitors nearby, I was not prepared to retaliate.

My head pounded, my body ached. I missed the touch of Nimue, that curious way she saw me. Since Arthur's rejection, I had known and embraced the power of my body, the way of desire, power, and sex. I had seen those I wanted and pursued them; they responded in kind. I had sucked the fairest bosoms, slid the finest lengths along and into my sex, and entwined myself between them all. My body had been worshipped, pleasure had been my goddess. But I had not worked my muscles in the way of a warrior, the way my mother would have done.

None of my merry players had followed me to Withiel—and as I helped the maid with the last of my packing, I was struck with the knowledge that I had finally pushed every last friend away. There, in my cold bedroom, hands full of furs and wool, the last of my self-preservation began to crumble. I felt so entirely alone, second guessing my decision to trust Ahès, unsure of how to broach the subject to Kian and Cador—and, more than anything, craving the fortified mead I knew was one bell away, wanting to obliterate the feeling inside of me. The gnawing had returned, insistent and true, now entwined with cold sweats and the pale ghosts of regret.

Perhaps that desperation is what sent me back down to the barracks the evening before our departure. There were, of course, guards set to protect me, to ensure my safety. But they did not know Withiel as I did, did not know her secrets and her winding passageways. I may have been twice the size I was as a child, and some of the narrow nooks no longer allowed me passage, but I could still find my way about.

As far as they knew, I was still in my tower room. But there was a reason I insisted I remain there, and not move to the Queen's Tier.

I felt tension in the whole castle, the rumbling voices in the distance, the shuffling of robes. In all my life I had never felt so completely untethered to my own existence. I never needed to belong; I built my personality and my reputation around a lack of connection. And for a time, that had worked. I indulged in every way possible, using my proximity to power to broker a life of freedom.

Now, with my players and gambolers gone, Gweyn long dead, and my father in the throes of a final, desperate madness, I had nothing left. Not even Nimue. I could not go back to Carelon. Mawra would not come rescue me, and I had no desire for it. The last person I wanted to be indebted to was the Queen of Braetan and her pompous king.

At least here, I had a purpose. Even if it was for show. I could play one last game and then—

Alone in the barracks storage room, I sat before the suits of armor and thought of my mother, who had abandoned me. But the story had changed: she had no longer departed without a gift. She left this gift from Lyonesse, the far-off kingdom where my uncle Meliadus ruled as regent, stubbornly refusing to acknowledge my mother's death. I knew so little of them, but I wondered if we had more in common besides—if I could write to them of Avillion's plight, if I could have time to do such a thing.

Perhaps my mother had abandoned us to live life on her own terms. My father had never spoken about her departure before, and he would take those secrets to his grave. But these suits of armor were waiting for Tregerna's daughters. It could have been any of us. Perhaps, in another world, it was Gweyn who discovered them, or even Mawra—though the idea of her ever wearing such a raiment was strange, indeed. I wondered what my mother would make of us, now.

There was no doubt which suit was my own; each suit was built for a daughter of Leodegraunce, three possible threads of Fate.

Perhaps I was not Arthur's queen, and only a Queen Regent out of desperation. But I was a daughter of Lyonesse, as much as I was a child of Avillion. And it was high time I began my own story rather than paddle helplessly behind the rest.

THE LION'S MANE plumes shivered in the cold wind, the faceplate off for now, but the metal was plenty frigid against my skin. After making my decision the night before, I had strapped the entire suit to my back with lengths of leather and old rags, and crawled the passageways one step at a time, then polished every piece until the sun rose while I shook off the worst of the effects of sobriety.

When I had exited my rooms, Kian looked shocked, almost hurt. I had planned well, and the *goursez* could say nothing;

for Sir Gareth was there, with Sir Bors beside him. Kian could not look weak before them, could not express the frustration I undoubtedly caused.

With few words between them, they escorted me to my horse and our large retinue.

The armor clattered with every step I took, no doubt alerting the entirety of the castle to my presence far ahead of me. The fit was far from perfect. Still, every eye turned to me as I walked onto the field. The Skourr Council's veiled faces showed little expression, but I knew well I had done much to upset them, judging by how their shoulders tensed and they worried their hands. A Queen Regent of Avillion arrayed in the colors of Lyonesse! What could this mean? Well, perhaps they would not forget that I was a daughter of two bloodlines, and a queen twice of my own right should I choose it. Though it was not a power I wanted, it was not a power I would waste.

Sir Palomydes, who would remain behind, tried to suppress his smile as I passed him by, to little avail. He ended up coughing into his cloak.

Sir Gawain glared at me with something like contempt. But I did not want to think what it entailed, especially considering he would be traveling as my personal guard—along with Sir Lanval, Sir Bors, Sir Yvain, Sir Kahedin, and the priestess twins Elowyn and Wenna. No doubt he had expected me to play the delicate maid to his brute.

The skies were clear for the first morning in weeks, periwinkle blue streaked with white, still pink on the eastern horizon. I could see flashes of my armor refracted on the gathered crowd, rainbows and motes slashing across cloth, skin, hair, burnishing them all.

Wenna, who wore her Skourr habit over her riding leathers, leaned over to me and said, "You certainly know how to make an exit."

The crowd pressed closer, onlookers trying to get a better view of me. Clothed as I was to the last inch, I had never felt so exposed in my life. I would have felt more comfortable wholly naked in that moment.

But it was working.

I swung up on my gold brindled palfrey, shooing away Sir Cador as he tried to help me up. If I had not considered the weight earlier and tried my hand at a mount before returning to my room, I would have fallen back. But I had thought ahead. Perhaps it was on account of my clearer mind, no longer at the mercy of drink.

Not that the ascent was easy. When I righted myself above my horse, my arms burned from the effort, my thighs shuddering. The armor was well-crafted, but heavy, and though I had spent many years riding horses for enjoyment, never so encumbered.

I slid my attention to Sir Palomydes for a moment, and he raised his dark brows to me. I could read his expression: *They are expecting you to say something.*

As my caravan took shape behind me, carts and knights clattering and squeaking, I raised my hand to quiet the crowd. Kian tried not to glare, but he was not doing a very good job of it. I had offended him and alienated him; we would have words when I returned. But I pushed those thoughts aside knowing that he—perhaps *most* of my closest confidants—had knowingly withheld information from me about my mother, and my inheritance. Not to mention the chance of a sorcerer of Ys in our midst.

The crowd was a mix of court servants, workers, and townsfolk. So few I recognized in that sea of faces. But they gazed at me with a look between confusion and wonder. Perhaps it was anticipation.

"We go to treat with a threat in the north," I said, training my voice to resonate as I had been taught. I had a low voice, and I used it to my benefit. "Avillion has been a kingdom of peace for a thousand years, and I will do all in my power to prevent any conflict, as your Queen Regent, and as a child of this sacred isle. Sir Cador, Kian, and Skourr Ahès will be my representatives in my absence, and Sir Gareth and Palomydes, along with nearly two hundred remaining knights of Arthur, remain among you. May the orchards bloom."

A few cheers arose. Not thundering applause, but it was good enough for me. Rather than linger, and assuredly just make a fool of myself, I edged the retinue forward and began our journey forward to meet Prince Ryence.

CHAPTER THIRTEEN

GAWAIN

I WAS WELL and truly fucked.

When Palomydes told me Hwyfar had found armor, I imagined the sort I had seen Queen Mawra in, and even my own mother, for ceremonial events: more jewelry and embellishment than protection, symbolic and not at all practical.

No so Hwyfar's armor. I had fought toe to with armored men that looked three steps from a crucible, and with men who were arrayed like metal peacocks. But I could say with utmost sincerity that I had never seen armor akin to what Hwyfar wore.

The metal was a rose bronze, inlaid with cloisonné accents in a sigil I had never seen before, all styled like the hide of a lion. Not a lioness—the plumage on the helmet caught the light, the surcoat and sash of a silk that moved like liquid metal.

And yet, she *wore the armor*. It did not wear her.

I realized, gazing over at Hwyfar as I mounted my own horse, that I had never truly seen a queen until that moment. And I had never wanted one so desperately, either. Thoughts of her made my skin hot, my heart thrum—gods above, thinking of Hwyfar made me feel *alive*. Even if she hated me, even if I could never have her, it did not matter. For the first time in years, I felt as if I was walking into the unknown. This was no tilting field, no minor land scuffle. Every moment near Hwyfar of Avillion felt dangerous, unpredictable, and real. And I relished it to my marrow.

We made good progress the first day out, on our way to the Plain of Maeldoi, an ancient fortress now in ruin which once served the last peaceful treaty between Avillion, Braetan, and the surrounds. It had been a thousand years since it was last used, and that alone was cause for concern on my part. I did not want us walking into a trap. I knew Ryence only by reputation, and admittedly he had a considerable claim. Leodegraunce, as a native of Avillion, should have had a longer life—not as long as Merlin's, but certainly far beyond his current expectation.

There were spies in the court of Avillion, Ryence's men and women waiting for the right moment. And there were Arthur's spies, too; for what else were we?

"Your face looks like a crumpled walnut," said Lanval, coming up beside me as we came to the narrow pass between the craggy Logodenn Mountains—which were somehow named for mice, and yet looked more like broken teeth—and Brocéliande forest.

"I always look like that," I said. "Years of being punched in the face with gauntlets."

Lanval laughed. His easy air always amazed me, no matter the circumstance. "I am willing to guess the source of your consternation has one of two roots."

"Are you, now?" I asked. Aside from being almost insultingly sunny, Lanval had a perilous window into people's thoughts and moods. Palomydes called him a "soul reader," but I think he was just good at guessing.

"First of all, I could not help but note the expression on your face upon beholding the Queen Regent so arrayed," said Lanval. He always spoke like that, too. Like some marooned poet left in knight's armor.

"I was scowling."

"You scowl when you attempt to conceal wonder and amazement. And I cannot blame you. Indeed, who among us would not be moved?"

"Her armor is impressive." I was trying to sound as if I had barely noticed, but my voice, deep as it was, hitched a little.

"Ah, yes. Her *armor*." Lanval sighed. "It has been a long time for you, my friend. Just exercise caution."

"I have no plans for conquest. And you should know better. Like all royals, ourselves included, she is just a person. She shits and pisses like the rest of us." Conquest? No. She was not a person for such a word. But I was indeed preoccupied with thoughts of her, whether or not I wanted to admit it.

Would she truly choose one of my knights as her husband? I looked at Lanval—handsome, affable, lithe Lanval—and the idea of him having access to her twisted my guts. Which made little sense. Hwyfar belonged to no one, man or woman. I knew that. And yet jealousy prickled at the back of my neck like an unseen ghost.

Lanval nodded, though his expression was far from convinced. "Ah, well, even I could not say that Hwyfar of Avillion is like the rest of us, and I only know her from my brother's stories—as he used to partake in the delights of her merry band—and my own limited, but fantastically memorable, experience. I am merely looking out for you, as my brother in arms, and adding a word of caution."

I groaned, and not just because of the conversation. The chill was making my knee ache. "I do not need cautioning, Lanval. Arthur already gave me plenty of that before I left, and so has Gareth." Indeed, my uncle had been very clear about where I needed to keep my attentions. And my loins.

Lanval let out a little hum. "And, historically, you have been so very inclined to follow Arthur's advice. Or anyone's, for that matter."

He had a point. "I would not do anything to compromise this mission, which is to assist in the protection of the Holy Isle and leave as soon as she's wedded, bedded, and contained." I said this low as possible, as it was not the sort of talk I wanted repeated. But even so, I felt that same sick churning of jealousy and dread. It had been easy to consider neutralizing the threat of the Avillonians from a distance, but the longer I was among them, the more time I spent around Hwyfar, the more difficult it became.

"I don't mean compromising politics, Gawain. I mean compromising yourself. You are a prince. You are attracted to power, and there is no shame in that. Just be wary, aye? Avillion is a strange, wondrous place. But the witches here, ah, they come with wiles that eat us alive."

"As if you have never had a dalliance," I said with a laugh.

"Ah, well, I am not the king's nephew."

Forever Arthur's. "Indeed, and you ought to remember that. I'm capable of making my own decisions and looking after myself, and you have naught to worry about. I've made it this long without bringing lasting shame to my family. I can hold on a little longer."

I was not meant for court politics. Which was another reason I'd left Gareth behind with Palomydes—my brother was looking not only for signs of intrigue at court, but hints of the *graal*. I would get close enough to Hwyfar to ask her directly. The idea of skulking around myself was laughable.

"Of course." Lanval bowed his head deferentially. "It is only—again, from my personal experience—that the farther we are from our regular lives, the more we become forgetful. To say nothing of what it will be like once we cross into Brocéliande."

"You believe in the old tales, do you?"

"I believe that old tales arise for a reason. And the longer I am here in Avillion, the more I begin to consider those possibilities."

"They cleared the monsters out of Brocéliande centuries ago."

That humming again from Lanval. "Well, perhaps the Skourr priestesses are just being cautious, then. They have insisted we camp early, to prepare ourselves for Brocéliande. As I understood, they need to perform a ritual for safe passage—it is a longer way around to the Plain of Maeldoi, but once we are within, we will be safe."

"We travel with the Queen Regent of the whole Isle," I said with a snort. "Strange that she would require permission from her own wood."

"But it is not her own wood," said Lanval. "That is why we bring Sir Yvain—his mother Modrun lives within."

That name gave me such a sense of foreboding, recalling one of the tales my nurse shared with me as a child. I had begged her, night and day, for tales of strange witches and magicians, and she told me of Modrun, the witch of Brocéliande, who turned misbehaving boys who had come to steal her prized flax into topiaries and wild pigs. At the time, I had never heard anything more blood-curdling: the idea of being frozen into a plant for all eternity kept me up at night. For a child who could not stop moving, it was as much of a nightmare as those which actually plagued me at night.

"*The* Modrun?" I asked.

"The one and the same."

I looked over where Yvain stood, holding the reins of his black palfrey and speaking lowly to the twin Skourr priestesses. He looked plain enough, and I know he had a good reputation—we had both been young squires together at Carelon. I had no idea his mother was the witch of Brocéliande.

I clapped Lanval on the back, his breastplate rattling. He had never been the sturdiest of knights, but made up for lack of brawn with finesse and speed. "Then we shall proceed with our eyes open, and our hearts fortified against the wiles and whims of women and witches."

CHAPTER FOURTEEN

GAWAIN

IT HAD BEEN years since I had set up my own tent, but given our small numbers, it was timelier for me to do so. The smell of old hides, clearly unused for years, reminded me of my childhood, climbing through the old military stores at Orkney Castle, trying to figure out new and better ways to pitch a tent. Avillion, for all its beauty, was truly poor in goods, and it was a miracle the tents kept out any rain at all in their state.

The tents also made me sneeze. Beautiful as they were—embroidered, though many of the threads had long deteriorated and faded—the mildew was grown so thick in places it flaked off. What remained was a testament to craftsmanship, to be sure, judging by the silver and gold floss woven in. But it hardly made a difference now. Fuzzy mold chewed off the faces of the warriors and nobles depicted. There might have been a dragon on the side of mine, but its hindquarters looked more like a withered snail's.

As the sun slipped down over the hills, casting our caravan into dusky tones, I absorbed the smells and sights. This was no war campaign, it was true, but I could not help but revel in the familiarity. Most of the men were clustered around small fires against the cold, or else piled in their tents with furs. Bors and Kahedin were in the throes of loud passion, finding other means of warming. I had thought Bors was looking at Kahedin in that way, and I was glad love still flourished in the hearts of some.

One of the twin priestesses found me meandering toward the wood and pulled me back with a hiss.

"The Queen Regent will see you now," she said, her tone coated with enough disdain to send a dry log into flame.

I followed her to the Queen Regent's tent, which was the only one that appeared in working order and could easily have housed a dozen men.

To my surprise, Hwyfar was sitting, her back to me, dressed as plainly as I had ever seen. Her long hair was brushed out and plaited loosely down her back; I had not realized how long it was, nor how bronze. Without the trappings of gowns and armor, she was still an impressive woman, but rounder, softer. The sight of her left me a bit breathless, and warm in places I'd rather not consider.

"I am told your men are afraid of the wood, and its so-called witches," she said, not turning around to look at me.

I took a glance behind me; we were utterly alone. Certainly not the protocol commonplace in Carelon. Then again, Hwyfar never cared for propriety in Carelon, and I supposed she had no plan to do so here. "And a good evening to you, as well, Your Majesty. Our journey was well enough, thank you."

"Sir Kahedin gave me a brief update," she said. "And I am tired and feel no need to waste both our time with pleasantries."

Opening my mouth to speak, I shut it again and nodded curtly.

Hwyfar continued. "Regarding the wood: I promise you, Brocéliande will keep you safe so long as you follow my priestess's directions. And Sir Yvain's, of course. He will arrange the meeting with Modrun."

"We are not accustomed to witches in Carelon," I said. "But I do not have to tell you that."

She turned, then, and I saw she had been weeping. Oh, it was not an obvious thing. But out here, away from her powders and the lighting and attentions of staff, not even Queen Regent Hwyfar could hide the puffiness in her face and the blotches across her throat and chest.

There was more awry, as well. The dark smudges under her eyes, the way her fingers twitched. She appeared ill at ease, almost fretful.

"No, Arthur has made it abundantly clear that women of power frighten him," she said, tight-lipped.

I did not rise to her goading, however. "The ladies of court have enough venom, to be sure, but few of them have the reputation of Modrun."

"Modrun is no common witch. And our visit to her is strategic. Or did you believe I would put all my hopes in a handful of knights from Arthur of Braetan?"

"We are a bit more than a handful." The words were out before I realized what I was saying, and my face flushed hot at the implications.

Hwyfar laughed through her nose. "Oh, I have no doubt of that, Sir Gawain, given your proud stature. Now sit, before you embarrass us both. Your looming makes me feel unsettled."

I complied without comment, and she handed me flask with mulled cider. Rather than further implicate myself in forbidden flirtation, I drank slowly of the sweet drink and tried not to think of the growing strain in my breeches. "Thank you. I am growing accustomed to it."

"It has that effect on a person. As does Avillion in general. Even our exhausting insistence on peace rather than slaughter feels natural after a time."

"Though my reputation may precede me, I promise I will do all I can to broker peace," I said to her. "You have my word."

"And if peace is not attainable?"

"I will fight for you, Your Majesty."

"And give me counsel, I hope." She nodded, eyes unfocused, as if she might be looking through me. "Yes. I know your general orders. And you likely know my predicament even more intimately than the rest of your knights. Your help is, of course, most welcome; I am grateful for the assistance. But once this matter with Ryence is settled, I must select a future husband. If

I do not select one of your number, Arthur will choose one for me. I'd hoped you might help me make a judicious decision to spare throwing myself on the king's discernment once again. It did not end well for me last time."

Her marriage. To one of my knights. I had never anticipated we would broach the subject so swiftly, and certainly not that she would seek my guidance. "Of course," I said. "I am happy to discuss with you."

In this tent? In this moment? Speaking of matrimony?

"If I am to suffer the bonds of marriage, I only choose to do so to save my country. No other reason would ever compel me."

"You do not find love compelling?"

Hwyfar wrinkled her nose at me, as if the mere mention of love left a stink. "I do not have time for affection, nor do I have the leisure. I would think, more than anyone here, you would understand that."

My throat was dry, and no matter how many sips I took it would not relent. "Then what do you seek in your future husband?"

She held out her hands, admiring her fingernails and the large, blood-red stone ring she wore. After a moment, she said: "I do believe character is the most essential component in a marital contract, especially between those of noble birth, if it is to last. Do you not agree?"

Character?

"I suppose," I said, though I had not given it much thought. Avoiding marriage altogether had been my greater preoccupation.

The Queen Regent leaned forward. "And you, like me, are a prince."

"I believe you are a *princess*."

"I am Queen Regent. I can be a prince if I wish." She gave me a merciless grin. "Who will tell me otherwise? I wear the armor of a lion, do I not?"

Should have known better than to challenge her. Still did it anyway. "You can call yourself a prince all you want, Queen Regent, but your form will betray you."

"True. But I like to think I have the *spirit* of a prick." Hwyfar spoke the word with no hesitation, no blush, no concern for propriety. As easily as if she had been commenting on the spirit of righteousness.

This woman would be the death of me. A slow, arduous, exacting demise. And knowing her, I would even enjoy it, and thank her afterward for leaving me in ruin.

Hwyfar leaned forward, her shift sliding down her round, sloping shoulder as I went to take another sip of cider. I was betrayed, and my mug was empty. So I pretended to swallow, then scratched my beard as she kept watching me.

"Tell me, why have you evaded marital machinations for so long, Sir Gawain? Proximity to Arthur? Lack of interest? You were a prince; you could woo any woman. Surely you have hopes and dreams, aspirations."

"I have not given it much thought," I said honestly. "I've been afield most of my life."

That amused look again, her brow quirking. "The nephew of Arthur, not given marriage consideration? Romances?"

"Not in many years," I said. "I had a few flames, but they died out. And since then, it has not been a priority."

What the living flame was wrong with me? I could not keep my mouth from draining confessions like a leaky bunghole from a barrel.

"What a luxury. Even Lanceloch du Lac did not escape the bonds of marriage."

"Lanceloch du Lac does not spend much time at the front."

I could tell Hwyfar wanted to say something more, but then she pressed her fingers to her forehead and sighed, standing, so that her hair fell in a crimson fall down her back.

Never would I understand how Arthur had overlooked Hwyfar for Gweyn. I *adored* Gweyn, but on a first glance? Even struggling, as she clearly was tonight, Hwyfar was power and presence and wit. She was clever, and intelligence and grace— and gods, her form.

"I suppose marriage has always felt like an end of something," I finally said. "And I have ever been an adventurer. I did not want to stop my adventures—but it seems even Arthur's giant nephew has limitations. It may be that marriage comes my way whether or not I desire it."

For a brief moment, I saw the pity in her eyes. Then her expression hardened again. "Ah, so the warrior is given freedom so long as his body is without flaw, and the woman given none so long as her womb is unclaimed." She held a hand to her own belly, the fabric clinging against her ample curves. Ah, to be that silk.

Sitting as I was, I could not help but watch the line of her body unfold, the soft draping of her robe catching in the low candlelight, shot with gold, flashing threads of silk dancing.

She turned gracefully on her heel.

"If you so desire, I will answer any questions you have about my knights, Queen Regent," I said at last. "But as to their character, I can attest to them all as good, loyal men, to the last. I would never have brought them here otherwise."

"Well, then, let us get them comfortable with Brocéliande and Modrun. Perhaps as I watch them travel through the unknown forest, I will find one or two more intriguing. Nothing quite demonstrates true character like duress."

"Anything you can tell me of Modrun would indeed help quell their concerns."

Relief washed over me, cool and calming, at the final change of subject. I could not withstand much more of her alone, not without doing something wholly idiotic.

"Your knights must remember that Modrun does not tolerate any men save her son," Hwyfar said simply, as if she were speaking of avoiding meat or disliking a particular feast day. "I can tell by that look on your face that you find this strange; hers is not my story to tell, but I daresay you can imagine what she might have endured to come to such a conclusion. You have fought in wars. You have seen what men can do."

Indeed. I had seen it. From men I had trusted, never thought capable of such things. My mother had tried to warn me; Bedevere had tried to warn me. I had not listened. I had not believed these good men, these friends of the hearth, when driven by bloodlust, would take women against their will.

Palomydes had once taken a man's life because of it. A fellow knight. We had never spoken of it again.

Not that I was free of guilt—or *sin*, as the Christians called it—in any way. I had just never maligned a woman so. Though, in my darkest days, drunk and furious, I had threatened it. To Nimue. I felt sick at the memory of her small form cowering before me, vanishing into the dark hallway in tears as I continued to shout at her...

I was not a good man. But I had tried to be better.

"Very well. What would you have us do?"

"You are not to look her in the face," said Hwyfar, her eyes meeting mine, as if daring me to do the same. "You are not to look at anything, really." Her voice was a command. In that moment, if she had told me to stand outside the room and wait until the next rain, I might have.

And that was when I understood it: I suspected Arthur was afraid of what Hwyfar might be, who she could become, that he would be diminished in her presence. He did not want an equal; he wanted a subordinate. Gweyn would never have spoken in such a way, would never have commanded a room. Her nature was to give, to serve, to love. Hwyfar was a tempest.

"You are to keep your eyes trained on the ground," said the Queen Regent, stepping closer to me. "All your men. No matter what happens. You are not to touch steel. You are not to draw your weapons. If you hear or see anything, you are to trust my priestesses, and Sir Yvain."

"I give you my word, Your Majésty," I said, for what that was worth. "But why bring us at all?"

"Modrun must measure you to protect you," Hwyfar said simply. "Otherwise Brocéliande will consume you."

"Ah," I said, apparently all I was capable of managing.

The Queen Regent grimaced, standing above me, like an impatient lover, her hands on her hips. I had heard stories of her, filled with such sensual detail that it would make the most passionate knight blush. And I did not doubt it for a moment. I had once believed her the most beautiful woman in Carelon. Now, gazing up at her, I realized how wrong I was. Carelon was too small a box for her; she was, in truth, the most beautiful woman in the world.

I stood slowly, wincing as my knee twinged from the long day's ride. For a moment, she reached out to steady me, then snapped her hand back.

Even standing before her, her eyes not too far below my own, was a dizzying experience. Being in Hwyfar's presence was not about sultry wiles. She did not try to tempt me, not as I had seen her do from a distance at court dozens of times. No, she let me gaze upon her, see her truly. And I saw a glimpse beyond the power, the command, the bravado: I saw a sad woman, alone and frightened. No, I didn't just see her, I *felt* her, like a tether in my heart.

I could reach out and touch her braid, if I wanted to. Gods, I wanted to. I wanted to touch many parts of her—longingly, lovingly. I stirred, and I did not care if she noticed the look on my face.

I wanted her. Not because it was expected, not because other knights had had her—not because of her reputation. But because it felt right. *She* felt right. We felt inevitable.

And I sensed she knew it, too.

"Do you require anything more?" My body ached with need, blotting out all my sense.

Her lips parted. "Gawain..."

My name on her lips broke the spell, and I realized how close we were, how close *I* was.

"My men need me. I should leave."

Hwyfar was trembling, and she had moved closer to me. Her hand remained lightly on the sleeve of my gambeson, pulling slightly at the cuff. I felt her breath on my neck. It took every ounce of strength in me not to kiss her, to cover that final, treacherous distance.

When she answered me, her voice was quiet. "Yes. Tell your men that the caravan departs at dawn."

Then she turned away.

"Very well," I said to her. "Thank you for—the discussion." I swallowed my pride, or grief—perhaps a bit of both—and stole one more look back at her before I departed.

In a daze, the cold air making my eyes stream, I stomped over to my tent, trying to come to terms with the fact that I just offered myself to the Queen Regent of Avillion. In spite of Arthur's warnings. In spite of my better judgement. In spite of my duty to my own mission. Never had I ever considered such an act in my life. Never had I needed to. Lovers came to me!

I sat outside my tent for some time before sleep came, thinking of Hwyfar's amber eyes and the woman I had glimpsed behind them.

CHAPTER FIFTEEN

HWYFAR

ELOWYN WALKED WITH me at the front of the procession into Brocéliande, and Wenna at the back. There were a half dozen other priestesses with us, and we decided it was best that they were interspersed throughout the group. I did not want to take any chances with wandering eyes. Even if my warning to Gawain had been somewhat extreme: Modrun would not murder them for their trespass, but they would put our attempts at peace at risk. And we had precious few bargaining chips.

"Did you not sleep, Your Majesty?" Elowyn asked me, voice low, as we passed under the bent yew branches that marked the beginning of Brocéliande.

"Do I ever?" I asked.

"I had wondered," she said, glancing over her shoulder, where Gawain rode, that big, shaggy red head higher than the rest of the company, his boisterous laugh rising up as if on purpose. Her tone was full of curiosity. "Perhaps I had hoped."

I snorted. "I do not need any more complications in life."

"There is no shame in a bit of good friction," said Elowyn. "From a knight, or a priestess, or anyone of your choosing. As a daughter of Avillion, one might even say it is in your blood. Does he not please you?"

Oh, he pleased me just fine. Too well. But I was too proud to admit to such a thing, and smart enough to realize such a dalliance was a disaster. Though we had come painfully close. And help me, but I would not have stopped it. "One knight is much the same as the rest. Especially princes. They are used to getting what they want, and it is quite tiresome. I am Queen Regent now. My mind is elsewhere, Skourr Elowyn."

"I do not mean to pry," she said. "I apologize, Your Majesty."

"No need," I said. "I once made it a public mission to tumble my way through Carelon, and drink and carouse every step. I suppose it must be a bit disorienting to find me diminished."

"I am told your mother was much the same, before she came to Avillion," said Elowyn. "I suppose you do not remember much of her."

"I suppose you do?"

"No—my apologies, I only mean to make conversation." Elowyn looked away.

I sighed, wishing for a bit of hot mead to warm me up. Last night had been another clammy, fitful attempt at sleep. Though, and I would of course admit it to no one, there was a little personal friction. I was smart enough to keep away from Gawain of Orkney, but it did not preclude me from imagining what it might be like to entangle myself with him.

"My mother left when I was five." I began the tale with my minstrel's voice. "I recall so little of her. In truth, I remember more of my nurse. She was very beautiful, but I do not even recall her name. She would sing to me every night—songs of a far-off land with dark oceans and silver rivers, and ancient foes come from the mountains. When Mother left, the nurse went with her. I spent the next ten years preparing myself to be Arthur's bride. I learned enough of Avillion, but I was just a borrowed child, and was treated so. My father was distant, and now it is much too late…"

Elowyn nodded, patting her horse's neck gently. "Wenna and I never met our father. Just our mother. We were given to Avillion when we were eight, and it has been long since we have seen our families. But perhaps, in time, if all ends in peace, we shall meet them again."

Hope felt like an indulgence I could not even reach toward. What semblance of family did I have? Even with peace, where was I in the end?

"Perhaps we should ride in silence now," I said to Elowyn. "The forest has ears, I am told."

I shivered against the bitter wind, still thrashing through the branches. It had been an age since I found my way to this old forest, and then I was just a child, a curious girl of six accompanying her father to visit the weather witch, bringing gifts to the baby, Yvain, a bastard prince.

The memory of that day lingered as if through a fog, like a taste I knew but could not quite recall.

We progressed deeper into the wood, yew giving way to oak and then, at last, to holly and to the black-barked chestnuts that represented the beginning of Modrun's domain.

Yvain rode beside me, his angular face set in concentration as we progressed. If I recalled correctly, he favored his mother: black hair, blue eyes, and a dimpled chin. He was broad and strong, briefly trained in Carelon before spending the majority of his life among my father's guard. Quiet, perhaps, but trustworthy.

"Your Majesty," Yvain said to me, as the edge of the stonework fence marking Modrun's land came into view, "it is time for us to dismount."

Sir Gawain made the call, and the company followed suit. The wind had died down slightly, but the chill was still deep, the winter damp having soaked into my boots long before. I could only imagine what it was like to walk around with older, heavier armor.

Yvain addressed the group gathered. "The Queen Regent will walk with me," he said, "then the knights and priestesses together. Unless you are addressed directly by name, do not speak to Modrun. Do not look up. You may hear strange things—you may *see* strange things, out of the corner of your eyes. If you feel it would be easier to walk with sashes over your eyes, we can arrange for that."

None of the knights opted for such a thing. As I expected.

"Once we cross the threshold, and over these stones," said Wenna, her voice rising higher than Yvain's gentle baritone, "none will be permitted to speak other than the priestesses and Yvain himself. Not even the Queen Regent."

"No sounds," Elowyn clarified. "Only breath."

"Hear that," said one of the knights I did not know well. "Keep your wind to yourself."

There was a rippling chuckle through the company, and I tried not to roll my eyes. They were not my knights.

"These men will be the doom of us," said Yvain under his breath.

Indeed. I shivered again.

"We have no other course of action," I said. "Let us go forward."

Yvain walked before me, Gawain and Bors behind. I could see the top of Elowyn's head not far ahead. I trained my eyes to the ground, and clasped my hands together. Elowyn passed by each of us and put a branch of holly into each of our arms, which we were instructed to hold to our chests. I was glad for the armor now, for otherwise it would have pierced my skin. The red berries stained the plate, though, like blood.

We began the slow marching progress, our horses tethered in a long line behind us.

As soon as I stepped over the stone divide, the forest plunged into twilight. My instinct was to look up, but I gasped and looked down, catching myself, as dread slid cold fingers down my neck.

I felt Yvain's hand on my shoulder, heard his soft voice. "Modrun is angry. I do not know why. Caution, my lady."

It was warmer, as if the season's chill had not managed to permeate Modrun's magic. Such a thing made sense, even to me, as it was the weather she commanded. Yet it was not a comfortable warmth: wet, cloying, but not warm enough to remove our furs.

I could see dark roots, deep green mosses and cobbled walkways as we progressed, but little else. Sweat beaded between my shoulder blades, dripping down my back, and I could feel my armor biting into my joints. My whole body ached.

I wished I had opted for the blindfolds. But my pride had prevented it.

Sister.

Gweyn's voice.

No. I could not look up. This had happened before. It was one of Modrun's tricks.

Or I was going mad.

Sister, you must remember. Remember the face—

I heard Yvain sigh, then grunt as if in pain. He called his mother's name. The world shifted; I could smell lightning on the air. Someone drew steel—knights shouted, scrambled. I had been told to not look up, that to do so for any reason would doom us, our mission. I was not one of the priestesses, I could not pass through unscathed; I was no true daughter of Avillion, I was Sundered.

Once again, I was on a stone plinth, tied down, faces looming over me. A knife blade pressed to my skin, a hand over my mouth. I could feel my body breaking, part of me being pulled away— part of my own heart, my own life, ripping away, through the fog of potions. The sash they had tied over my eyes had slipped off; I should not have seen.

But my body *glowed*. Tendrils of light flowed up and around me, threads of silver, gold, and green.

I must have dreamed that. My Sundering was never so beautiful.

This is no dream. Sister—you can restore what was broken.

A roar split the wood, sinister and bestial: a lion. Every hair on my body stood on end, and I cowered, feeling strong arms around me, then a blow that shook us both. I had assumed it was Yvain. I smelled blood, turned earth.

"Mother!"

"Traitorous wretches among us!"

Yvain's voice, far away.

Then came the storm, and it was inside of me, and my mind fractured—and in that fracturing, I realized, it was not the first time.

CHAPTER SIXTEEN

GAWAIN

I LIFTED MY head when I heard drawn steel, knowing well enough that whatever spell was wrought had been broken.

Traitors among us.

I had been prepared, but both afraid and distracted.

Yvain was in combat with a knight arrayed in blood-red armor and a horse-head helmet and losing ground—assailants had emerged out of the thick trees. Behind them both, a fountain belched mist and icy clouds. I had never seen anything like it; I wondered if it was the source of the witch's powers.

But there was no sign of Modrun.

The priestesses had been separated from us; before us stood strange figures woven of thorns, arms moving in jagged, unnatural shapes. My knights and the Knights of the Body were attempting to detangle themselves from their grasp, but to little avail.

Hwyfar clutched her head, shrieking in a way I had hoped never to hear again. She would not look up. Her body convulsed. Was she taken by a foul spirit? Or perhaps it was the nightmare unfolding around her: I had felt that horror on the battlefield myself. Spells or no, she should not be alone.

I went to go to her when I saw Yvain twist and then let out a high whistle. To my utter shock, quicker than I would have thought imaginable, a beast came crashing through the thick woods, feet padding over the thick moss. The lion's mane was pale, golden flax, its curling lips drew back over sharp teeth, its eyes were wild and wide. And it came to Yvain's aid like a trained animal.

Hwyfar shrieked again, hands to her head, cowering to the ground.

And the storm within the fountain erupted.

I threw myself over her, and just in time. Gusts of wind tore at us both, casting all of the wood into mayhem. I could see nothing and hear nothing as debris scattered across us.

Darkness fell, thick as a velvet blanket. I heard breathing behind me and saw twin shadows convening upon us.

I had seen them before, skulking around Hwyfar, and knew their movements well. She might not have noticed how precise and fluid were their steps, but I knew trained soldiers when I saw them. Of magic I knew little, but I had a measure of instinct about these things.

Though I could not say I was surprised, I was mightily disappointed. Hwyfar had trusted them.

When the first twin priestess rushed toward me, silent as death, I was prepared, though she thought me distracted, bent as I was over Hwyfar. I clocked her under her chin with my shield, throwing her off her feet. She was the slightly heartier one of the two, but I did not think her head was in this business, whatever it was.

Gods, the rot was deep in Avillion.

The other twin came at me next, coming at my bad knee, which I'd expected. I made no secret of my weakness; the better to conceal my strengths. When I rammed my pommel into her chest, she twisted just barely in time to miss having her own legs kicked out from under her.

Just in time for the first to grab me around the throat. My eyes prickled with lights. She knew what she was doing, and I did not know how much longer I had in me. They would take Hwyfar. I could already feel the second twin making for the Queen Regent.

131

I backed up slightly, feeling my boot gently make contact with Hwyfar. She did not move. Then I twisted, and with main force slammed the twin to the ground. No matter the circumstances, power usually won out. Enemies always thought they'd measured my strength, understood it, but they rarely did, when faced with the full depth of my anger. And there, in the wood, with Hwyfar lost to me, my body vibrated with power.

I was not kind. I was not merciful. The scent of blood was in my nose, my brothers were dying around me; these women meant to kill me and to take Hwyfar.

Still, the sound of the twin's back breaking on the forest floor, the sad moan that left her when her life fled… I felt the guilt twist inside of me.

It was made no better by the sound of the surviving twin, scrambling in the near total dark to the unmoving form of her sister. Her howl rose with the gathering storm; no match for the din of the fight around her, but it still made the hair on the back of my arms rise.

I grabbed Hwyfar around the waist.

"Hwyfar," I said to her. "We have to move."

Her head bobbed against my shoulder, and she muttered words I could make no sense of. My knee ached and burned, but there was no choice. With battle fury in my bones, I dragged the Queen Regent of Avillion away from the fray.

A horse rammed into us, knocking the wind out of me, and I tried to grab the reins, thinking I could drag us alongside of it for a moment—a big horse, enough for both of us, but pacing wild.

No, it was too spooked. I would lose my arm, wouldn't be able to keep Hwyfar safe.

I screamed into the wind, and the maelstrom screamed back.

Hwyfar was no small creature, even without the added burden of her armor, and she was in a state of shock. She kept trying to fall, go slack. I might as well have been trying to haul a side of beef with me. At last, I grabbed her and hoisted her over my shoulder, and, using the edge of my boots as a guide, slowly felt my way along the trees as the wind, hail, and bracken hit my face.

My knee buckled, but I had tied it well that morning. I would regret the bruises later, but had little other choice in the matter.

My thighs shook with the effort, my back and stomach so tight that breathing was painful. The wind shifted to my back, making my pace faster but more treacherous. Roots and slippery leaves at every turn threatened to twist my ankle or break my knee for good. I gritted my teeth so hard I could feel my jaw cracking. Sweat poured down my collar, into my eyes, but I could see the faintest outline of light in the distance.

Damn my bad eyes. Damn this whole island. Damn that I had left my knights alone. And damn this woman.

Finally, I felt what I had hoped for—the edge of the stone barrier we had crossed. I took one step, then another... I was so close. Just had to make it one more foot, and the light came closer until—

We tumbled down into a snow-covered ravine, slipping helplessly into bright afternoon sunlight.

I had shattered my shield, but I think the shock of the cold had helped Hwyfar out of her fugue, for she was breathing regularly, and her eyes had a bit more clarity.

We were embedded in a snowbank, she in my arms, blinking through snowflakes on her eyelashes.

"Are we safe?" she asked me, her grasp tightening.

I listened. We had good cover, even if we had been followed. But that last fall... I couldn't explain it, but it felt as if I had traversed miles instead of steps. The whole world was different. Brighter. Crisper.

"You're safe right here," I said.

Burrowing closer to me, she lifted a hand to her face and hissed at the pain.

"I hope you aren't hurt too badly," I said. The pommel of my sword was digging into my ribs, and my knee felt like someone had gone in and replaced it with shards of broken glass and stinging nettles, but I did not mind the arrangement at all. "I tried to make a graceful exit, but I fear grace is not my strength."

Hwyfar licked her bloodied lips, eyes vague. "I think you broke most of my fall."

I was disturbingly relieved by her familiar humor.

She rolled off of me, groaning. Her hair had fallen out of its lace, and her fair face was a mess of cuts: besides her split lip, one of her eyes had nearly swollen shut. But gods, she was beautiful. Even with leaves in her hair. Maybe especially with leaves in her hair.

"You look like you were kicked by a cow," Hwyfar said to me, upon closer inspection. "And there is a bruise the size of an apple on your cheek."

"It was an angry horse, not a cow," I said. "Though I should have blamed the lion. Makes for a better story."

"I did not dream that part, then," she said, staring down at her hands as if they held answers.

We had no food. No packs. No tent. I had a sword, a handful of provisions. We had too much armor for two people. And looking up and behind us, even with my rudimentary understanding of Avillion, I knew we were not where we had intended to be. I could smell the sea, even in the chill. That storm had been magical in nature, and she had been at the very center of it.

"No, you did not," I said. "I had heard Yvain had a lion, but I thought it a tale, to make him sound more exciting. He's about as talkative as a yew hedge."

The Queen Regent did not smile. She looked up toward where we had fallen and frowned. Now she looked at me, as if for the first time in her life. "Did you carry me all this way?"

"Tried to," I said, scratching my beard, a nervous habit I had picked up in the last few days, it appeared, only around this woman. "Fell most of it."

"How gallant."

"There was no time, I am afraid. Whole thing went to shit, Your Majesty. We are both alive, but I am not certain I can say the same for everyone else."

She went blank again. She'd gone away. That look I knew, I had felt it, gone to that place too. The wind whipped her hair, and I shivered into my cloak, gritted my teeth against the throbbing of my knee. I doubt it would let me sleep tonight.

Best not to talk to her, or at least wait for her to speak again. Arthur's words clattered through my head then: *Determine if she is worth the effort; then either do away with her, or marry her off to someone who can cow her.*

The thought of anyone cowing Hwyfar was beyond laughable, and anyone marrying her... ah, my guts squirmed at that thought.

"We have to find shelter. Conjured or no, that storm is building, Your Majesty," I said, looking over my shoulder. "We'll have to move quickly—they may be just behind us."

I stood with more effort than I would have preferred, prepared for her scathing words, but none came. I grunted worse than an old cobbler coming up from a bench. My back stung, and I could tell I bled beneath my armor, but we would have to tend to it later.

Worse even, I did not know where we were.

"Queen Hwyfar," I tried, resting a hand on her shoulder.

Nothing again.

My men were missing. I was quite certain a few were dead or wounded. The priestesses, last I saw, were being skewered by murderous thornwood creatures.

I took a moment to take in the land a bit more, while I tried to figure out to do with the woman—nearly as tall as I was, clearly in shock, incapable of helping me, but intent on having us freeze to death on the outskirts of Brocéliande.

We were at the edge of the forest, but it was by no means open plain. The south of the island, I remembered from our maps and Gareth's constant prattling, was home to the apple orchards and old monastery—Nin, was it? Maybe we would not starve to death quickly, but slowly, on old, blighted apples.

If it was Nin, then we must have traveled leagues. *Leagues.* Which was not possible.

Boars? Were there boars here? I thought so. Chestnuts, which would be good eating for them. But the animals were territorial, too. On the other hand, this close to the sea, we were bound to find a few farms, and even if they were abandoned, shelter. And fish. Or feral pigs crossed with boars. We had seen some of those on campaigns. Rutting fuckers.

So much for an island of wonders. This was an island of horrors.

Carefully, more for my benefit than hers, I knelt down to look her in the eyes. She moved her gaze to me, but looked through me and not at me.

"Prince Gawain," she said, as if meeting me for the first time in weeks.

Another might look at her and see madness, but I recognized battle shock. Deep in my bones I knew it; not just as a man who had felt it himself, but who had seen it dozens of times in others. Arthur had never been on the field to see it, he believed it a failure of spirit, a weakness of soul. But there was no telling which men would fall to such an ailment, no matter how strong of body or mind they could be.

"Yes, Hwyfar," I said. "I am here."

"Tell them to stop ripping it out. Tell them, no matter how many times they come, to stop cutting me," said the Queen Regent, grabbing the fur at my chest, her hands like claws. Then she was sobbing in my arms, beating me, screaming, tearing at her face.

I held her as she raged, shocked at her strength—especially given her fall, and all we had just endured.

I took each blow as I could, only on account that I was a brute and built for such abuse, until she had screamed herself hoarse and was trembling in my arms, shivering in the cold, and a mess of snot.

"Can you walk with me?" I asked. "We have to find a place to rest tonight. Snow is coming, and fast. I wish I could keep you here, safe, and warm, but we cannot rest yet."

Hwyfar nodded, face still buried under my chin, but she did not look at me.

* * *

EVEN MY SOMBER assumptions of our situation proved hopeful compared with what I discovered. Hwyfar remained in shock: barely able to respond to simple questions, often incoherent and violent, half wandering off without physical redirection, and prone to shrieking. Which was the best possible way to alert any enemies to our position. Although, I had to admit, the sound she made was quite similar to that of a female lion, so we had that to our advantage.

We did not get anywhere near the Monastery of Nin. We made it about a league and a half before I knew Hwyfar would suffer too much on the journey to come back from. I could not bear the thought of that, nor the guilt.

There were no signs of life, which was both strange and disconcerting, and I wished to the stars I had listened to more of Gareth's map discussions. The day was waning, and our survival could hinge on whether I pushed to the sea or kept to the tree line. I went with what limited instincts I had.

When I spotted the stone cottage, half-collapsed with snow, it was a relief and a disappointment both. From a distance I had hoped it would provide more respite than a makeshift shelter. But the closer we got, the more I saw that it had long been abandoned.

It was the remains of a cider house on the edge of a frosted apple grove. I found enough frozen apples on our way to make a meagre meal, combined with the hard tack I had on me, but it would not do for long. Most of the apples were covered with a purplish rot even I knew to avoid.

Inside, half the structure was too rickety to even contemplate resting under, but part of the storeroom was still dry enough and out of the elements. The occupants had left very little in their wake: a few old baskets, worn-down benches, and the remnants of an old press. I put Hwyfar down on one of the benches and went to work peeling off the layers of my sodden clothing, knowing that too long in the wet and damp would be the death of both of us.

Pushing through the gnawing pain in my ribs, I made a small fire out of old bat guano, twigs, and dry grasses that had grown and died within the shelter of the old cider house. From my years of traveling with Palomydes, I had learned how to build a smokeless fire, or close to it, and I was glad. We could not afford to go without the heat, nor could we be a beacon to whatever had besieged us in the wood. Or to Ryence.

Once I was down to my woolens, still shivering but at least no longer clattering my teeth, I turned my attentions to Hwyfar. She was staring into the fire.

I was just about to start with her, at the beginning, in the kind, calm way Palomydes had taught me when we were both young and free of the wounds of war, when she held out a long arm to me.

"Take it off," she said, flipping her wrist so I could untie her vambraces.

Just touching that remarkable armor felt like a violation, but I put it aside with as much reverence as I could in a place such as this. Hwyfar did the same for every element she wore. It was a perfunctory business, her muscles slack, her body fluid. I was worried she was going to snap at me, awake from her strange stupor, but she did not.

When her armor was in a neat pile by the cider press, Hwyfar rubbed at her elbows, her knees, her neck. She pulled at the knots in her hair, staring at the fire as if the low-dancing flames held answers.

But she never looked at me. Not as I handed her hot apples from the makeshift skewers, not as I warmed her furs, not as I sang her the song my mother taught me on the high bluffs of Orkney as a child.

She fell asleep, though, curled up beside me on the bench, her head on my lap, an arm to either side of my waist, breathing deep and even as a child.

* * *

I WOKE WITH a start, having only found sleep in fits, to branches scratching at the windows. The storm had reached us, as I knew it would. What it would bring, I did not know. Winds buffeted the structure, wood creaking in its wake.

No, I never did much like storms. Always reminded me of my father and his drunken tirades through Orkney Castle. How he loved to find me when the thunder rolled, because no matter how much I yelled, no one could hear.

Hwyfar stirred in my lap; the fire had guttered to a low, amber glow, and there was little left for fuel beyond what we would have for the night. I had no idea if the roof over our heads—if one could call the haphazard beams and shaky debris such a thing—would take such a beating. We were buffeted from the worst of the winds, but not for long.

"Gawain?"

The Queen Regent sat up, rubbing at her face. I looked for signs in her expression, hints that she had returned from wherever it was we went when our minds could no longer hold on to the world's pain.

"Still here," I said to her. "Much, I am sure, to your disappointment."

She said nothing at first, looking down at her hands and flexing her long, fair fingers, as if they were unfamiliar.

"I still have some apples if you find yourself hungry." I poked at the sad basket with the knotted stick I had adopted as my very own. It was a good stick.

"Should we be risking a fire?" Her eyes had lost that glassy quality, and the question was far more rooted in this world than the one she had been visiting.

I shot a quick glance out the window at her imperious tone, as if the storm had been frightened away by it; but no, sure enough, the gales still blew, and the frost and snow crept across what glass remained at the edges of the leather flaps between us and the squall.

"Yes," I said simply.

"I should think it would attract unwanted enemies."

"Perhaps. But to do otherwise would risk freezing ourselves solid. And that is not an end I would wish on anyone."

Well, perhaps du Lac. Balls first.

Hwyfar gave me an appraising look. "You warmed and dried my clothes."

"I did."

She swallowed, worrying her bottom lip with her top teeth.

"There is no need to concern yourself with what happened," I said to her, handing her over one of the warmed furs. "Nothing untoward, on my honor as Arthur's nephew, for what worth that is to you."

Her look was enough to curdle milk in the teat. But Hwyfar took the furs, anyway, and shivered into them, coming a little closer to me on the bench. When I gave her a hot apple, she took it, nibbling thoughtfully.

"How long do you expect the storm to last?"

I tried not to stare at her mouth as she devoured the apple flesh so delicately, tried not to think of the warmth heading down from my spine and awakening elsewhere. "I can't say. I have no idea where we are. But every storm passes, doesn't it? We have shelter, we have food, and warmth, if you'll have it. Not to presume."

"You are not as I remember you in Carelon. You are—well, polite. Respectful. I cannot reconcile this Gawain of Orkney with the hot-headed brute I once know," she said, tossing the core into the sputtering fire. I would need to try and find more fuel, and soon.

"I promise you, I am still a hot-headed brute, but I have learned to hide it better," I said, suddenly fearful of what her answer might be. "Time changes us all."

"Not like it has changed you, Prince Gawain. You played the game well at first, blustering at me and acting the conqueror, but the cracks began showing quite swiftly. You are no longer a spoiled prig. Something happened."

I cracked around her, because I could not be other than myself. Besides, I was not ashamed of my own history. "War happened. And loss. I think you can understand that, too."

Hwyfar looked over at me, drawing one of her hands down the side of her face. "I suppose I do. And back there. During the fight. I went away. I... That has not happened to me for a very long time. How did you know what to do?"

"War and loss," I said again. "My men on the field—we would see things. Experience things. And no matter how strong a person is, there is always a point where the mind decides it is too much." I wanted to reach out, to touch her hand, but I did not. So I skewered another apple. "I lost someone."

"Did she break your heart?"

The words were out before I could stop them: "He died."

"Oh."

I had never spoken of Drian, not to anyone outside of Palomydes. He was our "utmost care." Now, though, I wanted to; needed to, even.

"You would not care for the tale."

"You'd be surprised. I lost a lover myself. Besides, if it helps, I will listen," she said, her palms now flat on her thighs, leaning toward the fire, eyes closed. "It is the least I could do, given you've saved my life."

Swallowing, I stared into the flames. Couldn't say why I spoke again, but she pulled words out of me whether I liked it or not. "Ours was a short-lived love. He was a prince, a son of Pellinore, sent to war as I had been. But he was not prepared for what we saw. And I was not prepared for him to die."

"I'm sorry."

"Wasn't just him." I considered what it would cost me to tell her, to open up myself. But we were in the middle of a squall, and half our company was possibly dead, including dear friends and comrades in arms. "For as long as I could remember, my mother would disappear for days, weeks—months at a time. When I came back from that campaign, when Drian died, she did the same. And when she emerged again, I had become a horrible monster in my grief. I threw things. Shouted. Threatened her handmaiden. I almost tore down the doors to Mother's apartments at Carelon. The marks are still there."

"I take it the theatrics were not effective."

"No." I took a bite of the hot apple. This one was a different variety, velvety and tart. It made me a bit nauseated. Enough apples for now. "I could have told her about Drian, I could have apologized. But instead, I drank myself into darkness, and nearly broke my family apart."

"How did you find your way back?"

I was beginning to feel dizzy, unaware if it was the beginning of my wound festering, or if it was proximity to Hwyfar. Or both. Pretty sure I was feverish, now. "I could not have done it alone. Palomydes. Gareth. Bedevere. They made me better."

And Gweyn. Always Gweyn.

CHAPTER SEVENTEEN

HWYFAR

No, GAWAIN WAS not the man I expected. Not at all.

It was rare in my life that men surprised me. I did not often take them as lovers or companions, for I found their ways tiresome and their jealousy exhausting. And I admit, I had judged the Orkney prince thoroughly and swiftly in our brief acquaintance.

His immense form seemed at odds with that gentle spirit. Perhaps *gentle* was not the right word. Broken, but not in the way of shattering—twisted, shaped into something new. The way one breaks stallions. Life had done that to him, and his response had shaped that new form.

"I have an uncomfortable request to ask of you, princess," he said, for the first time avoiding my gaze, and addressing our fire instead. Had he gone paler?

"Do tell," I said.

My head still pounded, but I felt more grounded now after I had eaten and warmed, and I felt capable of assistance. Though by the tight expression on his face, I was worried what it might be.

Gawain cleared his throat and turned to the side, moving his cloak so I could get a better look at his back. Even in the meager firelight I could see the dark bloodstains through the gambeson he still wore. It would have to be a lot of blood to make it through all that quilting.

The idea of putting a needle through his flesh made my bile rise. "I can make the attempt."

"I can talk you through," Gawain said, handing a small, waxed packet to me. Inside I found a delicate set of bone needles, likely just for this task. Judging by the sheen upon them, they had been used many times. Once, words had been embroidered upon the inside of the case, runic and strange to my eyes, but they had worn away with time.

I was about to make a comment upon the contrast between the beautiful bone needles and this oaf of a man, when Gawain began undressing with the efficiency of a soldier. He did not look at me, nor did he ask for help, and within a few breaths he had bared his great back to me without a moment's concern or resistance.

And at last, I understood his hesitation. It was not for his pride or his sense of propriety: it was his scars.

Without thinking, I let out a gasp, and his shoulders drooped.

"I have only seen it a few times, in the mirror—for obvious reasons, I try to avoid them," he said, voice low. "A short lifetime for such a story in scars."

"No, please." I swallowed some of my words in earnest. I could feel cold currents about my ankles. "I meant no offense."

"I take no offense," Gawain said, reaching up to touch the top of his neck, where I could see a notch of flesh removed entirely, healed over with silvered scars leading down his shoulder blade to his spine. "I can typically keep them hidden. But I do not want the new wound to fester."

I tried not to stare at the marks on his back, his arms, and the tracery that hinted at more. The man must have used his body to block arrows and sword blows like a human shield. No wonder I caught him limping occasionally. If his back held scars like this, the rest of him certainly would be akin to it.

A particularly horrid chunk had been taken out of his back down by his left lung, and I wondered at that. It looked almost purposeful, like a pound of flesh, and had healed at the edges like winter frost. The few places where his skin was not marred were covered in freckles, deep brown and red. Then I remembered his tournament joust at Lugh's Tournament, years ago, when Lanceloch du Lac had bested him—hadn't they said his rib had gone straight through his skin?

"What do you need me to do?" I steeled myself. As a girl, I had been a talented embroiderer, but this was quite another matter.

Gawain pulled a dagger from his waist and held it out to me. "You will need to clean it, then seal it. With this. You put it on the fire, and then brand it to my skin."

Another scar to add to the map of his body. Except here, there was little hope of escaping without some a miracle. And I was not made for such acts of healing and kindness.

I swallowed.

"Hwyfar." He did not address me by title.

"'Your Majesty,'" I corrected him sharply.

"There we go," he said, and he took my hand, pressing the dagger into it. His skin was so warm, and I felt that pull again, that need to draw even nearer. "First, you heat the water. Then you clean the wound. Then you heat the dagger in the fire."

"We need more of a flame," I said. "And we will need to wrap the wound."

"We cannot afford that," Gawain said, turning his face to me. His profile was striking, vibrant green eyes catching in the firelight, his hair burnished copper.

"I do not like being told what to do."

"I am aware," he said, weary amusement in his voice. "But I also doubt you would like to be trapped here with a moldering corpse twice your size."

My gorge rose, and the thought was worse than imagining his skin sizzling beneath the knife. Still, I countered: "You are not twice my size."

He chuckled. "Fine, then. Twice your weight. You would not be able to move me, I promise."

I worked fast, worried that if I stopped to think too long about what I was doing, I would swoon like some ridiculous maiden. I melted a little snow by the fire and poured it over his wound to clean it, until it ran clear as he instructed. There was nothing of special concern, but the gashes were deep. Brambles, by the look of them, from the fight in the forest. The skin was shredded at the edges and sliced in the middle.

Breathing deeply, trying to still my mind as I had been taught in my early days as a priestess, I described what I saw and Gawain, hands trembling from pain and the beginning of what I knew as a fever, showed me how to sew up the skin; he had the right floss for it in his kit. In embroidery it was called a love knot, but I did not tell him that.

"Then heat," Gawain said, gesturing to the dagger. "Not too long. Just enough to sizzle."

I shuddered.

When first I pierced his skin, I dry heaved and pain blossomed in my chest. He reached back and put a comforting hand on my thigh. In any other circumstance, such a motion would have been untoward—but it was not. It was grounding. A motion of camaraderie. If he could find the strength to keep me focused, I could continue.

"Gets better," he said.

Which was a lie. It did not. But I endured. I had to keep wiping away blood, for the light was bad enough already and the unsteady flame obscured my vision, blurred as it was with sweat.

Then came the worst part.

My hands trembled as I approached the fire, and I did as Gawain had instructed, holding the dagger in the coals for the count of ten. It did not glow or show any sign of enchantment, merely darkened in the heat.

"Do it quickly, before you lose your nerve," he said, in a voice used to command.

I turned, looking again at that great, scarred back, and pressed the blade to the wound. It was nearly a perfect fit. It sizzled, and I counted, smelling searing skin, hair, and blood. I retched, gagged. Then I pulled away.

Gawain shook from the pain, his jaw set, eyes scrunched shut, freckles dark against his cheeks. Without thinking, I took the long length of silk from my armor, still folded neatly on the rickety bench by the press, and tore it in half. His eyes shot open, but there was nothing he could do.

"Anything else would have done—and not cost half a kingdom," he said, as I gestured for him to hold up his arms, so I could wrap the cloth around him.

"Nothing else has purported healing qualities," I said, indignant. "Besides, you're my way out of here. I am useless with a sword, I have no magical proclivities, and… Gawain?"

Gawain stood up, as if he had an important declaration to make.

And then he collapsed.

He'd been right. I could not move him an inch.

CHAPTER EIGHTEEN

GAWAIN

I WOKE WITH a woman curled in my arms. Not just any woman, but Hwyfar of Avillion. For a brief moment, I was mightily confused, worrying that I had caroused myself into a mistake. It would not be the first time such a thing had happened, but it had been many years.

She snored softly, that mountainous red hair tickling my nose. Morning light streamed through the rooftop, and cold water dripped on my neck.

The storm had passed. My side ached, but the sick feeling was gone. I had endured enough infections and wounds to know the worst of it was gone; the clamminess had subsided, and I was thirsty, hungry, ready to move.

Every instinct told me to leave, and yet I waited in the early morning brightness with Hwyfar in my arms. It occurred to me in that moment I had never awoken with a woman like this, never curled together thus. Vulnerable. In the old stories, we would have slept with a sword between us, but in our terror and my sickness, we had cast away propriety.

Hwyfar stirred. My heart leapt in my chest, and I swallowed back on an emotion I could not identify. Regret? Grief? Love? It felt like jealousy, but for a thing I could never have—a thing we could never attain. A thing that was forbidden to me.

"Well, I see you survived the night, so that is a start," Hwyfar muttered, then disentangled herself from me. She shivered, pulled away, and I felt the absence of her like a blow to the chest.

When she turned, the look of concern on her face was devastating.

"Your face is pale as spoiled milk," she observed.

"My father called me worse when I was born," I said, which was true.

She went to the window, long hair half undone and tumbling down her back, and an utterly moronic desire rising in me to touch it—wishing I had spent time stroking that hair while she still slept, mourning that I had not.

Hwyfar shivered. "I did think you were going to die."

"Apologies for the disappointment."

"I had planned a burial and everything. Dragging you would have been impossible, of course, so I was going to build a pyre, right here."

"I appreciate the thought."

She pressed a long finger to the side of her head. "My father always thought my sisters were the ones with the Sight, but I do know how to plan." Hwyfar grinned, teeth straight and bright. "Though it is easier with you alive for all those manly tasks. I am only a passing herbalist, and I prefer game to vegetables. I would have perished chasing rabbits for dinner, I am afraid."

"I doubt that. You are a formidable foe." I could listen to her speak for hours. I wished I could.

Hwyfar snorted. "Hardly. Now. Before we discuss how we are going to extricate ourselves from this miserable cabin and make our way to wherever we must go on this island, let me take a look at your..." She gestured with her hand and made a sour face.

"You did retch a few times before. Are you certain you are up to seeing the wound again?"

Hwyfar put an indignant hand on her hip. "I shall have you know, I sewed you together so keenly, we shall display your pelt as a tapestry in Arthur's hall when you die."

"You are horribly macabre, woman."

"Thank you. I do try."

I turned and lifted up the edge of the furs, feeling much tighter of a pull on my skin than I expected. She might be right, judging by the sensation: I did not remember so many stitches, but then again, I had been under quite a fever.

When Hwyfar gasped, I looked at her, alarmed. "That bad?" I asked.

But she was prodding my skin, her hands flat on my back, as thorough as grooming a gelding.

I did not feel any pain, though. Just tightness. A little soreness.

"The silk—it has adhered to your skin," Hwyfar said, her cold fingers making me jump a bit. "It has *become* skin. There is no sign of your wound. It... it has vanished."

I had seen many wounds, and I had seen magic. But I had never encountered a wound healing so swiftly. It should still be red, seeping pus, enflamed. We should need to change the bandages, to add hot compresses, to hope for the best—which was, too often, putrescence.

Hwyfar sat cross-legged, examining me as I pulled my gambeson back down and wrapped my cloak around me defensively.

"It makes no sense," Hwyfar said, pulling the remaining length of silk to her. We had used about a quarter of the material, and though the edges had frayed, it still held its luster. "I made no spells, spoke no incantations. Palomydes said the silk had healing qualities, but I cannot imagine it could perform a miracle." She paused again, gazing at me, as if she expected I would turn into a ghast. "And you feel well?"

"Tired," I said. "But nothing unexpected after enduring a night of cold and damp and merciless storming."

"I did not dream." Hwyfar rummaged through my satchel as if it were hers. She tossed me a bit of my own hard tack, and two apples. "Not a single dream."

"Perhaps the storm is a dream-eater," I said, recalling a story my mother used to tell me.

She tilted her head at me, hand on her hip. "You say the strangest things. Perhaps you will explain on the way."

"Presuming I am in the mood for telling stories. It is not my strength."

"I will command it, and you will have to obey."

"Would that we could linger a little longer. I find this place not so terrible as I believed it at first."

Hwyfar went silent, pulling on her furs. The dripping of melting snow punctuated the quiet between us. Finally, she spoke. "We both know we cannot tarry long."

"No," I said, wishing for another life, perhaps. A life of stories for other knights and queens marooned together in abandoned cottages, wounded and alone. "We cannot."

Ah, I was truly addled. My mother would be ashamed of me.

It was slow going, gathering our things, but the sun shone brightly, and the snow began melting quickly, giving me hope that the path might not be so treacherous. Indeed, though there was little in the way of roads, the sparse woods around us had been well-traversed by herds, and we picked our way well enough. We had apples aplenty to eat, and fresh water, and the day moved on with a bright blue sky, a brisk, clean wind, and not a single sign of human life.

CHAPTER NINETEEN

HWYFAR

GAWAIN OF ORKNEY was a *good* man, and I did not know what to make of that realization, as we walked across the barren landscape together, toward what we hoped was a sign of civilization and, hopefully, toward our treaty point.

"My knights will know what to do to get themselves to safety," Gawain insisted when I expressed concern regarding the rest of our party. "As will yours, and your priestesses. *You* are the heir, and the Queen Regent; getting you to safety is paramount."

I knew it was not safe to go back to the forest and I had far better odds traveling alone with Gawain. But it did not rest well with me, still. I had almost no recollection of what had happened, and feared for the lives of my people.

What astounded me most about Gawain was how he looked at me, with bare, clear eyes, as if I was a goddess of old. As if I was cherished. Oh, I could not mistake the attraction there. But he did not let it cloud his pursuit of my protection—or, as odd as it seemed to me, my friendship. For we were becoming friends. I felt at ease with him, in spite of our perilous situation. Only the day before I had boasted that Gawain was simply another knight, boastful and pompous as the rest, but even then I had known that not to be true. He had a light inside of him I recognized, felt drawn to.

Our conversation grew easier, even as I began to tire. The sun was bright, the snow brighter, and I began feeling a sense of hope until I had to stop and vomit profusely against the side of a tree. Too embarrassed, I did not call after Gawain for help, but he noticed and came stomping back to me.

Gawain looked appraisingly at the patch of sour apples and bile in the snow. "You should have said you were feeling poorly."

"A Queen Regent never feels poorly. She is momentarily inconvenienced." I wiped the spittle from my face with the back of my hand. It came away green. Then I vomited again, barely missing Gawain.

Gawain's cheeks were bright pink, and when he squinted the lines around his eyes deepened. Which I found rather handsome.

Meanwhile, I was streaming snot down my face, and dribbling bile.

He leaned against the tree and waited until I was finished heaving. "The worst will be over tomorrow."

I spat to the ground, shuddering at the taste still lingering in my mouth. "What will be over?"

"The malaise. The nausea. Comes and goes for a while once you stop."

My arm was aching again, for the first time in a while, where the stitches rubbed against my vambraces. "I really hate it when you act like you know everything. I promise you aren't half as clever as you think."

"Oh, I'm well aware of my limitations. But I do have the experience enduring the week or so after stopping drinking in large quantities, and I imagine fortified mead is even harder to let go than ale."

I glared at him. "I hate you."

"Only because I'm right." Gawain handed me a small square of cloth. It seemed a very civilized bit of linen in this bleak world.

Snatching the cloth from his hands, I scrubbed at my face. "And I am slowing us down."

"Time for a break, anyway. And this is as good a place as any." Gawain turned over some snow with his boot to cover the remnants of my vomit. "Sit on my satchel. It'll keep your rear dry, at least. Take a nap. I have yet to see a single sign of an animal, human, or walking tree, but the dagger is there just in case."

I did not like the idea of him leaving, but my pride rose up in defiance, and I grabbed the satchel, threw it down on the other side of the tree, and sat down on it like a petulant child.

It took me no time to fall asleep. I jolted awake at the sound of hesitant footsteps, my heart racing.

"Gawain?"

No, it did not sound like him at all. I listened, slowly moving my head, straining my ears as I had been taught as a child. In Avillion, we were told that animals could sense our intent if we could extend it to them, and though I knew I had no connection to that magic, I hoped that by keeping calm and breathing evenly, whatever stalked me would not attack.

Four feet. But not the deep padded sound of a cat, nor the pounding of a bear. The sound was sharp, clear. I smelled fresh pine, suddenly, and fresh, sweet berries.

Then, I felt a warm, soft sensation at my cheek, and turned to see a white, equine face with limpid blue eyes. I startled, and it startled back, and then I gasped.

A unicorn.

Trembling, I leaned back against the tree, making myself as small as possible, while I watched the animal approach me again. She was no larger than a pony, paler than the snow, slightly blue, with an ivory horn rising from her forehead. Her delicate legs tapered to curly white hooves, just like the mane and lion-like tail. She had a long tuft of hair at her narrow chin, like a goat.

Every tale I had ever heard spoke of virgins and unicorns, purity and unicorns, grace and unicorns—and none of those terms applied to me, to Hwyfar the Whore of Carelon.

And yet the unicorn approached. And instead of cowering, I held up my chin and welcomed her.

She stepped closer, sniffing the air near me, and I realized I still had some apples. Slowly, tears obscuring my vision with a mix of sadness and hope, I pulled a small, golden apple from the satchel, and held it out to the unicorn.

The unicorn did not hesitate. She trotted over to me and, lips as soft as a butterfly's wing, nibbled at the apple directly from my hand. Then she looked at my arm, the one with the wound, and shook her head as if angry. It was true, it did not look like it was healing. The bruises kept spreading, especially where the stitchwork was done. I had considered that it was from rubbing against my armor, but even when I removed it, the bruises spread.

"Can you help?" I asked the unicorn.

Then she gazed at me, licked the tears from my face, and trotted off into the snowy landscape.

I sobbed for a good while.

I did not tell Gawain what I had seen when he returned, but I knew well the sigil of Orkney was a unicorn. To speak truth, I was uncertain if it was a dream or not. But I counted the apples and the golden one was missing, now in the belly of a beast who should not exist.

CHAPTER TWENTY

GAWAIN

AT FIRST, I supposed the storm had simply frightened off any would-be pursuers, but after a few leagues, I began to grow suspicious. We had stumbled into a kind of rocky lowland valley, grazed by wild herds, but—other than the abandoned cider mill—untouched by farmers.

I did not recognize it from my maps.

"Do you know what they call this place?" I asked Hwyfar, as we bent by a small river to refill our water skins. I was sweating, now, my cheeks a bit raw from the wind, lips already peeling and chapped. And I was tired of apples. To say nothing of what they were doing to my guts.

Hwyfar ran her hand over her brow. "I should have paid better attention to my studies as a child at Withiel," she admitted. "Alas, the area is unfamiliar to me."

"Well, I did study maps on my way here, and I do not recall anything such as this." I gestured to the high rocky outcroppings all around us. They looked like jagged teeth, akin to the standing stones Merlin had erected across Braetan for worship, mottled with moss and lichen. There were hundreds, if not thousands, of them, dotted across the landscape. "Would seem rather odd to omit it from a map, and I feel as if I would have remembered such an unusual formation."

"Do we have map-eaters, now? Is that an Orkney practice, as

well?" Hwyfar rubbed at her shoulder where the straps dug in. She was still not used to her armor. I had offered to carry it for her, but she would have none of it.

I rolled my eyes. "No, Your Majesty," I said. "We do not have map-eaters. Just dream-eaters. And dream-eaters are friends. You leave out offerings to them at night when you are plagued with nightmares, and they take the food and eat your dreams in return."

"They eat your food *and* your dreams?"

"Yes."

"Rather gluttonous."

"I had never given it such a thorough consideration," I conceded. "But when I was a little thing, my mother would set out a piece of honey cake for me to keep away the bad dreams, and in the morning, it would be gone."

"She probably ate it," Hwyfar said, fastening her water skin.

I laughed. "I assume so. Or the rats did. Orkney Castle was always overrun with the little shits."

"So are boats," she continued, holding up a finger. "Perhaps *the rats* ate your map with this section of land."

"Whatever the case, I am both confused and concerned." Finding food had been difficult, and I was giving the larger share to Hwyfar of the few squirrels I'd managed. Another day or two of this, and we would not be long for the world. What kind of storm frightens off all the game? To say nothing of the people.

We continued our trek along the river, since it was the easiest path, and we both agreed it was most likely to take us toward any remnant of civilization. I remembered enough of my maps to have noted the many tanneries, mills, farms, and villages along the rivers of the island. It was not so big, after all.

And yet as the day stretched on, and the smell of the sea all but vanished, I started to wonder if the illness of the night before had been more dire than I had thought. I began to think that we were no longer on Avillion. That somehow, by dint of some enchantment, we had traveled elsewhere...

I was considering sharing my addled revelation to Hwyfar when I sensed a shift in the edge of my vision. What I had mistaken for rocks were cleverly camouflaged leathers.

There was no time to warn her.

We were already surrounded.

CHAPTER TWENTY-ONE

HWYFAR

THERE WAS NO time to warn him. I could feel his distraction; I knew that look. Not that I was entirely opposed to our banter, nor was it entirely unwanted. The oaf was indeed stirring something within me I could not quite grasp. With no explanation to his healing, or our whereabouts, I could not deny our companionship held a certain *inevitability*.

I put those thoughts aside, however, as two dozen soldiers emerged from the high, snow-dappled rocks around us.

They wore motley leathers, meant to blend into the landscape, but allowing easy movement, and soft boots with better grip on the uneven ground. They cascaded down the slope quickly, spears and swords at the ready, braids and plumes streaming behind them, shouting in high calls like birds.

Women's voices, demanding and brusque, in a language I did not know entirely, but grasped snatches of. Inexplicably.

They did not point their weapons at me, but immediately encircled Gawain.

The idiot drew his two-handed sword, gritting his teeth.

"Gawain, stop!" I commanded, but he did not listen. He was a warrior, a soldier, and I was his... I was unsure exactly what I was to him, but he did have a very sore need to protect me.

The women soldiers pushed me back with their staves when I tried to intervene, though they clearly meant no threat to me.

They wore black stripes of charcoal across their eyes, so the blue and brown and amber of them stood out bright. I recognized none of their visages.

"We would prefer not to kill him," said a voice to my left, and I noticed a woman, a little shorter than me, grizzled hair pulled through her elaborate feathered headpiece, and a bronze circlet across her brow. Her eyes were green.

I sighed. "I would also prefer that."

Watching Gawain fight three of the lithe women at once was painful. They danced about him, ducking his swings. He was exhausted from our trek, his illness, and little in the way of food or nourishment for the last few days.

"Gawain, stop—we are sorely outnumbered!" I called out.

I raised my hand to try and warn Gawain again, the cape falling away from my forearm. I had tucked the bracers in Gawain's pack, but I was surprised to see that my scar was blackened, gruesome-looking, far beyond simply bruised.

The woman beside me saw it, alarm crossing her features.

Out of the corner of my eye, I saw Gawain fall to his knees and heard him cry out—of course, they had seen his weakness—but not before I let out a cry of my own. The grizzled woman had taken my arm in hers, twisted, and snapped my bone.

Pain seared through me, obliterating everything. I could not see for the blazing agony, could not breathe. A dim, mad thought in the back of my mind, like a tittering laughter, marveled that this woman, decades older than I, had broken my arm like an old, dry twig, and I had not even managed to fight back.

I longed to swoon, but I could not. I lived only in blossoming misery, tendrils of red and black before my eyes, and obscured faces. I heard shouting voices, saw meandering shapes and forms, but could make no real sense of any of it.

Someone poured a sweet, tangy substance into my mouth and though I tried to spit it out, I got my face slapped for it. I did not have enough fight in me to try it again, though I did manage to bite a finger or two before relenting. The pain shifted, my vision dappling with blue starbursts, and I thought I could hear Gweyn singing in the distance, beckoning me to follow her through a dark wood.

I swayed, a hot, wicked feeling coursing through my veins. My chest flushed under my armor, my loins tingled. I was glad Gawain was nowhere near me; I had not felt such a sensation in quite some time. It was drunkenness, but a kind of awareness, as well. The pain remained, but it spread and became a kind of ache, a wanting.

I might have moaned.

Get her on a horse.

Hands guided me, voices rose, arguing. I could smell blood. The figures around me were veiled in darkness, their eyes like hot coals, mouths like blue caves with glittering stalactites.

…should not be allowed to draw breath.

Danger to all of us.

Never again.

By my sword.

Silence him!

I could hear their words—hear Gawain's voice, too, amidst the arguing—but I was aware only of a soft, dark world about me. A shadow world, where wights walked between the shades of the living. It seemed a peaceful world.

Gweyn stood by my shadow horse, her long golden hair alight with fireflies. She turned her moon pale face to me, and her eyes were blazing stars.

I had no more pain, but I could no longer feel my broken arm.

"Sister…" I said her name, tasting blood in my mouth. "Don't leave me again."

Suddenly her presence felt more solid, the familiar smell of her rose perfume tickling my nose.

"Shh, do not tire yourself with words, my love," she said, and I could feel her soft hand on mine, silk on my skin. I knew she was not really with me, understood that I was seeing a world in between. They had given me a draught of poppy milk, but along with it, some seer's vetch, which I had used many a time as a young initiate, to travel these same pathways. In an untrained woman, it might have lulled her to sleep. Now it helped me hold on a little longer to her vision.

"You have many enemies, and many who seem like enemies," my dead sister said to me, her voice sending a murmuration of feathers through the air between us. "But those who walk with you now will not bring you death, though it will draw near to you again and again."

Her grasp on my good hand felt more solid for a moment, and though my body was barely responsive from the tonic, I looked down upon her, into her blazing eyes and the flickering firefly diadem upon her.

"The throne, Hwyfar," Gweyn said, her mouth red with blood, red with fury. "The sword. The cup. The shield. You draw closer every day. Do not let distractions lead you astray. A distraction may be a direction; do not confuse the two."

I went to reach her, to touch her hair, that hair I had plaited and combed for hours on end, those cheeks I had stroked as an infant. Once, I had loved her as no one else in the world, cradled her in my own plump arms. Now, she was all spirit and mystery. And still, she returned to me with portents and riddles.

"Do not forget the face of our mother."

I WOKE TO my mother's face in dim candlelight, in an unfamiliar bed.

Without her headdress, face paint, and warrior garb, it was easy to recognize Tregerna of Lyonesse; she was the elder woman, the one who had broken my arm. I suppose she had her reasons, but I was not yet prepared for forgiveness. Though I did want an explanation.

I started, for Gawain lay next to me, snoring, blissfully unaware of the world. The room was immense, draped with rich cloth, warm and comfortable and filled with the musk of expensive incense. The dark dreams fled, only shreds of them remaining as my head throbbed and I took in my surroundings.

"I did not take you for the sort of woman to flinch from her lover," said my mother, leaning back in her chair to examine me. Tregerna of Lyonesse bore a stark resemblance to me, and the longer I gazed at her face the more uncanny it seemed. I had the same high cheekbones, the very same shaped eyes. Our hair fell in the same pillowy waves, though hers was gone silver now. And her broad frame, long legs, and strong jaw were unmistakable. "If your reputation is true."

"Mother—" I said, holding out my splinted and bandaged arm.

"You may call me Tregerna," she said. "I have never been much of a mother to you."

Her calm, unbothered tone was disturbing, and I felt tears prickle at my eyes. Me, a grown woman, nearly weeping at my mother's indifference at her abandonment. I swallowed, smoothing the fine silk sheets before me as a distraction. "He is not my lover. And I did not *flinch*."

"Shame," said Tregerna. "He has quite the pedigree. Arthur's nephew. And quite a load on him. He would be a good stud, at the very least, even if he is half a Pendragon."

Gawain did not stir, but I could not hide my flush. My arm throbbed, and I swallowed on a very dry mouth.

My mother smirked at me with the kind of guileless grin I knew well enough; I had offered the same look to countless courtiers and challengers in my life. No wonder Father barely spoke of her and could not stand the sight of me.

"You broke my arm." I would have spat the words if I had the energy.

Tregerna's brows rose, as if I had made a regrettable discovery. "Yes. The curse within it was spreading. It is my duty to keep Lyndesoires Castle and its inhabitants safe. It had been within your body so long I had to break the bone to sunder it, and then we had to perform a rather exhausting spell to part it from you. You may thank us later."

I spared a glance at Gawain, who still slept as soundly as a babe. "I do not understand."

"Not surprising," said Tregerna. "Your father Sundered you, cut you off from your power before he shipped you off to Arthur. I had hoped you would be less dull-witted and more informed."

I rubbed my head. "I can make no sense of this."

"Well, at least you found the armor left behind for you."

"Yes, I did. But I thought you were dead."

Tregerna was quickly losing her patience with me. "Clearly not. Lost, yes, along with the entire castle. Dead, no. As to your injury, breaking your arm was necessary, and it further upset that one; it took us quite some effort to subdue him." She pointed to Gawain with her thumb. "I think he has taken a shine to you—I have never seen a man fight like that before."

That made my stomach turn in on itself.

"What is to become of us?" I asked.

Tregerna leaned back in her chair, the reeds creaking as she did so. She slapped her leather leggings. "You are now lost along with us. Though I left some of my generals in Avillion to help find your way to us, if it was possible—although he told us he had killed one of them in your flight. You might remember the twins."

"Killed?" I did not understand.

"That is what he said. Though he could not remember which one."

Wenna. Elowyn.

In the wood.

"We were beset with a storm in the wood—I do not recall what happened," I said. "We were meant to treat with Prince Ryence. He means to take Avillion."

"Prince Ryence is no threat to you." Tregerna was so sure of herself. "He is a minor inconvenience. You are meant for far greater things, Hwyfar. You ought to consider this accidental tumble into my realm, lost as it is, a great boon."

"I don't even know how I got here."

Tregerna looked at the pile of my armor at the foot of the grand bed. "I suspect it had a great deal to do with that. Powerful items call to powerful people. As I said."

"You have no idea who I am. You have no concept of what goes on outside these walls. You have been gone for almost twenty years."

"You have waded into intrigue, Hwyfar, and you need to keep up," my mother said. "Did you think this was all a game? That one may be an idiot, but he at least understands the cost."

I tried to stand, but Tregerna pushed down on my legs, keeping me still.

"Enough for now. You are in my castle now, and you require rest."

"No. I want more answers."

My mother, the woman who had abandoned me when I was five, stood and looked down upon me with a look between pity and wonder, and commanded: "I said that's enough for now. You will rest. I will speak to you in the morning. You will both convalesce here until I tell you otherwise. I have given you a room full of every amenity you could ever desire: decadent food, glorious velvets, a warm hearth, and time. Do not waste it."

I tried to follow her to the door, hastily disentangling myself from the sheets, but my arm was tied to my body and my balance was mightily askew. By the time I staggered across the thick carpeting and shoved my shoulder against the barred door, it was locked from the outside so securely that not even the latches rattled. I might as well have been a moth battering at the moon.

Her scent lingered, unfamiliar. And I burst into tears. I did not *remember* my mother's scent. I did not even *like* her. And, damn the gods, my arm hurt and my ass hurt and my heart hurt. I missed Gweyn more than ever, and wanted to go back to that dark place, where shadows and fireflies knew me as a sister.

CHAPTER TWENTY-TWO

GAWAIN

HWYFAR WEPT—DEEP, wracking sobs—as she threw herself against the door again. I'd only heard the last few minutes between her and her mother, but I knew better than to interrupt, even as the conversation turned down most tortuous avenues.

I should have told her about killing one of the twins—I had wanted to, but we had not had many chances to speak of such things. Even if we had, I had been too much of a coward to bring it up. We had started to become friends; she had started to trust me. I was afraid of losing that, losing her.

There were already too many impossibilities between us.

I moved, finally, and she turned around, fury in her face. "Gods, I hate you!"

I held up my hands. "I'm sorry, Hwyfar." I knew she did not mean it, not how her eyes blazed. The other side of the coin of hatred is love, and I knew that well enough.

Hwyfar wiped at her face, as if that could hide the tears, the snot, and the red blotches. "What is wrong with me? What is happening to me?" She gestured at herself with one hand, and I could not see what was so terrible, really. Only real. The more layers of herself she shed, the more I marveled at her.

"Mothers," I said, hoping it was a meagre consolation.

She let out a hysterical bit of laughter. "Your mother did not abandon you as a child. Nor does she refuse the name *mother*.

166

I am a grown woman! I should not shed tears over such a self-righteous bitch!" With this, Hwyfar kicked the door.

Before she alerted the whole castle—I was fairly sure we were in a castle, even if I had only seen a glimpse of it before being spelled to sleep—I got out of the bed. Grudgingly. It was the best bed I had slept in in an age.

"You waste tears, it is true," I said, gently as I could, coming over to her with hands in supplication. "Save the fire for later. We still have no mind for how we arrived here."

"She must be lying. We cannot be in Lyonesse—Lyndesoires was the greatest castle in the land. How could a whole castle vanish?"

"It *is* a very large castle," I said, gesturing to our soaring chamber. Dark though it was, its grandeur was quite obvious. "As I said before our capture, we were nowhere on any map I had ever seen."

"One cannot simply fall into another country."

I held out my hand and Hwyfar gently, tentatively, put her hand into it. It was ice cold. "Hwyfar."

"Do not speak my name like that." But she did not retrieve her hand.

"Why?"

"It is too comfortable."

I looked down at her, squeezing her fingers in mine. "Are we not comfortable?"

"You killed one of my priestesses."

I sighed. "They tried to take you away. If they were sent by your mother, that was not made clear to me. They saw me as a threat. They also tried to kill me. And, when people do that… you know what I am, Hwyfar. I did what I had to."

She pressed her lips together. "You had men to protect. You should have left me."

"My men have their orders," I said. "I had to try to get you to Ryence." That was mostly true. Except, in the moment, protecting Hwyfar had been a reflex, a need—a call.

"You should have told me."

"Then it was my mistake."

"I hate when you do that."

"Do what?"

"Admit to your wrongdoings so easily!"

"You hate many things about me tonight."

"I do."

Hwyfar drew closer to me, eyes still brimming with tears, the firelight catching the red in her eyelashes. I felt the presence of her again, like the first time I had seen her in the hall at Withiel, as if she filled up the room, the air, my lungs. I barely had to look down into her face, would only have to dip my head a slight measure to brush a kiss across her cheek.

We both went still, time stretching, a tightening pressure in the very center of my being. Her eyes searched mine, back and forth, that golden gaze full of promise and hesitation, and finally, acceptance.

Then, Hwyfar moved forward, pressing her leg between mine, and the sturdiness of her, the insistence, made the rising heat in me culminate fully. And I did not feel ashamed.

Her breath quickening, she took a fist full of my tunic in her free hand, lips parting. It was her eyes, though, that caught me, swallowed me whole with the desire written so plainly. I felt like a fly caught in amber glass. She had never looked at me like that, at least not while I was aware, not with such clarity.

I would eat her whole, gods above.

"Hwyfar…" It was all I could think to say. She clouded my senses in the moment, and I was glad to be leaning back against the bedpost.

She pressed her nose against my chin, tender but urgent. I felt the ripple of her breath move down my neck, and her grip on my tunic tightened, the material moving and straining.

"I think we have played this game long enough," Hwyfar said into my ear, her voice low. "And I am tired of games. I am tired of shadows. I am sick to death of magic and deceit."

Now her fingers were trailing their way up my forearm, every delicate touch making my blood rise and boil and push me forward, upward, outward, as I wanted to wrap her fully in my soul, devour her.

"You are injured," I pointed out, gently tracing the line of her shoulder through the delicate silk of her tunic, and she sighed in response. Was this whole forsaken kingdom draped in silk? Somehow her skin was softer, still. And I wanted to taste every measure of her. My head tingled, light and heady, giddy with desire.

Hwyfar, Queen Regent of Avillion, gave a throaty giggle and planted a soft kiss at the base of my neck. I should have stopped her then. I knew better. But her lips were warm, lingering, brazen, and I was tired. And lonely.

"Injured? Why, so are you, Sir Gawain," she countered. "I believe I can make the proper accommodations, however. I am quite deft at such things."

Hwyfar looped her arm around my neck and pressed her lips to mine, breathing in, before biting down. Sweet pain followed, and every inhibition, every smothered thought I had for her breached the surface while the litany of warnings from Arthur slipped away like dried leaves down a river.

She smelled of honey and autumn fires.

I was undone.

Kissing Hwyfar was like drowning. She met my strength, even with her injury, pulling me toward her, crushing her body into mine. There was no gentleness, no sweetness—just a mad passion, a roaring flame between us. Breathing was necessary, but came only in gulps between kisses, gasping as our mouths met again and again. She tasted sour, bitter, the tinge of whatever drink she had been given still on her breath, but I did not care, even when I felt my own lips numb. Her long legs wrapped around my waist with ease, two grasping tree trunks, and I moaned into the crook of her shoulder as I sank down into the silk and furs.

I would die from this if I kept going, I would go mad. Want pulsed inside of me, aching and spooling, tightening my throat and pressing against the thin fabric between us. Her hair was fire across my face, her fingers dragging nails down my back.

Fuck.

"That is the idea," she said.

I must have said that last bit out loud.

Thank the gods, she slowed a moment. I swallowed, licked my lip, tasted blood. This woman.

"I can't."

My lips were numb. We were not ourselves. I loved—gods, I *loved* her—too much to begin this way. No. Heart thundering in my ears, I groaned in frustration.

The strength it took to say those words was greater than any effort I had ever exerted in my life. When I tell you that it physically *hurt* me to push her away, to gently back away, to look her in the face, to stop myself when I had finally, finally touched her, it is no lie. My heart cramped with pain from that separation, my stomach roiled.

"What?" Hwyfar's face crumpled into an expression of hurt and confusion.

I put my hands on either side of her hips, bowing my head so that I was just a breath away from her. "It isn't because I don't want you. Because *obviously* that is not the case."

Hwyfar squinted at me. "Have you never had a woman before?"

"Ah, no, that is not it either." Now, I was flushing with more than arousal, but glad for the firelight. "Look—you and I, we've both been given tinctures. I can feel it. I know you can. I can see it in your eyes. They're glassy, and you've been crying and slurring your words, and you don't usually do both of those things at once."

She snorted. "I fucked all the time with my potions and powders before, I don't see how this would be any different."

I could not say why that hurt so much to hear, but it cut me a bit. "I know."

170

"Gawain, that isn't what I meant." Hwyfar scrambled closer to me, put her hand on my shoulders. I must have expressed my thoughts on my face again, for she looked truly panicked.

The feel of her hand on my skin made me shiver, and she traced the lines of my scars almost reverently. But it was not a touch of passion, it was a touch of intimacy—a touch of apology, perhaps, without words.

"I do not want to begin like this," I said at last.

"No one has ever asked me to stop."

"Then let me be the first."

She swallowed, and I could hear the tears, thick in her voice. "We will sleep a while, then. And perhaps, when we wake, we will have clearer minds."

Gingerly, still sore from riding, from fighting, from days of travel and terrible sleeping arrangements, I found my way under the thick furs and quilted silks, Hwyfar slipping down easily beside me. How we had gone from bench mates to bedmates without a word, I could not quite say, but my whole body relaxed as she curled up beside me. She faced away, her spine pressed against my side, but still near.

Slowly, my blood settled again, my breathing slowed, and though I thought of little else but what it would be like to be united with her at last, I fell asleep, strange twisting shapes moving in the darkness behind my eyes.

I awoke to the feeling of Hwyfar's hands running slow circles on my stomach—languid, gentle, and moving slowly downward. I cracked open an eye: only the first blue rays of morning lit the room from the high, narrow windows, casting her red hair a dark hue. Her eyes were clear, and she had taken the liberty of removing every last stitch of her clothing.

Gods below, if this was a dream I would die of disappointment upon waking.

My head ached to the underworld, starting behind my skull and ending somewhere in my molars, but looking at the shape of her distracted me mightily from that inconvenience. She was sitting, cradling her broken arm on pillows, but making very good use of the other, every mountainous curve of her on display, somehow even more beautiful than I had ever anticipated.

I should have considered Arthur's warning. Gareth's warning. Palomydes'...

No, I did not care. They did not understand this connection, whatever it was. I was not merely chasing her for conquest. I needed the taste of Hwyfar on my lips like a dry bed needs cool rains in spring. My whole body ached and twisted in need, in recognition, in absolute relief to hold her at last.

Hwyfar angled her head. "I quite like your skin."

"You do?" I asked, taking her chin with my hand, smoothing my hand across her lips. She let me. Hwyfar let me have this gentle moment, this moment of perfect intimacy.

Then she tried to bite my fingers. "Yes."

"You are terrible."

Hwyfar wrinkled her nose, grinning, eyes pointed down toward my own rising. "Ah, you like it."

I swept my hand down her cheek, that sculpted, noble face turned so powerful in desire. Then I sat up, taking her in my arms, because I had to. She leaned into me, cheek to my palm, and I breathed in the smell of her hair. Someone had washed her, for she smelled of lilacs.

Tipping her face up to mine, I gazed into her eyes as my heart tried to fight its way out of my ribs. "No, I like *you*, Hwyfar. Every part of you."

"I have taken note. Quite a few times." Hwyfar took my hand to her mouth, kissed my thumb. "You are not very good at hiding it. Not even from the first time you entered Withiel."

I moaned when she brought my finger into her mouth, running her tongue along the side of it. My whole body responded, my mind buzzing, but no longer with the haze of potions. I barely grunted out: "I stopped trying to hide it. It was too exhausting."

"Poor mighty warrior. Too exhausted by desire."

I laughed. "You have invaded my mind, there was no point in

holding defenses you'd already breached."

"Hmm." She hummed softly against my cheek. "I have to admit, I have found myself taken with you, as well. From the first."

"Truly?" I wanted to giggle, but I swallowed my glee as she writhed against my touch. Her softness yielded so delightfully when I grabbed a handful of her ample, beautiful thighs.

Hwyfar leaned over me, whispering in my ear. "Come to me, Gawain of Orkney, prince and knight, delayer of the inevitable, singer of songs in the dark, and roaster of apples. I welcome you. I—I need you."

Tears threatened my eyes. Desire was one thing, *need* another. Love, a distant hope. "Gods, Hwyfar, I am yours. If I am who you want."

I slipped my hand down between her legs and she rose to my ministrations.

She sighed in relief and pleasure. "I want you entirely. As you are. Immediately."

Hwyfar ran her hand down between us, grasping my full length, eyes widening in response. She did not break my gaze, but she smiled wickedly as she explored what she discovered. Her palm pressed against the tip, expertly, drawing wetness, and I shuddered, pleasure rippling up through my belly, twisting up my spine. My whole body felt wrapped in wool, blanketed in silk velvet, alive and responding to her every touch. And ah, the sound she made when I moved my fingers inside her! Nothing else mattered but that I would make her glad.

There was just Hwyfar, and pleasure, and knowing she had chosen me—and that she desired and needed me—and all sense left me.

"Lie back," commanded Hwyfar, eyes glittering. My heartbeat thrummed in my chest as I pushed back, and she released me from her grip.

I would happily die of pleasure upon this bed under her watchful gaze.

CHAPTER TWENTY-THREE

HWYFAR

HE HAD WAITED until morning.

Never, in all my years, had a lover done such a thing. Especially not the first time. I watched him sleep in the morning light until I could take no more, until I would burst from emotions I could not place, when I woke him by gently touching him. Because I wanted to. Because, at last, the song in me had awoken, and I remembered the call of passion.

Not just any passion. A different pull of desire, one that had beckoned me the moment Gawain entered Withiel.

And more: I realized that Gawain, nephew of Arthur, beloved knight of the Table Round, had never lain with a competent woman. Or at least, never one who had been allowed, or taught, to embrace her own sensuality, to command a man in bed, to fight for her own desire.

Certainly, never one who was willing to take him on her own terms. And the way he looked at me—goddess alive. My whole body was slick with wanton need.

His reaction to this novelty, to my forwardness, was intoxicating. I could not tear my gaze from him, from his wide green eyes as they drank me in. No lover before had ever beheld me in such a way, in such a starved, worshipful manner. I had long lost count of my lovers, of our assignations and orgies. But perhaps I had lost myself in the act of it, perhaps I had forgotten that passion was a gift and not—what had Mawra called it?—hedonistic indulgence?

I had taken, I had commanded, but I had not been *wanted*. Not like this. He did not want the act; he wanted *me*. Not my performances, not my reputation, not my permission. Me.

Gawain of Orkney lay before me on the great bed in the shadowed morning light at the edge of a strange country, and he glowed like marble, all scars and freckles and knotted muscle. I gently peeled the silk tunic from his body, seeing him as if for the first time, basking in the brightening dawn. No lover of mine could match him for size and stature; few could even match my own. My breath caught in my throat as I beheld the breadth of his chest, the muscled, scarred length of his legs, the impossible rise of him before me.

In another lifetime, I would have so many plans, so many devious approaches, but with him, in this moment, I simply needed the feel of him. The immediacy made me dizzy. I kissed him again, his beard rough against my lips, feeling the strong line of his jaw against my hand. He gave me breath, comfort, safety. I felt complete in his arms, as if we were returning to a familiar intimacy rather than exploring something new.

Anticipation had me trembling as I slowly crawled forward, and I leaned to get closer, my braid falling near his face

"Undo it for me," I whispered to him. "Slowly."

I yearned for more, to take my time. But the wanting was so sweet, and his knowing smile so radiant, as he slowly undid the lace, that a flutter of wings cascaded around my stomach. My hair tumbled free, falling down across my breasts, down to my navel, the deep red of my hair meeting his.

"You've already undone me," he said to me, drawing the back of his hand down the peak of my breast.

I could wait no moment longer.

Rising to my knees, I pressed my good hand to the center of his solid stomach and leaned back, hovering just above his length. He ran his hands over my hips, thumbs delicately sweeping circles over my belly, and I felt so pristine, so perfect. I was no maiden—less so than most women outside a brothel—yet I was not quite prepared for the sensation of our connection in that moment.

In a breath, I rose and fell down the mighty length of him.

I was moaning, I was filling, expanding. The air felt like fire, my body shifting to make room for him, for us, for this connection. My ears rang; I heard myself cry out, felt Gawain's hands on my hips, steadying me as my legs trembled and pleasure flared in my core, hot and building. Part of me shuddered at the thought of rising and falling upon him again, and yet a languid, greedy part wanted more, wanted him in every possible way.

He closed his eyes, tilted his head back, and I saw the clean, exposed paleness of his throat beneath the shadow of his beard. I wanted to kiss that skin again, to taste the salt of his body, but my own sex throbbed with want, with pain, with pleasure, and I fell upon him again, taking him again, so deep I saw stars prickle my vision.

Gawain's breath came in ragged gasps, and he opened his eyes, catching my gaze. I could see a moment's concern there, but I nodded to him, let him know I was well enough. More than well.

I moved with him in me, and gods, the way alone that he watched me, with such barefaced passion, was nearly enough to set me to the skies. And when I slipped my hand to the sweet bud between my legs, I could feel the smooth skin of his member, slick with our mingled wetness.

"Hwyfar," he breathed, eyes glistening as he gazed at me. "I have been starved my whole life before this moment."

His words ignited my soul. I knew what he meant. I wanted it to last longer, I wanted more time to mingle with him, and yet my body had other ideas. As did his. Perhaps, if we were lucky, we would have time to try again with less urgency.

I felt the climax begin, my body clutching around Gawain's, and then heard him gasp in response, in surprise and wonder.

My world sang to life, a thousand sunrises of release—months of pent-up frustration—as Gawain's strong arms reached up behind my back and clasped me to him as we shuddered together, bodies drenched with sweat, laughing, kissing, tasting, breathing, alive.

I HAD NOT often woken in the same room as my lovers, but we fell asleep again; Gawain left the bed before me, and somehow, I dreamed on. When I emerged from my cocoon of blankets, yellow morning light streaked through the room, and I saw him, wrapped in furs, a massive shape at the doorway, speaking to someone in a low voice. A moment later, the chamber filled with the scent of bread, smoked meat, and fresh roasted fruits.

Gawain was limping, and I felt uncharacteristically shy as he caught my eye, carrying a platter of foodstuffs laden to the edges. It even looked large in his immense hands.

I would never look at those hands the same way again. A shiver of desire unspooled in my belly and I did not want to look so much at the food as on his form again.

"Good morning," Gawain said to me, sitting on the bed. "You slept so soundly; I did not wish to wake you."

I grabbed a small bun, streaked with honey cream, and took a bite. After days of apples, the feast before me seemed decadent, but I was too famished to eat slowly.

Watching him as I ate, I shivered, restraining myself from going to him again, taking him into my body, tasting him again. I had never experienced a connection like this before. Such comfort. Such ease. It was more of a continuation of our friendship, somehow, rather than the pinnacle of tension. I had joined with more skillful lovers, those who had studied the practice and made of it an art, but our lovemaking had been beyond skill. It was addictive, painfully sweet and, I suppose, *true*.

Gawain went for a small pot of apple stew and a hard oat cake, eating in silence, occasionally peering up at me while I ate with a half-smile.

Words. I should use them. But just watching him, the golden dawn moving across his body, was distracting and heartbreaking. I had thought such notions would flee once we had finally tasted of one another, but now it felt worse. Because it was impossible. *We* were impossible. And I only wanted more of him.

"I slept well, thank you for asking, Your Majesty," he said, eventually, into his flagon of ale. "I appreciate your attentiveness to my person."

I threw a bun at his head. He caught it deftly, not even spilling his drink. Then he ate it in one bite.

"The food is better than I expected," I conceded.

His grin was wicked, and I relished it. "Ah. Yes. *Delicious.* I have yet to sample all the delicacies of Lyonesse, however. I am just beginning my exploration."

"Gawain."

"Ah, I do love my name in your mouth. You say it with that accent."

"I do not have an accent."

He chuckled, deep and resonant. "You do. That haughty Avillion lilt. Especially when you're mad."

I wanted to play this game. Goddess, I yearned to mount him again right there. I had to ball my fist in the coverlet to stop myself.

"We're prisoners, Gawain."

"Hmm, indeed. But I have no complaints at present. I could do with a couple more days of incarceration, Your Majesty."

I dropped my voice, looking down at the food, for fear that looking at his eyes again—those bright, springtime green eyes—would let loose the rising tide of desire. "This is madness, you must realize that. We will be late to treat with Prince Ryence. He will think we have betrayed him. We have knights and priestesses out in the field, and—"

"Now you are the level-headed one," he said, though his tone was lighter than the words. "I know all of these things, Hwyfar. I know that the moment I looked at you, I was right and truly fucked in every sense of the word. But right now, I do not care."

178

"Gawain—"

"Hush. Let me look at your arm," he said, mouth still full of food.

"Did you hear me?"

"Aye. I've had many blows to the head, but not so much as to impede my hearing. You are correct, of course. But I have been informed we are to meet with the Queen and her consort shortly, and they would like us in court dress."

"What?"

"It's the game of court politics, you know. Of power. At least that part you understand. You might be rusty when it comes to the nuance of formal court conduct, but I don't have to tell you that Tregerna has us in her thrall at the moment."

He was right, of course. As so often, I forgot he was as much the courtier as he was the brute and the warrior. I had lived at court, but never within its rules.

"My soldiers—your men—"

"If we have any hope of seeing them, helping them, and— gods save us—mourning them, we can't risk putting ourselves in danger."

That did make a great deal of sense. "You want us to play along."

"I don't think it's a good idea to deny them at the moment. This is a very lovely room, and I did enjoy the evening's proceedings, and hope against all hope that I may be permitted more of you, and the sooner the better." His smile was guileless as I felt my skin flush. I turned away from him as he tried to untie my sling. "However, I would like a look at your arm, in case we need to arrange for an adjustment to your dress."

"Are you a tailor now, as well?"

"I realize, Your Majesty, that I look to you like a russet ogre who's been at the bad end of a rusty gauntlet, but I promise I was raised in Carelon among the most prim and proper, and made to learn every law for both ladies and gentlemen."

"I was not raised in a pigsty. I am the Queen Regent."

"You are, indeed, but you have never had any regard for rules, and if you did learn them, you clearly forgot them immediately when you learned you would not be Arthur's queen."

I would have kicked him, but that would have only belabored the point. "Fine. You think making a good impression is important. What would you have me do?"

Instead of replying, he leaned over and kissed me deeply, then ran his hand up my bare belly. The thrill of his touch had me utterly lost again, so swiftly I felt like I was about to swoon.

"Oh, the things I'd have you do," he muttered against my lips.

"I have ideas, myself," I reminded him.

Before I could act, however, he broke away to begin speaking again, grabbing another bit of fruit while I tried to find my own breath again. He was enjoying this, the monster.

"To your very valid concerns: We are outnumbered, outmanned beyond even what I can manage, and both wounded. For right now, we cannot simply escape. You have a broken arm, and there are two exceptionally armed guards outside, and gods know how many others. Even I can't fight my way through that many soldiers. So, we follow the rules. And the first step in that is getting into court clothes. Because Tregerna says so."

"I hate court clothes," I complained. "I prefer my own ensembles."

"I know. And, if I had it my way, I'd lay you out in your armor and then take you apart piece by piece. Alas, that is not my fate today. Let me see your arm, Hwyfar."

I frowned at him, turning away again. "It feels fine."

"It's me or their medic."

Finally relenting, I allowed Gawain to untie the silks that kept my arm firmly taught to my body. The knotting was impressive; though it had impeded my balance slightly during the night's activities, but he was more than capable of the work. I supposed he had done so many times on the battlefield, having endured many campaigns in his youth.

As the pressure relented, I was surprised at how little pain I felt. Soreness, yes, but not the burning, oppressive pain I knew well from broken bones. I had fallen from one of the lower towers of Withiel when I was seven and broken a leg, then later broken my collar bone after being thrown from a horse.

There were layers upon layers of herbs wrapped between the silk, and though it was not the same silk as I had used on Gawain's wounds, it appeared to have similar properties. It was a pale yellow, rather than golden, and when we reached the final layer—splinted with a rigid wooden frame—my arm was bruised, but largely healed.

Gawain stared at my arm as I cautiously turned it back and forth. It stung, but I had full movement. I could not explain why dread swirled in my stomach at the look and feel of it.

"Well," said Gawain. "Their healers are quite impressive in Lyonesse. I shall have to ask them about my knee."

CHAPTER TWENTY-FOUR

GAWAIN

THE QUEEN HAD a wife, and they made a fearsome pair. Tregerna wore a bright diadem upon her head, set with amber stones, and her wife, the consort Ymelda, wore golden silk and seven strings of pearls across her chest, which was bare save for a thin gauze.

As for the rest of their court, it appeared I was the lone man in all of Lyndesoires.

Hwyfar need not have been so irascible regarding her gown. This was not the kind of affair Queen Mawra or their late sister would have had her wear. Loose silk dresses were the fashion, banded with thick kirtles in bright plaids, coupled with high two-pronged hats. I thought they looked rather fetching, but Hwyfar said they looked like aurochs' horns.

Before we departed our quarters, the Queen Regent of Avillion had let me comb out her long red hair, then braid it into a coronet. She wore blue silk, strings of amber, and copper cuffs. Of course, I wanted to take it all off of her. Tried to, even. But though we had stolen kisses, the pressure of our imprisonment weighed heavily on us both.

My mind was preoccupied with thoughts of her—not just of having known her, but of protecting her, now that I understood her more, that I had someone to fight for. I was aware of our surroundings, nervous. Flighty. And out of my depth. Knowing I was outnumbered was one thing; living it was another.

Was this what loving a woman felt like?

I wanted to heave my breakfast at my feet. And sing. And weep. And perhaps take another nap. Once I was done with her.

Above all I wanted more of Hwyfar. There was no end of my desire for her. The moment I was out of her, I wanted to take her again.

As we strode across the black marble floors, streaked with veins of white and crimson, the warriors of Lyonesse fell into flanks on either side of us, their tall glaives snapping to attention. I had never seen women wield such impressive weapons, and I had no doubt they would slice us to ribbons at the slightest provocation.

Queen Tregerna lounged almost indolently on her throne, her long legs wrapped in glistening silk, a longsword at her side. Her throne stood on the floor rather than raised above us on a dais. She had a craggy, angular face, and though I could see the resemblance to her daughter, the bearing was all wrong. Hwyfar was proud, not haughty; bold, not priggish.

"What do they feed you in Carelon?" This was Ymelda, the queen consort. She was a small, pinched woman, with close-cropped blonde hair and even teeth. When she laughed, it was a high, strange titter that reminded me of the court girls who used to walk by me when I was training as a squire. "Darling, they are both so very tall."

Queen Tregerna looked a little annoyed, but nodded indulgently. "Yes. I am aware of our guests' heights."

"And they are so *red!*" The consort found this terribly amusing. None of the warriors were laughing, which was a mark in their favor. I had been teased as a squire for my hair, even though I was far from the only lad so blessed—though none had more freckles. Once I'd grown enough to beat them down, they'd stopped. I did not consider that an option here.

I scanned the hall for exits, but it was dark, with none of the splendor of our rooms. An old, timber ceiling, darkened from ages of fires, thick velvet draperies in deep greens and brown.

I had bragged of my hearing to Hwyfar, but my eyesight had never been particularly good.

"Ymelda, enough," said Queen Tregerna.

Ymelda pouted but fell silent in a clatter of pearls.

"Queen Hwyfar of Avillion, Prince Gawain of Orkney," said Queen Tregerna, raising a ringed hand, "you are welcome in Lyonesse under a banner of peace, so long as you remain here without ill intent."

Hwyfar's jaw was set so tight a blacksmith might be required to release it.

"Thank you, Your Majesty," I said, bowing at the waist, and pulling Hwyfar down with me. She resisted at first, but I pinched her, hard. She had agreed to play the game as I directed. At least until it was prudent to do otherwise.

What those terms were, I had not made clear. And I was likely the fool for it.

My tunic and hose were light, and strange in their fashion, but our hosts had given me a rather good cape. I liked it. Made of boar hide, I think, and embroidered with gold and green silk leaves. Princely. It had been many years since I had thought myself a prince.

"Queen *Regent*," corrected Hwyfar, when she stood straight again. "King Leodegraunce is not yet dead, and if the gods are merciful, he will make a full recovery."

I knew Hwyfar didn't believe that, but gods, she put on a good show.

"And more is the pity," said Queen Tregerna, and to our surprise, the entire gathered court erupted into cheers of support.

"I must return to Withiel," said Hwyfar, when the din died down. "We were meant to treat with a rival force when—when we..." She trailed off, looking at me, as if I could be of any help.

"When you found us," I said. "And made such an exciting introduction. You're lucky I was so outnumbered."

Queen Tregerna leaned forward, narrowing her eyes at me. "Queen Hwyfar is a daughter of Lyonesse. She wore the armor of her people, and *it* brought her here in her time of need. Truly remarkable make, that armor, and a treasure of our people. How *you* found your way in is more of a mystery, but magic can be strange that way. As I explained before, breaking her arm was necessary to dispel the curse upon her. As you see, she is none the worse for wear. And she has already healed, proving our point further. Time in Lyonesse brings out her true self."

"I already know my true self. I do not need your theatrics or your illusions," said Hwyfar.

"Oh, child, you are but a grub sleeping in the bark. You have not even dreamed of what you could become." Queen Tregerna's voice had a hunger in it I did not altogether appreciate.

"What do you want from me?" Hwyfar asked, taking a step forward. I went to grab her arm, but she was too quick. "If I knew how to leave, I would. Since you clearly do not want me as a daughter, speak to me as a queen."

"Perhaps we ought to speak privately," I said, keenly aware of the courtiers around us, listening well. "Rather than before such an audience."

Ymelda laughed. "Oh, Prince Gawain, you are ever a child of Carelon. We discuss openly, transparently, with our wider family, and do not leave speculation and gossip to dark corners."

"Then let us leave," Hwyfar said through gritted teeth. Her anger spiraled out of every pore, her long fingers flexing. I tried to catch her eye, but she was having none of it.

Queen Tregerna gave a mighty sigh, as if bored by her daughter's anger. "By all means, try to leave. We have been trying to for twenty years."

I felt the hair on the back of my neck prickle as she said this, looking again for exits. There were indeed windows with views. But just like our bedroom, the windows were too high, or else facing inward. I felt a pressing, uncomfortable sensation, what my old nurse might have called the *kenning*.

Hwyfar looked over at me, and I saw real fear in her eyes. Fear of being caged, of being trapped.

"Explain yourself," she said to the Queen of Lyonesse.

"If you are trapped, how did you find us?" I asked.

"You were inside the castle walls when we found you," said Ymelda with another giggle. "It looks outside, but it is within the perimeter. The castle and its grounds are… lost."

Queen Tregerna sighed. "Indeed. I was married young, to King Leodegraunce of Avillion. But I was not happy. When I discovered my brother, the heir to the throne of Lyonesse, had died, I wished to return home and rule. After five years, I escaped Withiel."

Hwyfar listened. If she had more venom, she kept it in, as I had advised her. Listening was more important now.

Queen Tregerna's expression grew distant. "But he knew—one among my retinue had told him of my planned escape. And so he placed upon me a curse so great, it lingers on us to this day."

Ymelda took her wife's hand, which now trembled, and stroked the back of it. "Leodegraunce gathered his priestesses, and sorceresses from afar, and attempted to break all of Lyonesse," she continued for the Queen. "But our powerful queen, amassing her own magic, countered it—keeping the country safe, but our court separate." She gestured to the castle, as if it was enough of an explanation. "She saved our lives, but we remain here. In Castle Lyndesoires, and its small surrounds. Alive, yet lost."

"I do not need to ask if you have tried to break this curse," I said. "You are formidable warriors and sorceresses."

"We have tried, but that brought us our greatest horror," said Queen Tregerna, shuddering. I could hear her teeth chatter against it. "We are kept here by a monster of corrupt power we cannot conquer. Our magic is nothing in its presence."

"You made my armor, certainly you can fashion greater weapons," Hwyfar said. "If your magic brought me here, across a hundred miles and more, surely you're capable of more."

Queen Tregerna held up her hands. "I fashioned your armor, Queen of Avillion, as a gift, and perhaps in the hope that it might lead you to us. I knew, even then, that Leodegraunce would not go without a fight, and so I poured my blood and power into that smithing—foolishly, for it weakened me forever. I can no longer make such things. But I am glad to know my sacrifice was not in vain, for you stand here before me now, back in Lyonesse where you can be useful."

"Though it still does not explain this one," said Ymelda, looking at me again, up and down, hunger in her eyes. I wished I had more layers of clothing on.

One of the women who stood behind the queen, who wore a dark red circlet, stepped forward. "He must be the child of a witch; the armor might have brought him through, had he but carried the spark."

"A witch?" I did not mean to laugh, yet it happened. "My mother, a witch?"

Hwyfar did not join me in merriment. The look in her eyes was more perplexed, ruminating, considering. It troubled me.

"Lady Anna du Lac is no witch," I said, when no one spoke. I could not say why I used her married name, other than I was growing angry, and thinking of Lanceloch helped stoke those flames. "My mother is—"

At the mention of my mother's name, there were some mutterings. Interesting.

"A sister to the greatest witch of the age?" Ymelda finished for me. "Niece to Vyvian, Lady of the Lake, whom even Merlin feared? Oh, Prince Gawain, tell me there is more to you than all that muscle and brawn. 'Twould be a shame for that handsome head to go to such waste."

All the words I tried felt like ash in my mouth, memories of my pale, haunted mother wobbly and dim on the edges of my mind. How many times had I sought my mother out, and she was gone? How many times had I found her, and she had been distracted, strange? Had I seen what I wanted, what *she* wanted?

"Men rarely inherit the gift," said Ymelda, nodding to the priestess who had spoken earlier. "But they say crimson hair is a mark of magic in some families."

Hwyfar snorted. "I was Sundered," she said. "It is too late for me."

"Indeed," said Queen Tregerna. "But not too late for you to help your people, if you can help me free mine."

CHAPTER TWENTY-FIVE

HWYFAR

THE QUEEN, THIS woman who had birthed me but wanted nothing to do with me, stared me down and dared to ask my help.

"You were not Sundered from the power of Lyonesse," said Queen Tregerna to me. "You were Sundered from the power of Avillion. It is not the same source. That you were able to use the armor to travel here indicates you have some prowess. We can move between places swiftly—distances long and short. Or we could, until..." She gestured again, at a castle with no exits, at a mountain pass on no maps.

"I promise you; I am a terrible disappointment in terms of magical capabilities," I said to the Queen of Lyonesse. "These hands are beautiful, but unskilled since my Sundering."

"Beg to differ," muttered Gawain under his breath. The gall. My stomach fluttered with recent memories.

This elicited a grin from Ymelda. "Well, Queen Hwyfar, you carry the blood of Leodegraunce in your veins as well as that of Lyonesse, Sundered or not. And Prince Gawain carries the blood of Pendragon."

A shocked murmur rustled across the gathered crowd, voices rising in surprise and dismay. Even Ymelda looked a little taken aback.

For the second time, I noted the unease around the name *Pendragon*. A quick glance at Gawain confirmed he'd noticed it too. As nephew to Arthur, he was in an even more precarious situation than I. With little Mordred just six years old, he was the next in line to the throne. Avillion was essential to Arthur's hold on Braetan, and though he had not come himself to help me, Gawain was his best bet—but he had never conceived of a situation such as this. How could he?

Gawain was a prize.

"I do not trust you," I said to my mother.

She grinned. "Good. You're paying attention. Will you consider assisting us?"

"Do we have a choice?" Gawain asked, a tinge of a snarl in his deep voice. I did not hate it.

My mother's wife looked as if she might devour Gawain whole, and he was pale as boiled silk save for the hectic flush at his cheeks.

Queen Tregerna shuddered a moment, shaking her head, and Ymelda put a hand on her arm. Then the queen said: "We need time to discuss the terms of your freedom together, as a court. Go to the gardens and await us. We will fetch you when we are finished deliberating."

MINUTES LATER, GAWAIN and I stood in a small chamber off the hall, before a pair of glass doors overlooking a winter garden. We could hear voices behind us, but the beauty of the glass and the ice-laced greenery made the space feel entirely apart.

I could not breathe for my anger.

Gawain was quiet, his own breathing even. The guards had closed the door behind us and instructed us to wait, that we could venture to the walled gardens if we wished, and that we would be called when the terms of our freedom had been agreed to by the entirety of the court.

The Queen of Lyonesse needed to consult with her people, and despite her proclamations of an open court, we were sent out of the hall like children overstaying their welcome at a feast. It seemed her dedication to transparency only went so far.

My heavy breath frosted on the glass, and I reached out to wipe it away with my glove. But it had already frozen over, and I flinched my finger back.

I was seething. I was hurting. My skin ached with it. No number of words or deeds felt adequate. But if I opened my mouth, only tears would come, and I could not bear weeping again.

This woman could not truly be my mother. This place could not be my inheritance.

Gawain's voice was soft in my ear. "What can I do?"

I turned slowly to him, and felt as if my heart would burst. I had no idea what to say to him. Had anyone ever asked me such a thing? Gweyn, yes. When we were children, she was ever looking after me, trying desperately to make me smile, to help me. But not in this way.

He saw my pain.

"What is wrong with you?" I asked, defensive only because it was comfortable. Because I did not know what to do with genuine concern.

"Many things," Gawain replied. "To begin, I, unfortunately, am missing a number of teeth. Which you may or may not have noticed this morning during your thorough attentions."

I turned toward him, away from the windows. I did not want to look at the beautiful garden, the frosted flowers, the impossible courtyard. I wanted a distraction, warmth between my legs again, a reminder of life, passion. I wanted him, apart from this broken kingdom, more than I had ever wanted anything in my life, and that made me furious.

But there was worry in his expression, the lines around his eyes crinkled, in spite of his playful words, and it damped my crackling temper.

His sigh rattled me. He rarely showed me how weary he was. Not like this.

"That is not what I mean," I said, knowing full well he understood that.

"What *do* you mean, Hwyfar? You don't have to push me away. Where would I go, anyway?"

"I am not accustomed to people perceiving me the way you perceive me."

"Perceive you? It is difficult to avoid such a thing when you are standing a breath away. Not to mention how our morning began."

"I—not with your eyes. I have worn many faces, kept myself together, my emotions smothered beneath laughter and passion and…"

"Lies?" he asked, picking a thread that had unraveled from the embroidery at my neckline.

Maddening oaf!

I slapped his hand away.

"And you have the gall to ask me what you can do for me," I said to him.

"Shocking," he said, brows raised. "You should report me to my liege. *Dear Arthur, King of All Braetan. My greatest appreciation for sending troops to assist me in keeping Avillion sovereign, but Sir Gawain, your nephew, asked me how he might help me, and I am offended to my core.*"

"This is no jape, Gawain. Truly."

"I know," Gawain said, his expression softening, taking my hand gently in his. "My apologies. I make light because I do not know the answer, not truly. Maybe walk with me in the garden a while? This cannot be easy for you. And… I would like to speak to you of something."

The way he said it, the pain I saw in his eyes—I felt it. A twinge in my stomach. He truly needed to speak with me, and merely asking made him squirm.

Beside us, two white fur cloaks hung together on wooden pegs, trimmed in golden silk and warm-looking indeed. I had no doubt that Queen Tregerna would watch us, but at least we would have more privacy than within the walls of her castle prison. Not to mention less of a chance of being overheard.

I nodded my assent, and Gawain wrapped the cloak about me as tenderly as if I were a new bride heading to my first showing. He quickly fastened his cloak, and it made his hair stand out like blood on snow, his beard stark and his green eyes glinting, like deep winter ice. In another tale, I might have leaned in and kissed him, but instead I nestled deeper into my cloak and followed behind him as he opened the great glass doors. Perhaps there would always be a sword between us of one kind or another. Now that we had begun this dance, we did not know how to maintain it.

The winter gardens were not as stark as I had worried and smelled faintly of roses. The courtyard was cobbled, but not icy, and the temperature was cold, but not damp. A breeze blew, moving our hair and reddening our cheeks, rattling the remnants of once-blooming flowers I could not recognize. Mawra would know; Gweyn, too.

Statues, and empty plinths, stood guard in uneven rows, covered in snow and ice, crawling with vines, curious onlookers. I had taken Gawain's arm and not even noticed it, reveling in the heat from him.

"Do you trust Queen Tregerna?"

That had not been the question I anticipated. But my answer was a ready, "No."

"Good," he said.

"I did not consider you took me for such a fool."

"Of course not. It is only—she is your mother."

I frowned over at him. "I am not a child."

"I am aware. I wanted to speak to you of parents. Of family."

"If you bring up Arthur again—"

"I will not."

He put his hand on my cheek, so familiar. And, goddess help me, but I closed my eyes and leaned into that touch. In that moment, I needed to feel rooted to the world, to this man. He brushed away the tear that fell with his thumb and spoke not of weeping.

Gawain took a deep breath. "My father..." His voice caught, and he tried again, and I felt his entire, massive body tense, as if preparing for a blow.

I clasped my fingers over his. "There is no need now, Gawain. This is about *my* family, about the woman who birthed me. I know your father was not a good man."

"No, he was not," he said. He worried his lip with his bottom teeth a moment, then continued: "You asked me why I see past your performances. It is because I know what it is to live in broken places. You were meant to be Arthur's wife, and cut off from Avillion—but your father, he had no more use for you once your purpose was served."

I could look nowhere else but Gawain's eyes. The vines above us shook in the breeze, a dust of snow falling about us. "I am my family's greatest shame," I whispered.

"You are no one's shame, Hwyfar. Your father—I cannot properly put into words what I think about what your father arranged for you," Gawain said. "And I know not what poison your mother has taken, but you cannot believe her treatment of you is natural."

"I suppose you are an expert in the relationships of mothers and daughters."

"My father gave me my first scars," he blurted, and I realized this was what he meant to say at first, for it came out in a rush, eyes closed, lips snapped shut after, bloodless.

My retorts fell dead in my mouth.

When he met my gaze again, tears filled his eyes, and he searched my face.

"Gawain..."

"When I told my mother, he hit her, too. So I stopped telling her. I made it easier for him to find me instead. Once, he caught me staring at a stable boy. He beat me until I could not walk, and he broke the stable boy's hands. I never saw the boy again. I couldn't be looking at men like that, he said. But this pain—he said it would make me a stronger man, a better knight—a future king. King of Orkney. My inheritance."

"Your mother gave the crown of Orkney to Arthur," I said. "You've never spoken of it."

"She knew I did not want it. It had tainted us both. I did not even attend my father's funeral. I only regret that I did not kill him myself."

Every hair on the back of my arms rose at the tone in Gawain's voice. I had seen a gentle, loving, attentive man in our time together. A lover, and patient friend. I had forgotten he was a killer, and that once plumbed, the thirst for blood rarely left.

"But your brothers, surely…"

Gawain raised an eyebrow at me, a moment's amusement passing his somber expression. "You know the gossip as well as I do, Hwyfar. Aside from the Pendragon height, my brothers bear very little resemblance to me. And I am glad of it. Their father is a worthy man."

Sir Bedevere, then. So, it was true. I admired Anna Pendragon more and more, it seemed.

He continued: "When my father died, I did not grieve him. But I was not free, either. I put my body in the way of danger time and again, because I thought I could bury the scars my father placed there with new ones—you have seen what price my body has paid for that. I squandered the love I was given, because violence was the only language I understood."

Put my body in the way of danger time and again.

I hated those words. I hated that I understood them. He chose violence, I chose performance.

"I will not ask what happened to change you, to bring you back to Avillion, but we spent enough time at court together that I know you are not the same woman you were," he said to me when I tried to pull away. "I know you left without a word, and then—it was not the same when you returned."

So close. My chest ached, the wound opening up. After Gweyn died, I had tried—I thought I had found love again. But loving Nimue was like loving a dream. I felt exposed, bare. Primal. I craved her love and feared it, and ultimately, my fear won out. She never seemed real, really. Never truly mine.

I left her before I could face what that meant.

When word reached me of her death, my light went out. But now, a new light kindled, and though I felt afraid, it felt *tended* in a way it had not been before. Reflected in those green eyes. Matched with fear and apprehension.

"My performances may have convinced everyone else, but inside I began fading away. I stopped feeling anything. Even desire," I said, reaching out to an iron trellis. Holly still shone green beneath the bars, each thorny leaf shimmering in an icy cage. The surface was smooth, melting slowly against the warmth of my fingers. "I thought my life could go on forever in debauchery and pageantry."

Gawain's laugh was sharp. "My body gave out first, and I am a fool for it. I still have penance to make, but perhaps that is why I am always reminded," he said. "The knee, then the shoulder. When the cold comes like this, 'tis a harsh reminder."

"Are you in pain?"

His answer came after a long pause. "Nearly always."

"So where does the anger go? The fury?" I asked, turning to him. My cloak caught on the holly, sending the hedge trembling behind me. "Where do I put this brokenness?" I pushed at my chest, as if beneath it was a living thing, crawling and horrid and pressing for relief.

Gawain straightened his back and put a hand on my shoulder, a soldier to a soldier. "Palomydes told me, the night I was strapped to a table on a dark field in Ascomanni territory, frightened out of my thick skull, druids around me casting ancient spells upon my shattered leg, that I would not be broken, I would be re-forged. If I chose it."

"But you are a warrior, a survivor—loved and cherished—I am—"

"So much more than I ever will be." He looked into my eyes and it pulled at my heart, those painful hooks of love. "You are every possibility of both lines of your family, and I have no doubt your story is just beginning."

I had never felt so. My story had ended the moment Arthur saw Gweyn. My reputation was ruined the moment I began bedding down anyone who would have me. I did not regret the pleasure, nor was I ashamed of it—but Carelon had bruised me, judged me, and moved on, and the marks still lingered.

"How can you say such things?"

"Because I see you. If no one else does, then I am all the more blessed. For when I look upon you, my whole world fills with light."

I pulled him toward me, into the alcove between the iron trellis and the corner of the marble gardens. Above us, a perfect canopy filtered the strange winter light into dappled, glittering reflections upon our clothing and skin. Cold as it was, the fire in my belly was sudden and insistent.

Need rose inside of me again, that fluttering sensation I had come to associate with Gawain's closeness. His lips found mine, his hand taking the full weight of my breast in his, and I moaned low into the kiss he gave me. I wished to be free of my clothes, of this place, of our duty, and my heart pulsed between my legs as I savored the feeling of his rough beard upon my lips and chin.

Ah, gods, I was shaking for want of him, desperate in a way I had never been accustomed to, behaving like a nervous maiden. Part of me reveled in it. Coupling had not felt new to me in a long, long time.

"Gawain, I need to feel you," I said hoarsely.

"No soul has ever desired anyone as much as I do you," he said into my ear, his hand slipping under my skirts and over the stockings he had so lovingly helped tie earlier. "No one could survive such a thing."

"Plenty have had me," I whispered.

"None have ever known you like this."

He watched my face as he caressed the crease between my thigh and sex, desire plain as he bit his lip. Then, without warning, he plunged his finger into me. Those big hands, those wide fingers, and ah, I gave him no resistance, feeling him smile against my cheek, proud he had prepared me with naught but words.

I fell back against the frozen wall, lifting my leg to wrap around him and ease the way for his ministrations. There was just enough of a lip to the wall whereon I could take pressure off his leg and allow for better access.

I writhed as he arranged his hand just so, his thumb brushing my bud with every thrust, then adding another finger, opening me wider. The warmth of him mingled with the slickness of me, and I threw back my head as he kissed and tasted the length of my neck. My stomach turned into a flight of birds, wings and air fighting for purchase, and tears of joy stung my eyes. I had thought desire was dead inside of me, but now understood it had been only sleeping, waiting for this man to see me and, perhaps, love me.

Though I wanted to scream, to call his name loud enough to shake the trees of snow, I bit back on every sound. And somehow, keeping quiet stoked the flames of my passion more—with every breath, the mounting climax coiled tighter, the muscles in my legs and belly fluttering and clenching.

But I needed more of him. As impressive as his fingers were, I needed to feel his own pleasure—I needed to give him pleasure in return.

I told him as much, and he let out a sound between a desperate sob and a growl, begging. Gods, I had never begged, but his doing so set something free inside of me.

"As you request, Your Majesty," he said.

All the air went out of me as he pressed into me, up and inward, and my whole body expanded to make room once again. The aching sweetness of him radiated up my stomach, and I moaned into his shoulder to keep from rousing the whole castle. He felt perfect inside of me, as if he belonged here, buried to his hilt in my body.

"Gods, Gawain. The feel of you."

He went still. "Is it—"

I laughed in his ear, clenching around him and said: "More."

Gawain complied and rushed into me with that glorious power of his, every inch deeper and more luxurious than the last, pain and pleasure fighting as I gasped, grabbing him through his thick cloak. What I would have given to watch him, barechested, the muscles on his body moving beneath his skin. In that moment I only relied on sensation, as clothing covered us both—cloak and dress and tunic and all.

But gods, the feeling of his whole length inside of me—it sent a wild sensation over my skin, like rain on my face, my lips. I felt him move inside, retreat, and go deeper, and my toes curled inside my boots, but it was not enough. Would it ever be enough?

My back hit the wall hard with his next thrusts, harder again, and I welcomed it. With every stroke I filled and broke, split and ached and arched. I could smell my wetness mingling with the chill air, with his own scent. Though I could count dozens, if not hundreds, of such intimate moments in my life, none were out in the open like this, nor so close—so connected.

Gawain was right. Every other conquest had been planned. I had taken what I had wanted. I had not been *wanted*.

"I could watch you all day like this," he said to me, between shuddering breaths. "One day, I shall."

He looked me in my face, green eyes heavy with lust, swollen lips parted between his short, red beard. That look broke me as I came, rising and arching under him, my mind emptying of everything but wave after wave of pleasure; a breath later and he followed, great shoulders shuddering.

Distantly, I heard someone calling us.

We giggled like discovered lovers in the Greenwood, arranging ourselves together, stealing kisses in between. I took his hand and licked his thumb, and the look he gave me was regret mingled with a kind of dare: *Later.* A promise.

* * *

I HAD DONE far more brazen acts before—once under a table at the Feast of Ayr, within arm's reach of Sir Cai—but now, standing before Queen Tregerna, my mother, having just mingled with Gawain in the gardens, I felt exposed and a little embarrassed. Giddy, too, underneath that, a combination that was both exhausting and new.

Gawain, on the other hand, looked attentive—and, dare I say it, glowing.

Now was not the time for such appreciation, as Queen Tregerna held what might have been the key to our freedom in her hands. I did not know what she had discussed with her court, but I thought she looked wearier than when we had entered that morning.

"We have discussed, and we will require a task of you, Queen Hwyfar," said Queen Tregerna, and her eyes fixed upon me. I did not look away. Looking at her was gazing into the mirror of my future. I had never seen much of myself in my sisters—and no wonder. I had taken after my mother almost entirely. "And you, Prince Gawain. And when these two tasks are done, and we are once again free, I will send my troops to help protect Avillion from Prince Ryence, or to show your strength to treat with him, if that is what you wish, or to obliterate him."

Gawain gave a bit of a bow. "We are pressed for time, Your Majesty. We have already gone significantly out of our way, and Prince Ryence is expecting us within the next day or so. I cannot agree to these tasks if they put Avillion at risk."

Queen Tregerna leaned forward, a spider with a fly caught in her web. Her breathing was measured. "Time is the one thing we do not have to worry about here in this closed palace," she said, her voice low. "This prison, which I forged in my final act, to hide and preserve us, uses our very magic to protect us. Time passes, yes. I cannot go back, cannot take you to where you once were. But time moves far more slowly where you were, and when you are ready, you will find but a few hours have gone in the space of days."

"We can show you," Ymelda said, snapping open a fan and fluttering it before her face. It was green, studded with yellow swirling shapes that looked like leering eyes. "But for now, we shall describe your trials."

I did not like the idea of trials, or quests. I was not built for such adventures and discomforts. But Gawain's face; ah, goddess's kirtle, there was hope there. Once a knight, I suppose, always a knight. Were he any other man, I'd have laughed at his dedication to old chivalric ways. But in Gawain, it felt natural, almost beautiful in its purity.

"I will need you, Queen Hwyfar, to go to Withiel. We will show you the way, and it will be done swiftly. You must retrieve a priceless object of great power for me that your sire stole—an object Arthur desires and cannot have." She looked at Gawain. "I am certain Gawain is familiar with it. Merlin sent spies to Lyonesse years ago, asking for a similar token, but we had it well-hidden. That one has since been lost. But now Arthur turns his eye to Avillion."

Gawain went to speak, and then closed his mouth.

The silence made my skin crawl.

"What does she mean, Gawain?" I turned to him, taking his hand. His grip tightened in mine, but he did not look at me.

Queen Tregerna leaned forward and caught my eye. "Hwyfar, Queen of Avillion, you must learn to think beyond your loins. Did you ever stop to consider why Arthur would send his own nephew, his most trusted and closest of kin, on such a trifling mission? A seasoned war veteran, a man known far and wide, to you, a hapless queen drowning in her own vices—one incapable of standing on her own feet, most nights, let alone commanding a kingdom?"

My face burned; my throat tightened. I let go of Gawain's hand and I heard him sigh, saw him drop his head out of the corner of my eye.

"Tell us," Ymelda said, her fan making crackling noises as it flitted back and forth. "Was your assistance against Prince Ryence your only mission?"

"You can always lie," said Queen Tregerna. "None of us will know, Sir Gawain."

Gawain was still as stone save for the movement of his shoulders as he breathed in and out. He looked like a lord of old, some great god, draped in that boarskin cloak, preparing to do battle. And perhaps he was.

At last, he raised his head and looked not at the Queen and her consort, but at me. "No," he said. "Prince Ryence and the support of my knights was not my only mission. But Hwyfar, let me explain—"

Queen Tregerna barked a terse, harsh laugh. "You should address her properly. She is a queen."

"Your Majesty, I—" he tried.

Tregerna interrupted. "So, given his hidden motives, Sir Gawain will not accompany you to Withiel, Hwyfar. Long have the Pendragons sought this item, and long have the kingdoms of Avillion and Lyonesse kept it from them and their scheming enchanters. The moment I saw Sir Gawain here, I suspected as much."

The queen held up her long, knobbled hands. "I have hidden this ancient object in plain sight and will give you more instructions in private. Return it, Queen Hwyfar, and I will grant you passage from my halls."

She turned to Gawain, whose face was a mask of anger. I could not bear to look at him. "And Prince Gawain: we are kept safe here, but we are prisoners. My magic is hedged in, for in my haste, I attracted a foe, a heinous creature who stalked these in-betweens long before I came. In two nights, he will arrive, and I will need you to kill him to free us. If you do this, I will give you our army to assist in running Ryence out."

My mouth tasted sour, my fists curling, my legs shaking with the need to run. My vision flickered. I wanted to scream, to fall apart as I had in the forest. And for a moment, I thought I might. For a moment, the temperature in the hall shifted, and I nearly let go of the storm inside of me, whatever it was. If it was real at all.

The cup, the lance, and the shield.

Arthur wanted them, too. And Gawain had not told me. My arm still ached, the muscles straining with the magic and my bones sore from knitting together so hastily. How very weary I was.

Gawain would not look at me again. He was staring at the queen, a look of shock and worry on his face. He could have lied. He *should* have lied. I had let myself know him, perhaps even love him, and the whole time he had been conspiring with Arthur. But of course he had. What a fool I was for thinking he was aught else! My skin stung with the betrayal.

"I am no monster. I understand the two of you must have need of conversation before you begin your journeys. We shall discuss more tonight," said Queen Tregerna. "At dinner. For now, you have free rein of your quarters."

CHAPTER TWENTY-SIX

GAWAIN

DREAD AND SHAME vied for my attention as I followed Hwyfar and our guards back to our rooms. I could not look at her; she would not look at me. The silence stretched between us and into our rooms, and into my bones. I tried to rehearse what I would say to her, how I could explain—how I had changed, how the mission had changed, how I no longer cared what Arthur wanted. Or didn't care as much. Didn't care in the same way? No, the words weren't there.

But she felt betrayed—she *was* betrayed. She would not even acknowledge me, not when I tried to touch her shoulder or call her name.

I had broken us, just as we had started to heal together.

As soon as the doors to our rooms closed behind us, she quietly requested time alone. The calm in her voice was just as devastating as if she had screamed at me, and watching her close the door behind her into the bower felt like a death knell to our relationship.

Arthur was right, I suppose, in a way. I never would have believed, never in a thousand centuries, how much more Hwyfar was than I had known in Carelon. He was right to warn me about her, he was right to predict her involvement with the *graal*—but he did not understand why. As much as he feared her, he had underestimated her.

If Hwyfar only knew how alone she was.

Should have told her before. Yet my mind had been—what? Not my own? Filled with her? I couldn't use that as an excuse. When I was around her, there was no room for logic and reason. No room for Arthur and schemes, no room for loyalty to the crown.

Even now, my heart thundered treacherously as I thought of ways to preserve what we had, knowing I could not have it.

Gods, what had I done? I wanted to be a better man, I wanted to choose the right path, but I could not be part of her life and remain loyal to my king. Even if I doubted him, even if I doubted myself.

I wanted to break something. Drink something. Kill something. If there ever was a time for the brute to return, it was now.

But I did not wish to frighten Hwyfar, and though my body shook with anger, I kept the worst of me at bay.

Our chambers were more spacious than I had first realized, and I discovered a balcony overlooking the courtyard gardens that might have been pleasant in warmer climes. My knee ached with a ferocity I had not endured in years, and when I sat down in a soft leather chair by a carefully banked fire, I spent a few moments just waiting for the icy burn to leave my leg, breathing through the pain and anger.

We all know your days behind the shield are limited. Arthur's words. *A wife is what you need, even for show. Just a decent mark in the books, good lands and good connections; I prefer a marriage of convenience, so you need not worry about progeny. I have Mordred for that. Given your proximity to the throne, it would be good for the Table to see you as neutralized.*

Pendragons. Gods, their obsessions with prophecies and succession—and now *graals*—had brought us to this point. And I had believed it, once; had fought for Arthur's vision so long, felt so certain that no matter how much blood I spilled, how many died, it was for a the right cause. Because Arthur had seen me as no one had before. He had never asked me to be other than myself, had never shamed me or hit me, or maligned me. Was that enough to give him control over my life?

I gazed into the flames and thought of my mother and uncle, thought of all the spaces in our conversations where their closeness should have been, as brother and sister. She never spoke of him. I had seen them together at events—she played the game as well as any, and as the wife of Lanceloch du Lac, she was expected to perform. But we all knew theirs was no marriage of love.

Neutralized.

A thousand years, my ancestors had ruled Orkney, and my mother and I had cut off the head of that dynasty. And now, I was on the precipice of ushering in a new age for Avillion by the same tactic. But Hwyfar held more—she held the key to the beginning of Arthur's supreme dominance, his power to spread the new faith to the edges of the kingdom. The *graal*. The first was in Avillion. Now I knew.

And I was certain it was what Queen Tregerna was sending Hwyfar to retrieve for her at Withiel.

The pain in my knee would not relent, so I stood and hobbled like an old man into the apartment, and found that someone had drawn up a hot bath for me. When I saw that steaming hot water, I made a sound between a sob and a laugh, and it took no time or thought to take off my clothes and submerge myself. Somehow, the bathtub was deep and high enough for me, and the foamy water made it up to my chest.

I sank down, eddies of lavender-scented water whirling about me, and closed my eyes, letting the heat soak through my skin and into my muscles as I practiced as Gweyn had showed me: I felt the water moving around my toes, swishing the hair at my legs and stomach, noted the slippery sensation about my fingers, the floating of my manhood. It was so rare that I ever felt *weightless* in this world. I was always being dragged down, pulled this way and that, by my body, my duty, my anger.

When I was calm, I could speak to Hwyfar. I would give her

space, let her think what she needed of me, and then we could, hopefully, piece together what we had left.

My reverie ended with a splash to the face.

I opened my eyes, surprised the water was still warm, to see Hwyfar standing, arms crossed, looking down her nose at me.

"I got a chill," I said.

She raised her brows. "Is it your habit to take a lavender soak when preparing to fight a faceless ancient foe?"

"All knights do. It is in our ancient tomes." I leaned back in the tub. There was no point in trying to cover up any bit of myself, so I did not. "You would not be privy to such secrets."

"We need to speak."

I flicked water at her. "We are speaking, Hwyfar."

"You are indecent."

"Not a complaint you expressed about an hour past, but if you have suddenly taken holy orders, I can respect that."

Her face flushed, and I nearly laughed. How the flow between us had changed so quickly, I did not know. Days ago, the idea that I could make Hwyfar blush at all would have seemed impossible. "I cannot take you seriously when you are like this."

"It helps my knee," I said, lifting my ugly, knotted, scarred leg out of the water. It was red, freckled, and swollen. But it did not hurt anywhere near as badly as it had before. "I hurt. Everywhere. And I wandered this way after you turned into a pillar of ice."

"I did not turn into a pillar of ice."

"You retreated from me, and made it quite clear you needed space. So I gave you space."

"I'm ready now. So, grant me clarity, Gawain. Tell me that Queen Tregerna is just goading me into misery. Tell me she's wrong."

Gods, there was no way out. "I can explain."

"Good." She was absolutely seething, her lovely lips pulled back in a sneer. "Tell me: Why did Arthur send you to Avillion?"

Well, Hwyfar was right. This conversation would have been far better suited to a drier environment, with me feeling less vulnerable. But I could see by the look in her eyes, that furious smoldering, that any inching out of the situation would not serve me well. I had, once again, deftly put myself solidly in shit.

The relaxation I had felt moments ago, the weightlessness, evaporated. I could not fathom what Arthur was thinking, sending me on this task with this woman. Those amber eyes, that simmering wit and impossible temper. That pain. Did he have any idea how alike we were? How deeply I could love her?

Arthur had thrown her away, discarded her like chattel. He had made her into this, reforged her.

No. I could not give Arthur credit for what Hwyfar was. That was not fair of me. But she did not yet see what power she held, what possibilities, who she could be.

Avillion was not Orkney, not some backwater territory ruled by a brutal dynasty. It was real power, and Arthur hungered for it. He wanted to take it, to mold it, to command it. Marriage to Mawra was not enough. Hwyfar's claim to the throne was greatest, unless he backed Ryence if she fell out of line.

Would he?

I could not get the idea out of my head that he would. That he would risk anything, even me, for the promise of power. Never had I entertained such a thought before, but then, never had I been anything but useful to Arthur. What good was I to him now?

"Do you trust me?" I asked her.

She stared me down, resolute. "I thought I did."

"Do you at least trust me to tell you the truth now?"

Her nostrils flared. "I thought I trusted you. And more the fool am I."

Every word felt too thick in my mouth, my throat constricting around my passions. "You cannot tell me this did not feel inevitable, you and I, because I know you felt it, too."

"Oh, because I'll lie with anyone? Hwyfar the Whore again, are we? I suppose Arthur told you to do anything to find out more about the *graal*, knowing full well how easily I would take you between my legs."

"Gods, Hwyfar, no! Arthur told me to *avoid* you. To keep away. To focus on my mission."

"Then you must truly have been desperate to fuck me for information."

"No, I—I did it because I love you, Hwyfar. And you know that." I slapped the side of the tub, splashing more water, the copper ringing in response. "You don't want to hear it, but you know it's true."

That stopped her. When she spoke, there was less fury in her words, but more hurt. "How can you love me if you've been spying on me?"

I was so weary. "Are we truly going to have this conversation right now?"

For the first time I noticed she had a dagger in her hands. Not just any dagger: *my* dagger. Ah, that was poetic. Murdered in a tub, naked, by my lover, with a weapon I had carried with me since I was a squire. If she *was* my lover. That was still unclear, as was much of our relationship. But if it had to come to an end, I supposed it could be far worse.

"Why did Arthur send you?" she asked again, biting each word out, crisp and clear.

I wanted to drown myself in the lavender bath, to hide under the water and never resurface. Instead, I growled in anguish, because every other word I tried to say felt false, inadequate, our entire connection teetering on the edge.

Then I tried again: "I am King Arthur's nephew, Hwyfar. I have no say in these matters—I have a *duty*. I have been bred for duty every moment of my life, groomed for it since I could speak or hold a sword. When he asked me on this campaign, I never imagined that we would end up here, with your *mother* of all people. But most of all I never imagined *you*."

The dagger clattered to the stone floor, and I knew, in spite of how hard I tried, I had chosen all the wrong words.

CHAPTER TWENTY-SEVEN

HWYFAR

I HAD DONE this to myself. I should never have allowed Gawain into my bed, into my mind, into my body. *Never trust a Pendragon*—I had lived by that every moment since Arthur had shunned me, nursed that promise. And Gawain, in spite of all his kindness and his professions of understanding and his damned stories...

He was still a Pendragon. He was right: his duty would preclude all else.

I could hear him splashing out of the tub, calling my name, padding over toward me with wet feet, a hitch in his gait as he struggled not to slip and fall. They had locked us in the room again, so there was little chance of avoiding him, but I would not tolerate a Pendragon in my life again. I could not endure the shame again, could not be broken so.

"We need to work together to see this done," I said, knowing he was a few steps behind me, naked and drenched in water, "but know we are working on opposite poles."

"Tell me what you want, Hwyfar. Is it the crown of Avillion? Is it freedom? Tell me why we should not give this *graal* to Arthur, and then perhaps this will make more sense. You never cared about it before."

The *graal*. I wished I had never heard that cursed word.

I should have been furious, and I was. But my anger was no

tempest—it was a deep, churning sea, far below soft surface waves.

"Arthur takes everything he wants," I said, finally turning to look at him. Thank every goddess, he had grabbed one of the coverlets and tied it around him. The man was addling my brain. "The *graal* is not his to take. It is the inheritance of Avillion. He can have the Isle, but he cannot have that. What more does he want of me? How much more can I bleed? I cannot understand how you stand by him."

Gawain shook his head, droplets falling. "He's my blood, Hwyfar. He gave me a home when I had none, gave me a purpose. He accepted me as I am. Avillion is part of his grand plan, and he wanted me to ensure you were—" He stopped himself, jaw flexing. "Arthur does not know you, but he understands you have power and potential, and that you could sway Avillion to your side."

"This is not his story. I am not his quarry!" I stalked over to him, and Gawain stepped back from me, as if expecting a blow. I had come at him with a dagger moments ago, but I had not intended to use it. It was protection. In case the façade of him melted away to reveal someone worse.

He did not flinch. "You're right. And I knew that the moment I saw you—the moment I *felt* you—that I would fail him."

Even if I did not believe it. I was furious. I knew who Gawain had become, but Arthur did not. And he did not deserve him. Tears came, hot and angry, and I could barely contain myself.

"I should have known better. Goddess! I have spent my whole life preparing myself, building walls to keep men like you at bay. And here I let you in through the front door. Who should I choose now, Gawain? Who would you like to see me married to? Bors? Lanval? Perhaps Palomydes and I would be a good match."

"Hwyfar…" he begged, dragging his hand down his wet beard. Bits of lavender clung there among the red, coarse curls. He smelled fresh, bright, lovely. His hair, usually in a short plait, was loose and long on either side of his face, and goddess help me, but he had never been so beautiful.

"Arthur asked me to see if you knew anything about the *graal*. He told me little, but knew it was in Avillion, and Queen Mawra confirmed. If I'd known it was important to you, Hwyfar, if I'd known it meant something to you, I would have come up with some nonsense to put him off. Arthur can always be distracted by a good story."

"I will never be able to trust you again."

"I don't understand why the *graal* is so important. I love you. I have broken every promise to Arthur, and I have protected you with my life. But there is so much about you I do not know, and... explain to *me* why this matters so much to you. You have never wanted the crown. Why do you want the *graal*?"

I wiped snot from my face with my jeweled sleeve. I hated everything about the dress, the room, and myself. But I could not hold onto this any longer. I would have tell him about Gweyn; it was the only way to make him understand.

I could not forgive him, or trust him. But I could help him see the depths of this betrayal.

"Gweyn came to me the night of the Fire Feast." I closed my eyes, clasping my hands under my chin. My stomach felt cold, tears burning my eyes. "She told me I had to keep the *graal* safe and away from Arthur."

He did not mock me, or laugh. Instead, his expression sobered, eyes going wide. "You spoke to Gweyn?"

Nodding, I looked at him again. "The last time I spoke to her before she died, it was in anger, and I never had a chance to apologize before she left this world. I fell to pieces when she died, Gawain. I thought I must have dreamed her, but then she came to me again in the wood, the night you saved me. I have to listen to her. I have failed in everything—as a priestess, as a princess, as a sister, a daughter. I cannot fail at this, too."

Gawain gave a great sigh, his broad shoulders falling, head dropping low. "I visited her grave every year at the side of the apple tree, you know. I would answer her questions, the ones she always asked me when I could not break away from my own darkness."

I smiled through my tears, and recited: "*What brings you joy? What brings you peace? What brings you pain?* She said all life's mysteries were in those three questions."

Never had I seen him so stricken with grief. "You asked me what changed me. *She* changed me—when it was too late for her, I suppose. When she was gone, and we no longer could share walks together or practice her archery or tend to the kennels. She always brought out the best in me, even when it was just a spark. Gweyn always brought me back from myself."

"She had a way of doing that."

"I know," he said, voice breaking on the words. "She was my greatest friend, and I cannot help but think she led me to you, somehow. So, if the *graal* must stay in Avillion, we must ensure it does."

It seemed too easy. My heart began beating, softening toward him. "Your greatest friend."

He nodded. "Her death broke me, too. I have forgiven Arthur many things in our life, but not how he kept her. Not what he had her endure—going to childbed, when he knew it threatened her life, when he knew she grew sicker and sicker."

I was so surprised at Gawain's confession, I reached out to touch his bare shoulder. To Gweyn's pain, I could not speak. But to the *graal*, I could. "What will Arthur do if you return home without it?"

"No worse than he has already done."

I did not understand what he meant, and my words were harsh. "What has Arthur ever done to his precious nephew?"

Gawain flinched. Pain, I realized, and shame. "Arthur decided that this is my final campaign before I am married off and settled on my own lands."

Perhaps he understood me more than I thought.

"You can pick whatever plump, rich maiden you want, Gawain."

"I do not want another wife."

I could not say why my stomach twisted at those words. "Then consider that you are just a man, still. Surely all knights' careers come to an end."

"Not like this. Not for me!" He shouted the words, and I saw the anger in his face again, far more than a glimpse. "What am I, if I am not Gawain of Orkney, commander of Arthur's army, and champion?"

He was so much more, yet I knew better than to argue with him. "Gawain…"

"You see how I am, what I have become. I am nearly as crippled as Cai, but he was nigh on thirty when he stopped going on campaign. I was once the most celebrated knight of Carelon, the pride of the Pendragon line, and now Arthur does not want to even look at me, no matter how close I am in blood. I am his shame."

"He does not deserve you as you are now," I said, squeezing Gawain's massive arm. I felt him tremble beneath my fingers as tears rolled down my face—as my heart broke for him. "And he will not reign forever. Not even Merlin could achieve eternal life, and certainly no *graal* shall grant that, either."

"I know. And yet I live in fear of a world without the order he has brought, even if it is an uneasy peace. And what will you do, Hwyfar? You are a *queen*. You should not let anyone take that from you. Least of all me."

He looked down at me then, that bare, plain look he had given me in the frozen courtyard. It stilled me to my heart. I had never known a person with whom I could communicate wordlessly, and yet we managed in those moments when words failed.

"So, the knight balks at betrayal, but not at treason?" My heart beat in my throat, and that inevitable pull began again as I watched his face, his expression. He was in agony.

He spoke slowly: "If you trust Arthur with Avillion, tell me, and this is far easier."

I screwed shut my eyes, pressure mounting behind them. "I trust him with nothing, Gawain."

"Then know he will stop at nothing to get what he wants. If I fail, more will come to seek it. Once Avillion is his, no one will be able to stop him. Your father tied your marriage contract, and your sister's, to this surrender. But Avillion is more than Arthur's plaything—I know that, and you know that more than anyone. Even if you don't want to be queen, you are the one thing standing in his way."

The weight in those words broke me. Something vital to my own preservation cracked open inside of me, and twenty years of protecting those memories no longer mattered. That fragile framework could withstand no more. I had been wounded from the beginning. How could I fight for an Avillion that was already slipping from me? How could I be a good queen, or even dream of being one, when I had grown weak and distant from my crown? Of course he had done everything in his power to keep me in Carelon: I was the least threat to him when drowning in fine flesh and food, drunk to the world around me.

And worst of all, I had been Sundered. My gifts were gone. I was nothing.

The ringing began in my ears. Distant at first, then closer. A clarion whine, coupled with the rushing of the sea. The firm flagstones beneath my feet fell away, my world narrowed to the thin connection I held onto: Gawain's hands on my shoulders.

I did not find my footing, but I found my voice.

"A week before I was meant to marry Arthur, I was Sundered."

"Sundered?" Gawain's voice was rough, pained. He cupped my cheek, searching my eyes, but I could not look at him.

"They told me it would help loosen my ties to Avillion, help 'tie me to Braetan and Carelon.' That my father had agreed to the procedure, even though it was new magic." I had never spoken of my Sundering. Yet in that moment, if the words stayed inside of me, in this place, with this man, I felt I might perish, or else choke to death on my grief. "They promised a deep sleep, from which I would arise changed but still whole. I do not know if the doses were wrong, but the draught they gave me did not keep me asleep as intended. I lay awake on the stone table in the High Priestess's tower, chained, aware. My magic was strong. Stronger than either of my sisters'—though that is all I remember. I no longer remember what I could do—"

I felt the sob before it poured out of me, but could not see Gawain's face for my tears. Could feel nothing but the warmth of his hands on my skin. "There were so many faces, and vicious daggers, shaped like sickle moons, to cut thousands of places upon my body and pull... pull out *strands* of me. I could feel each and every one as they were removed and broken: golden strands and deep crimson, opalescent and green. Each one a part of me, a part of my power, that had been nurtured on the Isle since the day I was born. It felt like dying. Like losing a sense—like losing my sight or my touch. The whole world dimmed and has never come back."

Except, perhaps, when I loved Nimue. Except, perhaps, when Gawain saw me. When I made Gweyn laugh.

"Breathe, Hwyfar," he coaxed gently, brushing damp hair from my face. "Breathe."

I did, and the air was hot and strange. "When I walked through the world after, I forgot how to cry, how to feel—I had spent three years of my life prepared to be Arthur's wife. It was destiny, foretold. But after my Sundering, I lost myself. I had no voice for days, even when they packed me onto a ship, wrapped me in silks and trinkets, perfumed my body with oils, and presented me to Arthur. I had a palanquin of cloth-of-gold, sixteen white palfreys, and twelve ladies in waiting... I counted them all over and over, as if that knowledge could anchor me to this new, washed-out world. The whole way, they assured me, again and again, that it would be worth it, because I was to be queen. Queen of all Braetan." I gazed up at him, relishing in his closeness, his attention. "But when Arthur came to the balcony to see me, he saw only Gweyn."

"Oh, Hwyfar."

I continued, leaning into his hand. "I could see my future

216

then, a mere footnote in history, the testament of a broken, sorry woman left in King Arthur's wake. But I decided it was not for me. Not for Hwyfar of Avillion. Instead, I made myself larger than my damage—I built my own legend."

My vision swam back, and I opened my eyes to see Gawain's face before mine, gazing down, tears streaking his freckled cheeks. His spring green eyes blazed from red rims, a mix of anger and grief.

"I remember you that day, Hwyfar. I could look at no one else. But I will never forget how I saw you—triumphant and sad," Gawain said softly. "Now I understand why."

I leaned into his strong arms. "I sought pleasure and gossip, I lay in the arms of knights who told me their deepest secrets and gravest fears. I never thought of Avillion again, because Arthur had Gweyn, and Father's death seemed impossibly far into the future.

"They called me whore when they thought I could not hear. The butt of their jokes. I was no lady, no princess. Not at home in Carelon, nor welcome in Avillion. I tasted so many pleasures, but I could never hold on to them. But it was my story. *Mine*."

"As if you could ever be anyone's but your own."

I breathed in and out, his hand slipping to my chest, reminding me of the importance. "You told me you put your body in the way of violence to drown out the pain from your father, Gawain. I sought out pleasure with my body, every kind you can imagine, and though the taking, the having, kept me afloat— the next mornings, the empty beds, the cold indifferences, the headaches..."

"The moment never lasted," Gawain said, leaning his chin on my head. "No matter how many times, how many ways, how much you sought it out. It is the same with killing, Hwyfar. I went to that well time and again, but it never ends, and it never satisfies."

I curled into him, into his warmth, and he wrapped his great arms around me.

"I don't know if it happened to other priestesses, but I know power exists to negate the magic of Avillion. I cannot let Arthur near it. He would bow to no one."

Gawain took in a sharp breath. "No man should hold that kind of power."

"But I think I can prevent the Sundering from happening again, I can stop it if I have the power of Avillion behind me— and perhaps the *graal*, too. Gweyn knew," I said slowly, "and she, too, broke from its effects."

"She still had the Sight," Gawain said softly. "Like you, they could not break her completely."

"Gawain, if you knew you could stop other boys from the horrors of men like your father, would you?"

He did not even hesitate. "Yes."

My mind felt so clear. I had pushed away responsibility because I felt I was powerless. Yet here I stood, carrying the key to untold power, enough to bring my sister's spirit back from the Underworld: I could heal what was broken. She'd known— she knew.

"The longer I stand as Queen Regent, the more I become aware that great powers seek Avillion, and I would be a fool to give up without a fight. But I do not know if I can trust my father, or Arthur. Or my mother. Or you, really."

"Then trust yourself." He kissed my head. "Start there."

He traced circles on my back as I breathed in and out, the exhaustion of the last few days and the pain in my soul expunged. Softly, he hummed, rocking me back and forth. I wept again, and he did not let me go, but held me as my body shook with sobs. Then he kissed my forehead, my nose, my cheeks, until I managed a small smile. His attention and care, his ability to remain with me in the quiet, was a magic of its own.

"How can I hate you forever?" I asked, pressing my cheek to his chest, the curling hair soft on my skin, comforting. His heart thudded beneath my ear, slow and steady. "How can I hate you for being a piece in the game, just as I am?"

"I hope, in time, you will forgive me. I tried to do what I thought was right. Now I see that, for all the twisting pathways of my life, I was meant to be here with you," Gawain said.

I was almost back from that precipice.

"And what are we do to do? We are both to be married away. Arthur would never—"

"No. He would never allow us."

His words hurt more than they should have, not least for their swiftness.

"We should be enemies," I pointed out.

"You will never be my enemy, Hwyfar. But for now, we must work to escape this evil place. You must find the *graal*, and then we discuss what we do; we will have Tregerna to reckon with and her games to play. I will fight to free us from the danger within this castle, and you will fight to find the *graal*, and we will face Ryence together."

"And then what do we do?"

Gawain ran his hands down my arms, and I reveled in the closeness, the touch without demand. "We reforge the future."

I glanced out the frosted window above us. Sleet pattered the thick glass, droplets streaking and freezing before their final descent. We might never mend, not fully. But it was a place to begin.

CHAPTER TWENTY-EIGHT

GAWAIN

QUEEN TREGERNA'S GREAT hall was a dismal affair, even when decorated for a guests' dinner, but I was certain my mood played a part in my perception. Still, Hwyfar and I were sent formal attire—in matching green and gold silks—and seated each to the side of the queen and her consort at the end of a long table hewn from a single tree. For reasons I could not fathom, it was I who sat beside the queen and Hwyfar beside the consort. In some courts, such an arrangement would be considered a slight or an offense. But given our precarious situation, and the exhaustion of the past day, I didn't belabor the point. I was more concerned that Hwyfar would manage a taxing formal dinner after her exhausting afternoon, but, stubborn as always, she insisted we continue.

The meal was humble: baked porridges, berries, honeyed figs, and stewed vegetables. It occurred to me that they were the sort of food the castle could grow, since they were cut off so from Lyonesse. Although, clearly, there was *some* kind of connection between the two countries. Too many mysteries, not enough answers. The magic was a palpable presence, like a sneeze I could not quite release.

There was no music, no troubadours. Just the clatter of old cutlery, the clanking of wooden platters, and the roiling din of conversation between the three dozen or so gathered members of court. I noted another two dozen guards posted around us as well, most of them paying exceptionally close attention to me. I nodded to a few of them, but there was no humor in their faces. It was good to know I at least held some threat to them.

"I hope you find your quarters amenable," Queen Tregerna said, just as a gelatinous paste with green flecks in it was placed before me. It smelled faintly of mint.

Conversation was a good distraction from having to eat. "The room is very spacious. And the baths quite warm."

The queen smiled over her ale cup. "We have some excellent improvements here, though many limitations. We have ensorcelled our pipes to provide hot water in the tubs when desired, in every chamber. Should you prefer a certain schedule, we can accommodate it."

I had never heard of such pragmatic magic. "Truly?" I asked.

The Queen of Lyonesse nodded. "Indeed. We have had time for such work, and the materials."

"Then I shall not feel guilty warming water again," I said, thinking of retreating back to that bath as soon as I could. "I was wounded on the way, bringing Queen Regent Hwyfar, and it has done me a world of good."

"You have been wounded many times over," said the queen without looking at me.

"Well, the silk from Lyonesse was a significant balm for the most recent wound," I said, tapping my side in an attempt to avoid eating whatever it was they were masquerading as food. "I would not have come this far, I think, without it."

Now I had Queen Tregerna's attention. "Silk from Lyonesse?"

"Yes. Queen Regent Hwyfar—she used it to heal my wound on our way. She sewed me up, and in the morning, I was good as new. Just as you did with her arm, I presume."

Queen Tregerna looked at me, eyes narrowing. Her eyes were not shaped as Hwyfar's, not quite as catlike; and their color was green, not deep amber brown. But I recognized that look. She was puzzling something out.

Then, without warning, and to my utter embarrassment, the Queen of Lyonesse produced a jeweled dagger from her side and drove it into the center of my hand, pinning me to the table. The pain dazzled me, and my vision sparkled, shock keeping me still at first. She could have plunged the knife into my heart, I realized dimly, unprepared as I was.

My battle rage simmered inside me, muscles tense and ready, but there were dozens of her guards, weapons in hand. I could brawl my way through half of them, if I could wrest my hand free, but would likely bleed out before I managed the rest.

Bad odds, even for me.

I suddenly felt faint, like the ground was moving under me.

"Queen Hwyfar," said Queen Tregerna, as Hwyfar stood, shouting my name. "Tell me about this magical silk of Lyonesse."

Ymelda looked on, concern in her features, and from my pain-dappled perspective, looking a little sick. Sometimes, pain could lend clarity, and as I felt the blood pooling in my palm, I thought perhaps this might be the exception. The heady smoke in the room, the unpalatable food, and the strangeness of the last few days conspired to make me feel as if, perhaps, I truly was going to swoon.

Hwyfar was by my side in a moment, the scent of her wrapping around me, welcome and familiar, cutting through the shock of pain. I had endured many wounds in my life, both creative and merciless, but I had yet to be impaled through the hand by an incensed, mad queen.

"By the Veil," Hwyfar said, turning fiery eyes toward her mother. "What madness is this?"

"Curiosity," said Queen Tregerna, her exacting gaze never leaving me.

"Darling," Ymelda said calmly, as one speaks to a bucking horse. "This is no way to treat our guests."

Blood oozed through my fingers, and Hwyfar ripped at her sleeve to begin sopping it off, meeting my eyes.

"I can pull it out," I said, reaching over to grab the hilt. This was a great upset, and a greater insult, but in a moment it would be over. I could control myself; I did not need to spill their blood. Just another scar to add to the long list.

Yet when I touched the hilt, I recoiled: it was molten hot to the touch. I hissed, smelling my own scorched skin, looking around with alarm. Magic. I could smell it now, feel it. Bile rose in my gorge, and I had to steady myself with my free hand.

Queen Tregerna laughed, cold and deadly. "This simple dagger pins a great beast like you to the table. Strange, is it not?"

"You sick wretch," Hwyfar said to her mother. Her command was a thunderclap: "Release him."

Ymelda's hands shook as she beheld the reddening pool beneath my hand. It was a great deal of blood, and in spite of the heat from the dagger, it was not stopping.

"No," said Queen Tregerna, leaning back in her chair, and pulling her knee up, as if she were preparing to watch a minstrel show. "I want *you* to, Queen Hwyfar."

I have never seen such anger in Hwyfar's face. She was still kneeling, yet her presence grew in a way I was now familiar with. I was growing to suspect it was a part of whatever power she had been born with—or left with—tied to her emotion. If she was a weather witch like Modrun, I would not have been surprised to see storm clouds gathering above her head, and lightning in the distance. She had been part of that storm in Brocéliande, if not all of it.

My arm was going numb. Bloodless. Head light. Lips buzzing. Shit.

"Gawain, hold on." Hwyfar put her hand to my face, turning my attention from the wound to her. "Breathe. Breathe with me."

She regarded me with true concern, fear. I thought I saw little witch lights in the amber of her eyes, floating and dancing, beckoning me...

CHAPTER TWENTY-NINE

HWYFAR

I WOULD MURDER my own mother.

Gawain had been felled by her dagger, rendered weak and useless. My mind raced with the implications: if we were to fight this nameless horror that haunted Queen Tregerna's halls, there was a chance it held some of the same powers as this. We could not win in the face of those odds. Gawain was already weakened from our escape, his knee on the verge of incapacity.

His eyes, always so bright and expressive, were sapped of life. Dull. He spoke words, but they made no sense. He said his mother's name, told me I was beautiful, that there were butterflies in my eyes.

My mother watched from her great feasting chair, goblet in hand, while Ymelda and the rest of the court looked on.

One of the maids leaned forward, concern on her face, catching my eye. Then she looked away, hiding her face.

"You are a daughter of Lyonesse, are you not?" Queen Tregerna bellowed, raising her arms. "Our great prince tells me your hands healed him—how romantic!—and yet you tell me he is not your lover. The garden wall might bear another witness."

"You think you can shame me?" I snapped at her. My skin felt too tight, my breath too hot. "I have made shame a weapon. I will not stoop to your petty tricks."

Queen Tregerna frowned slightly, but as usual, my barbs

glanced off her like hail upon armor. "Heal the man, Queen Hwyfar, before he bleeds out upon this floor and you are left to both tasks on your own."

I looked down at Gawain's hand, the wound now pumping blood in time with his heartbeat—he slumped forward in his seat, eyes fluttering. I was moments away from retching upon the table; it had happened before, in the cider house cottage. Try as I might, I could not abide such quantities of his blood.

No one moved. This cursed hall with no music, no laughter, no light. It was wrong. *She* was wrong.

"Or has his prick addled your mind so that you have forgotten yourself?"

If Queen Tregerna meant for me to perform, it certainly worked. But I did not heal Gawain. Rage poured forth from me as I stood, placing my hand on Gawain's shoulder. I could *feel* his strength as I did, a living, wild thing, and it moved within me, mingling with another sensation I knew as familiar, but distant.

The world went white hot, and all I could see was the hilt of that poison dagger, glowing a sickly grayish purple in my sight. The hall, the people, all but Gawain and that dagger, were washed away. I screamed; Gawain bellowed. I closed my hand around the hilt and pulled with strength so great it cracked the marble table, shattered the glass windows, and took every last breath from my body.

I threw the dagger from me, color rushing back to the world. The guards surged toward us, but could not — for somehow, I had raised a ring of glass and clay shards around Gawain and myself, a protective arc they dared not enter.

How? How was I doing this?

"Well, she did not heal you," said Queen Tregerna to Gawain across my deadly conjuration. "But she finally showed us what she is capable of."

The woman I had noticed before shimmered blue in my sight, yellow around the edges. She felt like the healing silk, cool and welcoming. A few of the others in the hall felt the same, but I dared not reach out for them. I did not know what this power was, nor how long I could keep it. She caught my eye, put a hand on her chest, and I nodded to her and said, "If you are a healer, please help him."

"Elayne, go to them," Ymelda said, voice strained and curt.

Elayne crept slowly through the ring of glass I still kept about us. Only when she had wrapped Gawain's hand in scraps of her own dress, muttering a prayer that staunched the worst of the bleeding, did I begin to loosen the grasp.

"Breathe, Hwyfar," Gawain said, and I was not sure I heard his voice in my mind or in my ears. "You can let go now."

He put his good hand over mine, and slowly I released the fury that had been mine. Ours? As glass and potsherds rained down upon the marble floor, I fell back into my chair, cold air rushing into my lungs again.

Snow fell in through the windows, bitter winds covering the great hall in a fine white dusting.

ELAYNE HERSELF TENDED to us in the healers' apartments after the disastrous dinner, with two handmaidens who I recognized from when my arm was broken and mended.

Gawain was no worse for wear, save for a new scar on the back of his hand. Their poultices and healing powers were astounding. In fact, I would say that Gawain flushed brighter, his skin almost glowing, as we sat face-to-face in adjacent beds, Elayne and her maids examining us.

"This truly was uncalled for," Elayne said, coming to sit by me. "You must forgive Her Majesty. This is all highly unexpected."

She looked younger than her age, but now in the candlelight I saw Elayne had fine lines around her mouth and lips, though her long, flaxen hair was still full of luster, the long braids turned up and back in a thick twist at the back of her neck. Her movements were quick and birdlike, but she was made of sturdy stuff.

"Aye," said Gawain, looking over at me with a scandalous smirk. "I wonder if any of us expected to be impaled at dinner."

I tried not to smile. It did not work. Tired as I was, down to my bones, the look in his eyes... goddess. I was glad Elayne was between us, for I might have expended what energy I had left mounting him there on the sick bed.

Elayne relaxed, tutted. "And to think you tried to convince me you were but friends while I tended to your arm, Your Majesty."

"I did?" I did not recall much of my time under the care of the healers of Lyonesse. Just dim shadows before my mother's visit.

Gawain's grinned through the pain as Elayne tightened the wrapping on his hand. "I'm afraid there is not yet a name for what Hwyfar and I are."

"Oh, but there is. You are *carioz*." Elayne perked up even more, taking on the air of a scholar. Her maidens nodded in response. "It was not the outcome Queen Tregerna expected, brutal though her methods were. You *are* a daughter of Lyonesse, Queen Hwyfar. But that magic you displayed, and the magic between you both... that is magic of Avillion."

"I have no magic of Avillion, Elayne," I said, rubbing at my collar bones. They ached. My skin felt as if it had been boiled. Gawain looked at me, concerned.

"It would seem you do," said Elayne. "And I would know. I came from Avillion, but I have been fostered in Lyonesse since we were lost, as I showed a prowess for healing at a young age. There are healing properties in the silk of Lyonesse, you are right. But *carioz* is old, older than the pillars of Avillion you know now."

"I was Sundered," I said to Elayne. "It was taken from me."

The look on her face was doubtful, sad, and a little conflicted. She lowered her voice. "You are a daughter of Lyonesse. You are a *healer*. Not all healers are the same. Some heal the land; some heal the sick; others heal livestock, or blighted crops. I think you healed your Sundering, or part of it at least, through the *carioz* bond with Gawain."

"What does *carioz* mean?" Gawain asked, examining Elayne.

"It is a word in the language of Avillion," I said to him. "It means *beloved*. Or *friend*. But I have never heard of it used in this way."

Elayne gave me a small cup of fragrant chamomile tea and I drank it greedily. It was sweet, comforting, and quelled the shivering remnants of whatever I had done in the great hall.

"How do you feel?" Elayne looked at me intensely, searching my face for clues.

"Better," I said. "Tired." What I wanted to do was crawl over to Gawain and fall asleep on his chest. More than anything. Just thinking of it was almost unbearable, like a thirst I could not quench. Glancing at him, seeing his expression mirroring mine, I knew he felt the same way. Knew it more strongly and deeply than I ever had before.

"I would expect so," Elayne said with a sigh, but she looked nervous, now. "A thousand years ago, before what they call 'the great peace'—there were different magics at play. Not just priestesses, but priestesses and knights, together. Pairs, triads—sometimes more. *Carioz*. They would work, live, and train together as a unit. They were bonded by magic and made stronger together."

"Why did it change?" I asked.

Elayne took my hand gently between hers. "The world changed. The ancestors of Uther Pendragon went to war and wanted more knights, and Avillion had them. And so... our great peace began. And the *carioz* were no more."

"What I did..." I swallowed, looking at her. "That was *carioz*."

She nodded. "I saw you beside Prince Gawain, twisting together the broken strands of your Sundering, repairing yourself—and he, freely giving of himself."

"You saw this?" I asked.

Elayne nodded.

I shivered. "I thought the silk healed him. I stitched his skin together. I retched the entire time."

"Your body was reacting to your connection," Elayne said. "To his pain. Your connection, as *carioz*. It takes a toll. You spent your own power, gave your own health unto him. Were you sick the next day?"

"She couldn't keep food down. We thought it was effects of another kind," said Gawain.

"Likely, her body was recovering from the magic," Elayne explained. "And silk of Lyonesse is an ideal conduit for such magic. It was good intuition."

I gaped at this woman, amazed. "How do you know such things?"

"Few among us still do. Not even the queen herself could see it. She believes you are solely responsible for that power, Hwyfar. And for now, I believe we should keep it that way." Her voice went low, eyes looking back and forth between us. Even her maidservants looked uncomfortable. "Do not tell them of your *carioz*. Do not let them know."

Them?

This was a strange change of discussion. Fatigue wound about me, thick as wool, but I steeled myself to remain awake. We had two days until the unnamed horror came to these halls, and perhaps less until my trials with the *graal*…

I sensed Elayne had more to say to me.

"You do not remember me," she said, and there were tears now in her eyes. "I understand, of course. Lyndesoires has a habit of making us forgetful."

I felt the sharp, bitter taste of guilt—a rare emotion for me. Nothing about her fair face was familiar, however, try as I might. Yet, in my heart, I felt a twinge: regret.

"Elayne!"

The doors blew open and Queen Tregerna came in, flanked by four of her guards.

Elayne fell into a bow of supplication, "I was just finishing up with Queen Hwyfar, Your Majesty."

Queen Tregerna scowled at the healer. "You are overdue."

"Of course, Your Majesty."

"This is no time for idle prattle." Tregerna never once addressed me; it was as if I did not exist. "Your report is due to me, Elayne. Now. Delen, Hedra. Take Queen Hwyfar and Prince Gawain to their chambers; they are not to rejoin us until tomorrow evening, when Hwyfar is due for her first trial."

I wondered if Elayne knew me as a child, and if she remembered my own powers. I had been drawn to her, among all the attendants at Lyndesoires. Had we been friends? Gweyn told me once that the Sundering did not just remove our abilities, but some of our memories as well. Who was Elayne to me, all those years ago? And why would they have wanted me to forget her?

CHAPTER THIRTY

GAWAIN

WHEN WE FINALLY returned to our chambers, Hwyfar was half dead on her feet. She collapsed in my arms, so fatigued I had to carry her to the bathtub. Her skin was hot to the touch, her lips chapped, but Elayne and her handmaidens had assured me this was expected. I was given hasty instructions to prepare a cool bath, to soak her in a mix of herbs she had given to me in a wax bag, and to get her to drink as much tea as possible.

Easier said than done.

"Go to bed," was most of what I could get from Hwyfar as we slowly limped toward the bath.

"Those handmaidens will impale me to the wall with daggers if I fail to follow their instructions," I said to her, biting back on my groaning knee as Hwyfar went slack again. Hauling her bodily was becoming more and more of a pastime. But I did not mind so much.

Despite my whirling mind, I wanted to hold her and touch her again and more, draw her legs around me, and bury myself in her until the sun vanished, rose, and vanished again.

Her wants were far different. Though I never was a gossip, I did wonder what my brethren might think of this vulnerable Hwyfar, this creature being reborn before me. The woman I loved could command power of a like I had never seen; and judging by the faces at court, a power few expected of her. And she allowed me to care for her. That was a greater gift than any bodily intimacy.

And we were tied together. We were *carioz*.

I hoped she had more thought, more insight, into this *carioz*. The idea that I could be capable of wielding power beyond my own body's strength made me uncomfortable, thinking again of what Tregerna had said of my mother: a witch. Laughable, I had thought. Except that my grandmother Igraine had been of Avillion, had she not? Her daughters, all save my mother, had trained there, too.

Shivering, I began helping Hwyfar out of her clothing. No, that was a kind way of saying it. She was no help. She kept batting me away, falling asleep in between my attempts to untie the delicate fabric without spoiling it. In another circumstance, the disrobing might have been arousing. As it was, the struggle was grimly funny.

Certainly, if this was the cost of *carioz*, this could not happen every time. Yet, I recalled, after she healed me in the cider house, we had both fallen deep asleep, awoken in each other's arms for the first time. It had felt more natural than breathing, and now I was beginning to understand why: we had uncovered an ancient bond. Perhaps it had been there between us from the moment she entered Carelon. Part of me knew that to be true.

"I really do hate you," Hwyfar moaned as I lowered her into the water, the flakes of mint and buds of chamomile clinging to her fair, dimpled thighs. I felt her body respond to the chill, bumps rising along her arms, as the water rose to envelop her. Beneath the water, her skin looked blue, her breasts buoyant and ready for...

"Aye, you have said far worse to me," I said to her, turning my attention elsewhere and watching her eyes widen as the water began its work almost immediately.

"Goddess's cunt!"

I had never heard her swear like that before, and could not help but laugh, even though I got a mouthful of water and herbs from her splashing. "I do not want to know which goddess you refer to."

"This water is like ice, you oaf!" Hwyfar squealed and started hitting me again, making a very sorry attempt at getting out of the tub. It was deep enough for me, and therefore too deep for her to get out of in her current state without assistance. It was like watching a fly stuck in a mug of ale.

Pretty fly, though.

I opened another pouch into the water, and it looked like rendered fat and dirt, though it smelled of lemon and lavender.

"Forgive me," I said, watching her cringe as the gelatinous mixture swirled around her chest.

"Please tell me there is method to your madness, Gawain, and this is not simply torture for being incapable of healing your hand."

"Healer's instructions. Very clear. She said a good soak here, in this combination of herbs, until you begin to wrinkle, and then you may be allowed sleep."

She truly must have still been exhausted, because Hwyfar's shoulders slumped forward, she drew her knees up to her chin and did not argue. "Then we should get it over with," she said quietly. "But please, comb my hair?"

"I—of course," I said. I was halfway to the table by the bed— was it *our* bed now?—when I noticed the pain in my knee was a fraction of what it had been earlier in the day. Before I had been impaled by a poison dagger to a table.

I had endured longer days, but not many.

When I returned with Hwyfar's brush, she was quiet, distant. It did not take a trained healer to see that Hwyfar was in a fragile place, and I had seen her through enough dark moments to know that much.

So, I combed her hair while she sat in the stillness, working out the tangles one by one. I found some chips of clay and glass still in her curls, leftover from her magical theatrics, which she was clearly not prepared to speak of yet. But it did not matter to me, because she had asked me to comb her hair, and it was personal, and the beginnings of trust, and enough reward for me.

I found rose oil nearby, and worked it into her scalp, helping some of the worst tangles. She relaxed finally at that, and I watched as her hair made damp curls, dark as fresh blood, across the pale expanse of her skin.

When some of the oil slipped down to her neck, she exhaled in a way that stirred me, and suggested she needed more work on the area. So, again, without words, I kneaded her neck and shoulders as the fire crackled, focusing on the patterns of her curls and not the throbbing elsewhere.

A time and a place, I told myself.

To make better work of my hands, I then plaited her long hair in a simple triple chain, like I did my own hair.

"Show me your hands," I said, and she held them up. I nodded. "Appropriately pruned."

We had enough furs and silks for an army, and in spite of her half-hearted attempts to dissuade me, I lifted her up out of the cold water and dried her thoroughly, wrapped her in a silk robe, and then carried her again to the bed.

"Your knee is going to give out, and then you will be angry at yourself," she muttered, eyelids already drooping as I pulled the fur coverlet up to cover the lovely angle of her shoulders.

"Aye, it might," I said. "But the pain will be worth it."

I lowered myself to the bed beside her, and she looked up at me, thoughtful, mysterious. We had not spoken much, yet I knew she wrestled with all we had before us, and all we had between us.

"Thank you, Gawain," she said to me, and held out her hand. She had never done such a thing, so small, so intimate.

"What brings you joy, Hwyfar?"

She gave me a faint smile. "The color of your eyes."

"What brings you peace, Hwyfar?"

"The touch of your hands."

I took her hand in mine; it was not a small, delicate hand. Not a fragile thing. The hand of a warrior queen. Long, deft fingers. Wide palms. Suited to a sword, to wielding spells. But I still loved each and every fingernail, cracked and split as they were.

You begin with joy, and you end with pain. Because some days, you may never get to the end, Gweyn would say.

"What brings you pain, Hwyfar?"

My heart hurt; gods, all of me ached.

Hwyfar did not answer, and I was glad, for she was asleep.

SLEEP DID NOT come easily for me, but after my own, warmer bath I crawled into the enormous carved bed beside Hwyfar and eventually found a few hours of dreaming.

I saw Arthur there, in the bleak halls of dreaming, pacing his chambers in Carelon, a broken unicorn horn in one hand and a goblet spilling blood in the other. Beneath him, Mordred played in the blood, tracking it all across the golden marble floors, and Mawra laughed from the balcony, overlooking a blighted field.

I started awake to find Hwyfar on my bare chest, a spreading wetness where she still snored softly with her mouth open. Again, that pain. My whole heart twinged with it, more than my old pains. This woman, this soul.

This person I could not have, yet I was bonded to.

She moved beside me, and I ran my hand over her back, over the waves of her hair before it met the plait.

"Good morning, Queen Hwyfar," I said to her as she raised her head to look blearily at me. There was crust at the corner of her eyes and mouth, but she was still beautiful.

"I fell asleep on you." She looked down at my chest. I had not bothered dressing.

I scratched at my beard. "Well, I fell asleep next to you after you tried to assault me, but then at some point in the night you crawled over here, yes. I did not have the heart to move you."

I was grateful she did not move away. Instead, she just leaned into me, breathing deep. Never had anyone do that before. I could imagine getting used to it.

Hwyfar's hand rose and rested briefly on my chest, just above my navel. Her fingers found the ridged scars there, the little indentations from axes, daggers, arrows... I had once been young and foolish, counted them and known them by each and every dent. Now I had no recollection of most of them.

"I must stay apart from you tonight," she said at last, her breath tickling the hair on my stomach. I did not want to squirm. "Gawain—what will become of us?"

"Death, most likely," I said.

She raised her head to glare at me. "This is a trying time, and you opt for dramatics?"

"It is inevitable. And probable, for me, tomorrow. If I survive the nameless horror your mother keeps as a pet, then Arthur will kill me. Or Mawra will. Or perhaps I should let Lanceloch have the death blow; he's been hoping for it since he nearly did me in the first time."

Hwyfar pursed her lips. "Surely Arthur will not be so sour about you coming home without the *graal*."

I kissed her forehead. "He will kill me for losing my soul to you. Especially after he gave explicit instructions to avoid you."

The look she gave me was full of surprise. Perhaps I had said too much. Her lips curved into a smirk. "Arthur would never kill you. He loves you too much. But he does not know you as I do. If that is the reward for owning a bit of your soul, then I shall take it."

"I am already entwined with you, Your Majesty," I said. "You took my heart. How much more is a soul, truly, on the scales of fate?"

She propped herself up on my chest now, folding her hands under her chin, and giving me a very wicked smile. "Well, whatever will we do now?" When she rolled her hips, she slid her thigh up against my leg, and the clear rise of my prick.

My whole body, already perpetually aroused in her presence, seared to life.

I slid my hand behind her neck, feeling the strength of her there. The challenge in her eyes was clear. That tug between us sizzled, insistent and clear.

"You're certain?"

"Do I seem uncertain?" Her long, tender body undulated over mine, punctuating her words, as her hand slipped further down, grasping me. She gave me a throaty laugh.

Clearing my throat, I struggled to find words amidst the fog of lust Hwyfar always brought with her. "I never want to assume."

Never in our time together had I heard Hwyfar giggle. But she giggled then, a high, tittering noise, which ended when she buried her face in my neck.

"You said you—you used your body. This morning," I said, hands up and away from her, as she continued laughing. "I—Hwyfar. Stop."

Peering up at me through her fingers, Hwyfar then hoisted herself up, slinking free of her robe at the same time. That might have been magic, because in one smooth motion she was bare to me, those full breasts just a hair's breadth from my mouth. I had not tasted her skin as thoroughly as I had wanted to, and wondered if the mint from her bath lingered, what it might be like mingled with her own flavors...

"Whenever the day comes that I do not want you between my legs, you will have no doubts. I am fluent in the language of pleasure, and we have just begun to converse." Her hand moved up and down, now, tantalizing, gentle, not quite enough pressure to undo me, but more than enough to distract me.

I forgot how to swallow. To breathe. "Ah, gods, Hwyfar."

Then she shifted, and she was sitting on top of me, straddling me as one would a horse, pinning me down between our hot flesh.

Hwyfar leaned forward until her lips were nearly brushing mine, teasing, breath tickling. "When I was younger, I behaved like a knight, and I became infamous. It is not shame that brought me here, Gawain. It is experience. Though, I must say, our *conversations* are beyond anything I have experienced before."

"Then what is your pleasure, my Lady Knight?" I asked her, sliding my hands to cup her full buttocks, teasing my fingers inward. I could feel her muscles beneath, and ah, she moved me.

Hwyfar came forward to kiss me deeply, and as she did, she slid me into her, moaning against my mouth. That scrambled my thoughts as surely as eggs over a cook-fire. Her tongue was a living tool of passion, and when she pulled away from me to brush a hand down my cheek, I saw her eyes were wet with tears: brilliant, shimmering.

"I never wanted to come back to my lovers before," she whispered, her face flushed with pleasure, lips swollen from kissing. "I tasted their sweetness, I had their pleasures, and I was done. But you, Gawain. You feel—like—"

No more. I would have her know me fully, and I met her movements with an upward motion of my own, watching her face melt into ecstasy and words leave her completely.

We crashed together, language no longer capable of conveying the need between us. She gave me a sly grin of appreciation as I slipped my arm around her waist and swapped positions, so I was above her now, looking down upon her form.

I had not her storied experience, but I could see the challenge in her eyes. My full strength was a wild thing, a power I did not bring into the bedchamber. The first woman I had bedded had goaded me on, and then shamed me for going slowly with her. Another had cried when I caused her pain. My lovers afield had been hectic, passionate, but I had withheld myself from them, too.

We may never have this time again.

In a matter of hours, she would leave me; we could both be dead.

First, though, I would taste of her. I began at the inside corner of her knees, her long legs descending to her wondrous middle. I was rewarded with sweet lavender mint, not to mention her encouraging sounds.

She did not expect, perhaps, my knowledge in this area, for the sound she made when I began my ministrations was of surprise, dissolving quickly to pleasure. Hwyfar reached down and took hold of my hair, which I had not tied back. I did not mind that at all; I rather felt encouraged, my own flames rising as her hips lifted up to meet my tongue and lips. I could be patient. I did not need to be inside her to find my pleasure.

Her nectar was bright, honeyed, ripe. I could drown myself in that sweetness and die a happy man.

Then she was pulling at me, insistent.

"You. Now," she said. "All of you."

I swept my arms under her thighs and picked her up at the knees, as if she were feather light, pressing her against the wall. My whole body buzzed with desire, and I had no thought to my own pain as I lifted her up and let her hover, just above me, poised, and took one of her nipples into my mouth and bit down. Gods, her breasts were perfect against my hands, soft and ripe and yielding.

Then I buried myself in her fully, her heat wrapping around me, muscles clenching in response, and her back arced in my grasp—she went taut a moment, a sound like a stifled cry in her throat—

"Again."

I complied.

Hwyfar dragged at me, nails scratching, as I took her again and again. She bit my shoulder, pulled at my hair, and I grabbed fistfuls of her flesh in between, kneading her between thrusts. She was strong, but she was ample, too, and gods, I loved every inch of her. I was drowning in the fullness of her.

As we moved together, growling and rutting like feral beasts, a sizzle of power arced between us—a live current of strength. Hwyfar's eyes shot wide and she stared at me, shivering. Light shimmered over our bodies, whorls of gold and green around our arms and legs.

Then she pushed back. *She pushed back.*

We fell off the bed with the power of her, tumbling and laughing in a tangle of limbs and magic.

Hwyfar's eyes glittered, and she pinned one of my arms to the thick wool carpet.

I could move it, but just barely.

"This is *your* strength," she said, breathless. Wisps of her red hair made little circles at her brow and cheek. "I can feel it. I can feel *you*."

It was more than that. I could feel *her*. Feel what *she* felt. Like we shared one skin, not two. Pleasure of a kind I never considered flowed through us, expanding us by a measure without calculation. We became more, opening up and joining and growing into an experience beyond either of us.

And nothing else mattered: not Arthur, not our current tribulations, not the future, nor the doom that would befall us.

Her cries became more insistent, and I reached down to touch between us, feeling her body tremble with anticipation. My own pleasure was near its peak, and the moment I heard her cries of passion, felt her body flutter around my own, I was undone along with her.

"Perhaps it is the *carioz*," Hwyfar mused when we at last were spent. "But I must let you know, I have been lost to passion for some time."

"Lost?" I did not know what she meant.

She expelled a short breath. "I have been two years without a lover."

"Two years?"

Hwyfar nodded slowly, her nose touching mine. "And now, wanting you never ends. It is a constant melody in my mind, one I cannot stop hearing—and I do not want to stop." She licked my lips open and kissed me again, as consuming and as full of fire as the last time.

"All the time," I said in agreement, as she began kissing my chest. "Gods, Hwyfar, I have never desired anyone so much."

She giggled again. "Every time I see you, I want you like this."

Hwyfar gestured to my chest, the rise of my stomach. She let out a little moan, and gods, my whole body responded with want again, as if we had not just concluded. "I think I might be going mad. Are we going mad, Gawain?"

I stirred again under her touch. "Maybe. But I will gladly go into madness with you, so long as you will have me, and I can feel your pleasure alongside my own."

Gods, what a gift and what a curse.

CHAPTER THIRTY-ONE

HWYFAR

MY BODY FELT liquid, detached, as I lay beside Gawain on the carpet, the shimmering light fading from our bodies. We still clasped hands, both gazing up at the thick-beamed ceiling, trying to breathe, to comprehend this connection.

I had never felt such a thing, never shared such a thing. I had not just had his strength—I had known his *pleasure*. I shivered at the thought of it again, knowing that if there was still time I would take him again, and he me. And there would be no end to it. Had I been seeking this all my life?

After years of passion and conquests, I did not want to run from my lover. Running felt a punishment, a danger, a kind of unbearable death—a sudden fear gripped me, and I threw myself into his arms. Gawain held me, and dread slipped over us both, heavy and complete. The smell of his skin reminded me of fresh cut fields of wildflowers, his scars like tributaries to new lands. I wanted to remain in this little world of our own making forever.

"Ah, my beautiful, proud Hwyfar," he said to me, smoothing my back with his broad, callused hands. It soothed me as nothing ever had, and my sobs stuttered to an end. When he spoke again, I could hear the tears in his voice. "This cannot be the end for us."

I curled into his lap, as much as I could, and we rocked together.

"This world will not make a place for us," I said.

Gawain rested his chin on my head. "I know."

In the distance, thunder rumbled in the dark night. This time, though, I was not tired. We had used our magic, and though I was cold, and afraid, I was not spent.

I was angry.

"Will you fight for this?" I asked him, pulling away to look him square in the face.

He looked so torn, so broken as he gazed into my eyes, clasped my hands, kissed them. "If you do not run, I will not falter."

That was it. Our promise, our bond. I felt my heart stutter, a sweet hot sensation pouring through my blood.

If you do not run, I will not falter.

We did not pledge our troth; we did not even pledge love. Ours was a connection deeper, down to our marrow.

I gave him a token, a narrow length of green silk from the dress I had worn the night before, as if we were a knight and maiden upon the tilting field. He braided it into his queue and promised to keep it there until we were united again.

THE EMISSARY CAME to me an hour later, announcing that I was due to meet with Queen Tregerna and her First Weaver at dusk. Alone. At least there was no judgement in the eyes of the woman who delivered the message, though I was red-eyed and disheveled, and wore nothing but the robe I had been given the night before.

We ate, and fed one another; we came together softly, we came together with fury.

Then Gawain helped me dress. He combed my hair with a silver comb we found in a chest delivered to us, along with a hammered copper circlet, and smoothed every tangle with care. Then, with a delicacy I now understood, he tended to each long braid, threading ribbons through them, and helping to fasten them through the circlet.

My gown was green, flecked with silver floss, the bell sleeves long enough to touch the ground. Were I home, I would have insisted upon leather riding trousers, a garment I felt most at home in for practical reasons. I did not understand how I would get to Withiel, nor what this sort of work would entail, but the gown felt fitting, somehow.

"I wonder if this is the beginning or the end of our story," I said to Gawain, as I looked at the two of us in the mirror. Regretfully, he had dressed in his grey tunic and belt.

I enjoyed seeing us in the reflection before me. Aside from our proportions and the hue of our hair, there were few similarities between us. He had a body of lines, cuts, angles, save for the beautiful curves of his lips, the roundness of his middle that I had come to adore beyond reasoning, and where his cheeks and chin dimpled when he smiled. I, in turn, was all long curves—but for the edges of my eyes, the sharpness of my teeth, the cut of my cheekbones.

"Can it be both?" Gawain stared at my eyes in the mirror, rubbing his hand down my neck. I leaned into his touch. It never would be enough, I knew. And it would never last.

"I wish I could stay. I wish I could dig down to the Underworld with you and escape this madness," I said, and it was the most ridiculous thing I had ever said to a person in my life. How I would have laughed at myself to hear such words!

He gave me a smile, his cheeks flushing a bit pink. "You would write us the greatest tale, my love."

"Say it again."

"You would write the—"

"That's not what I mean, you oaf."

I turned to shove him, but he caught my wrist and kissed me deeply, drawing me in by the waist. I did not mind—or I minded only its brevity. Time had slipped away from us, no matter how much we had tried to still it.

"My love," he said.

Holding his face in my hands I looked into his eyes. If only we had more time, if only the world was fair. But neither of us had known fairness. Neither of us expected it. In a way, our stolen time together was a miracle.

"My love." I had never uttered those words to another before, but when I spoke them, I felt a lightness in my soul. I pressed my forehead to his. "Woe that we had only these days—but joy that we had them at all. I will not run from my duty, and you will not falter in yours."

I DID NOT need to look back down the length of the hall to know that Gawain stood at the threshold to our room, watching me go. He understood why I did not spare a glance; I feared my resolve would crumble. Arrayed as I was, queenly and poised, it took every inch of my focus to remain that way. My heart thundered in my chest, my skin ached with longing; I was one bruise from top to toe, and if I dropped the mask, all would be lost.

So I became a fortress: the fortress I had lived for years. I became Hwyfar the Prideful, haughty and resolute, unashamed and unflinching. It was a familiar mask, yet it took more effort. In all my performances before, I had little to lose. Now, I felt everything hinging on this moment. Would I succeed, and return to see Gawain fight his foe? Would he know if I failed? Would he, then, take up the fight for me?

I did not recognize my escorts, nor did I know what part of the strange castle we turned into. Though I had a near-preternatural ability to find my way through even the strangest structures, this unnamed castle had me disoriented within moments.

The walls were normally hewn of a dark, pebbled stone, but they transitioned to red as we came to a narrow passageway, and were joined by additional hooded figures. It smelled of pitch and incense, but distantly. Even if I had been paying attention, I had no concept of where I might escape. And then—where to?

A strangling, uneasy feeling pressed into my chest, but I swallowed it down. Weeks ago, I would have reached for my powders, for drinks and tinctures, at the merest hint of such a discomfort. Now, instead, I sank further into myself, armoring myself with more layers, preserving a still, calm center.

They would not break me.

I had already been remade.

One of the robed figures pressed the wall, and it slid sideways, revealing an immense chamber, empty save a cluster of figures around a tall silver mirror.

I knew that mirror, or at least, one like it: I had spoken to Morgen in it, not long ago. I had brokered a deal that I thought would save Avillion, a casual agreement to assist in our preservation through my father's illness. It had felt so easy, so simple. I would do this one thing, and then...

The woman who had made that deal felt like a different person. Had it been as Elayne said? Had I, indeed, reforged my bond with Avillion?

And the *carioz*...

Queen Tregerna stood, armored in a plate of bronze, a crown of gold set with spikes of jet in her silver hair. Her face was a jagged mirror of my own, lit by hundreds of beeswax candles scattered about the dusty floor. I could smell the burning wicks, feel the thickness in the air, sense my mother's gaze on me.

Ymelda stood beside the queen, draped in what I assumed were the robes of her station as consort: blue and yellow, the same colors I had seen her wearing in my rage during our last dinner, with a large ammonite pendant at her chest.

I expected a commentary from the queen, perhaps on how I had spent the last few hours since our parting, but she set her lips in a grim line and ushered me forward.

The immense door behind us came to a thundering close, and the dozen or so women slipped into formation behind me, herding me toward the mirror.

"Before Avillion was in chains," Queen Tregerna said to me, "there was another magic, another Way, when there was no divide between magics. These mirrors are a last reminder of that path, the Fated Web. Long has the web remained untended, her mysteries lost to time… In Lyonesse, we kept the Paths open, but the Byways and Strands went dark."

I listened, trying to puzzle out what she was saying. Ymelda's eyes were wet, and I wondered if they were from tears. She would not meet my gaze.

"The Paths give us access to mirrors all throughout the realm, including the very same inside of Withiel," said Queen Tregerna, as I took a step toward their mirror. It was a darker metal than the one I had known, the surface pitted with wear and time. "But recently, the Byways and Strands have awakened. Now, the Spinner awaits you, and you must pass through her web before you arrive in Withiel."

The mirror before me looked plain enough, but there was no reflection in it at all. Once I passed my hand over the glass, I saw nothing but a faint shadow.

I shivered, even in the eerie warmth of the room.

"And how do I begin?" I asked. I kept my voice even, commanding, as if I were speaking to Arthur himself. "You expect my blood to guide me, Queen Tregerna?"

A ghost of a smile passed her lips, and Queen Tregerna nodded. "We find a few things helpful in the Paths—or they once did. My spell keeps all residents of Castle Lyndesoires bound for our safety. Even myself. But we can read the web. Ymelda, bring Queen Hwyfar the tonic and implements."

Ymelda came forward with a small platter, upon which sat a silver goblet that smelled of anise, a very familiar dagger now secured in an ornate sheath, and an ammonite amulet.

Finally, the queen's consort looked up at me. I could not read her expression beyond vague concern.

"The tonic," said Ymelda softly, "is meant to fortify your mind and open your senses to the Path. That awareness should prevent you from getting lost, which is always a concern for those new to its pathways—and as we cannot provide training, it is the best we can do."

I lifted the goblet, surprised to find it warm. I sniffed; it was tea. Ymelda nodded almost imperceptibly, and I drank it in one go, scalding as it was. It tasted like hot, sweet piss. I wished Gawain had seen it, the look on their faces. Certainly none of them had expected to see me do such a thing. He would have laughed that deep, musical laugh of his.

The dagger had been cleaned of Gawain's blood, but I knew it well, for I had thrown it across the great hall the day before. In the candlelight I had a better view of the interlacing filigree and cloisonné: two lions wrestling, surrounded by a dragon on either side. There had to be some symbolism there, but at the moment my heart was not stirred by it.

"The dagger is for protection and defense. We do not know how safe the Path is, and against unforeseen attack," said Queen Tregerna. "Tomorrow, our beast returns. If you are not back by then, you may need to fight your way back."

I sheathed the dagger into my belt.

Ymelda held up the ammonite amulet, the chain glittering. "This will bring you back to us if all else fails," she said softly.

"It is a trinket," said the queen, dismissively. "Forgive Ymelda's sentimentality. She has taken a fancy to you and your knight."

But Ymelda's face was drawn, serious. "Listen to your heart," she said softly to me. "Do not risk all for bravery's sake."

If you do not run, I will not falter.

"We will await you on this side," said Queen Tregerna. "Find the *graal,* bring it to me for safe keeping, and then we shall deal with the beast in the halls. Then, with our foes vanquished, we shall return to challenge Prince Ryence at last."

WALKING THROUGH THE mirror felt like passing over a ghost's grave, then dancing across the web of a great spider. Even though I wore layers of clothing, every inch of my skin felt the tickle of magic. Fear gave way to wonder, as the world about me dissipated like mist in the sunshine—yet it was a dimness and darkness that was revealed to me, silvery and grey, and not the golden light of day.

I felt a path beneath my feet, but it wavered, like thick lily pads on water. When I glanced down, I saw nothing but eddies of mist, whorls obscuring the bottom of my gown.

I heard nothing, saw nothing clearly, but walked on. I *felt* a pull forward, and so I proceeded in that direction, wrapping one hand around the ammonite amulet and resting the other on the hilt of the dagger. To my surprise, the dagger did not feel foul as it had the night before. Instead, the cool bone hilt centered me.

No sooner had I felt the hilt cool against my skin than I heard Gawain's voice.

Is that you?

I released the dagger from my grip. Nothing.

"Gawain?" I asked into the dark.

Taking a few more steps forward, I thought I saw a shimmer of light in the distance. I squinted, shivering into my cloak. My ears filled with pressure, and I winced as it ached.

So I stopped. Curiosity got the best of me, and I grasped the dagger again.

If this dagger is still crusted with your dried blood, I shall be quite cross, I thought.

I felt a ripple that might have been laughter. *That really is you.*

I am lost in the middle of a forsaken darkness, covered in mist and dim, bouncing lights. Queen Tregerna claims I should be on my way to Withiel.

An impression of Gawain flickered in my mind, the faint smell of his hair, warmth on my skin. He said: *Is that what the dagger is for? Murdering flickering lights?*

Not as far as I am aware, I said to him. *It was intended for protection; I was warned other creatures lingered here. But I believe Ymelda knew it might connect us, through our...*

Making more progress toward the light ahead, leaves brushed across my face, but when I reached up to push them away, my fingers passed through air. An unwelcome sensation among so many others.

I wish I could help you be less afraid, said Gawain. *But fear is a constant companion here, too. They have come to fit me for my armor for tomorrow. They have tried to tend to my knee, but assured me that nothing can be done in such short a time. If they had weeks—months—perhaps, but not now.*

My heart dropped. I wondered if he could feel it.

Gawain again: *If you do not wish me here, I will not linger. We have shared much, but your mind is very much your own.*

I loved this man. I loved him so much it was pain: joy, peace, pain, all at once. And in this oppressive darkness, I had not expressed my relief enough. My surprise, my fear, had clouded my judgement.

Please stay, I said. *I can keep you company, too. Tell me of your armor. It must be splendid. Is it like the one Tregerna fashioned for me?*

As I walked, I listened to Gawain describe the armor in my mind. And with his words, I could see faint outlines of it: burnished red bronze, interlaced with knotwork patterns, set with amber drops about the breastplate. He told me that it was articulated with scales like those of a dragon or a fish, and they had incorporated the Orkney unicorn on the helm, but not in a way that was cumbersome: an emblazoned star at its pinnacle. They had found Galatyne, his sword, cleaned and repaired it, and it gleamed anew. He had found a shield he liked, he said, and they would paint upon it a unicorn, as well. Once, he had fought with a similar one, and lost to Lanceloch du Lac.

I hoped that was not baiting Fate. He had survived that battle, but never truly recovered. I know, I had been there, watched him fight like a man possessed. Until Arthur himself conceded on Gawain's behalf. When they dragged Gawain off the field, I remember seeing them peel his armor off, a rib punctured straight through his side, where a horrible chunk of missing flesh remains now. He had fought through that pain, through that pride.

You remember that, do you?

It was easy to forget Gawain was in my mind. *It was hard to forget,* I said. *I recall cheering for you in the stands, even though I—wishing that you would fight harder. Now, I wonder if I knew, then. No, I was likely too drunk to sense anything profound. Ah, well, I need you to be careful. Do not let your stubbornness destroy you, Gawain, not while I am gone.*

I am not the fool I once was, Hwyfar. Thankfully. My body is not so reliable, but I have more to fight for—and a bit more sense. Not much more, but enough to tilt the scales in my favor, I think.

I sighed and sent across a distracting image of what I wished could transpire between us, in excruciating detail.

You will be the end of me, woman.

The light before me beckoned, but Gawain's words did not hearten me as much as I hoped.

Be brave, my knight. Soon, you shall bring me to my knees.

I let go of the dagger and went forward. This was my burden to bear, and my quest.

The brightness was shaped like a door: a door I knew. Carelon had many doors, and I had lived there long enough to learn each and every one—it was, in some ways, my gilded playground. One moment, I was living the memory of the streaming banners of Lugh's Tournament grounds, and the next, here I was.

This was the door to Anna Pendragon's—Anna du Lac's—apartments in Carelon. Gawain's mother. Once, briefly, she had shared them with her husband, Lanceloch du Lac. She favored sky blue, and the outer rim was carved with interlacing apple blossoms and orchids. I had passed by that door a thousand times and knew it well.

Instinct took hold of me. I was here for a reason. This was not my final destination. Had they not said that Gawain's mother was a witch? Though I had never considered such a thing, I did not doubt the women of Lyonesse. I may not have agreed with their methods, but their judgements were true.

I swallowed, focusing only on Gawain for a moment, clasping the dagger again.

Gawain, I must pass through where you cannot follow. I will come back to you. The way is dark, but I am not afraid. I will not run.

I felt his presence rise up, protective. But he relented. *Take heart, my love. I will not falter.*

I released the hilt of the dagger and the strand connecting me to Gawain snapped. Pain sizzled in my chest, and tears pricked my eyes. I had not expected that. Losing him all over again left me unmoored. But I knew he could not follow me here, even in my mind.

Touching the door, the Path behind me dissipated, and before I could even turn the latch or knock, I was standing inside the room, no longer lingering upon those dark pathways.

It was evening in Carelon, and Anna du Lac sat in a high-backed chair, with a spindle in her hand, by a roaring fire. She looked much the same as I remembered her: a tall woman, nearly as tall as I, with flaxen hair and the same high cheekbones and keen eyes as her brother, King Arthur. She had full lips and sharp shoulders, the picture of poise and beauty. I had more than once hoped to seduce her to my bed. Alas, she had never seemed keen on such a conquest, always chasing Bedevere.

I had never seen Bedevere among my revelers, though, so that was to his credit, I suppose. Many other knights had taken their turn among my merry band.

But now I also saw where Gawain's eyes came from, where the angles from his face, the shape of his nose. They were so close in age. She could not have been more than thirteen when she'd birthed him. Such was the curse of some noble houses: bled, wed, and bred. Not always in that order, as the old saying went.

"I admit I was surprised when I felt your stirrings upon the web," Anna said to me, not looking up from her work. It was an old spindle, the sort that village women would use, and the thread was fine and pale. Her long, slim fingers worked it well, though. "Hwyfar of Avillion. We have some unfinished business, so I suppose Fate would bring us together."

Taking a step forward, I was surprised to see the edge of my gown transparent. I was ghostly, a strange wisp of myself. Startling, I held up my hand.

Anna glanced up at me. "Yes, strange. It does take some getting used to. But if you speak up, I should be able to hear you."

"Lady Anna," I said, and my voice echoed, as if in a great cavern. "I did not intend to come to Carelon."

"I know. But I am the Spinner, so I directed your steps."

"You?" I tried not to sound indignant, but I failed.

"It does seem strange, I know. And I appreciate you leaving Gawain to his strengths. He would not understand. Not yet, anyway. He sees me the way most men see me: a shadow. I have spent the last ten years of my life dedicated to the work of my mother's line. And older magics. Magics left to the wind by Merlin and his ilk. Magic cast out from Avillion, and Lyonesse, and even Ys."

"The priestesses of Ys tried to have me killed," I said.

Anna did not look surprised, or even upset. She shrugged, placing the spindle on her lap. She wore the same periwinkle blue as the door. "Yes, they did. Theirs has become a largely corrupt power. And in a way, I understand that. I very nearly did the same. I, too, sought corrupt powers to serve my purposes, and it nearly killed me. But it was worth it. Women like you and I, Hwyfar, we are often pressed to desperate measures to change our circumstances. Some, like Nimue, do not survive the battle."

There it was. The challenge in her eyes.

"Ask me," said Anna. "And I will tell you the truth. I know you loved her."

The longer I lived without Nimue, the more I wondered if she had been real at all. The more I questioned my love for her—the more time I spent with Gawain, the deeper our connection, the less solid my connection felt with her. It had been like loving a tempest.

"Who was Nimue?" I asked. "I—you know she was my lover."

"You had many lovers, Hwyfar. What made her so different?" There was genuine curiosity in Anna's tone.

"I loved her. And I believe she loved me."

Anna closed her eyes, turning her face to the fire. Her lashes and hair flashed bright, her veil casting a shadow on the opposite wall. For a long while she said nothing.

Then, slowly, she said: "Nimue was a creature of air and darkness. I fashioned her from ancient magics—a daughter with no past, no future, and only one purpose: to serve me. But she became more."

I clenched my fists, tried to swallow, but my throat was dry. "I don't understand."

"Nor do I. But I do know that she was more real than I ever imagined, for you broke her heart, which meant she was capable of love, of regret, and of great pain," Anna said softly. "But you were not alone in that. She fulfilled her purpose before leaving this world, back to the mud and the ash she came from."

"I loved a shadow," I said.

"No, you loved a dream made real. Not many can say the same. And now, that love brought you here, in some way. For both her loss, and the loss of your sister, changed you, did they not?"

My body felt light and heavy at the same time. Like I would sink or fly away. It was grief, I knew, yet a long-lived grief I had not been able to experience in full since I heard of her death. There was resolve in it as much as there was pain.

I had loved a spell made real.

And where are you, my Lady Knight? I recalled Gawain's words, though I did not need to speak to him. After Arthur's rejection, love had never seemed possible; Nimue had changed that. Perhaps, if I had never felt love for Nimue, the door to Gawain, to *carioz*, would have remained closed.

"We do not have much time before you must continue on your way," Anna said, standing and placing the spindle in her chair. "I have but interrupted your passage."

"Do you read the Fates?" I asked. The last time I had been this close to Anna Pendragon, I had tried to seduce her. Now, I felt like a child in her presence. Even standing as I was, a watery vision, I knew she had power beyond my understanding.

The smile she gave me was fleeting, but almost kind. "No. But I sense the web. I give it structure. I make it easier for others to travel, to divine, to move. Though you see but one worker here, I am not alone; there are dozens, if not hundreds, of others, awakened, learning. Soon there will be more. But you are the first to follow this particular path in many years. For it is not just your quest you have brought this day, but my beloved son's."

My quest. *My Lady Knight.*

I did not know what to say to her. It was not shame, but a sense of judgment. My heart was squeezed to the point of pain, before this woman, who had constructed a being I had loved, and birthed the man who had taken a part of my soul—blended, somehow, with my own power. That could not be a coincidence.

"I love him," I said to her. They were the truest words I had to offer. "I need you to know that."

"Ah, love in Carelon is treason, Hwyfar," Anna said to me, an edge to her deep voice. "But only because it is the single power capable of toppling its foundations. And alas, you both are at the sword's point of crisis, and you are ill prepared for the sacrifices required."

I knew the truth of it, but fear still gripped my heart at those words. "Such power was never meant for me. I thought I understood my place in the world, my purpose, but I was just hiding behind my grief, numbing myself through life. Now I have a reason to fight."

"Nimue saw that warrior in you. And my son does, as well. He is, after all, a great commander. Gawain has never given less than everything, yet his greatest challenges are still before him, though he would not listen when I said as much. And if he loves you as I believe he does, he will rage until the stars go out."

The image her words conjured in my mind made my blood run like frost, and I took a step back. "I will fight for him."

Anna clasped her ringed hands. "Alas, for all the joy you bring to one another, be aware that Arthur will only see my eldest son married to a woman of status, and of his choosing. To do otherwise would imperil us all."

This we knew, and Gawain most of all. I did not know Anna's relationship with her brother, could not tell her what I would do to see Arthur put in his place. But I also knew that Gawain could not abandon everything for me. To abandon his family, his brothers, mother, Bedevere—it was too much.

"I will never ask of him that which he cannot give."

This seemed to satisfy Anna, and she nodded, holding out her hands. "Then we have an understanding. Should you desire passage upon the Path, we must bargain. What do you bring me, Hwyfar of Avillion?"

"I have little, Lady du Lac, but I will offer it humbly," I said, knowing well the price of the items I had upon my person: the ammonite amulet. It glowed purple, and when I grasped it, the material solidified. I handed it over to her.

There was a look of surprise on Anna's face as she beheld the jewelry. "Do you know what this symbol represents?"

"It was given to me on my way here. I was told it was a way back. Protection."

"This is the symbol of the priestesses of Ys," said Anna, taking the amulet from me.

The hair on the back of my neck rose. Ymelda had given me that amulet. But she was of Lyonesse. Certainly she did not know what it meant.

"I see where the Path takes you, Hwyfar. I grant you passage. But prepare yourself to be torn in twain, again and again. Your choices are your own. Never forget that."

When Anna stepped aside, I saw another mirror behind

her—tall and slender—and in it, the Path lit in a bright amber glow. Withiel, I knew, lay beyond. I could feel it, almost smell it, memories of home, of apples, Braids of Una baking in the ovens, and my father's favorite incense.

I passed through the mirror, and I felt Anna's hand on my shoulder briefly as cold air blew at my face. I closed my eyes against the breeze, and when I opened them again, I was in my father's chamber. That explained the incense.

"Your sister Gweyn said I should expect you," King Leodegraunce said.

CHAPTER THIRTY-TWO

GAWAIN

I LAY AWAKE in the bed I had shared with Hwyfar and counted my breaths one by one. We had spoken, I was sure of it, but she had gone silent since those few exhilarating exchanges, and now I felt worse than the last time I had seen her leave.

Just as I was preparing to get up and check to see if there was any update on my own challenge—they had come and measured me for armor four times already—I felt Hwyfar's presence slide under my skin, keen as a cat.

I will not run; do not falter.

Then, nothing. An abrupt stop. I was breathless, like I'd been punched in the stomach, dread creeping over me, a net of melting ice over my skin. Cut off. Since I had seen Hwyfar walk down that corridor I had not felt too distant from her—it was more akin to being in adjacent rooms. Now I felt a void yawning between us, as vast and incomprehensible as death.

I reached up to touch the thin band of silk braided into my hair and closed my eyes. We could not pretend ours was a story so simple as the tales told: a knight, a lady, a token. Yet it steadied me in that moment when I felt so adrift.

Carioz.

The thundering clamor on the door startled me, the iron hinges rattling: five shuddering knocks. At least they gave me warning. I steadied myself, shaking off the nerves that came with the anticipation of a fight. In my early years, I went from battle to battle without concern—it was exhilarating. Now, after my injuries, after losing men, losing lovers, losing parts of me I could never reclaim, I could not recover so easily.

Something about the shaking hinges brought back a memory from a camp years before: an angry mob of Ascomanni, piles of stinking corpses, biting flies at my neck and a burning hot sun...

With clammy hands, I pulled open the massive door to find Elayne, dressed in pale moss green, her flaxen hair braided long and coiled about her ears. She carried a tray laden with honey cakes, fruits, and cheese.

Taking me in, she tilted her head so the horned hat she wore went askew. "You do not look well, Prince Gawain," she said softly. "I am a healer, I can help."

I glanced behind her, hoping to see the source of that monstrous hammering, but the dark hallway was empty, the nearest torch smoking and guttering but otherwise unremarkable.

"I am quite well," I said to her, taking the tray, and trying to shoulder the door shut. "Thank you."

Her slight, pale hand slipped through, and I barely avoided crushing it. I went to apologize, but she instead followed me into our room, her wide eyes taking in high ceilings, plush pillows, and untended linens.

"I appreciate the food, Lady Elayne. My aunt is called Elaine, you know." And the woman I nearly married once was also named so, but I saw no need to tell her that.

"She must be a fearsome woman for you to pale so," said Elayne, taking a seat in one of the leather chairs, as if I had offered it to her. "Is she treacherous?"

Glancing at the door again, I noticed no additional accompaniment. I heard no sounds from the hall, no sense that anyone else was near.

"Not treacherous, no. I have only met her a few times. She is small. Smaller than you. And rather pinched." I found a place by the window which seemed the farthest possible distance from Elayne.

I was not enchanted by her. I was not tempted by her. But I was terribly suspicious of her. That she had appeared precisely at the moment I had felt my connection to Hwyfar vanish. Hungry though I was, the food she brought smelled *off* to me, a little too sweet. Like fruit just about to turn. And if there was one thing my Aunt Morgen had taught me, it was to trust my instincts— especially since she claimed I had none. *If even you feel like you have an instinct,* she had told me, *it must be a strong inclination indeed.*

Then an odd thing happened. That placid, restrained look on Elayne's face slipped, and she gave me an absolutely exasperated look, and hissed at me in a whisper, "Please come over here so I may speak with you."

She flared her eyes. I had seen that look many times before— from my mother, from Gareth, and even from Hwyfar—and it meant I was being very dense.

I strode over to Elayne and she looked up at me, not even the slightest glimmer of fear in her eyes. Irritation, yes.

"You must be cautious, Sir Gawain," Elayne said to me, barely a whisper. This close, I realized she was older than I had thought, though she still had the bearing of a maiden. Older than I was, perhaps. It was difficult to tell, exactly. "They do not mean to fight fair tomorrow evening. They can forge weapons greater than that dagger."

"I was not expecting a fair fight," I said, gesturing to my knee. The pain had returned once again. "But the armor should help some."

Her expression made me immediately reconsider my words.

"Be wary of the smiths of Lyonesse," said Elayne, pressing a golden apple into my hand.

"That's ominous," I said.

Outside the door, voices rose. Elayne stood, nodding to me.

"I will be but a moment." Then she was gone into the hallway yet again.

The apple was uncomfortably warm, and that cloying aroma rose again, filling my nose. I closed the door, checking the latches, and then examined the fruit. Along the side I noticed a slender scar, and so I cracked it open.

A ring fell out, set with an immense ruby signet. It would not fit any of my fingers save my smallest, but I gasped when I recognized the double Pendragon crest. The metal was hot, as if it had just been forged.

I put the ring on the hand Queen Tregerna's dagger had scarred. If that single dagger had caused me such pain, I could only imagine what an entire suit would mean. Was Elayne suggesting I fight this creature without armor? The thought of it shook me at first, but as I began pacing the room, worrying my thumb over the stone on the ring, I wondered if there was some wisdom to the suggestion.

The weight of armor would strain my knee, not to mention my old shoulder wounds. I had not been in training for weeks, unless you counted bedroom adventures with Hwyfar—which, although exhausting, were not the kind of exertion I required— and I had little confidence in myself save for what I had always had: my size. My strength. My rage.

I had been given no details of my foe. Only that it was the mechanism by which the castle remained cut off from the rest of Lyonesse, and Queen Tregerna and her court with it. So it was likely a being of magic. What good was armor against such a foe?

Never had I wished harder for more time, or for the reversal of time. For Hwyfar to come back to me, back down the hallway; for a glimpse of her, that wicked smile. Once, as a young squire, Bedevere had told me that Merlin was rumored to age backward, so great was his magical acumen. I would try and catch glimpses of him in the dark halls of Carelon, catch proof of his hair darkening or vanishing caverns on his face. But no matter how hard I looked, I only saw him age with every season, as sure as all the rest. No matter his power, not even he could stop the progress of time.

Still, I was no Merlin. I was no longer a great warrior, even. I stood alone in the empty apartment chamber, staring at the empty bed, thinking of battles past, my uncle's kind words, my mother's warnings, and my lover's sighs.

CHAPTER THIRTY-THREE

HWYFAR

I COULD SMELL Avillion burning. It was not incense, but the orchards afire. This time, I had passed through the path fully corporeal. This was Withiel. Ashes fell across my face through the broken window, still hot in the cool winds.

My father stood behind me, still as a planted oak, holding the side of his great bed for support, as I looked out the window across the craggy fields at Prince Ryence's army swarming our defenses. I thought I could see Palomydes out on the north battlements, saffron garments blowing in the bitter wind as he shouted out orders.

King Leodegraunce was much diminished from his illness, deep hollows in his face, scraps of his hair pulled back into a single braid in an attempt at maintaining an air of elegance. Yet his robes fell from his spindly body, his shoulders curved, and his spine twisted.

"It was a clever ruse on Prince Ryence's part. A long plan. I can appreciate that, in some ways." When he spoke, I recalled long evenings by our hearth, sitting with my sisters, while he recited epic poems from memory, and my mother... I did not remember where she was, but I knew she was present. I could almost remember her.

"You were mad," I said to him, looking through the thick glass, unable to tear my eyes away. Fires burned in the distance.

I tried to make sense of the time—they would have to have been within days of us when we'd headed out to make peace.

Had it all been a lie?

"I was being poisoned," said my father, wearily. "Slowly. Cleverly." His long silks rustled as he carefully made his way toward me. He dared not touch me; we had no such bond. "One of the cooks, I think, was an agent of Ys. The concoction put me in a strange madness, but progressive, over years. It looked very natural. I suspected Ymelda, but at the time, Tregerna would hear none of it. Now, I know my fears were correct."

"Ymelda?" She seemed a bit simpering, but certainly not evil.

"I could not see the connections then. The *graal*, you, your mother, Ymelda. But now it is come full circle."

King Leodegraunce sighed, and the sound was so full of anguish and regret that I turned to him. He was worn away, like a statue set beneath a fountain. So little of the brawny man I knew from childhood remained, just a hint of the red beard and mustaches amidst all the grey hair and cavernous wrinkles.

I wanted to see a monster in my father. The kind of wretch I saw in Arthur. It would be easier to hate him.

But that's not how I remembered him. I recall he wept when I left for Carelon. Perhaps he was not a good father, but he was not malicious, either; no matter how many years I had nursed hatred for what he had done, if what he said was true, he was misled as much as I. And after decades away, seeing him lucid, but so reduced, tore at me. I could see the pain in his eyes.

He was stooped with age, but still a tall man. He moved along the windowsill to keep upright. Those broad hands were just sinew and bone, wrapped with silk bandages and woolens to keep warm.

Even so, he had allowed his daughters to be violated. "Be that as it may, you Sundered us. You gave them permission. You invited the agents of Ys in to Withiel."

That terrible sigh again. "I did, Hwyfar. I did all of those things. I listened to the wrong people, and I governed out of fear. I worried that if you kept your powers, you would be unhappy, as your mother was."

"And now Withiel is going to burn. I came here—"

"I know why you came here. I tried to tell you where the *graal* is before. Even in my madness, I knew it was yours. Gweyn knew you must take it to Lyonesse. To keep it safe. And she always knew your mother was not lost. As did I."

Someone knocked on the door to my father's chamber, and I knew the sound well: a familiar rattling and creaking. For the first time since I had appeared to him, my father looked concerned.

"Keep hidden for the moment," he said to me. "I am afraid your presence will draw questions. Not all of your company has returned, most especially your red Orkney escort, and there is great concern as to his safety."

Though I was none too pleased with the idea, I did as he commanded, and slipped behind the velvet drapes. This, too, was familiar: I had hidden here many times as a child, hoping that Gweyn would find me, or trying to outsmart my tutors.

"Come in," my father said, and Gareth of Orkney entered.

I had forgotten just how tall he was and marked how similarly he was built to his brother, but with the lean lines of youth still present in his form. Weary he looked, though, blood splattered on his face, as he strode into my father's quarters. I saw in that set of his brows the sure mark of his father, Bedevere, intense and brooding.

Your brother is here. I am fighting for him, I wanted to tell Gawain, I wanted him to understand this peril. But my instinct said to wait. Unlike in the Path, I was not certain that the dagger would not impede my way. There, it had felt natural; now, the drawing on a powerful item of such provenance could imperil my quest.

Gareth bowed, wincing as he did so. "I bring grim tidings, Your Majesty."

"I know," said King Leodegraunce. "You do not need to

blame yourself, Sir Gareth. You have fought with all the power you possess. You have done what you can. If only we could have tipped the scales."

"The moat has so many narrow points for the invaders to vault," Gareth said, his voice catching with exhaustion, emotion. "And though we hoped Gawain and the Queen Regent would return with the missing party, along with Yvain and Modrun, there has been no sign of them. Palomydes remains, but half your own court—"

"Were traitors?" the king finished Gareth's sentence. I had a sense they had this conversation before. "Yes. Yes, they were. Cador was hardest to take, I think, since we have known each other since we were children. Branor was expected, his family had ties to Ryence and to Ys—and poor Kian, died protecting Ahès. I suppose she has not yet awoken?"

Kian dead? Treason from within the Knights of the Body? My blood ran like ice in my veins—and Ahès hurt? I grabbed the velvet drapes, squeezing the fabric tight to keep myself grounded. Queen Tregerna had lied: time had flowed faster, not slower. We were late, far too late. Avillion was lost.

"I wish our emissaries had got to the High King in time," Gareth said woefully. "And my brother..."

My father put a hand on Gareth's shoulder. "Do not blame yourself, Sir Gareth, that route is naught but darkness. We will fight, and we will hope, until the last light."

Again, I saw the image of Gawain, raging against a dappled firmament as each star guttered and died around him, and I bit back on mounting dread.

Gareth bowed his shaggy head, wiping at his dirty face. He looked like a lost little boy, and I wished I could have told him that his mother was but in the next room—I wished I could have taken him back on the Path, to Carelon.

Yet even in that moment, I knew the Path did not function in such a way. No, I *understood* it did not, as if it whispered to me from beyond.

Breathe, Hwyfar. Breathe.

"How long do you think we can hold?" King Leodegraunce asked Gareth.

The knight met his eyes for a moment, then he shook his head. "Tomorrow evening. If Fate favors us. The early morning if she does not."

"Then go to the kitchens and get the best honey wines," said the king. "They are stored in a hidden compartment under the wheat casks. Do you know your way around a castle kitchen?"

Gareth gave a short laugh, sardonic and a little cold. "I do, my liege. And I will."

Once Gareth was gone at last, my father had returned to his place at the windowsill, strangely calm again, arms clasped together as he watched the carnage unfolding in the fields below us. As the evening deepened, the sound of fighting had lessened, but I knew as well as he that the threat was still quite real.

"Is this how it ends? I take the *graal*, I leave you to ruin?" I asked.

My father looked over at me, kindness in his eyes, and a little sadness. "Ah, yes. You have realized where you are, but I do not think you see *when* you are."

"I…" I glanced back to the mirror from which I had emerged, which had once stood in my mother's chambers. "Queen Tregerna said time moved slowly where I was."

"She is correct," said my father. "And, if I recall, walking the Path for the first time, uninitiated and untrained, can tax the mind. It is easy to overstep. But I believe, in this case, you were meant to."

"You know of the Path?"

King Leodegraunce winced as he stretched his aching body. "As king of Avillion, no power is unknown to me."

"Lyonesse and Ys. Ymelda—I did not think she was a threat, but she gave me an amulet that I now know as a symbol of their sorceresses, and it seems that the agents of Ys were here long before even you knew."

"Indeed. I am wise, but it does not mean I am not a fool. Take my marriage—I knew your mother did not want to be my wife. But our parents would not be swayed in the match. So, Tregerna and I agreed on a five-year contract, after which I would let her go. Foolish boy that I was, I fell in love with her."

"I do not understand how she could have left us. She told me she left you, that you pursued her, and she became entrapped and lost because of you."

He gave me a weary look. "I never did such a thing. Her loss broke me. I granted her freedom. It was the only gift I could truly give her. She never meant to leave *you,* Hwyfar. You cannot believe that."

"She—" I could barely form the words for my swelling emotions, the desire to trust him rising but my own mind pushing back. "Nothing moves her. She is a soulless creature. But so are you."

King Leodegraunce frowned deeply, worrying his withered hands. "This is all Ymelda's doing. I know it in my bones. I swear upon the roots of Avillion, Hwyfar."

That was as sacred as anything. Not even I would blaspheme that. And if he was lying, he would be marked as dead. You could not defame the Isle without consequence.

"Gweyn knew I would be here," I said. "Did she tell you? Did she know I would hold the crown and our fate?"

He continued. "Gweyn's gifts developed young. I knew there were things I could not change, portents I would meet—I was an interpreter, you see. Like Merlin. Once. Before my brother and mother died, before my father married again and Ryence was born. I, too, lived a life politic."

"I wish she would have told me. Prepared me."

"She knew she could not intervene once the thread of Fate was woven. Yet I do believe she knew you were strong enough to spin your own."

"How can I stop this?" Avillion was burning, dying all around me, cinders flying past the windows. "I am nothing. I am no better than a performer. I have no true skill in diplomacy, and a power that regards me not. I am broken."

My father watched the embers cross our view. "No one has ever been able to break you, Hwyfar. Surely you see that. You are here—you are the heir of Avillion. This may be my end now, but it is not yours. "

"I will fail."

"If you try and do it alone, yes."

Gawain. My *carioz*.

"Tregerna will never let us go without the *graal*."

"No, but you will take another gift meant for her. The *graal* must be delivered to another. And then I shall tell you where to look for your missing party, in hopes you can come to our aid."

I looked at him, confused. "In hopes? You said you knew."

"I *interpreted*. You remember, my daughter, that there are many outcomes. Every prophecy is like a branch of a tree, or a capillary from the same vein. Many outcomes. For I think you begin to see that this was not only about the *graal*, Hwyfar, my little spirit. It was about getting you out of the way."

Gawain was alone at Lyndesoires. I could not protect him.

My hands shook, and I went to grab the bloodied dagger, to reach Gawain, but my father put up his hands and I stopped before I touched the hilt.

"It will not work now. That has already passed. If you listen to the dagger here, it will break you."

The realization, the darkness, that fell in my mind in that moment, nearly felled me. If I touched the dagger, if I reached out to Gawain, he would be—

"You are protected by the Path now, kept separate. It is a powerful web of magical safety," said King Leodegraunce. "But that dagger, forged by your mother, would pull you to the truth of this world. And I do not think you can bear it, new as you are along your journey."

He limped to the edge of the bed where the great chest, inlaid with elaborate cloisonné, had rested for time out of mind. I had sat there just days ago while he screamed at me, strapped to the bed, lying in his own vomit and shit, calling me a whore. As a child I had traced every garnet-eyed dragon, each endless spiral and intertwining knot. Time had removed some of the gleaming glasswork, but it remained lovely to me still.

The lock released under his grasp quickly, and King Leodegraunce shuffled through a stack of thick velvets, casting them to the floor, before he came upon a carved box as long as my arm. I had never seen it before, but the insignia was familiar: the standing lions of Lyonesse.

"It was a wedding gift," he said to me, handing me the box. In the distance, I heard a horn, clear and bright, shouting in dismay from the battlements.

Doom was at hand for Avillion.

"Tregerna would never ask for the *graal*. If the woman I knew remains within her still, this shall suffice. She thinks it is destroyed. I will tell you where the *graal* is, but you must give it only to one woman. Her name is Elayne of Astolat, and she is among those still with your mother at Lyndesoires."

None of my emotions made sense to me. I had planned to confront my father with fury if we had crossed paths; I had meant to take the *graal* and return to Gawain straight away.

But looking into my father's eyes, I could not see the cold calculation of my mother, nor her judgement or disdain. I could sense no betrayal. He did not want the *graal*. He was tired, old, worn away by his mistakes. When I blamed him, he accepted it. Like Gawain, he was a faulted man who had learned from his mistakes at a dire cost, and he no longer held the pride that had poisoned him.

I opened the box he gave me slowly, trying to buy time, even as I heard the portcullis gate shudder below, and a ripple of flame kindle on the horizon. It was a glorious instrument, made of black, carved horn and embossed with silver and gold. The work was old, older than any generation alive, of a smith with far less precise tools, yet it held a rustic beauty in the shaping:

snakes and beetles crawled the edges in interlacing patterns.

"You said you'd already told me where the *graal* was," I said, not looking up from the horn.

He laughed, a low, musical sound that brought me back to my childhood. To summer evenings among the fireflies and long walks by the lake under the stars. "Yes. It lies in a leather case, behind a clutch of old brooms—a simple spell keeps it hidden, but you will see it. I have known it lies there for years upon years and have decided it best to keep it within easy reach and plain sight. The servants' entrance is behind that wall, and there is another portal mirror in the wine cellar."

The brooms. The brooms. It's nestled amidst the brooms!

Down the hall, shouting resounded. I could smell burning hair from somewhere. Gareth had been mistaken: Fate would swallow them whole this night and spit them out, ground bones and all.

"Go, Hwyfar, run as quickly as you can," said King Leodegraunce. "I am so proud of you, and have always known this day would see you crowned in flame and fury. Carry them with you to the end."

He did not ask, but I rushed into his arms and held him, feeling the fragile bones of his body, and sobbed into his shoulder. He smoothed my hair and kissed my head, and I was no queen of fury, no bright crowned deity—just a child who had been lost in the lies and machinations of court, in need of her father.

CHAPTER THIRTY-FOUR

GAWAIN

MY FOE WOULD arrive at dinner.

Neither Queen Tregerna nor Ymelda were present, but the table was set in a crescent in the great, smoky hall, and a bonfire placed in the very center. Walking in, accompanied by four guards, I counted two dozen in attendance, all brightly and colorfully armored. It seemed, for my arrival, they had donned their most impressive harness.

It would explain, as well, their look of shock seeing me. For I was wearing no armor to speak of and carried only Galatyne in its scabbard.

I had little time to prepare myself, but the more I thought of Elayne's warning, and the longer I looked at the massive armor delivered not long after she left, the more it made sense. Even if I did wear the mail, even if it was simply solid armor, I was not accustomed to it. I knew well enough that new armor took time to get used to. The weight of it alone would buckle my knee, and I would be useless.

The best hope I had was in ease of movement.

Which, for me, was no easy task, even without any clothes. There was no time to fit me for chain. My old gambeson was all I had remaining, so I washed it in the tub, dried it by the fire, and then took my sewing kit out and got to work. I patched the gambeson with bits from Hwyfar's green silk gown and added a trimming of gold to it, so it would at least look the part. I wore the remains of my miserable traveling boots, and wrapped what remained of Hwyfar's gown around my middle like a belt in the fashion I had seen Palomydes wearing: a thick knot around the center, and much tucking.

I removed the ribbon she had given me for my hair, and with the extra floss I had, I embroidered her name upon it. Years at my mother's knee had taught me the basics, and she had never discouraged me. Then, I plaited my hair again with the ribbon, this time in the fashion of Orkney, as I had seen the old warriors do, tight and to my skull. My beard was not long enough for plaits—Arthur preferred his knights with tidy, short beards if any—but time away had left me a bit more unkempt.

My new ring—the one from Elayne—I slipped onto a measure of leather lace and put it around my neck.

In the mirror I looked like a green hedge. But it would have to do. Gareth would laugh at me, call me some strange puffed-up prince. Or a roadside minstrel.

But what else was I to do? I could not win by brawn alone. I had to do as Hwyfar would: I had to *perform*.

So I walked into the hall as if I wore a crown upon my head, which I had not done since I was a child. I pretended I could feel the metal warming my brow, feel the weight of it on my head, as I felt eyes drawing to me. All my life I had wished to shrink from sight, betrayed by my height. But this time, I welcomed their stares. At first it made me feel exposed, but with each gradual step I became aware that there was a power in attention. It was not unlike feigning moves in the sparring ring: drawing the eye away so your opponent does not detect your actual intent. Gives you an advantage, that.

Understanding washed over me. My mother had done the same her whole life. I never understood how she could shrink away in a room—this bright, tall woman—but she could. She could melt away, or tower with terrifying power, all at will. With men, like my uncle Arthur, she was demure, playing the game of quiet housewife. But I had seen her with her sisters, with me as a child, around Bedevere.

It occurred to me that I could *choose* who they saw: the prince or the brute.

Today I would be the prince. And a prince did not need armor.

"A fine dinner on this fine evening," I said, holding my arms out wide, breaking the silence. I dropped my voice low, letting it ring through the hall. "I have come on the request of the Queen of Lyonesse and her consort, the Lady Ymelda. Are they not here to greet me?"

If anyone was looking elsewhere, they no longer had the choice. My voice began a little unsure, but by the end, even I was surprised by the resonance.

I spied Elayne standing beside an older woman. They were both dressed in silver and blackened armor, but with long, pale grey skirts that fell to the floor in pools. Mother and daughter, perhaps? The poor light was no help to me, so I could not pick out details.

Perhaps she nodded toward me. Perhaps not.

No one spoke. Knives clattered on pewter plates; silk rustled, and armor creaked. Chairs strained. The bonfire hissed and crackled, and no one answered me.

"Come, now, the Prince of Orkney has come calling," I said to the crowd. I did not draw my sword, but I gestured to it. "I have been waiting in anticipation for days."

Someone coughed. I supposed this was the sort of reception many bards and players were accustomed to in their travels, but I felt my courage begin to waver, none the less. Nerves had given way to excitement, then to a strange kind of bravado. On the field and even in the jousting tournament, I always had my armor to shield me, to protect me from my own worst fears.

Now, I was a man with naught but quilted fabric between me and imminent death. If any of the guests before me threw their own daggers, which I was certain they carried, I would be grievously wounded. And still, they were not my foe.

What would my Hwyfar do in such a situation? She would command the room, somehow. Whether armored by her wardrobe or her performance, she would shift the attention and spin her own time.

So, when no one answered, I began to sing.

I sang about the dream-eaters, to a tune I remembered from childhood. It was not a long song, and I was not a terrible singer, but just when I was prepared for at least some response from the gathered crowd, the massive doors to the great hall shuddered, and I heard the court gasp and move into clusters, pressing back into the dark corners of the hall, but in an ordered way that spoke to a routine. This was a familiar pantomime for them; I was the only element out of sorts.

I should have felt a bit embarrassed, I supposed, but other than a growing dread, I was proud of myself. I only wished Hwyfar had been there to see.

As I turned to look at the closed doors, straining against the creature behind it, I remembered a day early in my time at court. Arthur was young, a new king, and had been convinced to bring a bear into the ring to fight a grifflet. Once, the forests were teeming with the beasts, a magnificent cross between a lion and a bird. I was only thirteen years old or so when it happened, and I barely could recall the details, other than the sound it made on the other side of the small portcullis gate: a high, keening wail, and an eerie scratching sound with its talons.

The sound I heard reminded me of that but greatly amplified. There were so many other undertones I could not place, sounds my ears had never experienced before. It was like a scream from the bowels of the earth itself.

A green mist leaked out from the edges of the door, covering the floor of the great hall and smothering the fire for a brief moment. Then, in a ghastly blaze, the fire burst into light again, but now a blue-black column of flame rose high into the roof. I saw now why it had been so charred, if this had happened every month for the last twenty years.

The curse of Lyonesse.

"Prince of Orkney," said a voice from the other side of the door, deep as ocean waves, but tinged with the buzzing of flies and the chatter of carrion birds. "You have come to rid us of this curse."

Still I did not pull my sword, but I planted my feet firmly on the ground and faced the door as it swung open, shuddering on its thick iron latches.

I could not comprehend the enormity of what I beheld immediately, the curse of poor eyesight, but as the form came forward—an enormous knight upon a steed twice the size of my own formidable Gringolet—I slowly put together the horror before me and got my answer of where the Queen and her consort were.

The Green Knight upon the horse, for they were shaped so, was woven of tree and leaf and branch, all hues of green and grey and a sickly moss hue too eldritch for nature's hand. Their face was blank save for two black eyes, empty as the void, and they wore a crown of white ice, twisted and flecked with red drops of blood. Each arm was as thick as a tree trunk, and within the cage of their enormous chest curled the Queen and her consort, like two sides of a red beating heart.

A great cape of old leather flowed over the back of the knight's steed, dark as night waters, and they carried a great axe glittering with frost the color of verdigris. Their nails were black against snow-pale fingers, white as bone or sea-bleached wood. It filled the hall with the scent of cedar and pitch, of old fermenting holly berries and the copper hint of blood. At the great steed's feet, beetles crawled, squirming out of the marble floor like burbling water.

I shuddered at the sight, never much one for such crawling things, let alone the horror before me.

"I have come to fight as Queen Tregerna's champion," I said, finally unsheathing Galatyne, and clutching it with both hands. "I am Sir Gawain, Nephew of Arthur, King of All Braetan, and I am compelled to challenge you by duty and by honor."

Did the Queen wish me dead? Had she been corrupted by this being? *Was* she the being? I certainly had no way of knowing, but I knew well why they had not described the foe to me. Knew it in my gut. Wished I'd had my armor, too.

The Green Knight laughed, beetles skittering in concert with it, a murmuration that went on longer than I would have liked: a million chittering shells and expanding wings opening and closing at once all around me.

Hwyfar would laugh. *No, my love,* I would tell her in the afterlife. *'Twas not the horror of bone and branch that broke my courage, but the common beetle. In my defense, there were more than I could count, and I think they were saying my name.*

"Prince Gawain," the Green Knight said, drawling out the syllables. "You come without armor. Do you come without honor?"

I swallowed, then twirled my sword. I could do that. A good flourish to quiet my nerves. Once, I had been full of such arrogance and surety. "I cannot imagine your captives are enjoying this arrangement, but I have pledged to free them from this plight."

"You know nothing, Son of Orkney," hissed the Green Knight.

There was a beetle on my boots.

"I know that the rightful ruler of Lyonesse remains a captive in her own spell, and she has asked me to challenge you. And here I am. Arthur's best. Well, very nearly; you've likely heard of Lanceloch du Lac, but alas, he is otherwise occupied," I said. Never in my life had I engaged in verbal riposte in such a situation, but I found that it was slowly unwinding my nerves. Again, I could feel Hwyfar's influence arming me with another kind of protection.

The horse snorted at me. I decided to take that as a sign my sense of humor was appreciated by at least someone.

Still the Green Knight approached, and I could see the pulsing on Queen Tregerna's skin, a sickly green at her neck, and I was worried I might just piss myself in front of the entire crowd. Which would be even more embarrassing than usual, since I had no armor to hide the mess.

No one outranks you here, I heard Hwyfar say to me. *You are Arthur's nephew, the beloved of the King himself. They cannot dare to challenge you.*

I felt her, whispering, that connection between us sizzling to life again, a rush of life coming back to me that I had been lacking from that terrible moment in the room before Elayne's appearance. Relief.

Can you see what I'm seeing?

I tried to project the enormity of the Green Knight to her, hoping she could understand the scale of my enemy.

Her cool, distant response was: *You were born to fight. You do not falter.*

If Hwyfar believed in me, I could banish my own fear of failure and at least try. I forced my face into a placid expression, knowing all too well I wore my emotions on my face.

So I squared my shoulders and felt warmth spread over me, an assuredness that I had not had before. The mask slipped into place, and I was no longer Gawain the hobbled. I was Prince Gawain.

Rather than respond directly to me, the Green Knight came to a halt, that colossal steed just a breath from my own face, and dismounted. Their body moved in an unnatural, liquid way, stretching and re-assembling to make space for their internal quarry, then re-forming again to tower over me.

I could not recall, in all my years in harness, staring *up* at a foe like a child looking up at a full-grown man. Confronting this eyeless bastard was like staring into the bowels of the Underworld itself. Which made me wonder, given the stench, if that was where it had come from. We knew that some event had befallen Queen Tregerna when she had hidden from Leodegraunce, separated the castle from Lyonesse—had she awoken the ire of some ancient god?

They did not look like any god I knew, not from any of the pictures I recalled from my childhood; and even if I was far from pious, I knew my pantheon front and backward.

Hwyfar...

I heard nothing. I felt *nothing*. As sure as she had been in my mind before, she was gone.

Panic replaced relief.

The Green Knight stepped back and their horse moved away to give us more room. Our crowd emerged slightly from their cowering, likely hoping to get a closer view of my demise.

"Shall we begin?" I asked.

And begin we did.

I was prepared for the axe, and easily dodged out of the way, the heavy head clanging into the marble floor with an ear-splitting wail of metal upon stone. My knee was tied well and thoroughly, and I knew how to move without aggravating it. That would change when it came to the clash, but for now, I wanted to see how this creature fought.

Alas, the Green Knight needed just one hand for that axe, and the knight hefted the enormous weapon—more than two thirds my own height—with as little effort as I would lift a soup spoon.

I heard their body whine with the effort, however. I suspect they had to compromise a considerable amount of movement to prevent crushing their captives. Which had me consider there was a benefit to the two women being there, some parasitic connection. It would explain the Queen's reticence on the subject.

There was no point in going for speed, but I could try for precision. Though I had never had to fight someone larger than me, I had still spent most of my life trying to outsmart fighters doing their best to undo me. So, I did not opt for an assault on the Green Knight's body, but went for one of the thick rope-like tendons at their feet.

I could feel the meat of the creature: it was not like cutting through the leg of a man, or a tendon, even. As my steel made contact with the woody exterior, it sank at first into a softness, and then stuck into a harder core. I had to jerk Galatyne out, and when I did, it was slick with greenish gore, thick like congealed blood.

The Green Knight chittered and backed up again, defensively. Hitting it made even more beetles swarm about me.

"Did you get a taste?" The Green Knight's lightless eyes now glowed dull violet, deep and fathomless. Inside, I heard Ymelda muttering.

"Haven't ever developed a palate for bugs, I'm afraid," I said in reply, squaring my stance. It was difficult to read the knight's body language. "But steel cuts just the same."

This time when the Green Knight lashed out at me, they did not miss. That, too, was by design, but I was not prepared for the power in the blow. I blocked the axe with my sword, but it drove me down, and I collapsed agonizingly to my knees. I felt the shock clang down Galatyne and down my arm, through my chest, up my throat, even. Might as well have been struck by lightning. I had taken more blows than most, and never had I felt a sensation like that.

It woke something in me. Cracked me open. The world dappled red, and my blood simmered. I turned to right myself, twisting my head to the side to dispel the dizziness.

And then I felt a helmet shoved over my head, and the world went dark.

CHAPTER THIRTY-FIVE

HWYFAR

I TUMBLED THROUGH the mirror in the great chamber of my mother's fortress in Lyonesse, the edges of my gown smoldering, the *graal* spear I'd found among the brooms in Withiel's kitchen tied to my back. I did not recall walking through fire, but my mind was in a panic. Rolling, heart frantic in my chest, I beat at my hems.

The last thing I remembered was running, running so fast, across the path, thinking only of Lyndesoires, of Gawain, of my mother.

Elayne was there to greet me in the cavernous room, her pale hair fallen from what was once a most complicated twist of braids.

"Am I too late?" I gasped, grasping at my gown with a trembling hand.

Elayne frowned at the sight. "No, no—nearly, but not quite."

"How did you know I would be here?"

"Do you really need to ask?"

"You're Elayne of Astolat."

"I am. And I hold the second *graal*. I have kept it safe here, beyond the reach of our captor."

She held up a small, abalone cup. It shone a pale silver in the light. Just gazing upon the artifact made me feel the sorrow of a thousand generations, anguish and pain beyond reasoning.

Though it was small, I knew it had carried tears I could never count, never measure, never even understand. Looking at that bare, small bowl in Elayne's hand, I knew even my anguish, was irrelevant in the scheme of the world.

The other *graal*. The *graal* of Lyonesse.

"Why did you not tell me earlier?"

I could tell she was struggling to speak, her lips shaking with effort. "The spell upon Lyndesoires weakens, for I am able to speak more plainly, but it still causes great pain. I have kept the Cup here, safe, at a great cost," she said softly. "And your father has kept the Spear."

I wiped tears from my eyes. "How do you endure the pain?"

Elayne put her hands on my arms. "I am merely its emissary, not its keeper. The pain has protected me these twenty years and kept me from the worst of the spell. Now, unsheathe the Spear, and listen to it."

The spear was still in its leather case, and though I could feel the thrum of its power, I knew not its strength or its purpose.

I looked down at the spear in my hand, noting the simplicity of the weapon. Silver though it was, the construction was plain: there was no etch work, no design, no symbol of its power.

Yet, as my eyes adjusted, I began to notice small spiraling patterns, worn almost smooth with time. When I ran my fingers over the implement, I knew immediately what it was—whose it had been—and I gasped.

"A unicorn's horn." My voice was so small.

My friend who had found me, comforted me, in that snowy glade. They had known. Gweyn, it seemed, was not the only messenger pushing me into this new realm of Fate.

Elayne nodded. "One who freely gave up its life, for the horn cannot be taken otherwise. A creature of a forgotten world, an implement of great power and responsibility."

Holding the spear was like holding a rushing river, its strength careening into my body, cold and unrelenting. I looked at Elayne and saw her as she was, limned in yellow, body holding back a tide of pain, Ymelda's spellwork pressing around her on every pore, but never quite making contact.

"The Spear is truth. Peace. Center." Elayne looked at me with kind, understanding eyes. "It has already been guiding you all along, I see."

"I saw—I dreamed—I can't explain it, but there was a unicorn. It came to me, slept in my lap. I could not tell if I woke or slept, but I know it happened."

"Only you would recognize this, then. You have been granted its power for a short time, but do not let it consume you. The magic of Ys has broken this kingdom, and you must fight it from within, with this ancient weapon. Gawain awaits, but he is flagging fast. Together is your only hope. *Carioz* will guide you."

Trust never came easily to me, but I knew Elayne as a friend. Even before I had held this great weapon, I had known. Now, as I blazed with the flame of truth, I was relieved to find her unchanged. She was my ally, fully.

Without hesitation, I followed her. We moved as fast as we could until we breached the second flight of stairs down to the great hall. It was then that I felt the wind knocked out of me entirely. If Elayne had not been beside me, given the state of my legs, I was certain I would have toppled over.

I could feel Gawain's pain, taste blood in my mouth—his blood. Dread returned and I resumed the stairs, my lungs trying to pull for air. Exhaustion—not just my own, but his as well—pulling down upon me.

I heard shouts, and a roar I knew immediately as Gawain's, down the hallway. It was a place changed from my last visit: dark stonework designs rose overhead, bathed in green and gold light, grappling vines growing so fast I could bear witness to their march across the marble and timbers.

"She did not expect you to survive," Elayne said to me as I searched the antechamber leading into the great hall, gripping the spear with both hands. "Remember that. You were meant to fail."

I kicked open the doors, rage propelling me forward, my body imbued with strength unlike any I'd ever experienced. I was fury and power and judgement, and I would not bow down.

Gawain knelt upon the great marble expanse, a burnished copper helmet upon his head, Galatyne on the ground before him. Above him stood the creature I had seen through his eyes in glimpses as I had tried to reach out to him; now rendered in its full, resplendent horror. Between them pulsed lines of coppery light, flecked with ruby-like daubs of blood. Members of the court crouched in corners and under upturned tables, pressed down by spells and fear.

Yet in that moment, all eyes turned to me, and the air shifted. Because I commanded it.

"I am Queen Hwyfar of Avillion," I said to the Green Knight, "and I come to rescue my beloved, Gawain of Orkney."

But the scene before me did not change. Though I heard my voice echo, Gawain did not raise his head, nor did the Green Knight turn to survey me.

I reached out with all my strength to Gawain, but our connection was tinged with smoke. Like he was burning up on the inside. And he was lost to me.

CHAPTER THIRTY-SIX

GAWAIN

MY WORLD WAS green, a mad, crawling landscape of desolation that lived in every corner of my mind. I was no longer in the center of the great hall at Lyndesoires, but in a bleak killing field. I knew it well. It was a field, deep in Ascomanni territory, where I had nearly lost my leg. Where I had lost Drian to the worms and mud.

Queen Tregerna stood before me, pale and grim against the mossy green sky, her lips and eyes sewn shut with rough-spun red thread, blistered where the skin had cracked and bled. Her hands were tied much the same, sewed palm to palm, and she shuddered every now and again, with a pitiful, muffled whimpering.

Ymelda, the picture of health, golden and bright, stood between us both, her skin glowing an unnatural hue beneath that eldritch sun.

"At last, we can speak more plainly," said Ymelda, giving me a mocking bow. "Prince Gawain, so gallant. But you could never have managed against our knight—that was never my hope, really, though it was impressive to watch. You really are as strong as the stories say. Shame about the knee, though."

Gone was the sweetness in her voice, the simpering innocence.

"I came here on a presumption of honor," I said, knowing already she cared for no such thing.

"You really believe Hwyfar will return to us? With a *graal*?" Ymelda laughed, a titter that made my stomach turn.

My intuition was worth about as much as a pile of fresh horse shite at a joust. Aunt Morgen was right.

I had no sword in this green world, this place in our minds. And I had no answers. Distantly, I felt the pain in my body, but where I had thought I felt Hwyfar, there was nothing.

"What did you want, then?" I asked.

"Why, *you*," said Ymelda, taking a step toward me. She looked me up and down like a prize ox at auction. "Or, more precisely, what is inside of you. I sensed it the moment that Hwyfar pulled you in, and the reality was so very much better than my hopes. *Carioz*."

Not for the first or last time, I was utterly lost in the conversation, but now I felt a creeping suspicion.

"You can never have what connects Hwyfar and me," I said.

"No, but I can *dis*connect you. And I can be free of this one"— Ymelda pointed at the Queen of Lyonesse—"and finish what I began." She tutted like an impatient nursemaid, and pulled an amulet from under her gown: an ammonite shell. It was the source of the glow. "You see this? It means I am a servant of Ys. I have worked for time out of mind to secure Lyonesse for my nation. I gave one of these to Hwyfar as well, hoping she might edge closer to her inheritance. I have plans to bring her to our cause, in the end. My agents have been working on her for years."

No. Hwyfar would never. I had to believe that.

"And the Queen of Lyonesse? What of her?"

Fear rattled me, but Ymelda liked speaking, so I let her continue. There was no place to run to. I was in a nightmare of my own making. I could smell the corpses, feel the sun beating on my skin, hear the flies buzzing and the sound of carrion crows ripping flesh from bones.

I did not want to look.

I did not want to remember.

"Oh, she is strong enough to carry on as she stands, so I may be rid of this curse," said Ymelda, brightly, clapping her hands. "You see, *that* is why you are here. You and Hwyfar have a natural *carioz*. It will be so very easy for me to knit you and Tregerna together. As you can see, she is my puppet. It took some effort, since I had to force our connection. What you see now is a reflection of my work on her inner mind—I am able to direct her to my will. Mostly. When she broke Hwyfar's arm, I had to do some clever work to throw you off the track. I had underestimated the strength of her memories. Little matter; I see all through her."

I felt ill. "So the queen we met, she is not Tregerna."

Ymelda pouted. "Well. I like to think of her as Tregerna as she *should* be. I must be both Tregerna and Ymelda, and it is exhausting. Alas, our magics are enmeshed, and I am unable to extricate myself from the Green Knight; for in our entanglement, we attracted their attention."

"You did not bargain for that, then."

The Queen let out a muffled cry.

"Hush, love," Ymelda simpered.

"Then you are to blame, I imagine. Got more than you thought, playing with corrupted magic."

Ymelda sneered at me. "No. I did not. The spell was old, and vaguely worded, and I inadvertently allowed the fiend access to us. Our *carioz* fuels the knight's rage. Every full moon, they capture us, no matter where we are, and we present as you have seen us, imprisoned in the belly of the beast for a night. Many have tried to challenge them, and none have succeeded."

I dragged my attention from Ymelda and gazed again at Queen Tregerna, taking a closer look at what I saw. My gut told me that the blisters at the Queen's mouth meant that she was still struggling, still fighting.

But then, my gut had not been terribly reliable as of late.

"Our *carioz* is strong," I said, biting back on bile as the sound of wet veins snapping rose up behind me. Vultures. There were vultures everywhere. And crows, crows with green eyes. "I will not falter."

My ears began whining, a high unceasing whistle. The heat seared my skin, sweat slipped down my armor, sun blinding my eyes. The sweet stink of rotting bodies filled every breath, and I knew I was standing knee-deep in the bodies of men I had known, dined with, danced with—all reduced to naught but sacks of decomposing meat. I glanced down: I knew that face. I knew those hands.

Drian.

I heard worms in the ground, felt their mucous slinking bodies curling around pebbles. I felt flies tickle my face, caress me lovingly, tangle in my beard and pry open my lips.

"It is already gone." I heard Ymelda's voice rise over the rushing blood in my ears. "Why would she stay for a knight, broken as you, when she was just given her freedom?"

"She said she would not run."

"Gawain, child. Hwyfar has lived a life of passion, pleasure and renown. Do you believe a bit of fated magic will change that? You are a momentary distraction. I gave her freedom. You will be like all the other knights and ladies in her long litany of lovers: conquered and forgotten."

I did not want to believe it, yet under the growing weight of Ymelda's influence, unskilled as I was in the way of magic and worn down by my own doubts, I began to crack.

CHAPTER THIRTY-SEVEN

HWYFAR

THE TOWERING CREATURE stood over Gawain and made a tortured, strangled noise, shuddering and twisting in a kind of half-paralysis. Inside the Green Knight's great ribcage, my mother and Ymelda were curled up together, floating like babes in the womb, suspended in pale green light. The long, pulsing tendrils of copper-glowing luminescence reached toward Gawain, and I saw them enter his eyes and mouth, and encircle his hands.

I looked around for Elayne and found her tending to one of the young ladies of the court, who was crying out in pain from the growing briars. The thorns, I realized, were meant as a defense against the Green Knight. I did not believe they were intentional—this being was in great pain, carrying this strange burden inside. The power from within was damaging, damning.

"I have to reach him, Elayne," I called out, over the shrieking that now seemed to come from every corner of the castle.

She was wiping tears from her eyes. "If you cannot, you must use the Spear."

I understood. It was a strange thing, connecting with the Spear. When I had beheld the Green Knight through Gawain's eyes, it had been with fear. But now, holding this great relic, I knew a kind of bare truth I would not have known with my own eyes, blinded as I was. The Green Knight was not a monster—it was a god.

But Elayne meant more than the truth. I could not comprehend the fullness of the spell before me, but I understood my mother and Gawain were not the source of the evil. I recognized the magic of Ys commandeering the Green Knight; my arm throbbed in memory of a similar spell.

Grasping the spear in one hand, I took a step forward, carefully, looking straight at the Green Knight as I moved toward Gawain.

"I do not wish to harm you, good knight," I said to the Green Knight as the piteous sound continued. "For I feel you are as much grieved in this as I."

The Green Knight turned their fathomless eyes toward me, and where Gawain had seen the void, I saw the maw of life and death: I saw the beginning and the end, springtime and deepest winter. I saw the eye of a newborn babe and the chasm of a skeleton's gaping mouth, full of beetles and worms. This creature, this marvel of bone and briar, was a power far beyond anything I had encountered in my short life.

I doubted Ymelda had known what she was dealing with. I doubted Ys knew what they were dealing with, either.

Taking another tenuous step forward, I gasped when I felt the Green Knight's arm lash out at me, wrapping around my forearm. I felt my skin split under the pull of briars and thick vines, and a brightness filled my vision, the taste of new moss and fine sun and deep-water wetness on my tongue.

My first instinct was to pull away, but as I did, I caught a glimpse of Gawain, and the pain raging through my body ebbed away, replaced by wonder: I could see our connection. I could see our *carioz*. Each thread, finer than silk, twisted and braided together in opalescent fibers that glittered like infinitesimally miniature stars. They swirled, whorled, breathed between us, from heart to heart, head to head, hand to hand.

The Green Knight gave this to me, adding to what the spear had already granted.

One look at my mother and Ymelda, and I understood a new horror: what lay within was a mockery of our *carioz*. It had a structure akin in form, the pattern on the loom drawn in the same hand. But the thread was sickly, bone white, the blue of corpse skin, bloomed with verdigris. And deep within their connection I could see three Sundered threads floating from the back of my mother's neck, frayed and silver as a new-forged blade. My heart ached, and I understood to whom those had once tied her: Hwyfar, Gweynevere, Mawra.

"He awaits within," said the Green Knight, their voice low and rumbling, but weakening. "You must follow."

I was growing cold, weaker. Grasping the spear in my free hand, I slowly reached toward Gawain, the Green Knight's tendrils still firmly pulsing through my arm, giving me this new green sight. The rest I would have to do—*could* do, because the magic of Lyonesse had never left me.

At last I reached Gawain, and I knelt. His eyes were closed, hectic movement beneath his lids. Sweat beaded upon his brow, lines of worry there; his skin was cold to the touch, and a slow trickle of blood fell from one of his ears, staining his beard red as madder. I touched my brow to his, whispered his name, but he made no response. I could not *sense* him, even as our *carioz* danced between us.

For a brief moment, I knew I could leave. My body was so full of pain, with exhaustion, and a desperate, selfish part of me knew well enough that I could seek comfort elsewhere. The woman I once was still lingered within me, old habits tempting me.

With this *graal* implement in my hand I could sunder the connection between the Green Knight and myself. In a moment, I could end its suffering—or not. I could leave the scene to play itself out. Hwyfar could cease to exist in the story. All would remain was Sir Gawain and the Green Knight, whether he lived or died. The mirror, the Path, was before me. There was escape. I owed nothing to Lyonesse, to Carelon, to Avillion...

The *graal* spear showed me the truth of myself. And I was a coward. Yet even cowards had choices. I had run my whole life from any shred of responsibility, from trust, from true connection. Now, though, I began spinning my own Fate, no longer resigned to impassivity.

I kissed Gawain's lips, cold as death, and spear in hand, I breathed in our *carioz* to follow where he had gone.

Sun overhead, blinding and hot. I squinted, confused, choking on the smell of rotting flesh. I was on the ground, my hands sinking into sucking red mud. Black wings obscured my sight for a moment, and when I raised my hand to cover my eyes, it dripped fetid fluid upon my face.

I looked down slowly, my vision slowly coming to focus, making sense out of what I beheld: I was in a bed of rotting corpses. A battlefield.

Standing, I scrambled away to a patch of clearer ground, and wiped at my face with my forearm. I wore yellow gauze robes, tied at the forearms with pale silver cords. My hems were covered in gore, dried as if from long hours in the sun.

In the distance, more crows gathered, black flecks upon the flat fields, rising and falling as clouds darkened the horizon. But it was not the welcome of impending rain, but of death, like a haze of locusts come to devour flesh from all our bones.

Dread came at me then, clear and sure. The spear! I turned around and saw it, still wedged in the pile of bodies behind me. Steeling myself, I approached those bloated, mutilated corpses and I retrieved the *graal* spear, the pointed end making a sucking noise as I pulled it from a man's groin.

The spear gave me new sight to the truth: among the dead I saw eyes where they ought not be, teeth along an earlobe, small fingers growing across what should have been a spine.

These were more than dead men. These were nightmares made flesh.

"Run, Hwyfar... Queen of Avillion..." whispered those unnatural mouths, their unclean tongues full of yellowed sores, belching clouds of putrid magics. "The decay of Carelon is on the wind."

I ran as I had never done before, never quite as fast as I wanted. This dream space, this land of nightmares, tamed me in a way I could not express. Even with the spear in my hand, I could barely cut through the foul magic of the place.

The spear guided me to Gawain, to the beating of his heart, like a drum in the distance. My lungs burned, my throat threatening to close, and I choked back dust as clouds rose against me, flying into my face. I shouted into the wind, trying to grasp at what dregs of magic I still possessed, but my attacks were useless.

My heart leapt, just as I spotted what I knew to be Gawain, standing in gleaming armor upon a small hill, facing two figures, when a murder of crows descended upon me. I choked back a scream, not wanting to reveal my presence to Gawain yet—I still could not sense him, not really, other than the vague beating of his heart, the pervasive dread of this place.

Birds flew in my face, wings shining beetle green, and I batted them away, wondering if I had the courage to pierce them with the spear, until I stumbled backward. Then my perception shifted again, and I understood: they were giving me cover. They walked with me. I stumbled back, they clicked and cawed, moving in time to swirl and obscure my path, smelling of loam and green things.

I stood still, hundreds of green-eyed crows encircling me at once, and I understood. They were emissaries of the Green Knight, even here. We were still connected, too. Though the creature was under duress, captured in Ymelda's corrupted spell, they reached to me here, helping me through the last trial.

Soft breezes cooled my face, gentle feathers caressed my skin. I felt pain, of course, but their presence, around me like a great globe, was renewing, comforting.

I had closed my eyes, and when I opened them, I was not surprised, somehow, to see my sister Gweyn standing before me.

I suppose, for all the places she had visited me, this was the least strange. Gawain had been close to both of us, once. We were in a crossroads of great magics, both ancient and profane.

She, that golden queen, still lost and unresting in death, blazed in soft starlight, framed in thousands of black feathers, all tinged with iridescent purple and green.

"Sister," she said to me.

"Gweyn..." Her name on my lips. I never called her *sister* as she called me.

"I am so proud of you," she said to me, walking closer. Her skin was translucent, where before she had been ghostly, frightening. Those luminous eyes, though, shone like sapphires. "I wish I could stay longer, but you have come close to our truth now, and that is my last will."

I missed her face. I missed the feel of her, the way she would embrace me even when I rebelled against it, how I would relent anyway, and enjoy it in spite of myself. Gweyn made me feel safe, made me feel seen. I should have hated her for marrying Arthur, but I was grateful for her. Every day. Arthur never would have made me happy. And even though she died...

"I miss you," I said to her, for it was all I could think of in my grief. "I miss you every day. I left you alone. I hate myself for it."

She smiled—so kindly, so wise. "I know. But I am not far. We are sisters. We were woven together with thread that cannot be undone. Not even by Fate."

I held out my hand to her, and she took it, but I could not feel her skin. Just a light coolness. "I wish I could have helped you."

"I knew my Fate, sister," Gweyn said, her voice causing scintillations on the wings of the birds behind her. "But yours was never woven so tightly. And perhaps now you see why."

"*Carioz*," I said.

She nodded. "It is ancient, older than we. Older perhaps, than these crows and the being who sent them. I am their guest. But *carioz* is not Fate, sister. *Carioz* is still a choice."

Ymelda had told me of *carioz*. She had also broken it, created a broken mockery of it. Yet I had never considered it was a *choice*. Or what that meant for Gawain and me. If we could not have a future together, Gweyn perhaps meant we could undo the work of it.

I felt the pain of that knowledge slice through me, and I said softly, "I understand."

"I know you do," Gweyn said, sadly. "It is unfair that we so often bear the burden of the men of this realm. Again and again. But we are the keepers of the Loom, the Spindle, the Web, and the Path. You are here, sister, and you will stop the scourge of Ys if you have the courage. It is not just for Carelon that you do this, but for the future of Avillion. For your future."

"Gweyn…"

"Sister."

"I am so sorry."

Gweyn tilted her head at me. "For what?"

"For never being the sister you deserved."

"Oh, Hwyfar. We both deserved so much more than we were ever given. So, too, all the daughters of Avillion and Lyonesse, of Ys and of Carelon and beyond. But Fate, at least, gives us a chance, even in its cold calculation, to choose what we desire. I love you, sister. And I will wait for you in the arms of my Lord, the arms of your Goddess."

"Gweyn—what brings you joy?"

"All I have now is peace, my sister. For that is what remains when the pendulum stops."

She pulled away from me, back into the gyre of wings. I thought, for a moment, that I could see another figure near her, smaller and stouter, just a hint of a shimmer, but then they were both gone.

The wings parted, and the hill rose before me. And there Gawain stood, resplendent in his armor, a golden god towering above the figures beside him. I could not see the others, for they were some distance away, but he gleamed in the noon sun and my heart leapt, for he began to run toward me at once.

Hope flared in my heart, fanned by my conversation with

Gweyn. Wiping tears from my eyes, I began to run toward him.

"Gawain!" I cried. "I've come!"

But I halted, for as he came closer, he drew steel, squared his shoulders, and began to charge.

My world flared to life with fear; fear he was lost to me, fear that he would destroy me, fear that I would fail. We had no future. I knew that. We both understood that in Arthur's world, we could never find peace, never live as our souls longed. But nor could I allow an end like this.

I dug my heels in, stilled my breath. Though every instinct told me to flee, I forced my eyes open, not just to watch the oncoming assault, but to understand what I saw, to hunt for any hints in this macabre landscape of Gawain's imagination.

His armor shone bright as the sun, near blinding me, and he ran without impediment. In this place he was a younger version of himself, leaner and smoother. Though the armor must have weighed as much as me, he wore it like leathers, and his movements were liquid. As he drew closer, I heard his breath, ragged and bestial, and there were spirals over his breastplate and pauldrons, like the ammonite necklace.

I did not move. I did not run.

Gripping the spear, I pushed into the space I knew Gawain and I shared, that place we knew in our minds. I felt nothing, but there was an echo there, a memory in my muscles. I pivoted my foot back, adjusted my grip, and saw with my green sight that the helmet he wore was brighter than all the rest of his armor. Barely. Just a slight aura, a hint.

He was ten strides away. Six. Three.

I screamed, and a tide of green-eyed crows screamed with me as I flipped the spear and jammed it into the edge of his helmet, lifting it off his head and sending it in a glittering arc behind him. The crows had obscured his sight, and the death blow had only grazed me, but even as I looked down, the world of this making faded away. I heard my mother's voice, howling in agony, and then I was flung backward.

My head hit marble, vision sparkling with a thousand blooming white flowers, and the heady green smell of Queen Tregerna's hall flooded my senses. I tasted blood, thick and salty, at the back of my throat, and the pain from my burns rushed back with a new intensity. The weight of my own body had never been such a burden.

I went to lift my head, and there was Gawain, bending over me, eyes full of tears and terror. But I could feel him. Our *carioz* was restored.

"What have I done?" He was touching my face gently. I winced.

"You didn't do anything. But I am glad you still have a head attached to your shoulders," I replied. "It was close there."

"You came for me," Gawain said, and I could tell he had been broken in a way I did not understand. "I was sure you had gone."

I took his great hand and kissed it quickly. "But this is not finished yet."

Across the hall, the Green Knight pawed at their gruesome middle. Ymelda shrieked and bellowed long plumes of purple flame, and my mother was glowing a soft green color.

Elayne was still working to evacuate as many of the guests as possible, but the relief on her face was palpable. But guards were closing in on us, and there was a significant distance to cross before I could reach my mother.

I needed more strength to perform any kind of magic, but my body was failing me.

"We need to subdue Ymelda," I said to Gawain as he helped me up. I was unsteady as a colt on my feet. "She will destroy the Green Knight if we let her. And my mother."

He set his jaw. "Take strength from me," he said, taking my free hand and placing it on his chest. "I have plenty to spare, but a body that will not hold it."

A flush of understanding swept through me then. "And I will give you the spells, what I know of them. She will not expect it, I do not think. Her link was forged with broken, corrupted magic. It does not share, it only takes."

"Do you think it will work?"

I can feel you; it's working already.

Gawain nodded, eyes widening with wonder, and my skin prickled as if showered with cold spring rain. Blood rushed to my limbs, my muscles, and I felt the pain in my legs lessen. The spear felt light in my hands, and I saw its sharpness in a new dimension. I understood, as Gawain understood, how best to wield it.

When he handed me Galatyne, startling at how easy it moved in my hand. Like a practice sword.

"Let me guide you," he said, stepping back. "But first, tell me what it is I see."

CHAPTER THIRTY-EIGHT

GAWAIN

SHE HAD COME for me.

It was I who had faltered, in the end. I had not the strength, not the will, not the faith in her. But Hwyfar had, and she ventured into my deepest nightmare to pull me free.

Never had I felt so unworthy of trust or love, yet there I stood before the towering Green Knight and saw them for what they were: a god of old, not an adversary. Had I lost faith in Hwyfar? Myself? My duty? Now, staring across at this indescribable creature, I wondered how I had ever beheld them otherwise. They were no fiend, merely ensnared by the corrupt magic of Ys. Hwyfar's powers granted me a new vision, a world of light and magic, apart from the dim shadows I had known before. I had seen what Ymelda wanted me to see.

"I will need you to tell me where to strike," Hwyfar said, as she began her assault forward. She spoke through me, at me, with me. Her voice came from so many places it made my head hurt.

My body felt so strange to me: light, but not unpleasant. I wondered idly if I had shrunk somehow, for the pain in my knee lessened. And Hwyfar—she was a giantess already, but now she bellowed and moved with the rage and purpose of a lifelong warrior. And I suppose she was: my rage, my purpose.

Ymelda is trying to hurt your mother, I told her, reaching out in my mind, trying to translate what I saw, but finding words painfully inadequate. *I don't quite understand, but when Ymelda bonded herself to Tregerna, she awoke the Green Knight, and Lyndesoires was trapped along with it. Time, too. Lyonesse is the power of time. Ys is the power of connection.*

Hwyfar turned, her long braid an arc behind her, and she charged forward, spear in one hand and sword in the other. Her movements were so natural, so beautiful, I found myself following behind her both out of need and a kind of worship. She wore the mantle of a warrior better than anyone I had ever seen: her face blazed with power, her muscles flexed and tensed as she took off at a run toward the Green Knight.

The court was as much enslaved as my mother, but there are agents of Ys among them, besides. I was nearly felled on my way here, Hwyfar's voice shimmered back at me, just as two guards appeared to her right. *Look, and you will see.*

I had forgotten. Someone had put that cursed helmet on my head; Ymelda was not alone in her deception.

And as we approached, I watched as a handful of court attendants came forward, their ties to Ymelda clear in ribbons of thin light running through the room like currents. It was not as bright as what I beheld inside the Green Knight, but clear: the green sight showed me the flow of magic, both corrupt and pure.

As expected, our assailants set out with me in their sights, but Hwyfar interrupted them.

Like me, Hwyfar was not quick on her feet, but the first attack did little to concern her. The first guard, the brightest in Ymelda's sway, did not anticipate Hwyfar's backhand, nor her barely perceptible reaction to her shield bash. Even without a gauntlet, she caved the first guard's nose in, and by the choking sound she was making, her shattered bones had lodged themselves in her nasal cavity.

I'd done that once in a fight. Also, the reason I never wore those helmets so popular in Lyonesse with the nose guards. Once you bent the guard in, there's little chance of bending it out.

The Green Knight aided Hwyfar by sweeping up the bloodied

guard with one of their long vine tendrils and throwing her across the hall. She crashed through the long dining table and did not move again.

The second guard was wilier. The sort of assailant that I always struggled against: lithe and quick, likely one of the women we had first seen on the ridge days ago.

Hwyfar needed to calm herself and not lose her head.

Strength will only get you so far, I said to her, but as a scream tore from Queen Tregerna's throat I knew my words meant very little. *Hwyfar, you must focus. Find peace in the rage.*

She was not listening, and I had the distinct realization that both Cai and Bedevere must have had a similar difficulty with me for years.

The second guard dodged, dodged again. She was all energy and movement, and Hwyfar could not even set up a decent stance, let alone get a blow in. Without a shield, Hwyfar would have to resort to blocking with the spear...

A little help would be much appreciated, Hwyfar said to me. *It's like trying to deal a blow to fog. Maybe you can distract her with a page from my book.*

All I had seen of Hwyfar's magic was close to obliteration. What had she done? Unlike my decades of martial training, or her powers of persuasion, spell work was new.

When the second guard's short sword sliced across Hwyfar's thigh, and blood blossomed across her gown, none of that mattered.

I had experienced battle rage many times before, and this was nothing like it save in the completeness of abandon. Every measure of my body prickled to life, a thousand cold stars of awareness. Now I truly saw the hall before me, not just the streams of magic and life, but time. I could *see* where the second guard was going to move. Oh, for such insight on a battlefield.

I had no shield, but I had air. So, I would make a shield of it. In that moment, air did not seem soft and easy, but a gale I could shape into a small space.

It was enough to take the guard off her assault, and Hwyfar kicked her in the side. Once the guard was on the ground, it was all over.

Except it was not, because drawing Hwyfar's blood had aroused the rage in her as it would in me. I felt it sizzling across her mind, like spices and hot tears and the blazing sun.

Hwyfar was on her downed assailant, punching her face, blood splattering.

"Hwyfar!" I yelled.

The guard was clearly unconscious, arms splayed in motionless defeat. And the spear and Galatyne were both gone, cast across the room in the altercation.

The Green Knight was on their knees to the ground, desperate vines rising up out of the marble in a bid to free them, great cracking sounds shaking the hall. And I knew why: Ymelda had freed herself from the cage inside the Green Knight and was now clawing her way across the marble floor, her body slick with grayish fluids like some newborn horror.

She was a woman changed: no simpering consort, no golden companion as in my dreams. She was a narrow thing, whittled to strange angles. It took me a moment to grasp that her skin had hardened to bone at her cheeks, her forehead, her chin, her brow. When she held up her hands to command a spell—I knew this before I could fully comprehend it—I noticed the tips of her fingers were bare bone, smoothed away to deep brown.

"You should have stayed in Avillion, princess," Ymelda said to Hwyfar. "You should have taken the gift of freedom. You should have run away!"

That got her attention. Hwyfar rose slowly, brushing hair from her face, and strode toward Ymelda, her mind a jumble as I tried to reach it. She was shutting me out.

"I was too late, it seems," said Hwyfar, a strange amusement in her voice. The connection between us blazed with anything but mirth. "Avillion is no more."

I could see fires in her mind, fires over Avillion, and it did not bode well. For Gareth, for Palomydes, for her father and the rest. I could not ask her what it meant, because I understood.

She was performing. I knew she was lying, yet I knew what she had seen was real.

Trust me.

"A shame," said Ymelda, wiping sweat from her brow. Her hair came loose in chunks as she did so. If it was a concern, she showed none. "But I will offer you one more chance at freedom: Leave this brute to me and come with me to Ys. You can have Lyonesse. I have no need of it now."

"Explain what you did to my mother, and I will consider it."

Gods, the sound of her voice. The way it rang from every corner of that hall. How Ymelda did not cower and shrink just from that command, I could not say.

"Hwyfar—" I would have to play the game.

She snapped her head toward me. "You nearly killed me. You have no say in this, Orkney."

I prayed that venom was not real.

I'm sorry, she said. Faint, But genuine.

Still, my own guilt brought real tears to my eyes. We would have to delay.

"I paid Queen Tregerna back. For all the years I served her." Ymelda favored Hwyfar with a smooth smile. "She loved me once. We believed we could unify the magic of Ys and Lyonesse, once we were free. But three whelps, and suddenly sweet Tregerna no longer spoke of *our* plans, *our* magic, *our* connection. But I was loyal to Ys. I was always loyal. So I Sundered her from you so we could build our life together—but in my haste, I attracted the Green Knight."

"And now you have a solution," said Hwyfar. Queen Tregerna still lay within the confines of the Green Knight's chest chamber, pulsing a low, sad, blue light.

"I can take this brute off your hands," Ymelda said, giving me a scathing look again, made worse by the eerie, fever bright glow in her eyes, sickly yellow. "A replacement. A solution for a time. Until I find a more permanent solution to rescue the rest of my court, of course."

"Your agents have plagued me," said Hwyfar, raising her sword. My sword. Our sword. "They poisoned my father. They conspired with Prince Ryence. They dare to challenge Arthur and the sovereignty of Avillion. You send a confusing message."

She was stalling. She believed that last part no more than she believed I could speak to salamanders. Which was truly more plausible than her praise of Arthur's sovereignty.

"Ys seeks no sovereignty—and you needed to be tested. Besides, you did not strike me as sympathetic to Pendragons," said Ymelda.

"I regularly bed the grandson of Uther Pendragon. Or did we not make enough noise for you?"

What was she playing at? But whatever she planned, she was not allowing me in.

"Your mother was lusty too," said Ymelda, extending a long hand toward Hwyfar, the bony ends catching in the green light. "But she is past her prime, and I cannot be free of this curse without a strong bond. Surely this aurochs of a man cannot mean so much to you, what with all the promise you have? He is blood *carioz*. It would be so easy."

Aurochs? I snorted. Which did not help my case in the least. But I felt Hwyfar's connection calming me, warning me, to stay the course. The Green Knight whined, and Queen Tregerna moaned, and I wished we were any place other than here.

"You believe I have promise?" Hwyfar asked, taking a tentative step forward. "I have heard many things said about me before, Ymelda, from many mouths fair and foul, but none have ever suspected me of greatness."

Ymelda stared into my eyes now, so intent, her gaze roving over my body, bony fingers running down my chest. Even through the fabric of my gambeson, I felt the chill, fetid touch of her, the wrongness. She wanted me, but for something more nefarious than possession.

Forgive me, my love. The best lies follow the current of truth.

Swallowing, I focused on my breathing, Ymelda's breath like carrion baking in the sun. "I will grow plump and strong again," she said, her purpled tongue slinking out between broken teeth. "And he will live many years—I can even make his dreams pleasant."

"He can dream of me." Hwyfar worked hard to keep her breath even, but I could feel her pain rising up through the performance, her fear. "He will know no different."

Ymelda looked affronted, but hungry, too. Like Hwyfar might have a tasty strip of meat for her—or might be the meal itself. "If you insist. Meanwhile, you, the heir of Lyonesse and Avillion. You, the carrier of *carioz*. You, the wielder of the *graal*. And perhaps, with the right marriage—say, to a young prince with an eye bent on a throne—*you* could challenge Carelon."

"Of course. Ryence is only my half-uncle, after all," said Hwyfar, not missing a step. Behind me, I heard a soft, slinking sound, but I could not take my attention from Ymelda, as she continued to paw at my arms, taking great, greedy breaths over me.

Ymelda shrugged. "And such alliances certainly aren't unheard of among the Pendragons."

I had no mind to what that meant, but when Ymelda said it, she drooled through her missing teeth, staining her chin with a congealed grey material like old brain matter.

"Then I would unite Ys, Lyonesse, and Avillion," said Hwyfar. "You will be a queen among queens."

I knelt, bowing my head. Ymelda held up her hands, gleefully, until Hwyfar said: "I already am."

Hwyfar stood just behind Ymelda now, and I at last understood. The sword—my sword. The Green Knight had slid it toward Hwyfar as Ymelda roved over me.

Ymelda turned around, irritation on her face, just long enough for Hwyfar to behead her in one swift slice, with Galatyne.

Ymelda's head fell to the ground with a *thunk*, hollow and dead, her body still convulsing, geysers of brackish purple blood splashing to the black marble. So for good measure, Hwyfar ran Ymelda's body through with the Spear.

With a high-pitched whine, Ymelda's body inflated, grew, and exploded into ash.

But there was no peace. For though the sorceress was dead, her magic was not: Queen Tregerna and the Green Knight were still tied together, and the sounds they made shook the foundations of the hall. I reeled, bile rising in my throat, and I felt my grip on Hwyfar's magic slip away.

No, she took it from me, slipped it free as easily as one would take a pair of stockings off a child. She had been storing it, healing it, inside of me, as I had been healing her body with my strength. I knew this, understood this, as she looked at me.

And I knew what she would do next even before she spoke the words.

CHAPTER THIRTY-NINE

HWYFAR

"GAWAIN."

There was not enough time to tell him, to thank him, to give him the right explanation. There were parts of my magic he would never have: the spear had opened up my mind, given me pathways to the truth that existed outside of us. Outside of *carioz*. Every part of me ached to see this moment happen, though I had known it would come to pass since I had understood what Ymelda had done to my mother, and what the Green Knight was.

Carioz was a beautiful, brilliant connection. It was wild, impossible magic, and I did not understand how we had it, but I knew why we did. In another world, another life, Gawain and I could have ruled side by side, wife and husband, prince and princess, of a great realm forged with our magic. We could have raised children, governed a kingdom, loved each other until we were old and tired, and died blissfully bored.

But our love, even with *carioz*, could not endure this world Arthur had wrought. Our *carioz* was just a glimmer of the real power that lay beneath the world. To love me would mean his dishonor; to love him would mean losing everything.

"You… Hwyfar…" He tried to make words, but his throat just tightened, his hands moved helplessly. His anguish flared.

"There is no other way to help them," I said softly, the sounds of my mother's pain joining with the Green Knight's anguished cries.

The briars growing around the great hall shuddered, enhancing the horrid sound, gnawing and cracking, moaning and whining.

I went to Gawain, finally, knowing well that it would be more difficult this way, but that I could not live with myself otherwise. I needed to feel him around me one last time, to know the touch of our *carioz*.

My heart burned with the pain of a thousand knives as I held him, hot tears on my face. I had never known love such as this; I never would again. *Carioz* was not meant for another love in this lifetime. We would have this one glimpse, together. This last chance.

"I love you, Hwyfar," he said to me, hot breath in my hair. I could feel his tears, could feel him tremble. "I love you so much that my soul feels on fire. I love you so helplessly, and I cannot stop myself."

Even beneath his thick gambeson, I heard his heart beating, so deep and so fast. "And I love you like no other, Gawain," I said. "No other before, and no other after. Never doubt it again."

I felt the weight of his chin on my head. "I won't."

"You are my answer, and you always will be," I said to him. "You are my joy, my peace, and my pain."

I kissed him. I touched his face, felt his rough beard, his braid with that scrap of my dress in it, and I thought I might break to pieces. I sobbed into his shoulder. I grabbed onto his arm, and for a moment I was certain the whole world was ending. My body felt foreign, numb. But he looked me in my eyes, kissed my forehead, took me by my waist, and pushed me back, away from him.

Until that moment, I did not know how strong Gawain of Orkney truly was.

Then he fell to his knees, head bowed, hands upon the hilt of his sword. Thick with tears, desperation, he said: "Tell me what to do so I can help bring them peace."

With *carioz*, I showed him.

Ymelda's corrupt spell, which kept my mother and the Green Knight entwined and in agony, was a vast net of braids. A million braids, now Sundered, the ends wild and open like the roots of teeth in the wind. The ones Ymelda had made were ragged, thorned knots, but we could undo them, and replace them with patience with our own *carioz*. Only when the bonds that were broken were re-woven would they find peace. We had an answer to the puzzle within us, the only way to set the Green Knight free and give life back to Queen Tregerna and her court. For each tendril between her and the Green Knight led away, to those she led.

Removing each luminous tendril between us felt like untethering a vital bit of ourselves, a pain that reached deeper than bone. But every time Gawain and I worked a new braid into the network of my mother's aura, both she and the Green Knight calmed a little more. We were healing corrupted magic, returning life to what was broken, willingly. And that was not without reward, without a feeling of *rightness*. I understood that the *graal* was not for me, but it had shown me this path. And there was a measure of relief amidst the grief.

We had, for a time, lived magic of a rare, impossible kind. Together, we had become more than we were alone. The Green Knight was older, wiser, and more powerful than any of us would ever be, and though it was no small sacrifice, their life and their balance was the greater.

Time slowed until we were down to bare threads between us, our hands raw and our bodies hollow from the work. My breath felt like fire in my lungs, and I looked over at Gawain and saw blood trickling from his nose again.

Then I lost my connection to him entirely. The line between us faded away forever. And it was so much worse than I knew, so much deeper than I reckoned. Worse than Sundering, because I was awake for every moment, staring it in the face.

I choked back a sob, and Gawain grabbed my hand, squeezing. *Look*, he seemed to say. *Listen.*

The hall was silent inside, but birds sang outside. Queen Tregerna stood, surrounded by the long, vined tendrils of the Green Knight, and they gazed up at one another, peace and understanding on their faces.

Then I looked back at Gawain, at the small space between us: one small thread remained. Barely visible. Almost nothing. It was thin as spider silk, not even enough to braid. Just a whisper of a memory of what once bound us like sun and moon. But we were done.

Side by side, my mother stood with the Green Knight. Her face was much the same, but lit from within by a different spirit, one I recognized.

The Green Knight, now renewed, towered over us all, their abdomen healed and smooth like jade. They stretched, then sighed, and I felt my body warm, then cool, and my exhaustion evaporated like mist. I felt renewed, awake, and restored, even though sorrow still coursed through me like an unrelenting spring.

"Lyonesse is free," said my mother, and she came to me, embracing me, and now memories of her came to me in a flood: her smell, I knew her smell. *This* was my mother. I would have known her anywhere. "Thanks to you, Hwyfar. And to you, Prince Gawain."

Her voice was so different. Gone was that hardness she had under Ymelda's spell, gone the judgement.

"You have done us both a great service this day," said the Green Knight, bowing low in a strange way, like a willow bending over a river. "And we are indebted to you now. The price you paid is beyond measure."

"There was no other course of action," I said, taking Gawain's hand. I needed his solid assurance, more than I ever had. "Not if we are still to save Avillion. We need Lyonesse. And we need you, Green Knight."

"You need my gift," said the Green Knight, looking at me with eyes that were no longer so fathomless, but old and godlike all the same. If this tale was told again, would anyone even believe us? "I give you two. One, armor for both of you, and matching axes. You will find them in the foundry here. While you wear them, you will have my protection.

"Second," they continued, "you will be welcomed to my hall

in one year's time. Ride north of Lyonesse until you find the Green Chapel. I expect you both there."

Then, without warning or fanfare, the Green Knight dissipated into a fine green mist, and all the briars and thorns throughout the hall along with them. Elayne rushed over to us, joined by the remainder of the court in the hall, and the relief and shock went on for some time throughout Lyndesoires.

"We must leave in two days' time if we are to arrive in time to save Avillion," said Queen Tregerna to me, once she had finished greeting her subjects, who had been similarly ensorcelled—even Elayne, who had only been able to break some elements of her spell, which meant she had not been able to reveal Ymelda's true treachery. "We can use our power to move some leagues faster, but the Path will not move us all as you can do."

I could not bear the thought of traveling the Path alone again, and an unexpected relief came to me. My duty was to Avillion and to Lyonesse, but to the *graal*, as well. This was not yet finished.

"I have so many questions," I said to my mother, kissing her hand. "You… you were still in there, somehow, while Ymelda controlled. You left hints for me. And Gweyn."

"I suspect the Queen was fighting to find her way back to you every moment," Gawain said, holding me close, stroking my hair. I let him. I leaned into the touch, choking back a sob, for he did not feel as close as he had before. Our *carioz* was truly gone. "You *had* been cursed, tracked, followed."

"I saw all, but could do little. A fate I would not wish upon anyone, let alone at the hand of a person they once loved." Queen Tregerna looked out across her great hall and sighed. "We will have time to speak on our journey. For now, you and Gawain must heal and rest. We have a few days yet, and you have both worked old, strange magic. Though the Green Knight has blessed you with healing, your minds and hearts need comfort."

CHAPTER FORTY

GAWAIN

WE SAT ON the floor of the room in Lyndesoires we called our own, legs entwined, staring at each other as if for the first time in our lives, wordless. I drank in every line of Hwyfar's face, each damp eyelash, every bruise down her neck and line of worry. There would be time to wash, but first, we had to speak. And yet words did not suffice.

I choked them out after watching her try, desperately, ending in tears.

"You were always there," I said, my voice catching. "Gods, Hwyfar, we were connected the whole time."

This was the weight of this price: she had been part of me all along. She was what sang to me at Carelon, a distant bell that brought me joy when I was in my darkest days, a spark I could never quite reach. I had never had a name for it, yet we had lived and dined and fucked and danced in the same keep for half our lives. It was only in the last months, when she had left for Avillion, that I had felt truly unmoored—or when I was away on campaign. And the closer I had come to her, the more I had come into myself. The more I had *understood* myself.

And when the bonds were cut, it was not just that the *carioz* was gone... part of *me* was gone. Like losing a sense, as she had said when she had been Sundered. And now she had been through it twice.

"Gawain, I cannot bear this," she cried, and fell into my arms. The weight of her was so foreign; I could not sense her as I did before, and it broke me. I wept into her hair, shook until my soul felt dry, my skin burning.

"We did what we had to," I said, even if it was not fair. Even if I did not believe the choice was right. "There was no other way."

Hwyfar's sigh was so ragged I felt my insides ache with it. "No," she moaned into my chest. "No." She lifted her head to look at me, and gods, my heart still beat to see her honeyed gaze. It would never end. It did not matter if our *carioz* was gone. "Arthur would never have allowed us. We would have been followed to the ends of the earth. And I must help my father. I must—"

"What brings you pain, Hwyfar?"

I held her shoulders, pining for the sense of her, feeling the emptiness in me like a chasm opening wide. Like death itself. She felt it too, I knew she did. I had never seen her so afraid, so diminished. We should be rejoicing. Victory was within our grasp. Ymelda was dead. We had befriended a god, or a being with powers close enough to one; Queen Tregerna was free, and Lyonesse saved. The rest of the kingdom would know soon.

"I want what I cannot have," Hwyfar whispered, crawling into my lap. Even to me, she was not small, but she managed to curl up, and I was strong enough to hold her. "I want our bond back. I want you, every day, with me. I want to live a life together without Arthur."

"He will keep coming for the *graal*, even when I fail him. And if he ever finds out about this, our lives—your goal of keeping the *graal* from him—could cost you the lives of those left here on Avillion."

It was not simply that Arthur had forbidden my involvement with Hwyfar, it was that we were quite literally on opposing sides of a silent war. "If I keep the *graal* from him as long as possible, if I work to summon the power of Avillion and destroy the knowledge of the Sundering in Ys, I can be more than the Whore of Carelon, even if no one knows but me. But, by doing so, I would risk your life. Your duty. Not just to Arthur, but to your mother, your brothers, your whole life."

There was no use in false promises. No longer would we let lies into what remained of our love, our connection. That slender remainder between us could not bear it.

"I will fight for you. For Avillion. I will never fail you again."

I meant every word, even if the web of our own future lay cut and blowing in the breeze.

"Fighting for me is not worth losing your life. For what is Hwyfar without her Gawain, even at a distance? I could never live with myself, knowing I had ruined you."

I kissed her forehead, my body aching with the loss of our power, with the heavy cloak of dread about my shoulders. "I will never stop loving you."

We washed each other, combed the tangles from our hair, cleaned the dirt and blood from our bodies. I rubbed her skin with oils and salts until it shone bright. When she had to stop to weep, I held her and waited; when I had to do the same, she stroked my hair and rubbed at my scalp, and sang softly to me.

Naked, bodies gleaming with oil, clean and bright, we slept in each other's arms, deep and dreamless, eyes still raw from the salt of our tears.

When we woke, the fire was low in the hearth and our hair had dried. Hwyfar sat at the edge of the bed, fingering the end of her braid, a nervous motion I had never seen from her. The soft down of her body lit from the fire, and I saw the sharp profile of her face cast in gold, leaving me breathless.

"No dreams," I said to her, kissing that shoulder softly. "Did you leave something out for the dream-eaters?"

She touched my cheek with her hand, relaxing. "I was too hungry. I ate it."

THE NEXT MORNING, we met Queen Tregerna in the foundry, and I could see the concern in her eyes when she saw her daughter.

I was worse for wear, half lost to meandering thoughts that felt unfamiliar and deadly, but Hwyfar was broken in a way I could not quite reach. If there was more time for healing, we could work together to help her, but this was not the way of things.

"I have never seen armor like this," said Queen Tregerna, walking us toward a small room off the foundry proper. She walked differently now, with more confidence. "The armor was my idea—before. I knew the spell was happening. It was over months, you know, and I was unable to stop it once it began. The magic of Ys is that way, and it has infiltrated deep into Skourr, but it can be of use. Your body is suited to it, as evidenced when I broke your arm."

Hwyfar turned her head sharply. "Then it's true, what Ymelda said."

Queen Tregerna nodded slowly. "The magic of Ys is not inherently corrupted, Hwyfar. But yes. You hold all three magics within you. Ys, Avillion, and Lyonesse. That is remarkable, indeed. No other person living has such claim that I am aware."

"Surely Mawra does," Hwyfar said.

"No, she was too young to be exposed to Ymelda," said Queen Tregerna, as she unlatched a small wooden door. There were scars on the wood. They must have been from the Green Knight's roots and branches; they had reached all the way down here. "Ymelda was your nursemaid. Before she became changed, she was a teacher, a nurturer. She really did give you a gift. The mark you were given was meant to activate part of the corrupted side of your powers—and it would have. If I had not intervened."

Queen Tregerna pushed open the door and revealed a single remaining thatch of the Green Knight's presence, and upon it, two suits of armor made precisely for us in deep forest green. They were not forged by a human hand—I saw no seam or nail—but must have been *grown*. All over the smooth surface was a dizzying masterwork of braids, covering every measure, now and again flecked with silver or gold—I saw upon mine dragons and unicorns, and upon Hwyfar's the lion, the apple blossom, and the ammonite whorl.

Beside them were axes, as the Green Knight had said. Mine was enormous, even by my standards, and forged of a single, solid, smooth measure of metal. I could see no hammer marks, no dents—the head was charred black save for the edge, which was nearly white. Hwyfar's was smaller, and double-edged, and perfect. But I could still wield it with one hand. With practice.

"I have no desire to work the spells of Ys," said Hwyfar, scowling at her new armor.

"You already have," said her mother. "How else do you think you saved me? Ys is the power of connection, the bonds between us—what we see and think, feel and perceive. *Carioz* belongs to all powers, yes, but the manipulation of it, that is the work of Ys, and it is work you both did."

I picked up the axe and found it lighter than I would have guessed. The metal was warm against my palm.

Looking at Queen Tregerna, I asked, "And you—how do you fare, now that you are free? You and Ymelda... was it always a false love?"

The queen looked thoughtful, glancing between the two of us while she considered her words.

"Corrupting powers, as I said, can take many forms," said Queen Tregerna. "Even love. Especially love, perhaps. I did love Ymelda. And she did love me, and we did plan to make a life for ourselves together here, in Lyndesoires. A castle of women. All of this began with good intent. Leodegraunce was no monster, but like many of our station, ours was not a marriage of love; and the moment I saw Ymelda, my heart was hers.

"It took me ages to understand that she was encircling me with spells, slowly binding me, much in the way Leodegraunce has been poisoned, I think. So, while I still could, I left traces of myself behind: the armor, the silk, Ahès. And Gweyn came to me. Comforted me. First in my dreams, while she was still alive, and then after, while she roamed, flitting in and out of the web. She knew you were the key to my freedom."

"And the *graal*," said Hwyfar. "She told me not to forget my mother's face."

"And you nearly did. Like Gawain, you forgot what was real." Queen Tregerna touched her daughter's face, smoothing the tears that had fallen once again. "But now, we live to fight again. Together. And to undo the ills woven into the Skourr. For it is deeper than we know, I fear, if they were nearly able to destroy the both of you, right under Modrun's nose. We will find her first, with our army, and then we shall fall upon Avillion and free Leodegraunce."

CHAPTER FORTY-ONE

HWYFAR

I FOUND ELAYNE later that night, alone. Gawain fell asleep, his body and mind still reeling from the fight, and though I felt the sting of guilt leaving him, I knew I had to return the Spear and bid farewell to the Lady of Astolat.

She was still in the healer's ward, tending to a handful of the court who had suffered injuries, but when she saw me, she took her leave and sent her handmaidens to finish up her work.

The *graal* spear was wrapped in silk, but the feel of it burned at my consciousness. A world of truth was difficult to bear, even on a short journey.

We walked together in silence to the Spring Chapel, as she called it, one of the small gathering places meant to worship Oyenne, the goddess of spring in Lyonesse. Unfamiliar gods, unfamiliar powers.

"My father knew you," I said to her, handing the *graal* spear over to her, reverently. The moment it left my hand I felt both relief and regret. "He assured me you would take the cup as well, when we go to Carelon."

Elayne nodded, taking the spear. "I knew your father well. He saw me through my pregnancy."

I had not expected those words. "Pregnancy?"

"I had a son, twenty years ago. I was only fifteen myself, at the time. As a priestess on Avillion, it meant I would not be welcomed in those halls, as I could not marry the child's father. So I agreed to leave, once the child was born, and Ymelda helped me arrange for his fosterage. But even then, I knew this would be my calling. As did your mother. As did your sister."

"I wish Gweyn was still here." I wished it every day.

"The final piece of the *graal* is hidden far away. But Hwyfar—"

I stopped her, putting my hand on her knee. "I know. It is not my quest."

As with so much about the *graal*, that had been made clear to me. Its future was in peril. Like the Green Knight, the *graal* power was old, living, a wild, strange force that could not be bent to the will of man. That Arthur believed he could use it to his advantage was foolish and dangerous. Not to mention the Christian priests, who wished to fold it into their own stories. Still, I could understand what possessing them could mean: being near them brought a sense of reverence, a clarity.

Elayne took my hand. "You have done so much. I wish I had been stronger, that I could have helped you earlier. But Ymelda's grip was strong. I had learned a few ways to push through it, to help you nudge closer, but she always seemed to find me."

"How did she grow so powerful?" I asked. "We managed it, in the end, but it was a close thing."

Elayne frowned, her pale brows knitting together in harsh lines. "She took our power, siphoning it out, much in the way she did with her false *carioz*. The spellwork was ornate, built over decades, with very few chinks in it. And many of us believed Queen Tregerna sanctioned it—but I knew her better. I only wish I could have done more, sooner."

"You helped as you could, Elayne. And I am forever grateful."

"I fear you gave too much." Elayne's eyes filled with tears.

Perhaps I did. Had I been trained better in Avillion as a priestess, perhaps magic would come to me more easily—perhaps I could have saved the Green Knight and my mother without sacrificing *carioz* to do it.

I did not have an answer for her. But we embraced in the Spring Chapel, and I felt the sting of truth through us both, and understood I had a friend. I had not lost all.

CHAPTER FORTY-TWO

GAWAIN

ALL TOLD, THERE were nearly one hundred soldiers gathered outside Lyndesoires. It was a transformed place now that Ymelda's spell was broken, and though I wanted to feel sorry for myself, to allow the depths of despair to drag me down, I could not help but rejoice a little in the faces of those surrounding us. Already, people trickled in from the borders, reuniting with loved ones. As the queen had said: for years, the castle had been suspended, as if in amber, apart from Lyonesse as a whole.

The queen sent word to the capitol, Lyoz, where her brother Prince Meliadus ruled in her stead. Lyndesoires and its surrounds were now restored, and its rightful queen alive. To my knowledge, in spite of Arthur's great pressure, Meliadus had neither claimed the mantle of king, nor surrendered to Carelon. This, at least, my uncle would not expect. Surely, the adventure would count for something.

We gathered at the gates of the keep, and I could not stop staring at Hwyfar in her green armor. It molded to her body as if she had been born to it; she had confirmed it was as light as mine, and just as impenetrable. It wore like driftwood, yet resisted every attempt at injury, not even scratching. And I tried. Certainly, it had its weaknesses, as all armor did, but gone were my days of fighting the weight of protection in battle.

Strangely, since the battle, my knee did not hurt as much. The new armor seemed to cradle it, giving support I had not felt before.

"The power of Lyonesse," said Queen Tregerna, to the gathered forces, "is time and distance. Until the curse was broken, we could not traverse our sacred Path. But now, restored, we may once again."

Hwyfar held my hand, her grip unrelenting, but she did not look at me as Queen Tregerna's priestesses encircled us: there were nine of them, and each held a horn similar to Hwyfar's own. I was told this was one of the sacred magics of Lyonesse, built upon the very same power Hwyfar had harnessed to walk the Path and travel to Avillion's bleak future, so we can prevent our future.

"Now, this power will take us forward in distance, together."

The horns began, and I felt the sounds tickle my ears first, then as each horn added to the clarion chord, even my teeth started rattling. My eyes watered. I could see nothing of the power, but I could *feel* it down to my bones, in the very air around us. The snowy landscape shimmered, shifted, and I closed my eyes against the strange brightness.

Then I could smell crisp pines, the sharp scent of a nearby river, the loamy undergrowth of a large forest.

Brocéliande.

I gasped, felt sick, barely managed not to vomit. Good start, that. The priestesses did not fare so well; many were on their knees retching. This, the queen told us, was expected. Such magic took its toll. Hence, we would stay the night. Time had passed, but not as much as if we had walked.

It did not take long to find where we had split with our company, the night of the attack. The trees were a mass of thorns and branches, which I now recognized as extensions of the Green Knight's magic: somehow, Ymelda must have used her abilities through her agents, amplified by the Green Knight's powers.

The signs of struggle remained, but there were no bodies. I guessed two full days had passed since we had been taken to Lyndesoires, which meant Prince Ryence was well past us and on his way to striking Avillion by Hwyfar's calculation. We had all fallen for his deceit. In an age of chivalry, the churl is a mastermind.

Of my men, though, there was no sign. Nor of Modrun.

"Let us not wake the wood tonight," said Queen Tregerna, when our scouts returned after a third sweep of the forest, covered in burdock and pulling thorns from their feet. "We shall rest, and travel by horn in the morning. We will make up for time then."

Hwyfar had not joined me in scouting, but had taken time to set up the tent we shared. She had been uncharacteristically quiet, but given the events of the last day, I did not wish to press her into discussion. I knew how fragile was the edge upon which she balanced.

Which is not to say that I was well. But I kept myself busy in the world I knew, of moving armies and training soldiers, and reading the road. Even though my body ached as it had not ached in years, the trackers were patient, and the conversation was familiar. I held out hope that I would see Yvain, Bors, Kahedin, and the rest, soon. We would need every last knight if we were to have any hope of saving Avillion. I would take every able-bodied warrior.

To say nothing of Modrun, if we could even find the old witch. Providing she had survived.

When I entered the tent, I expected to see Hwyfar red-eyed and exhausted, limp upon the furs and bedrolls, but instead she was sitting on a large chest, the Green Knight's axe in her lap, running a whetstone over the edge of the blade. She was covered in a fine sheen of sweat, curls clustered to her brow, rivulets of sweat staining her dress, pale silk clinging to her shoulders as she moved, muscles defined with each stroke. The way her hands clutched that long stone, ah, gods, I had never seen such a more suggestive sight. I wanted to watch her for an eternity, gleaming candles about her, eyes focused, brows down. No—an eternity would be torture. I would expire from arousal. Turn to a mist, die a happy man.

"You can stop staring," she muttered, not looking up from her work.

"I would prefer not to," I replied. "Your every movement stokes my desires."

The sound of the stone against that fine blade shimmered against my spine. Her breath punctuated each stroke.

"Mother showed me how to keep up the blades before we left," she said, taking a moment to admire her work. "I know it is pristine right now, but I thought I might learn the feel of it. I have never had such a weapon of my own before, let alone one gifted by a godlike being made of vines and thorns that somehow knows my exact measurements." She glanced at our twin suits of armor, stacked together by the makeshift bed. "Disconcerting, really, when I think about it."

I savored every word she spoke, for they were a bridge between us, filling up the space that had been so violently ripped open.

"You sound a bit frustrated," I said, taking a few steps closer. Her long hair was down, red waves down past her waist. Not a plait in sight. "Preoccupied."

Her eyes snapped to mine. "I am."

Honesty. I could do with that. I remembered what it felt like, when she was being honest. Sweet, like raspberries. Lies were like sour milk, just on the edge. When we were still *carioz*, I would never have been able to identify those tastes. But now, Sundered from her, I remembered.

I went to open my mouth and she held up a hand.

"If you ask me what you can do to help, I shall throw this whetstone at your thick skull," she snapped. "Though trust me when I say I am uncertain as to which is the denser."

"Very well." I walked around behind her. I leaned over to her ear and whispered. "Will you allow me to rub your shoulders, then, princess?"

She slapped me away. "Stop doing that."

"Doing what?"

Her glare was devastating. "Stop acting comfortable."

Gods, this was exhausting. "Hwyfar, do not punish me for this. I cannot bear it."

323

CHAPTER FORTY-THREE

HWYFAR

How could he stand there, gazing at me with such love and understanding? We had lost so much, and I could not quench the fury inside of me. Nothing I did could stop it. It obliterated my every thought.

Because no matter what we had done, what I had gained in saving the Green Knight and releasing my mother and Lyonesse, I knew at my core that the greater tide of Arthur was inevitable. Elayne had the *graal* now, yes. Our victory in Avillion was mere days away, if we moved fast enough. My father would soon be healed, Gawain reunited with his men, and Arthur outsmarted.

We could fail, we could win. In neither world did I have a future with Gawain.

Our story was over. I was still bound to marry. Gawain was still bound to leave.

"This is our twilight, Gawain," I finally said, mustering as much kindness I could, though my anger demanded a much sharper tone.

"If this is an attempt to frighten me away, it will not work," he said to me, going over to a small chair, deciding it would not hold his weight, then settling on the trunk instead. I had struggled to get it to move a handspan, and he pulled it with one hand, effortlessly.

"Do not presume to tell me what I'm doing," I replied.

He laughed at me. Laughed! "Hwyfar, you are one of the most stubborn people I know. You cannot tell me you are ready to give up so easily. Besides, I've seen the way you were looking at me. Let me kiss you until you forget."

"How do you remain so calm?" I barely managed not to scream at him. I flung down the whetstone, along with the axe. I half expected the Green Knight to crash into our tent at the insult, but no such thing happened.

Gawain raised his brows, the single scarred brow rising just slightly higher than the other. I loved it. Loved kissing that space, touching the scar that ran down his cheek. But what did it matter any longer?

"And why do you assume I am calm?" Gawain asked, folding his arms and leaning back a little. He did not hide the desire in his eyes, but he would do nothing until I relented.

"I hate it," I said, because it was true. I pushed at my chest, where I felt it the most, the void that gaped wide where the *carioz* once lay. "I hate this feeling, this distance."

He reached out, taking my hands, softly rubbing his thumbs over my palms. I resisted, but with a few breaths I found my rage simmering down to a more manageable rumble. Gawain and I were together now. We had this night. I could breathe again, even if it felt like fire.

"If you do not run, I will not falter," he said to me softly, not with the fervor of a new lover, but with gentle reverence. "Unless you feel differently now. Unless, without *carioz*, you cannot see me the same way. Then I would never ask it of you."

"What future do we have?" The fear gnawed relentlessly at me. "Can you still love me when you cannot feel me as we once were?"

"No magic will ever keep me from fighting for you."

I wanted to be strong, I wanted not to need him. But I was broken in a way I had never been: finding Gawain had made me whole for the first time in my life, and our Sundering had brought me to a precipice I had not anticipated. And now, we were preparing to go back into a world without roasted apples and lost castles, where our actions had very real consequences.

There was no choice, really, other than to crawl into his arms.

I folded into his body with such ease, and his arms wrapped around me so completely, there was no fighting it. The damp silk on my body melded to his, and I buried my face in his chest. I kissed him with tenderness and without demand, branding my love for him on his skin.

"I love you." I whispered it into his neck as he brushed away the sticky hair from my face. "Especially now."

"I know."

I wanted his body, that connection, but I was too afraid. What if we did not connect as we had with *carioz?*

He rubbed my back and sang softly, his deep voice reverberating through my whole body as I melted into him, clutching to our last moments before the world turned against us.

I must have fallen asleep, for I awoke in the pile of furs that made up our sleeping pallet. Gawain was beside me, not sleeping but resting, arms behind his head and staring up at the angled roof of the tent. It sounded like deep night, and I heard the crunch of boots on cold ground in the distance, as someone kept rounds.

"There's word of Modrun in the woods. A message arrived, from one of our scouts," Gawain said. "She is asking for you. She has given you dispensation to travel without a blindfold, but no guard may accompany you."

"Oh," I said, blinking back the confusion of sleep. "You truly think it's her?"

"Not in the least."

"I figured as much." I said, sitting up. The night chill pawed at my skin, and I groaned to leave Gawain's warmth, knowing how numbered our hours and minutes were.

He sat up with me, nudging me. "Our spies think someone may be posing as Modrun, and they may have the missing knights. They want you, powerful royal as you are, alone."

"I am no queen, Gawain. My father will rule Avillion for many years once this is set to rights," I said, the words a relief and, strangely, tinged with regret in the back of my throat. Like smoke caught in my hair the morning after a bonfire. "And as for Modrun, I fear she is in great danger if anyone is allowed without a blindfold into the wood. Clearly, they are interlopers, and Modrun's own magic is subdued."

"We will not be far, but they must *believe* you are alone."

I understood and shivered at that revelation, wondering if the living twin—Wenna or Elowyn—remained. Wondering where the rest of the knights were. I knew well what responsibility lay on my shoulders, and was glad for the rest I had managed, but rueful that Gawain and I had left too much unsaid. That we could not even have a night to ourselves.

But that was how it would always be with us. He was right: we never had a future.

I touched my fingers to his lips, to his brow. I dared not begin, knowing we could not continue.

"When we get back, I will show you how to use that whetstone properly," he said to me, his arm around my middle, pulling me in tight. The air went out of my lungs, so deliciously. Gods, I wanted to melt into him.

"I will allow it," I said, and touched his nose with mine. Never, in all my life, had I been so comfortable, so easy, with another. I yearned for this closeness, this easiness, forever. Ah, to live a life of such simplicity with another.

I wanted to tell him that he deserved a happy ending. That our sacrifice gave us every right to take what was ours, demand it from the gods. Even as I thought it, though, I knew he would never agree. He had a duty to his brothers, to his kingdom, and our happiness could never cost that. Gawain of Orkney was no perfect man, but he was not selfish, not like I was.

"Now, help me into my armor. I wish to make an entrance."

THE FOREST BREATHED, empty of the power of its enchantress, like a sentient, sprawling being composed of trees and leafmold and living creatures. The moment my boots crossed into the loamy ground marked by Modrun's stones, darkness embraced me and the living realness of Brocéliande enveloped my senses. My armor sang with it, humming against my skin, recognizing a twin power. And as I glanced down at my chest, I saw the embellishments and whorls glowing faintly.

I carried my new axe, bolstered by our previous adventure. I was uncertain of the path in the night, but shortly I noticed stout white mushrooms tracing a line to the East. They had delicate gills and greenish speckles on top and given that nothing else in the wood stirred or gave me any other direction, I took it for a sign.

As to my own abilities—those famed powers of Avillion, Lyonesse, and Ys—I felt nothing. My mother was certain they remained inside of me, but since severing our *carioz*, I felt only the loss of Gawain. I had been tied to him for so long, longer than I had known, and the gulf felt insurmountable.

My eyes continued to adjust, my own armor giving just enough illumination to gleam from the mushrooms. I found that, unlike the great armor my mother had crafted for me, my limbs did not grow weary or sore. Nor did I find myself chilled, even though the Green Knight's armor was made of mere wood. I was indeed quite comfortable, almost enjoying the nighttime sounds, when I heard growling behind me.

Not just any growling.

A lion.

"Yvain?" I barely managed the whisper before I saw the shape of the lion approach me in the dark. "Are you near?"

Oh, but he was massive. I saw no sign of Yvain, or of Modrun. I watched as my armor glinted off of the lion's eyes in the dark: silver and yellow circles flashing at me.

Fear caught in my throat, but I knew better than to challenge this beast. I had watched Yvain raise it from a cub and knew well their bond. And Yvain was not here. I knelt down to look the lion level in his eyes and lay my hands flat on the ground as I had seen Yvain do in the sparring ground when we were children, a sign of peace.

The lion's growls turned to a whine, and he snuffled, then placed his shaggy head between his paws and came over to me.

I realized, as he drew closer, that he was thin, hungry. How could a lion go hungry in the wood? Modrun's powers had done more than keep Brocéliande safe, it had kept its animals fed and nourished. Still, I saw no sign of the great storm that had roiled about us on our last journey through.

I tensed, and began to understand that I was perhaps, once again, far too trusting of the word coming from Brocéliande.

The mushrooms. I knew enough about mushrooms, and how they grew, to understand that what I could see was just a small part of their growth. Like the Path itself, their filaments reached underground, for leagues.

I wondered if the mushrooms were leading me away from my captor, or toward something else.

The lion did not seem part of what Modrun's captor would want me to seek out.

I reached over, the lion tucking his big head into the crook of my shoulder and touched my hand to the top of the glowing mushrooms. At first, I felt nothing but the cool, fleshy contact of the fungus on my skin, followed by that familiar earthy smell.

But then my armor flared green, and my vision shifted. I could see the whole of Brocéliande before me, but as if a net had been cast upon it in silver and grey light. There were thousands, millions of mushrooms, from the most delicate and minute to the most massive, sprawling all around me.

And they showed me Brocéliande, and its inhabitants. This was true connection. This was the magic of Ys. Not the corruption I had seen, but its purest form: the network of a forest, the tributaries of a great river system, the threads on a spider's web.

There, not far, I saw shapes moving, battling. Not close enough to hear but moving in such a way that I understood: conflict. *Gawain.*

I pulled my hand away in shock, and immediately the vision faded. Without hesitating, I took a small mushroom into my mouth, and allowed the power of Ys to flow through me, leading the way.

With the lion on my heels, I went toward the waterfall at the heart of Brocéliande.

CHAPTER FORTY-FOUR

GAWAIN

HWYFAR ALL BUT vanished in moments, Modrun's wood swallowing her whole. I was not far behind her, trying to mark her every move. At first, I kept myself calm, knowing that Brocéliande was a place of deception.

We awaited Hwyfar's signal, but none came. When we went to follow her tracks, even with our torches we could find no sign before us. With three priestesses in our number, and Queen Tregerna in our ranks, not even spells revealed her to us.

Worry swirled in my gut.

"Do not doubt her, Gawain," said Queen Tregerna, clapping me roughly on the shoulder. "She can do this."

"I know," I said, which was true. Yet, without our *carioz*, I had only trust to rely on.

The procession into the forest was still dim and despairing in the bleak early morning darkness. My armor glowed a strange pale green, the unicorn and dragons like eerie ghosts on my chest. We numbered twenty, and we had reliable steel, but the wood was sleeping, and I was fearful.

All was covered in moss: every surface, every rock, like a great blanket knitted over. The temperature was deadly cold, but I stayed surprisingly comfortable, and my knee clicked but did not ache for once. I closed my eyes and tried with all my might to reach out to Hwyfar, but felt nothing but a sharp emptiness where *carioz* once lay.

"Be on your guard," I said to the soldiers behind me. "The wood is full of strangeness."

Queen Tregerna, back in her remarkable gear and paint, nodded to me in agreement. "Yes, Sir Gawain."

When she had been in thrall, she had always called me by *prince*. This felt better. I had never known how little I had wanted to be a prince until I'd been called so routinely, and by a queen at that.

We walked on a while, side by side, until Queen Tregerna leaned over to me and said, "I sense there is something you wish to ask me."

Her intuition was strong, and I felt a bit embarrassed I was so easy to read. Without Hwyfar's connection, my ability to perform was eroding away.

I sighed, hesitating. "It does not concern your daughter."

"Good, I was wondering if there was any part of your brain left to you," replied the Queen of Lyonesse. "The way you two look at each other is practically indecent."

I felt my cheeks heat, but I was not ashamed. "Well, it does not concern her *directly*."

"I spoke too soon."

"It concerns Sundering. If you are connected with someone, but not *carioz*, can you still be Sundered from them?"

I could not see her expression, but I felt her hesitation. "As in, a blood bond?"

"Aye."

"No. Not in the way you and Hwyfar were undone. Blood is not magic, not in the way that *carioz* is."

"I didn't think so." Even speaking of it made me feel queasy again.

"That sort of breaking of the bonds of blood takes time and—alas—perhaps can never truly be broken. For it is not an arcane connection, a spiritual connection as between a mother and her children. It is a bond that grows up with us, in every bit of our bodies, in the way we learn how to think and see the world. If you and she had been raised together, as *carioz* bonded once were, it would have been so much harder, nearly impossible, for you to do what you did, for that reason. We cannot choose our families, but *carioz* is—should—always be a choice."

Tregerna was a wise woman; she knew what I meant. The time approached when I would need to speak again with Arthur. When I would need to face my future, married to a woman I did not want, to tend a land I did not care for. Perhaps I was a coward, but part of me hoped that the lingering loyalty, the guilt I wrestled with still, could be severed with this magic.

I could not speak for the thickness in my throat, threatening to rob me of my composure. Worried as I was about Hwyfar, thinking on my future felt fickle.

Queen Tregerna adjusted her gear, every inch the prepared warrior. "If I could have Sundered myself from Leodegraunce, I would have."

"But you did from your own daughters," I said. "And they were your blood."

"Ah, yes. But they were not yet fully-formed people—they were children. I suspect you speak of someone you have known a long time."

To my shame, I nodded. I had hoped to take a coward's way. If I could stop feeling loyal to Arthur, perhaps I could keep Hwyfar myself.

She sighed, wiping at her eyes. "We had no real history, save those few early years. With Hwyfar, it was the most difficult, the most painful, the least successful. She found me, after all. But I walked away to preserve them, and myself, from a madness I knew was impending, as Ymelda's poison was slow and unrelenting. I still felt the pain every day of losing Leodegraunce, my dear friend, even in captivity. But I *survived*. And I will still bear that pain. But it was a price I will continue to pay. Leaving Leodegraunce was never the wrong choice."

I ached at the thought of that. "So I must simply endure it."

"You must ask yourself, Sir Gawain, even if this power was available to you: where would it end? Could you break every tie—your mother? Your brothers? Aunts, cousins? Then your friends, your fellow knights? Would you give up everything? And who would you be at the end?"

Her words felt like a lance to my heart. "I love her enough that it could be worth it."

"You both know that is not true. Love has nothing to do with responsibility. You are nobles, of two great lines. I was given to Leodegraunce, and I wanted to be his friend, but not his wife. I did put my people at risk, ultimately, and I will never forgive myself for it. I would not wish that upon you, or my daughter. Not for any love. No, I think some powers are too dangerous and teeter too close to the corruption Ymelda fell prey to."

That, I understood, and Queen Tregerna's warning made my heart sink. "I wish I could give Hwyfar a future."

"No future is predetermined, no matter what the priestesses of Avillion say. Why do you think they brought in others to interpret their prophecies? It is an ever-moving horizon. I have never taken much stock in the prophecies of Avillion. How can I, when all three of my daughters were foretold as wives of Arthur? Such foreshadowing has a habit of becoming a powerful paradox."

"So I have learned. And for those with minds like mine, that's a dangerous path to tread. I'm afraid I was not made for such complexity."

"Ah, but you have what Hwyfar does not. You carry influence. You carry, by simple virtue of your birth, the ability to tilt the scale in one direction or another by simply speaking or staying silent when the chance arises. That is not prophecy, and it is not magic, but it is power. Leodegraunce understood it, and Merlin fashioned it into a brutal weapon. Consider it well, Sir Gawain, and do not take it for granted."

I had never considered myself a man of influence, and was prepared to tell Tregerna as much, when she held up her hand.

"Water. Up ahead."

We walked on in the mossy dark, slowly now, as that water was the first real sign of life. I wondered where Hwyfar was, but tried to swallow down the thought, knowing how much she would detest my behavior. If any woman was capable of this— any *person*—it was Hwyfar. We all knew things would likely not go to plan here, and she was well aware of the risk.

"You're crouching," said Queen Tregerna, as we knelt beside one another, willow fronds only swaying when we touched them, unmoved by breeze.

"I am," I said.

"How is the pain in your knee?"

I paused, realizing again how little it suffered. "Better," I observed. She was asking me for a reason. In all my distraction and moping, I had not really considered what it might mean. "You don't suppose Hwyfar might have healed me?"

"No," said Queen Tregerna. "I told you already, wounds like that cannot heal. But it can be, with the right power, shared. She could very well have taken some of the burden onto herself. That is the power of Ys: the power of bargain, exchange, balance, connection."

That hit me in the gut surely as Gaheris's fist might have.

"You mean, she could take on some of the pain," I said.

"Not just the pain, the injury itself. When she Sundered you."

"Gods…"

"How long do you think you were aware of her, Gawain?" Queen Tregerna asked. "Within *carioz*?"

I tried to speak and found my throat too tight again. Gods, how many times had I wept in the last two weeks? More than in my entire life, I would say. And this woman seemed to summon it from me with the ease of a blade teasing blood from a blister.

"I remember a feeling the day her caravan arrived at court," I said slowly. "This sense of anticipation I could not place. I thought it was joy for Arthur—for the king. He was everything to me at that time. And I saw Hwyfar, of course I did. I thought she was the most beautiful woman I had ever seen. But I had also not seen so many women. She stayed on at Carelon, but we rarely saw one another. And I was angry all the time. It felt like my insides were wound tight. It only got worse when I left—in war, I was a monster."

She put her hand on mine. "You were given a gift in the wrong time," said the queen.

"The last few months, after she left Carelon for Avillion, I was not myself," I said. "When I saw her at Withiel, I… I don't know if I can go back to who I was before."

"I saw glimpses of that pain you endured. Do not blame yourself, but trust that bond. It is not entirely gone. Do not falter now."

Before us, I finally saw pale yellow light and a glimpse of water: a pool, glimmering strange. Curious flowers, like upturned vases, rose out of the shore of the water as we watched, and I saw the whole scene come to life: figures lined upon the waterfall edge, armor reflecting that faery lantern fire. Bors, I knew by the plume on his helmet; Kahedin by the slight drop in his right shoulder; and Lanval, of course, by his slender frame and tousled hair.

There was no sign of Yvain, though, nor his lion. And I knew enough that this was not Modrun's magic. Hers was a private kind of power. If she was still alive, she was hiding, waiting in the shadows.

Two figures stood in the center of the pool, thin and wan, draped in long rags, hair pale and plastered to their sallow skin, perched on a rock with their hands outstretched.

It took me too long to realize they were singing, and longer still that those songs were spells.

CHAPTER FORTY-FIVE

HWYFAR

MY LEGS BURNED from the exertion, but the waterfall came no closer, though I knew it was near. This way of seeing the world made my head ache, and I had to stop, shaking all over, the lion licking at my face, to try and collect myself. I drank the remaining water from my flask, keeping it down through sheer will, though nausea gripped me.

There were mushrooms everywhere, of more variety, shape, and size than I had ever seen or known possible. Their tiny spores rose around me in glittering clouds, like sand catching in some invisible sun. I breathed it in, felt the chalky residue on my face. I knew where I needed to go, but the vision in my head was deceptively drawn. How had I become separated so far from Gawain and the other knights?

I stumbled forward, passing through low-hanging willow fronds, when I at last saw the shape of a person against the misty spores rising about me in a rainbow of pearlescent hues.

It took me a moment to realize I was looking at Modrun, for in my strange mushroom-sight, she was rendered to me in lacework and tiny pinpricks of light. But the way they settled on her hair, and the outline of her robes, was familiar. When I was young, she had not yet retreated entirely to the woods, and she would come to Withiel now and again.

"Princess Hwyfar, you found me," said Modrun, and there

was true relief in her voice, but weariness, too. "I was beginning to think you lost."

"I found mushrooms," I said. "And a lion. Is Yvain with you?"

She hesitated, then nodded. "I have kept him safe. But the lion was lost to me in the conflict. Along with the other knights. You found your way into my fold."

"Your fold?"

Modrun stepped toward me, tilting her head, the darkness moving like a constellation come to life. "May I?"

The witch of Brocéliande raised her arms up, and then whispered a few low words I could not recognize. When she lowered them again, I felt a strange tickling sensation all over my skin. Then my vision shifted, melting from the outside, and the darkened wood revealed itself to me once again. My nausea retreated, and I could breathe easier.

But it was not the same wood I had entered upon. Here, the wind blew upon my face, the branches creaked, and the leaves still rustled. In my previous state, I had not been able to sense those things, but nor had I upon entering Brocéliande—all had been rendered silent in her absence. I rubbed at my eyes with the edge of my cloak, peering at Modrun's face again.

She was missing an eye, the socket raw and red, pocked with scabs and angry looking marks down the side of her face.

"I will heal," she said, and then laughed. I could not imagine laughing at such a wound, in such a place. "Well, I will never have that eye back. But it will not look so frightening in time."

Modrun had aged little since I last saw her, only a few glimmering streaks of white in her hair. She had a round face, dimpled and kind, with a wide mouth and dark brows. Her form was rounded: wide hips and breasts, and sturdy legs. Beauty, yes, but in a way that felt rooted to the earth, powerful, commanding.

"Where are we?" I asked.

Modrun flinched slightly as she turned her head, likely from the pain of her wound. "My fold, as I said. I bargained with the wood for Yvain, and this is what I got. A bit of a fold within the curse for us both. But I could not get the lion. Thankfully, I was able to send out my spores, and you followed them here—and of course, the lion goes where I cannot. I am glad to see him again. But you shan't be able to linger long, I'm afraid. The wood will know."

"I thought there would be more time," I said.

"We always do." Modrun patted me on the shoulder, giving me a kind look. "And you have been through enough already."

As she moved, my eyes were drawn to her collar bones, where I caught the glitter of gold on her skin. Modrun followed my expression and nodded, pulling aside the grimy collar of her shift.

She had an ammonite amulet embedded in her skin. I recoiled, but she grabbed my arm, amusement—and perhaps a little pity—on her face.

"I am a priestess of Ys, Hwyfar, but you need not be afraid," she said softly, clasping my fingers gently. The motion was so motherly, so disarming, that even though my heart pounded in warning, I slowed. "You followed my magic here, and it is from the same root. And you sensed it, which means you know of it, too."

"The priestesses of Ys are to blame for all this," I said.

Modrun nodded slowly. "I know."

"I suspected the mushrooms were of Ys. But I am wary. The agents of Ys nearly killed me, and my mother."

"Yes. They have been well concealed, and they came so swiftly, I did not have time to warn you. I protected my son, but he was gravely wounded."

No, not Yvain. "Modrun, tell me how I may make amends. I know your son is precious to you—he is precious to me, as well, a friend from my own childhood."

"The wood will take care of him, and you have returned, have you not, Melic?"

The lion gave a huff, which I interpreted as a glad agreement, and then pressed his shaggy head against Modrun's thigh.

"The ammonite," I said, trying not to look again. "You seem to have no need of a chain."

"No, indeed. I am the last of a long line of sorceresses from the west of Ys, known for our connection to the forests, the waters, and the bargains of nature. Your father invited me to Avillion after the last war in Ys burned our sacred forest to the ground. The priestesses you now know come from the south of Ys, and it is they who now rule."

"My father?"

"Indeed, Leodegraunce of Avillion has made many mistakes, but he has tried, where he can, to also set to rights some of what he has broken. He knew you would need a teacher, once he suspected Ymelda's treachery. And only you could find Queen Tregerna and free her."

I gripped my axe a little tighter. "It frightens me, this power."

"It should," said Modrun. "It is life and death itself. That is why we choose the ammonite as our symbol, the great spiral. A dead creature, beautifully preserved for all time: death endless, beauty in decay. For what greater bargain is there than life and death, what greater connection?"

"They seem a brutal, merciless people."

"I believe some among them can yet be saved. I believe Ys can rise again."

I thought of the twins. One of them was dead, at Gawain's hand. One still remained. Could she ever trust me again? Could any of the Skourr, who had plotted against me and my father, who had opened the door to Prince Ryence, be willing to be start a new life here, with Modrun?

"What would they gain?" I asked. "They have committed to their cause long enough."

"They need someone to give them hope. A champion. They have been abused most of their lives, forced into bargain after bargain, with powers profane and corrupt. They are weary, Hwyfar. You could be that champion."

"I am merely a lost princess," I said.

"Who conquered one of the most powerful priestesses Ys has ever known, and was given the favor of a god," Modrun said, looking down at my armor. I followed her gaze to see the spirals shimmering as if they understood.

That the Green Knight knew gave me some measure of comfort.

"What comes next?" I asked.

"Connection." Modrun looked down at the horn at my side. "Connecting yourself to Avillion and Lyonesse and Ys. A threefold braid of power. The corrupted priestesses of Ys look to delay you and your warriors; do not let them. You carry the horn with you, and it will clear the way. Separate your enemies from the wood, and Brocéliande will no longer fuel their power."

WHEN I REACHED the clearing, first light lit the forest in a blue-green haze, and the sound of clashing swords rang through the wood. Still unaccustomed to running, and struggling with my knee due to my act of selfless love for Gawain—which had better be worth it—I could barely breathe by the time I saw armor glinting through the willows.

The waterfall's mist obscured most of the scene before me, but dread filled me still. It was worse than I expected: the forces of Lyonesse fought against my own knights and Gawain's contingent, the latter controlled by the priestesses of Ys perched upon the rocks. I did not recognize their faces from where I stood, and could see neither Wenna nor Elowyn. I bit back the dread that I would finally learn which still lived.

I climbed the writhing branches of the willow, trying to get a better view above the mist. For a brief moment, I thought I caught a glimpse of Gawain's red hair, but I almost lost my footing and had to focus on gaining ground again. The loss of him, of our connection, sent my stomach into free fall again. I did not know for certain if he was there. I did not know for certain if he lived. For a moment, fear had me in its clutches. I needed to see more clearly.

Then I remembered that I had a plan, that I had *power*.

Touching the great bough of the willow, I found myself again, and blinked back the sweat dripping into my eyes. I gazed down into the waterfall and quaked at the sight: the priestesses I knew from Carelon were floating in the small pool, motionless, eyes wide to the skies, as the elder priestesses cast their strange spells in dazzling arcs of blue and white and red. I recognized Elowyn, face flushed, her eyes vacant, limbs floating around her, hair a black halo about her head. So it had been Wenna who Gawain had killed.

I should have focused more on my footing. My boot caught in one of the branches, and no matter how good my armor might have been, it could not save me from stumbling. I twisted badly, my knee already weakened, and I slipped backward. Panic seared through me and I dropped my axe, hearing it clatter to the rocks below, followed by alarmed shouting from below.

Then the world spun as I tumbled down, grasping at roots and mossy clods of earth, but unable to stop. It occurred to me that I would split my head open on the rocks below, a rather unromantic end, and that Gawain would have to see my pathetic demise. Perhaps it was my pride that awoke my magic, I cannot say.

I did not die, and I did not crash into the water. Though it was not as elegant as a trained priestess of Avillion, still the falls rose to meet me, mists cushioning my descent, so I tumbled in a roaring torrent of water, staggering to a stand on the middle shore where the priestesses of Ys stood casting their spells. I had taken one of them down in my descent, and for good measure I kicked her in the ribs.

Up close, I saw what a wretched ruin these priestesses were: lips deep blue, veins thick and purple against sallow skin, reddened knuckles straining in their movements, hair like worms against their skin. Modrun was right: even their most powerful priestesses were run down to the bone. If I had known them at Withiel, I could not recognize them in this desiccated state.

I only had to blow the horn to send Gawain and the rest back to Avillion. Modrun had explained it well: I could save them, but I would not go with them. I would have to travel the Path back to Avillion on my own. That was how all the priestesses went, and why they were so weary after. They followed behind the travelers, and this particular horn would transport me one way. It would likely not survive a second blast.

CHAPTER FORTY-SIX

GAWAIN

THE CLATTER OF a falling weapon from above drew my attention away from Lanval, who was still caught in a mad trance and intent on slicing every damn sinew in my body. That was always how he liked to fight, and though I knew his weaknesses, I still struggled to get past him. I was stuck on constant defense, too tired to do otherwise. Though my pride would say otherwise, I am certain in the fog and magical twilight around us he made contact more often than not, but his wicked blades turned away from the Green Knight's blessing.

His eyes were wrong, too bright. He looked into me when he saw me, seeing me too fully, as if being used by another as a vessel.

"Come now, old friend," I said to my friend. "Let us dispense with the sparring. I am happy to admit to your superior footwork to Arthur upon our return."

Lanval would have liked that.

This was not Lanval. Not entirely.

He was preparing to come at me again when the waters by the priestesses behind him started rising. I backed up on the shore, already feeling the cold water splashing on my face, but the priestesses were not fast enough for Lanval. He staggered back and was pushed aside by an unexpected tide and out of my way.

There was crashing, a yelp, and I looked up to see Hwyfar—

there she was, falling from the high crest of the falls, and the water rising up to meet her.

Well, she knew how to make an entrance. And thank every damned god above and below.

The falls rose in rippling layers of mist, almost like the petals of a flower, their edges limned in green, and instead of breaking her body on the rocks below, Hwyfar stumbled into one of the priestesses of Ys and gave her a wicked kick.

My heart leapt in my chest, and I fought every instinct in my body to run to Hwyfar, to sweep her up and kiss her, and that cost me.

Lanval gored me in the thigh, piercing my armor. I felt the dagger pop through my muscle, just after that horrendous moment where it caught in my skin before slicing all the way through. Pain lanced up my leg, and with it came a sensation I had welcomed gladly: the bubbling giddiness of battle rage.

I laughed in Lanval's face as my vision prickled with the red and blue embers I knew so well, remembered from my days in the Tournament and on the field. Pain? It no longer mattered. My body went numb save for a burning energy, and I grabbed Lanval by his neck as he came at me, and I threw him aside like a misbehaving puppy.

Bors was harder, though. His head, I mean. And really, every part of him. Just as Lanval went down, Bors came at me, barreling forward like a perturbed ox. Those same fevered eyes, though, delving through me. Not Bors.

The battle shifted, I could feel it, and I tried to see what Hwyfar was doing, but I could not quite find her again.

Bors pressed his attack, and his great axe clanged against the hilt of my own axe, ringing across the wood. I grunted, teeth snapping shut with the force, face flushing with the exertion. Lanval was faster than usual; Bors was certainly stronger.

Water splashed upon my back, soaking my cloak: refreshing, but certainly an ill omen. Then I caught a streak of red hair and a figure dressed in deep blue robes, sodden, tumbling over.

Hwyfar was in a wrestling match with one of the agents of Ys, a Skourr woman and a traitor.

If Bors were not so intent on removing my head from my shoulders, I would have realized sooner who pursued Hwyfar: the other twin from our first encounter in the wood.

No time to waste, I rushed over Bors, surprising him, and then knocked him backward into the pool. My friend Bors, on days not being compelled by deranged priestesses, never would have allowed such a tactic to slow him, but when he hit the water it appeared to confuse him.

I used the moment to jog over to Hwyfar, her mother, and the remaining vicious twin.

Never in my life had I seen anyone fight like that. It put into perspective what I had done to keep Hwyfar safe when we made our escape. Hwyfar was trying to blow the horn, but for all of Queen Tregerna's valiant efforts to get her daughter a moment of peace, the remaining twin was relentless.

Even when the twin saw me, she did not stop in her pursuit of Hwyfar. Surprising, considering I had slain her sister.

Battle rage still sizzling in my chest, I roared into the fray and tried to get between the two of them.

"Elowyn, stop this, now!" Hwyfar was saying. She caught my eye for just a moment, fear and regret flashing for a moment.

I wish it were different.

Just a whisper, but I felt it. I watched as Hwyfar got her footing and tried to bring the horn to her lips, her cheeks flushed and hair wild. She heaved breaths, fingers trembling to keep the horn in place.

Then Elowyn's fist crushed into Hwyfar's jaw, and the horn went flying from her hands, clattering near my feet.

Bors's axe came down over my shoulder, but I twisted to grab hold of the horn just in time to deflect it. Instead of a death blow, I got a crack to the shoulder with the haft, pinning me to the ground. No matter, I had the horn in my hands.

"Gawain, no!"

Hwyfar shouted the words, and perhaps I ought to have heeded her. But the rage was in my blood, and there was no time. Clearly the agents of Ys did not want us to use the horn, and one of my most endearing qualities in life was my tendency to do the precise opposite of what my enemies wished.

I blew the horn and thought immediately of Palomydes, blowing a similar horn, when we fought together up North. That day it did nothing but frighten our enemies, but I could see him, cheeks puffed and eyes wide, hoping for reinforcements.

The sound was clear, low, and bright, and my whole head shook with the strength of it. My ears tickled with the effort.

I felt lighter immediately, but when I opened my eyes to check on Hwyfar, I was utterly alone in a silvery dark nothingness.

CHAPTER FORTY-SEVEN

HWYFAR

THAT OAF BLEW the gods-cursed horn and sent himself to his doom.

Fury and frustration twisted inside of me as I grabbed Elowyn by the middle and tackled her just as I felt the horn's magic seize me, gods knew where, and threw us all forward. It was not like traveling with the priestesses of Lyonesse, who had precision at their side, years of learning and training. Gawain was capable, somehow, of directing the horn—likely latent magic from his mother's side—but we could end up in the middle of the ocean for all I knew.

Nausea rolled over me, sweat prickling my temples and upper lip. Lights dazzled my vision, and I could smell burned cedar. Then I was rolling downward, hay in my mouth and sod on my face, the familiar scent of fermenting apples and thawing earth all around me, wet snow and mud.

Everyone else, it seemed, friend and foe alike, was tumbling down with me. Such a clatter of swords, armor, and bodies as I had never heard before. What a sight we must have been in that early morning mist, tumbling down the hill like errant children running from temple lessons, some still fighting and cursing at one another.

But I knew where we were.

I could smell the fires in the distance, feel the wind in my hair: we were on the far east bank of Withiel, by the gravel moat. It was half built into the stone, and we had appeared on the grassy rolling hill there, perhaps out of one of the caves.

Gawain must have been thinking of Withiel. Home. In Avillion.

From a tactical position, I had to give Gawain credit. The enemy would be approaching from the west and south, as they could not do so from the east: all was caves and rock. We were in good cover. Aside from being bruised, covered in sod, and wet to my bones, so long as we could shake the enemies still struggling to get the better of us, we had made an incredible distance in a shockingly short time.

Without Gawain.

I was sitting on Elowyn, and she was struggling to get at me, but I outweighed her by a considerable amount, and she had twisted her arm badly in the descent.

"Stay down," I said to her, moving to put my knee on the middle of her back. "I have no desire to kill you." As if she were capable of relenting.

But when I looked down at her face, she no longer had that intense, harried expression. And a quick glance over at Sir Kahedin demonstrated the same: he was rubbing his head, dazed. My mother's soldiers were tying up the priestesses, the ones who had been casting and controlling our knights.

"This was not supposed to happen like this," Elowyn said, her voice raspy, words each punctuated with pain.

"No. It never should have, Elowyn. Wenna would still be alive if you had not lost yourselves to Ys. But I do not think you had a choice."

"Ys is all we know." Elowyn's expression was resolute. No apologies; no remorse, either.

Sir Lanval came to aid me in tying up Elowyn, rubbing at his head.

"Queen Regent Hwyfar," he said. "Thank you. I wish I had a more elegant answer for what befell us. But you saved us."

"Gawain and me both." I clasped Sir Lanval's arm. Perhaps later there would be time for more discussion, for redemption. But I could smell fire on the air, and we would need to move soon.

"Princess Hwyfar! Sir Bors! Sir Lanval!"

A voice, clear and welcome, rose from the parapet above us. I looked up to see Palomydes leaning down over us all, bundled in a thick blue cloak, the morning's chill misting about his face.

"Palomydes!" I cried. I had never been so glad to see his face. "How many days are we in the siege now?"

If he found my question strange, he did not show it. "Thus begins our second day," he said. "I see you have a tale to tell, and I do not spy the great Sir Gawain among you. Make haste— we do not have much time. I believe you know your way to the Barrel Gate?"

I nodded. "Yes, indeed," I shouted up to him. "And I will need an audience with my father right away."

Before I turned toward the Barrel Gate, I looked desperately up to the top of the hill, hoping to see a glimpse of Gawain.

The Path was so immense, so vast, even if I could find my way there, I had no way of knowing where he was. He had no training, no concept of what he was doing. But, willingly or not, he had bought us a good amount of time.

"My forces will be arriving by nightfall." My mother's voice startled me from my thoughts as she passed by me. "Perhaps he has found his way to them."

I knew it was a false hope.

THE BARREL GATE was a small grate built down by the gravel moat, barely large enough for a horse cart to go through. It was one of my favorite ways in and out of Withiel as a child, since no one imagined that a princess would dare risk the rats and roaches. But they did not concern me much. The Barrel Gate was once used for wine and provisions, but had fallen out of use during our centuries of peace.

Prisoners in hand, we walked single file through the cobwebs and into what was once an expansive wine cellar.

My mother took my shoulder gently. "Look at me, child."

I was not yet accustomed to a caring mother, let alone

one capable of anticipating my worries and emotions, but I followed her.

"You cannot be thinking of getting him, Hwyfar."

I glanced over at her, pushing aside the remains of a decrepit door. It looked as if Arthur's knights had done a good job of clearing out the place, but they were not aware of all the secrets. There was a quicker way to the dungeons from here, and we needed to get the agents of Ys to a safe location before I figured out what to do with them.

"Not immediately," I said to my mother. I explained to her what Modrun had told me, that when I blew the horn I would be put upon the Path and would have to find my way back.

"Except Gawain has no knowledge of the Path," my mother said.

"No, none at all. And, strong though he is, I am unsure that he can survive such a thing."

"He did use your magic at Lyndesoires."

"When we were *carioz*. And I gave him but a little." I could not let this derail our focus. Withiel. Avillion. My father.

"One step at a time." Queen Tregerna leaned forward and kissed my cheek.

"I did not expect to be here so soon. I am no commander."

"They respect you. You will do fine."

Her encouragement felt like the sun on my face. "Can you spare a few of yours to keep the priestesses secure for a bit? I will send down reinforcements, what I can—I know who to look for. But I am unsure of what I will discover up there."

My mother nodded, looking at the dimly lit corridor before us. "If it is all the same to you, I would prefer to stay here, myself. I left 'up there' a long time ago, and do not wish to make my presence known."

There were tears in her eyes. I understood. She had left Leodegraunce, a friend, and there was too much pain between them now.

CHAPTER FORTY-EIGHT

HWYFAR

I ENTERED THE Great Hall again, with Bors, Kahedin, Lanval, and the guards of Lyonesse in my wake. I had to stifle my shock at how few of the Skourr were left: Skourr Gliten, Skourr Sawena, and Skourr Ahès—the latter blessedly unharmed. We had not come too late, after all. Sir Erec and Sir Branor remained, flanking my father: Leodegraunce sat upon the throne, frail but clear-eyed, draped in yellow and gold, thick furs across his lap. Attending him were also Sir Safir, Sir Palomydes, Sir Gareth, and Sir Morien.

I entered in a rush, ready to tell my father of our arrival, heralding the return of our knights, prepared for battle.

My message of doom was delayed however, by a great cheer, and all those within the halls wearing the colors of Avillion—and indeed the knights of Arthur along with them—all fell to their knees, crying, "Hail, Princess Hwyfar! Hail, Daughter of Avillion!"

My whole world swam before my eyes as my father slowly descended the dais, helped by Sir Erec.

Who did he see, I wondered? I had hay in my hair, my braids had become undone. I wore armor made by the hand of a creature I was half-convinced was a god. Gareth looked at me with a mixture of awe and utter devastation. I wore my mother's longsword, and my knights met joyfully with their brothers.

I could not see our *goursez*, Kian. I could not see *anything* for tears, but I could feel my father's warm hands on my face.

"There she is," he said, looking me straight in the eyes. "Hwyfar has come home at last."

"Why are they still cheering me?" I asked him, leaning to his ear as he embraced me.

"You bring them hope, daughter. More than I ever could. I was blind in my pride, and it brought me here. You are their future."

"But I have failed. I came too late to warn you. I should have recognized you were poisoned, that you did not scorn me as much as I scorned myself."

"We have both failed. But perhaps, together, our failures will turn this tide."

RYENCE'S ARMY HAD not advanced, I learned, because he had requested a parley the night before. We had arrived at daybreak, and so there were still a few hours of peace before Avillion shook again. As I walked the halls with my father and our knights, I saw proof of the siege everywhere: men and women bloodied and injured lay strewn in makeshift infirmaries, local townsfolk banding together to seek shelter with burn marks on their faces and clothing, chunks of Withiel crumbled from incendiary fire. It was an old castle, and not used to withstanding such an onslaught, and with so few of the Skourr left to keep it protected.

Priestesses, who normally kept to their own in the keep, skittered about in their pale red veils, delivering healing supplies to rooms on silent, slippered feet.

The Boar Room's walls were cracked, the table covered in a thin layer of dust, and it seemed so much smaller than it had been even a few weeks ago.

We assembled a very small group to listen to my tale: just King Leodegraunce, Skourr Ahès, Sir Gareth, Sir Eric, Sir Palomydes, Sir Kahedin, Sir Lionel and Sir Branor. I did not relay every detail, especially about Gawain and my connection, and of

Queen Tregerna's current location—but of the infiltration of the agents of Ys, and my connection to the three lines of magic, that was essential.

"If I could have made it back sooner, I would have," I said, turning to Skourr Ahès. "You saw the signs."

She gave me an understanding look, folding her hands together on the table. "The rot was deep. Even I could not see what was happening in full. But I believe we had an advantage because you came to me. The uprising was clumsy, and I was able to slowly get the King restored to health with Kian's help."

"Where is Kian now?" I asked, dread uncoiling. In my vision of the future, he had died, and Ahès had been wounded—but she was very much alive.

"Lost to us," said King Leodegraunce. "He fought valiantly and saved Skourr Ahès from being abducted, but we could not save him. He has been taken."

I buried my head in my hands. "Do you think he yet lives?"

King Leodegraunce leaned back in his chair. It was the one I had been in, with my feet up on the table, just a few weeks before, when they had asked me to be Queen Regent. "If he does not, we will bring his body home, and his death will lie heavy on my heart. Our enemies' treachery was deliberate and long in planning. I was being poisoned and manipulated. The orchards had a blight. But Hwyfar, you return to us new made. *Reforged*, I should say, in armor such as stories tell of. With new eyes, I believe, to see the world anew. That, our enemies do not yet realize. And it gives me great comfort. And hope."

"Yes," I said, and that was just the half of it. The woman I had been felt like a stranger to me. "I am prepared to fight for Avillion."

Gareth, who had been near-silent the whole time, finally spoke. "And my brother? We simply move on while he is what— lost? I still do not understand where you left him."

"I did not *leave* him, Sir Gareth," I said, fighting the urge for a more casual address. "He chose to use the horn."

Gareth scoffed. "I do not see how Gawain would have ever *chosen* to put his life at risk for this. No matter your connection. He is a man of brawn and tactics, not of risk and magic."

"Be that as it may, I would not be here if not for his sacrifice," I said. What if I never saw him again? What if he was truly lost to me? I bit back my fear, masking myself in the raiment of a queen. "I did not ask it. I do not think he knew the price, but you know as well as I do that once he turns his mind to something, there is little persuading him otherwise."

"You speak so comfortably of him," said Gareth, a sharpness to his voice I did not like one bit. He was badly bruised along one side of his face, and I knew without asking that he had endured many an injury on the behalf of Avillion these last days.

"We have endured many hardships together, Sir Gareth, and I hope you forgive me my digression. I can never repay the debt I owe your brother. I still have hope I can find him," I said. "But I am so weary—we have been half starved and fighting for our lives. But I promise you, I will shake the foundation of the earth to find Gawain when Avillion is safe. And if we are blessed, and he is wise, we shall have word sooner than later."

This satisfied Gareth for the time being, and he gave me a solemn nod. "Then I will fight for you, and my men with me."

Swallowing back tears I looked around at the faces gathered near me. I ought to be brave, to show them I was strong. "For Avillion and for Gawain."

No, I would no longer pretend. I was not strong. I had managed this whole tale without weeping, and I had spent my entire life carefully crafting my performances. And I was too tired to keep it up.

So I wept before them, covering my face with my hands, still dirty with black sod, nails broken and bleeding.

Gareth did not apologize, and no one coddled me, but the room's feeling changed. I had changed. Gawain had changed me. The Green Knight had changed me. I suppose Ymelda had changed me, too.

Skourr Ahès was the first to speak. "Avillion is more than a cluster of old buildings on an Isle, Your Highness," she said to me. "Just as you are more than a prodigal princess. Have faith. We have endured thus far, and you have returned to us with reinforcements we thought lost forever."

"Well said, Skourr Ahès," said King Leodegraunce, reaching across to me to take my hand. He dabbed at my bleeding thumb with his handkerchief, the same hue as the gown I had torn to braid into Gawain's hair. "For now, you need to rest."

"Prince Ryence will be expecting a performance, I suspect," said Sir Palomydes, tapping the table with one of his rings. "He will not anticipate you being here, but none of us want to push you, either."

"Hwyfar, my daughter," said King Leodegraunce, squeezing my hand again. "This is your choice. War will come to Avillion no matter the result, I believe that."

I groaned into my palm. "I fear the moment I see Prince Ryence I will gouge his eyes out."

"As I said, war one way or another," said my father, laughing in a light way I had not heard since I was a child. I wondered how long he had been being poisoned. "But I cannot deny, I would be mightily entertained to see such a thing."

After I departed the Boar Room, I requested no attendants in my chambers, drew my own bath, and then waited for the inevitable: my father's visit.

My room had been cleaned and was back to its staid familiarity, and my clothes had been laundered and mended since my departure. Someone had rid my room of all the odd bottles and potions, but replaced them with a selection of small books of poetry, mostly songs, collected from around the countryside. I wondered if it was a hobby of his. The scribe's hand looked familiar.

And then I realized. They were Kian's.

I heard my father's tentative voice on the other side of my narrow door and went to welcome him into my small antechamber. Withiel, for all its magic, had none of the glamor of Lyndesoires, and the rustic angles made it difficult to navigate the small tower space. Only my father's quarters could be called kingly in any way.

He looked so very old, his thick velvet tunic falling over his wasted body, the bulk of his cloak oddly padded at his shoulders. Once, he had been a massive man, heralded as the Boar of Avillion. Now, we saw eye to eye, and his hands trembled on his staff.

Bringing one of my chairs to him, and a fur coverlet, I dismissed his guard and gave them instructions to wait outside.

"We do have more spacious rooms, you know," my father said, looking around my room. "The Queen's Tier is yours."

"Yes, but this is where I belong," I said, taking a seat beside him. "And without Gweyn here with me, it feels practically cavernous."

"The whole world feels cavernous without Gweyn here," he said, taking my hand again. He kept doing that.

I tried to breathe evenly, to avoid weeping again. My whole face felt raw from it. "Before, you did not seem so affected. You did not write when she died."

"The priestesses of Ys crafted a very clever potion. By the time Gweyn died, I could no longer grieve. I was lost. Much like your mother, it sounds like. Just a different kind of prison."

"How did you manage to turn out the Skourr?" I had not asked the question, but I knew it had to have happened. I suspected Palomydes, Gareth, and the rest had something to do with it.

My father closed his eyes. "Skourr Gliten and Skourr Ahès had been working to slowly subvert our infiltrators, and they used our new guests to help tease out the poison. But when they heard word of your disappearance, they had to flush them out fast. Sir Gareth and Palomydes fought valiantly for us, but Sir Morien was gravely wounded. The next morning, Prince Ryence's troops arrived—which we had wind of not long after your departure."

"I trusted too easily," I said.

"Such is the curse of peace," said King Leodegraunce.

I stared down at our intertwined hands. We had the same fingers, though mine were slightly more delicate, the skin smoother.

"I sense you wish to ask me something," he said.

"I need to rest, but I fear I cannot until I ask you if you knew—about the Sundering."

He licked his lips, then frowned. "I believed it would spare you from pain later in your marriage to Arthur. Without your mother to assist in the decision, I turned to the Skourr for assistance, and they were split on this suggestion, a technique from Ys. They argued that it would cause you great distress—you and your sister—to live in Carelon, and still feel the call of the Isle. Vyvian was imprisoned, Igraine was gone. Morgen was never quite a child of this place. And so I went against my better judgement, and I allowed it."

I could not look at him, even though I knew the truth already. Hearing him say it in such a way, so measured and sane, settled in my bones.

"It should have been my choice." I could barely whisper the words.

"I know, and there is nothing I can do to make up for it," continued the king. "But I know Avillion can never truly be taken from you. You said it yourself: you commanded the waters in the wood just yesterday, the most holy of all Avillion's gifts—and heeded the call of the Horn of Lyonne, and now bring with you Modrun's protection. I will do all in my power to give you what you need to find your heart's desire."

"I cannot have my heart's desire," I said softly to him, letting go of his hand. "But for now, I shall settle for an Avillion free of tyranny."

CHAPTER FORTY-NINE

GAWAIN

I WALKED FORWARD in the dark, feeling my way forward by following currents of cooler air and the fresh scent of pine. The ground was fine sand, but I never came across a hint of vegetation, structure, or stone. There was just the relentless night, the air, and me.

Though I had tried calling out, my voice was swallowed, muffled. No echoes. Like I was shouting inside a giant stocking. I kept remembering the look on Hwyfar's face when I took the horn, the disappointment and the irritation, the fear. So lovely. Even when she was watching me make tremendously dubious choices.

I really was an idiot.

Perhaps I would soon be a dead idiot.

I was slowly freezing to death. Could feel my fingers crackling from the end inward. Well and truly lost.

"Gawain. You have been walking in circles for an hour."

I turned around, startled by the voice, to see the outline of a doorway limned in light, and a figure standing before it. Warm firelight poured into the lifeless world I had fallen into, making me squint, but I could recognize that silhouette anywhere.

My mother had not changed so much since I was a child, and she had a habit of lingering in doorways.

What she was doing here, that was the question.

"Mother?" I asked.

She opened the door a little wider. "Come in, please. I was hoping you had an ounce of intuition in you, but clearly all my hopes are lost on you, and you will die of exposure otherwise. Though, I am not entirely unhappy to see you have some gifts of magic still lingering through your watered down blood."

I had no idea what that meant, but I did as I was asked, and shuffled through the door behind her, blinking and shivering as the temperature shifted.

My mother was right. When I looked down at my hands they were tipped with frost, the skin purpling with cold. The horn still clutched in my fingers in my right hand, ice connected the two. Shivering, I looked around her familiar apartment in Carelon, confused but relieved, as she handed me a thick fur coverlet and settled me onto an appropriately sized chair. With three sons like us, her apartment was one I could always fit right in.

"How did I get here?" I asked her.

Anna Pendragon—Lady Anna du Lac, by marriage but not by spirit—sat down across from me, her face set in that impenetrable way I knew meant an impending lecture. It did not come yet.

"You were with Hwyfar of Avillion," she said at last.

"I have been," I said. Because it was true. Regardless of how she meant the statement. "Until very recently."

"That horn is an artifact of Lyonesse," said my mother evenly. "Lost to the ages."

"Is it?"

"I read a great deal these days," she replied smoothly. "And the powers of Lyonesse lie in travel, movement. The uninitiated"—this she said with a very pointed glance at me—"ought to perish, or go mad, or become forever lost when utilizing their power. Unless they hold some spark of magic within themselves."

I looked at her, awaiting more of an explanation. "You did find me out there. And someone I recently met told me you were a witch."

To my surprise, she looked almost amused. "Did she?"

"I denied it, of course. But your sisters, and great-grandmother—well, I might be an Orkney and a Pendragon, but there's a bit of Avillion in there, still."

"And perhaps that is why you are still alive, my son."

"Though that is no explanation for how you found me."

My mother leaned forward, the wheel-shaped necklace at her collar glinting in the light. "Ah, no. That is no explanation indeed. All you need to know is that where you were, that place, is familiar to me, and I know who travels it. Hwyfar visited me not long ago. But she was more attuned to those paths. I thought, perhaps, as my son, you might have some predilection to this kind of work, but no."

She was genuinely disappointed in my lack of skill, but she was my mother—this was not uncharted territory.

"So you knew I was there," I said.

"Yes."

"And you watched me amble around for an hour."

"It was more than an hour, outside of time. But yes. I was hopeful."

I looked behind me, where I half expected a door to still stand, out into the dark world of sand and shadow; but there was just a silver mirror, and my terrible looking face. The man in the reflection was bruised, scarred, bright red, and weary. I had never seen such hollows under my eyes, such ruddiness in my skin.

"I need to get back to Avillion," I said, trying to stand. My knee buckled, though, and I shouted out in pain.

My mother did nothing but watch. Always a keen observer, and so full of compassion, Anna Pendragon. "Your knee still troubles you."

"It always will," I said. "But that is no matter. Avillion is under attack."

"I know," she said softly, and for the first time I sensed she was truly concerned about the situation.

"You know? And—does my uncle know?"

My mother sniffed the air as if a dog had just taken a particularly foul shit. "Queen Mawra is apprised of the situation. But it is delicate. Leodegraunce's madness has been unpredictable, and allowed the agents of Ys to penetrate deep within the Skourr. To say nothing of Hwyfar's utter disregard for her own inheritance. Prince Ryence has a compelling claim, and Arthur is hesitant to throw his full strength behind an uncertain future—especially when there is rumor that Hwyfar now seeks to claim the throne as her own."

"She's an errant princess who just wants to go back to charming her way through the next court, once Avillion is secured," I said, trying to affect all the arrogance of a disinherited prince who once thought Hwyfar a spoiled, indulgent princess. "You have nothing to concern yourself with on that account."

"Don't I?"

I swallowed. "She has no desire for the crown of Avillion."

"I hardly think you are a good judge of the situation. You love her, Gawain. You love her to your very marrow. It's as plain as the color of your hair."

I was now the color of my hair, I was certain. So much for my own performance. Without Hwyfar, I was back to a ruined old soldier, mule-headed and too easily cowed.

"I owe her my honor," I said. "She saved my life."

"You are a prince, if only by birth," said my mother. "You do not need to live by such a code. Your uncle certainly does not. I can open the door to the hall over there, and you can simply re-enter life at Carelon as you are meant to."

"Gareth is still in Avillion, Mother. And Palomydes. And the rest."

"Yes, and they will be home soon enough. Their king will not desert them. He never intended to."

"Arthur has forces waiting, doesn't he? Waiting to see how the tide turns? He knew all along?" Rage rose in me, and I grabbed the chair arms, waiting to hear the wood crack as I squeezed. But nothing happened.

My mother gave me a pitying glance. "You are not quite *here* yet. I have not yet let you in. 'Tis part of the magic. The blankets work because you are still air—but not enough air. Morgen tried to explain it to me once, but I admit I was not entirely listening. She does love to go on."

"Please, Mother," I begged.

"Gawain, what are you asking me to do?"

"I—I hardly know what to ask. Until now, I never..." I watched her, tried to think back to my life, our time together, to imagine all those times I had tried to find her, only to be denied entry, to be brushed aside, to find her missing. "I suppose I do not know you as well as I think."

Her smile was more than a little wicked. "Few do. You are not the first man to underestimate me. Nor will you be the last. But you are my son, and my firstborn, and so I am willing to entertain you, now that I have plucked you from certain doom. That, I will give you for free. My interference, however, if I agree to it, will come at a price."

"Anything," I said.

"Ah. Child. Be careful."

Child.

I breathed deep, even. "Send me back to Withiel. Tell me what I can do to help sway Arthur to Leodegraunce's side. Help me save Hwyfar."

"Hwyfar does not need saving, but her kingdom does. You are both on borrowed time. And I cannot sway Arthur. You give me far too much credit." My mother stood in a smooth motion, her silks rustling after her. She went to the hearth and rested her hand on her hip as she stared into the fire. "It would be safer for you to remain here."

"You'd have me be a coward."

"I'd have you use your brain instead of your prick for once," she said, massaging her temple.

Gods, but I wanted to rip the whole world apart, sitting there, enduring her. There was a reason that I used to drink more:

spending time around my mother drove me to it, surely as a fox turned back to the coop. I found the less time I spent around her, the less I needed it. Even now, the idea of finding some ale was more appealing than it had been in years. It blunted the sting of her words, her judgement, her godsdamned imperious glare.

I wanted to tell her what I had endured. That I had been tied to a woman—a person—in a way that felt closer, and more real, than anything I had ever felt in my life. That I had held her in my arms and experienced her emotions, her sensations, as truly as my own. That we had connected across vast distances for years and not known it… and that we had given it up, we had severed it, and done so together with a god at our backs, to save a life and restore a kingdom.

Only to fall into the ruin of another.

But my mother was not a sentimental woman. She had lived a life that made her hard in ways that I would never know and she would never tell. And, in spite of all, she had helped shape me into a good person—a better man than I should have been, given my father.

"I can send you back to Withiel, but you must promise me that you will marry whoever Arthur chooses for you when you return," my mother said to me, turning to look my way. In the light of the flames, she looked like a hearth goddess come to life, the graying streaks of her hair kindling gold. "You must return to Carelon as soon as it is done."

There were long years ahead of me, but not on the battlefield. Not even with Hwyfar's gift. Try as I might, my men could not rely on me: not on a horse, and not on foot. I knew all those things. But until my own mother spelled it out now, a part of me had still not accepted it.

My love… Woe that we had only these days—but joy that we had them at all.

I will not run from my duty, and you will not falter in yours.

I thought I had known what those words meant. But as I stared over at the ghostly form of my mother, I understood how words held so many meanings, and how women, in particular, seemed to delight in that kind of magic, in the flexibility and fluidity of language. I suppose they needed it.

"You have my word," I said to my mother. "Tell me what I need to do, and send me what aid you can. And I will consent to whatever match Arthur deems right for me."

My mother nodded. "Good. I will speak to your aunt Vyvian promptly. When you are ready, I will show you the way back through the gate."

I glanced at the mirror behind me. "Why do you call a mirror a gate?"

She laughed, a cold, amused kind of chuckle. "Oh, well, I shall share one more minor secret. It is not the mirror that holds the power, Gawain. It is the frame. Men pass by our mirrors, calling them instruments of our vanity. In fury they may break the glass, but they do not think to destroy the framework. So survives women's magic: in plain sight."

CHAPTER FIFTY

HWYFAR

I WAS AWOKEN from deep sleep by the smell of fresh Braids of Una. For the briefest of moments, I forgot all that I had endured in the last weeks and was again a young priestess rising in the early morning, prepared for another day at Withiel. Except that my knee seized in pain the moment I turned in bed, and my neck twinged, and the very real bruises down my back from falling into the waterfall basin and tumbling down the hillside throbbed in response.

Blearily, I detached myself from the thick layers of blankets and searched the room for the source of the smell.

"Still hot if you find yourself hungry," said Gawain. The big oaf was sitting on the chest across from my bed, mouth full of bread, as comfortable as if he lived there.

He was very real, and very pleased with himself. Also sporting a bruise on his cheek, and dried blood down his leg.

"You!"

"Me," he said, standing with a bit of a grunt, and handing me the horn. It was a bit worse for wear, but otherwise unharmed. "Hope you do not find that so disappointing."

"How?"

"May I?" Gawain gave a longing glance at the spot beside me in bed, still warm.

I nodded, and he lowered himself down to sit, the bed frame groaning in protest.

"Blowing the horn was not the wisest choice," he said. He had another piece of bread, and this he offered me. I snatched it from him. "Everything hurts."

"No. It was positively idiotic. You could have—*should* have—died."

"I appreciate your concern. But I live."

"Clearly. I suppose you're going to tell me you survived by wit and instinct." I knew Gawain capable of many things, but this was dubious at best.

"Not precisely."

"You could have died, Gawain. You had no idea what you were doing."

"That isn't true at all. I knew I was getting you to safety. I knew we were disrupting those priestesses, which would stop my knights from tearing you to shreds."

"Gawain…"

"Besides, there is no point in belaboring what did not happen. I found my way back here, regardless."

Cleverness really was not his strongest quality. "Your mother found you, didn't she?"

If he was planning to deny it, the words failed quickly. "…Yes. But I came straight back to you."

"You ought to have stayed in Carelon—I suspect she gave you that choice."

He looked wounded. "How do you figure these things out?"

"I am incredibly clever. Which has naught to do with my current plight. Gawain, Prince Ryence will be here in three hours," I said, not knowing what was worse: having Gawain here, or not having him at all. Three hours was all we had left. Had he come straight to my room? Had anyone seen him? "He wants to parley with us."

"We will win this, Hwyfar. Avillion will not fall," he said, with such conviction, such fire in his green eyes, that I almost believed him. "If anyone can broker peace without bloodshed, it's you. And if anyone can help rip that maggot-faced prick apart with a minimal, exhausted force, it's me."

"And then we are finished."

Gawain gave me a concerned look. "Hwyfar. We can continue in secret, we can—"

"I cannot marry a man I do not love. So I have decided to take the Vow of Passage," I said, looking down at my hands.

"What?"

"It is what priestesses do, to remove themselves from consideration for marriage, protecting highborn women and allowing them to pursue magic. While my father rules, if the Isle is saved, I can call myself a Priestesses of Passage, as did Morgen, and Vyvian. I have the magic to show for it, and as such I am out of the reach of the king. But I renounce my claim on the crown, and all ties to the throne."

"I have no such option, Hwyfar."

"But at least I will not be forced to bed a man on Arthur's command, to carry his children. I could not bear it. So, if Arthur presses, I will take the Vow of Passage." I looked over at him. "Then you can move on."

"I will do no such thing. I will still love you," Gawain said, taking my hand, and kissing my knuckles, as if I were the fairest, purest princess, his chapped lips grazing my skin with a courtier's delicacy.

I pulled his hand to my cheek, stroking his fingers, allowing myself the indulgence of his touch for what would be the last time. "I wish I had to the courage to let you go."

He straightened, and then turned my face to his. "Hwyfar, you have it wrong. You had *all the courage,* and all the heart. And on top of that, you performed a miracle: you took away my pain."

"Just some of it," I muttered.

"*Hwyfar.*"

"I could not bear the thought of you in pain forever," I said, the words cracking me apart. It had felt bearable before, when he had been gone. "I only replaced one pain for another. I do not know how to endure this alone."

"You are more than us," he said softly, kissing my forehead. "You always will be. The future is not written. Right now, I am yours if you have me, more than I shall ever be another's, decree or no."

How he could manage such sage words, and yet still have crumbs all over his armor—his precious, sacred Green Knight armor—I could not say. Gawain of Orkney was a man of contrasts. And I had never loved anyone as I loved him, even bereft of our *carioz* bond. Inexplicably, as I stared at him, our hands entwined, I loved him *more*. Without that magical connection, those brilliant braids connecting us to one another, we had to work harder for each word of comfort, each admission of fear, each moment of vulnerability.

"I am tired of being alone," I said, my voice a whisper. "And I am afraid of my future in that solitude."

Gawain's gentle fingers found my neck, the tense muscles there, and my skin responded in a frisson that raised the hair on my arms.

"Right now, you are not alone," he said, low and wild, daring. He encircled me with his arms, pulling me tight to him. "Make it count. Or have you forgotten how?"

Inside me, the challenge rose like a flame.

CHAPTER FIFTY-ONE

GAWAIN

GODS, HER EYES. Sun-caught amber, when awoken. *Carioz* or no, I knew how to move her.

We had not come together since we had been Sundered. I knew she had been avoiding it; but I knew, too, that we may never have a chance again. For all my words of bravery, the next few days were not guaranteed. And if I was to be sent out to pasture, and Hwyfar was to stay in Avillion—or become a lifelong priestess—the chances of us ever feeling our bodies mingle again were minute.

But this... this was different. I cannot explain other than to say that I felt it, the possibility of this part of her, on the edge of my thought, since the moment I crossed into her room, like a voice in the next room, calling to me. I could choose to awaken it—I could choose to give myself to her in this way. I suppose I always knew that I would be the one to give her this power, that she had sought such surrender and never yet found it.

When she kissed me, this time, it was to claim me. And when I kissed her back, it was a promise. Hwyfar rose over me, her long legs wrapping behind my back, and her lips and tongue and teeth, her hands and nails, her breath—gods, the sheer surety in that single kiss sent my body spiraling toward release. And she knew, and she pressed down on me, and she reveled in that knowledge.

Hwyfar pulled away for a moment, lifting her head, as she ran her tongue over her lips. "You had the honey along with the bread."

I nodded dumbly. "It came with a most glowing recommendation."

She leaned forward, licking at the corner of my mouth. Then she said: "Take off your armor."

I complied, not because I wanted to—though I did—but because she commanded it. My blood itself understood the call and response of the power, perhaps down into the roots of Avillion itself. This holiest of places *sang* with my heartbeat, moved with Hwyfar's breath.

Never has magic felt as thick as in that moment, in that space.

We were in a room, but we were elsewhere. Just as we had traveled together to free Queen Tregerna from Ymelda's parasitic grasp on the Green Knight, here magic began to sing through us both.

Standing, I pulled off the magical armor, bit by bit, until I stood naked in the middle of her small tower room. Hwyfar walked about me in a circle, watching with her glittering eyes. Under that gaze, I had never felt more desired, nor more perfectly made. I did not think of my scars, of my swollen knee and my thick middle. Nor did I worry about the blood still caked under my nails, the days' worth of sweat on my body. Perhaps it mattered not when magic was involved. It was not my power—I knew I was a vessel, a channel for our oath.

Hwyfar was still clothed in her long silk gown, blue as periwinkle, and I watched the outline of her body strain against the thin material. And oh, I wanted her. I wanted to be that silk, wanted to cling against her skin, damp and supple, warmed against her heat. Desire rose in me, unrelenting.

"You were given to me, and I was given to you, by powers greater than any that rule the earth," said Hwyfar, and I heard a ripping sound, bringing me out of my silken dreams. "We were tied to one another, through bonds stronger than those of blood and duty."

Then she was tearing long strips of her bright blue gown, determination in her features. When the work was going too slowly, she grabbed her dagger—the very dagger that had been lodged in my hand at Lyndesoires—and began cutting in earnest. She did not ask for help, and I did not give it. When she cut her own hand, blood spotting the cloth, I only heard her breathe in sharply, but the thick scent of magic flared all the same.

I waited, watching, the edges of the room softly glowing, until she was naked before me, tearstained and magnificent. Her muscles stood out more now on her thighs, her arms, but she still had a softness to her belly and buttocks that stirred me beyond all else. I wanted to taste her again, to get between her legs and drink her in. I trailed my fingers down her stomach, slipping a finger between the velvet folds of her sex, and found her ready for me. I groaned, needing her around me more than ever.

She knew, but she had other plans first.

Hwyfar handed me the ends of the long strips of silk, three of them. Without needing to ask, I began braiding, until we each had long ropes of braided blue cord, the fabric catching the growing light in the room, which seemed to emanate from the stones themselves.

"Come to me, love," she said.

The pain in her voice, gods, it sliced through me.

I wrapped around her, and she around me, our skin meeting at last in entirety. The braided rope fell to the ground, and we held one another, bodies flush. The press of her heavy breasts against my chest, her silken skin slipping across mine, I could marvel in the way we fit together all my days and never tire of it.

So entranced with the sensation of her, new for our lack of *carioz*, that I did not see the dagger still in her hand. She sliced across her own braid, just at her neck, severing it so easily it could only have been assisted by magic. All the length of her hair fell to the ground.

"Hwyfar..."

"Reforged," she whispered. "We make what we cannot have."

I held out my hand, and she paused, then slowly handed me the dagger. My hair still held the small scrap of green cloth, her favor. No matter, we would both contribute. I branded her lips in a kiss and then, in a moment, my own braid lay along with hers upon the floor.

CHAPTER FIFTY-TWO

HWYFAR

THIS POWER WAS born of passion, and yet it was born of sorrow, too. I could feel the charge of it, running up through the stones of Withiel itself, ancient and knowing, as solid as Gawain felt when he surrounded me in my weakest moments—as I had felt in my alcove as a child, when I hid to find quiet and escape from castle life. Perhaps it had whispered to me then; perhaps it whispered to me now.

I let the wild power call to me, and Gawain opened himself to me. I could feel him, a great channel of strength.

No, I would not rebuild our *carioz*, but together we could make a vow that would shake the foundations of Avillion. We would claim it now, and perhaps, it could reverberate into the future.

Before our Sundering, I knew the fluttering and spirals of his passion, but now I had to depend on his breath, his movements. I watched his eyes, the half-lidded responses to my touch; I felt the flesh prickle on his arm when I raked my nails down his back, listened to the rumble in his chest when I bit at his neck. I was so much more aware of him without our connection.

His hair, shorn clumsily from the dagger, sprung back in tight curls, and I ran my fingers through it, eliciting the most pleased purr from him.

"I am yours," he said to me, as I dropped one hand down,

dipping to the rise of his stomach and the length of him. "Gods, Hwyfar, you have saved me."

I reveled in the feeling of him, the tenderness in his voice. I doubted anyone in all the realms knew this man as I did, knew his gentleness and his rage, his humor and his fears. I had known them so long, longer than I had ever realized.

"We saved each other," I said, taking his hand, and sliding it up my thigh.

The response of his arm muscles, so unfathomably strong, as he hooked my leg up and over his elbow, turned my core to molten honey. I reveled in the ease of his strength, how effortless it was, remembering the few moments it had been granted to me.

My power, that strange, unbridled part of me I did not yet understand, swirled around us as it once had in Lyonesse, when I had saved him from the poisoned dagger. But now it was a kinder wind, and I knew how to command it to draw us closer, helping just a little to take away the stress from his knee, and from mine, as well. Our shared pain.

Gawain's other arm pulled tight at my waist, and he buried his head in my shoulder as he entered me, and I gasped in surprise as magic entwined with the sensations of our bodies connecting. But I did not flinch, and he did not relent; the magic between us, spiraling, unrelenting, a maelstrom of power neither of us truly understood but to which we both surrendered.

All became the rhythm of our bodies, the slickness of sweat, the desperate need to take more from each other, delve deeper, taste more fully. My body arched, aching and sweet, a curved line as he now held me up, and I wrapped around him. Where I'd cut myself before throbbed in pain and yet it did not detract from my passion, but fueled it.

It would never be enough, but I would try.

The joy of it was blinding, maddening, lost to the power of sensation, all that remained was my own pleasure, Gawain's wild response, and it obliterated all other thought. All but the magic.

I slowed the pace, moving so I was turned away from him, feeling the cool air at my back where my hair had once tumbled in long waves. Gawain ran his callused hands across my shoulders, the roughness at odds with the tenderness of his touch. He stroked my spine, my ribs, pausing in our frenzy to just absorb what he saw. I did not have to see him to know what he was thinking.

He was worshipping me, taking in all he could before we could no longer, fingers pressing deeply inside of me just to hear me moan his name. I did not need to turn around to know he was smiling.

In all my conquests, I had never been loved so completely, nor had I ever loved back so well in return. It was never the quantity of it, never even the having. Besides Arthur, I had never been rejected, never scorned—those I had sought had shared my bed time and again. In my youth, I had seen Gawain, found him intriguing, but shied from him. I supposed because I knew. Somehow, I knew this waited for me. And I was not yet prepared.

We loved well, we loved through tears. We loved tenderly and together, in power and in passion, and as we rose to the heights of pleasure, the braided ropes rose, alight with magic of ancient power, and began wrapping about us.

It did not seem strange, then. We turned to look at each other, to clasp closer, breath ragged, bodies trembling. He moved in me, and I sank down around him, and the castle tower room shifted with the force of our treason.

In Avillion, and in Carelon still, marriage meant the tying of a braided cord around the promised couple. It was a shred of an ancient ceremony, now polluted with dowries and politics and social alliances.

Clutching each other, gasping in the last throes of love, we bound ourselves in that power, the silk ropes and our own braids sacrificed to seal our promise. There were no words, no oaths—the language of our bodies, of our magic, was enough.

Tiny lights, like enormous fireflies, rose from the floor as we sank to the bed, entwined, gazing at one another. The silk and hair had wound over our right wrists in intricate cuffs, five-stranded braids, like in the great scrolls and books I had seen in Carelon's library. A gift from some unseen patron, a force aware of the incoming storm, the impending loss.

Gawain held me close. "By all the gods, Hwyfar. No one can take this from us," he said, kissing my shoulder. I could hear the tears in his voice.

My heart ached, my body fuzzy with the expiration of magic, but I was not defeated as I had suspected I would be.

He was right.

I turned my head up to meet his green-eyed gaze, kissing him deeply. "I love you."

The lopsided smile he gave me, almost shy, was more than I could ever ask for. "I saw," he replied. "None could ever compare."

"No. None before, and none after."

"Until our bones are ash."

Pulling away, I inspected his hair. "I will need to tidy that for you, or the whole keep will talk."

"To say nothing of yours," Gawain said, taking a lock of my hair between his fingers. "But I rather like it."

He looked deep into my eyes, waiting to speak. In that moment, I felt the passing of a lifetime. It was no small burden, no small ask of him. I was used to performances, and I did not have blood brothers and brothers-in-arms to persuade.

"This is my oath to you, and your oath to me." Gawain's voice was firm, his gaze unwavering. "I will not falter."

CHAPTER FIFTY-THREE

GAWAIN

WE CAME TOGETHER twice more after our binding, slow and careful once and wildly against the wall another time, but I needed to find my brothers-in-arms—and my brother—before we met with Ryence. Neither Hwyfar nor I could bear risking their lives for our passion. We knew, from the beginning, that our days were stolen, and perhaps these hours were the most illicit of them all.

When we were at last spent, we began planning the final stage of this great quest. She combed my hair, put perfumed oils on my body, and gave me the foul dagger of Lyonesse, forged during Tregerna's imprisonment, knowing it could incapacitate me, wanting no one else to hold it.

"Take it," she said, pressing the cruel weapon into my hands. "May it protect you if you find another foul wielder of magic."

If our magic and lovemaking disturbed the castle, none seemed to note. Hwyfar sent guards for more food, and painfully, impossibly, I was able to make my exit along the servants' corridor, well-cloaked. I kept feeling my wrists for the bracers we had woven; they were so light it was easy to forget they were there, and they warmed to my skin. But each time, I was rewarded by the intricate braids just beneath my tunic. As to my armor, I carried that tied to my back.

My muscles trembling from exertion and stress, I still made my way down to the barracks. As I expected, I spotted Gareth there, along with Bors, Palomydes, Lionel, Safir, Lanval, and the rest, running their afternoon drills.

There were enough soldiers about that even I, in my state and stature, did not stand out immediately in the rush. War was on the wind. I knew the smell of it, the anxiety in the air, better than almost anyone.

I should have known Gareth would spot me, though.

The sound of his voice broke through the afternoon din, and within moments, he was crushing me, muffled tears against my shoulder. I didn't even have time to get a good look at him before Palomydes showed up, shouting my name, and then came the rest. I suppose they had assumed me dead, but I had not expected such fanfare, so many tearful smiles.

Gareth sported a fearsome wound across his brow, and there was a weariness in his face I had never wished to see in my younger brother. Unlike me, he and Gaheris had been spared much of the horrors of war; they were young enough to have lived through Arthur's peaceful years, and close enough to the king not to have to go out on the smaller campaigns. But Prince Ryence had come well-equipped, with the element of surprise, and it had shaken them. To have lost half our men, and to think me gone, had taken its toll on my Gareth.

"We have our giants again," said Bors, hitting me on my back so my armor rattled. "You must tell us of your adventures."

"How was it that you were separated from the Queen Regent—er, from Princess Hwyfar?" Safir, like the rest, was still attempting to make sense of the quickly changing situation.

"Were you truly in Lyonesse?" Lionel asked.

Lanval stroked his beard and shook his head. "There must be some tale behind those shorn locks."

"There will be time for my brother to regale us with his adventures," said Gareth, taking me about the arm. "But you can clearly see, the man needs a bit of rest. Our enemy is due within the hour, and Gawain must look the part of a prince. For we would give him a show, as Orkneys united."

The words were pretty enough, but Gareth did not look at me directly, and his posture was stiff. Unlike Gaheris and I, we had many strained years between us, so I knew it did not bode well.

I took a deep breath, bracing for worry. But the worry did not come. Instead, calm fell over me like a cool blanket as I fell into stride behind my brother, following him into the barracks.

As princes, we had been afforded our own room, which might have once been the captain's quarters, and it smelled of old cider barrels—mostly what it had been used for in the years of peace—and dust. All through the barracks, though, I saw the signs of war: upturned beds, strewn clothing, broken weapons, mended and discarded armor, and bandages hastily draped over tables. It smelled of mint and poultices.

Our room had its own door, and only when it was closed behind us and privacy ensured did Gareth truly stare me down.

I put down my armor, glad to be rid of the weight, as light as it was, and then sat down to rest my knee.

Gareth continued to glower at me.

"If you're concerned that I'm a ghost, I promise it is not the case," I said, holding out my arms to touch.

The look he gave me, utter disgust and irritation, was pure Mother. "Gawain. I thought you were dead."

"I did, too, to be honest," I said, leaning back in the chair. "But, thankfully, I am not. Though, given the state of everything, I am unclear as to how long that will last. I hope you are duly suspicious of this parley—"

"I saw you in Withiel."

My stomach should have dropped.

The best lies follow the current of truth.

I did not even hesitate. "I was in the castle before I came down to the barracks."

Gareth rubbed at his jaw. That blow must be troubling him; I knew that sort of injury well. I could use it to my advantage. Which pained me. But the truth would be no good to him right now.

"I saw you near the princess's tower. I saw you walk toward her quarters," he said.

There was enough hesitation in his voice, enough quelling of his anger, that I could tell he was not entirely certain of what he saw.

The lies came so easily. Sweet. Delicate. Comfortable. I was up and out of my chair, hands on his shoulder, looking him straight in his clear grey eyes.

"Brother. Look at me. I come from a journey I cannot even begin to explain to you." The truth. Every word. "I risked a great deal to protect the princess, and the future of Avillion—which is the future of Carelon." Also truth. "Do you think I would risk my duty to Arthur, King of Braetan, after all that?"

He wiped tears with his fists. "I cannot say what I think. I did not expect to see you again, not after Princess Hwyfar's account of everything—it seemed so unlikely. A lost castle, a Green Knight, a roaring forest... I worried she may have ensorceled you somehow."

I squeezed his shoulders. "We are friends, Gareth. After what we endured, it was my duty to return the horn to her. Such is the honor of a knight. I did so and was given her blessing. I am sorry to have caused you such concern."

"You and the princess—"

"I am to be married as soon as I return home," I said, again, the truth. I did not have to lie to his face. I was performing as myself, as Gawain before *carioz* had changed me. The sigh I let loose was no act. "I am to be retired."

Gareth's eyes shot wide at this. "You cannot mean it."

"Gareth, we both knew this was my last campaign."

"Surely we can make some accommodations."

"War makes no accommodations that do not end in the deaths of others. I cannot risk that."

He shook his head, like a horse dispelling a frustrating fly. "But there are plenty of other knights still afield."

"Not with injuries like mine. I have been in the thick of battle for over a decade, and I can say, with utmost certainty, that my most recent journey been the most memorable of them all. I cannot be relied upon—my body is failing, Gareth. If we survive Ryence, I will let the fighting to my younger brothers and the next generation of knights. I am not too proud to step away."

"This does not sound like you. Gawain, battle fury has always run through your veins—you are the heart of our company." He paused, realization dawning on him. "Did Arthur ask this of you?"

I nodded. "He did." I was surprised to find that it did not sting as it once had, though I made it seem as if it did. "I am to be put to pasture with land, a wife with a title. I will visit Carelon, of course, for feasts and tourneys, but, Gareth, there are some fights you cannot come back from."

He rushed forward to embrace me again, and I knew I had won. I had managed to deflect his accusations with scarcely a lie between us. Gareth clung to me, trembling, and I understood that he had been hurt, perhaps a little jealous, that his brother had not run to his aid. He had been afraid I would not return, terrified of going to Carelon alone.

"Forgive me," Gareth said. "The last few days have been harrowing."

"I should have prepared you better," I said. The twins had grown up strong in a time of relative peace, their battles confined to tourneys and glory—small skirmishes, but not the terror of ambush, of onslaught, of mind games. "I ought to have been here. We trusted Ryence. We left you vulnerable."

Now Gareth was the one to sit, spreading his hands on his knees, staring out across the dusty floor.

"I killed so many men, Gawain. I have no idea how many."

I closed my eyes, tears burning. It had not occurred to me that he had never handed down death, never experienced the fury of battle as I had. I was the volatile Orkney brother, descended of Lot. I had hoped that the curse of it was mine alone, carried in my blood.

Carefully, I knelt before him, wincing as the pain lanced down my leg to my foot.

"It happens like that." I took his hand. "Sweeps you up. Like your blood is molten, your muscles freed and full of unspeakable joy. And in the moment, it feels right. Only after, in the aftermath."

"They cheered me on," he said, fat tears falling to our hands as he tried to get the words out. "Our brothers in arms. Like a young Gawain, like a young Lanceloch. Ayr's favored son. But Gawain—it was not me."

"Look at me, Gareth." He did, and I saw the pain in his eyes, but I knew he had to understand this. "We may not live out this day, but you need to know that you cannot run from the battle fury. You cannot make it your whole life, as I tried to, but nor can you pretend it does not exist. You must make peace with it. Today, the teeth are too sharp. But I can help you build your armor so as to blunt the bite."

His voice was barely a whisper. "I have been drowning in guilt, but all anyone wants to do is celebrate me, and I loathe my own reflection."

"In time, you will know yourself again. I'm here, Gareth. I'm here now."

GARETH WENT TO wash and prepare himself for the parley, and I used the small basin in the room to clean myself as best I could. My mind was a mire: I could not keep one thought long enough in my head to manage a coherent plan. We knew there would be a price: Hwyfar's future, whatever shape that might be. Her safety.

As the washbasin darkened with dirt from my body, an oily residue forming on the surface, I thought of killing the twin priestess, and what it would have been like for Gaheris if Gareth had died. What it must be like for that twin sister in the dungeons now.

But mostly I wondered about the tenuous future of this Isle, of Ys, of Lyonesse, and of Hwyfar's part in it.

It was difficult to worry for such a fragile thing, yet it seemed to me foolish not to plan: if I had to return to Carelon, if Mother was right and Arthur had additional troops waiting for us.

I had not spoken of it to Hwyfar because I did not believe my mother; and I did not believe my mother because I did not trust her. She had lived an entirely separate life from me. And she had not sent me back to Withiel out of love or kindness: she had done so for political reasons. To solidify Arthur's dream of a unified Braetan. And if Hwyfar knew the depths of Arthur's treachery—gods, if *I* knew he was there, waiting, my own brothers-in-arms lingering like vultures to see who lived and died... I did not think I could sustain that anguish. The world could not contain my rage.

What I needed was confirmation.

I could send out scouts, but we had so few men among us already. And they were so exhausted.

And did Ryence know? Had he already been in contact with Arthur?

Our best hope was in the talks with Ryence, but if they did not go to plan, we would again be in danger until Arthur's arrival: he would be our savior, no matter the circumstance. And if Leodegraunce perished in the process? If Hwyfar? That would mean Arthur's troubles were over. No more heirs to Avillion, no more complication.

Bile rose in my throat, and I took some lavender salve in my hands, brushed it over my beard, and took deep, even breaths to calm myself down.

Breathe, Gawain. You can always breathe through it.

I thought of Gweyn and wished I could tell her what had happened, how Hwyfar and I had found each other... but then I suppose she may have always known. She had been Sundered, but it had never quite worked as they had hoped. And a prophetess does not forget her prophecies, even if no one wishes to interpret them.

What brings you joy, Gawain?

"Nothing brought me joy before her, Gweyn," I said to the water. "Nothing brought me so much peace, or so much pain. I suppose you were preparing me for this all along."

Running my fingers over the braided bracer at my wrist, made by Hwyfar's magic—no, *our* magic—I wondered at the craft of it. In the light, it shimmered between blue and orange as I turned my arm, the complexity of the pattern almost dizzying. A miracle. It was enough.

Nothing would last forever.

Not even King Arthur.

CHAPTER FIFTY-FOUR

HWYFAR

I watched Prince Ryence's retinue from the window of my tower room, his cursed banner streaming as they entered the gates from the Grey Chapel. Before, I would not have had a clear view, but thanks to the recent siege, the tower now sported a considerable opening over the courtyard. The cold winter breeze did me good, helping me clear my head away from this emotional precipice and to the matters at hand.

Father would manage the terms, and I would be present; Gawain and Gareth would witness the discussions. If we could agree, peace. If not, tomorrow we would fight again. Not that we had much to offer. But Father seemed to feel we had the upper hand. I was doubtful.

Shivering, I pulled the thick fur-trimmed cape around me a little tighter. It was my mother's; I had found it in her old suite among the dozens of chests and wardrobes left since her departure. Before, I had not wanted to disturb them, worried her ghost might come reclaim them. Now, knowing she was just out of sight, fighting for me, I knew they were my inheritance.

It was agreed that Gawain would wear his green armor, but I would not. Instead, I wore the breastplate my mother had made for me, over a blood red and gold velvet gown, along with the thin circlet granted to me before my departure to Carelon. I braided what was left of my hair close to my head and chose a dark veil beneath the circlet to conceal the shocking change. Only heretics and criminals would cut their hair in such a way, and though my reputation was low, I was not so removed from court politics as to be unaware I needed to keep a low profile today.

Ahès knocked softly on my door, and I admitted her. She came to stand with me at the window and we examined the retinue as they spoke with our guards and welcoming party.

I noticed she no longer wore her veil, and I did not ask. If we had time, she would tell me.

"He does not look so intimidating," I said, assessing Prince Ryence. In my years in Carelon I had seen so many princes come and go, and he was no different. He was dressed impeccably, showing no signs of recent injury, though his men were certainly dented and gored, and one even wore a sling. I was oddly relieved that Ryence was blond, and not red-haired as my father and I were. His expression was vague, his features narrow and aristocratic, a little pale.

He rode in the company of priestesses of Ys, their ammonite charms bright against their deep maroon robes. And along with them, hooded individuals I could only assume were hostages.

"At least the agents of Ys are no longer hiding," Ahès said with a sigh. "I had thought myself beyond their influence—the great irony of my life. A foundling of Ys, betrayed by Ys itself."

"The root of Ys is not yet poisoned," I said to her. I had only begun to tell her my tale but had not been able to share my thoughts. I did not know if the priestesses of Avillion could understand. Lyonesse had found forgiveness, in a way, but the deep and lingering betrayal would take a long time to heal. If ever. "But it is very close."

Ahès' gaze was far away. "Ys has been poisoned a long time, Your Highness, but, if you have cause to believe any of its power is worth preserving, I will trust you until I am proved otherwise. Your story moved me. The Green Knight—he is a figure of ancient Ys, did you know that?"

That caught my attention, dragging me from melancholy

musings. "Of Ys? And yet I encountered him in Lyonesse?"

"Ymelda was using magic of Ys, and she must have been remarkably talented, if what you tell me is true. So talented, I suppose it is possible she may have awoken Gwerryn Marc'heg, or *gwerren doue*, as we called them. We know them by many names: the great helper, the guardian of Ys—and if they were bound to Lyonesse all this time, it is no surprise that the agents of Ys were able to rise up and corrupt the magic of that place as their own."

I slipped my hands beneath my sleeves, to feel the braided bracers there, reminding myself of what had transpired just hours before. Gawain was here. I had not dreamed it. Whatever magic worked in us was real, and lingering, and I was certain the Green Knight had something to do with it.

"I sense there is yet a word of caution lingering." I watched her carefully.

"The Isle of Ys has taken a great deal from me, Your Highness. The Gwerryn Marc'heg has been lost to us for centuries upon centuries, and their return does not bode well. It is as though Ayr himself, or Lugh or Iowenna, were to walk up the courtyard. The awakening of Gwerryn Marc'heg heralds the end of days."

The hair on the back of my neck rose. Had Gawain and I started this? Had breaking his bond to Arthur spelled the end of Carelon? Was our love worth such a thing?

"Thank you, Ahès, for always protecting Avillion first, even when it was not yours by birth," I said. I slipped my father's ring off my thumb and placed it in her palm. "May this give you courage today, if the skies darken."

She did not argue with me, nor did she try to give me back the gift. Ahès was the kind of woman who did not deal in falsities. Her loyalty was true, her reward deserved.

"We are due in the Great Hall. They have brought in the table from the Boar Room for the discussions," Ahès said, slipping the ring onto her thumb, then retreating her hand into her robes. "I will stand by you as long as you need me, Your Highness. It is my honor, and always will be."

I leaned forward and kissed her cheek. "The honor has been mine, Skourr Ahès. May we bring light while we yet can."

FLANKED BY THE remaining Knights of the Body, just a few strides behind my father, I walked into the Great Hall of Withiel to begin discussions with Prince Ryence. King Leodegraunce walked slowly but with purpose, the great jagged crown of Avillion glittering in its obsidian glory on his head. We had very little time to exchange words, but they were kind and comforting, though less confident than I hoped.

I did not mean to attract attention, and yet I felt eyes drawn to me from every corner. The sense of exposure was truly strange, since for the majority of my life, I had orchestrated every entrance, calculating the angle of my shoulders and the tilt of my chin. But this moment, I was simply Hwyfar, the princess of Avillion, too tired to be anything other.

Try as I might, my eyes still found Gawain's across the room. He stood beside his brother Gareth, who sported an angry scar across his fair brow. In the few hours since we had parted, Gawain had oiled his hair and his beard, and his green armor glistened like emerald, brilliant against his blood-red hair. Who else could I look at? Among the vista of silver, copper, and gold, Gawain alone looked real to me, felt connected to this world.

It pained me to pull my face into a mask of cold indifference, to remember how I had acted upon our first meeting. I passed by Arthur's knights without so much as a nod, and took my place at my father's right hand, beside the throne at the head of the great table, now set in the very center of the great hall. Gawain then took a seat across from me, and his brother to his right. Kahedin, Palomydes, Ahès, Gliten, and the remainder of our guards took up the last few seats, leaving what remained for Ryence.

The room was frigid, tense. I trained my eyes on the side doors, where I knew Prince Ryence's entourage waited.

Sir Lanval stood directly behind me, adjusting his armor. He leaned forward. "I am your personal guard this afternoon," he said. "Should you require a moment's reprieve."

"I assure you, I am made of hardy enough stuff," I said.

"Of that, I have no doubt. I have experienced it first-hand." Lanval straightened up again, just as the horns blew.

The effort of looking away from Gawain made me feel ill, and now I was awash in nerves. I wished I had kept the ring I had given to Ahès—I had found the smooth face comforting as I'd worried my thumb over it—but instead I had only the edge of my sleeve and the jagged jewels on my bracelet.

I could not recall the last time I felt *nervous*. Then again, were I Hwyfar of a different time, I would have been deep in my cups and powders already, that comforting tingle of detachment settling in my muscles, loosening my thoughts.

The antechamber door thundered open on its iron hinges, and a retinue of solemn-faced guards, headed by Bors, escorted Prince Ryence through the Great Hall.

We stood, all but my father; it was customary to do so as a symbol of peace and willingness to welcome another in good faith, even if I knew the man had no intention of such a thing. He had already murdered innocent priestesses and soldiers under false pretenses, and the only reason we entertained his presence at all was because we were outnumbered, even with Arthur's knights.

I watched Prince Ryence enter with purpose, taking in the details of our hall. There was no way of knowing what he was accustomed to, but I knew well that Withiel was no longer the great jewel it once was. What made the Isle powerful lay beneath, as I was so recently reminded, not the splendor of its structures. Come spring, when the fields were full of apple blossoms, magic again would reign.

Prince Ryence and his priestesses and knights, thankfully absent of the traitor Cador—for I would have taken out his eyes with my own thumbs if I had seen him—stood at their seats. Their clothes were fine, woven of good silk and trimmed in fox fur. Compared to our weary faces, theirs were free of dark smudges of exhaustion, lines of worry, the pallor of hunger.

"Prince Ryence," my father said, raising his hand. "Take your seat, please, as we prepare to discuss your terms."

There was no welcome, no formal titles recited down the line of attendees. We all sat, and my father leaned forward, scrutinizing his half-brother. I wondered if they had ever met, ever written. I did not know my half-uncle in the least, and there was very little I could see in his face that I recognized as familiar.

Except when he spoke.

The voice was my father's, only younger. He was perhaps Arthur's age, I saw now, full of the same haughty promise.

"King Leodegraunce," said Prince Ryence, holding out his hands. "Your time and attention are appreciated."

I could tell how much effort my father put into restraining himself. Every word was measured. "I prefer to avoid any pleasantries, Prince Ryence. Forgive us for our lack of hospitality, but your first pretense of peace nearly cost my daughter her life. To say nothing of half of Arthur's champions sent to us."

Prince Ryence gave us all a very pitiable expression, as if he were truly grieved. "War is not pretty, but Modrun's magic was more potent than expected. As an outcast of Ys, we had no idea her powers would so disrupt the balance. The false treaty was meant as a delay tactic, not as a mortal interruption."

"'Mortal interruption'?" Gawain scoffed, leaning back in his chair. "You speak like a palace chancellor. We barely escaped with our lives. Sir Yvain was gravely wounded and is still lost to us now. Princess Hwyfar and I fell into the hands of corrupted magic that brought us mere inches from death. And you brush it aside as if we simply took a bad pathway through the wood."

Admittedly, I was impressed with Gawain's composure. He was relaxed, in spite of the bold words.

"A miscalculation." Prince Ryence bowed his head. "As was our assumption of His Majesty's strength. Clearly he is on the mend."

"Your words are riddled with maggots," Gawain snapped losing his restraint without warning. His whole body tensed, such menace in his eyes as I had never seen in him. No, I had seen it, and been on the receiving end—when he was in Ymelda's thrall. He was barely contained in his rage. "You dishonor knighthood. You dishonor your title."

But Prince Ryence was a practiced courtier, and Gawain's barbs did nothing to perturb him in the least. Instead, he looked more and more curious, examining Gawain with renewed interest. "I apologize, sir, but we have not been properly introduced. Though I had not seen you upon the parapets—am I to assume, based on your appearance and exceptional enthusiasm, that you are indeed Sir Gawain of Orkney?"

Gawain nodded slowly. "The same."

One of the priestesses of Ys leaned over to whisper something in Prince Ryence's ear. I had the sense they did not expect us.

I also noticed there were no Braids of Una. My father was playing a game Prince Ryence did not even understand.

"And that armor you wear," said Prince Ryence, after a moment's hesitation. "Did you garner it in the wood?"

"No," said Gawain, risking the briefest of glances my way. I willed my face still, blinking back nervous tears. This game would kill me. "It was earned."

They knew. Of course they knew where the armor came from; Gawain wearing it was a silent threat, one he did not understand, but one that Prince Ryence, and the priestesses of Ys would see immediately. They did not know his limitations, his injuries. My heart began crashing in my ears, an incessant drumming, a roaring of the sea. I clutched at my velvet sleeves, trying to steady myself on my chair, but feeling as if the floor itself was slipping farther and farther from my own feet.

I swallowed hard, biting back on a mad laugh. They would appeal to his pride, his duty, and he would agree. He would try to save me.

"Then we shall make you a simple suggestion, King Leodegraunce.

A civilized term for a civilized age," said Prince Ryence, leaning forward on his chair. He had a hungry look in his eye. "One even great Arthur himself would find difficult to fault."

My father had not yet caught on, and I wanted to go to him, to shout, to shake him, to warn him off. But I was frozen, caught in a snare of my own making. My father had tried to outwit Ryence, but it had not worked.

"Go on," said Gawain, and I could tell he was proud of himself. He believed he had made progress with Ryence, that he somehow had broken through this man. He did not see the disaster barreling forward him.

Prince Ryence grinned like a wolf. "Our initial terms were to be an alliance of marriage, to Princess Hwyfar."

I snapped my head toward my half-uncle so fast that one of my earrings fell to my lap. "You loathsome slug. I would not stoop so low even to scrape you from my boot heel."

"Hwyfar," my father warned.

"He's my *uncle*." I sneered the words as best I could.

Prince Ryence was not deterred. "Half-uncle. Less favorable matches have been made. And truly, I considered it a service, and an eventual solution to this situation. You are far beyond suitable marrying age, princess, for reasons that are growing clearer by the minute."

I did not need to look at Gawain to know he was clenching his teeth to the point of discomfort.

I should murder Ryence. I should cut his heart out and rip it open on the table. I should—

"Princess Hwyfar's marriage contract is not for discussion," said King Leodegraunce, waving his hand. "Tell me the terms of your second offer before I escort you out myself."

"I want your temples. I want your land. I want to re-establish the priestesses of Ys alongside Avillion, with their power and my rulership. I believe I am suitable to do so. Your orchards, bare and blighted, hold testament to this dying land, and I believe the gods have blessed me with this purpose."

Gods, I wished for Gawain's power in that moment. Had I been born a man with such rage and power, I would have reached across the table and ripped Ryence's ears from his own head for daring to lay claim to Avillion, and to me.

Instead, I glared at him and imagined feeding his ruined ears to the kennel dogs.

"Yet we do not wish for more bloodshed. What we wish for are legends. And so, I will fight for it, champion for champion. Sir Gawain of Orkney, I challenge you to fight my champion tomorrow at midday, upon the Field of Perenn."

CHAPTER FIFTY-FIVE

GAWAIN

I WALKED STRAIGHT into it. An ox for slaughter. The words were out of my mouth reflexively, thanks to rules of courtesy trained into me for decades.

"I accept."

There was joy, elation, celebration, hope. My knights clapped me on the back, King Leodegraunce looked relieved; Prince Ryence looked sly. He was playing the game better than any of us, and I did not know how, other than he had likely more information than we suspected. Perhaps spies in Withiel, from Ymelda's informants?

I tried to find Hwyfar in the clamor that ensued, as Prince Ryence and his escort were showed out and Gareth gave me the only measured look of concern, but she was gone, her seat empty.

This was our future, and it was a bleak one. No wonder she had left.

But there was still hope. I had to get to Hwyfar. We had a day, and Arthur's forces waited at sea. I could let them know of the situation, send a message of my plight. Surely, if they knew I was at risk, they would intervene. There would be no need for bloodshed. Now was the time to act. I could use this to my advantage.

King Leodegraunce came over to me, taking my face in my hands. He had tears in his eyes. "This is a sacrifice I would never ask of you, Sir Gawain, and yet you give it freely."

I clasped his forearm. "Your Majesty, if we can avoid more bloodshed, it is a worthy risk."

"You do your ancestors proud," he said. "Your grandmother Igraine was dear to me. Please, know that you have access to whatever you need today and tomorrow as you prepare. Withiel is yours. I already am in your debt for keeping Hwyfar safe."

I shook my head. "Ah, well, we both know that Hwyfar keeps herself safe enough. I have her to thank as much as that. Our debts are settled."

For a moment, I thought I caught a glimmer of understanding in his expression. A worm of worry came to me, but then the king sighed.

"You are right. I forget my eldest is every inch her mother's daughter. If you'll forgive me, Sir Gawain, it has been a trying morning already, and I must attend to my duties. Please, stay in the castle tonight and make use of our accommodations before tomorrow. Make arrangements with Sir Kahedin if you will."

I watched the king go and felt Gareth looming up behind me as Lanval clapped me on the shoulder, and Palomydes gave me a rather appraising look.

"That was heroic," he said. "And heroism's hardly your first choice."

"I used to tourney all the time," I defended.

"Back when you had two working knees," Gareth said in a low voice.

We were almost alone in the Great Hall now, and indeed, there was no sign of Hwyfar, or of the remaining Skourr priestesses. And I should not make a show of looking for them either.

"We could dress you up in Gawain's armor," Palomydes said to Gareth. "Pad out your middle. From a distance, they might not notice."

"We need to speak somewhere else," I said to them both. Clearing my head was becoming more and more difficult. Hwyfar would be furious at the change of events. We had gone in expecting war, and this did not bode well. I had to get a message to her, and soon. But I did not know who I could trust. "I have a plan."

"You have never said four words that frightened me so much," said Palomydes.

"Come now, I am a decent war strategist, aren't I, Gareth?"

Gareth looked between us both. "When the options are 'murder' or 'not murder,' you're rather keen. But when nuance is involved, I'm afraid your strengths lie elsewhere, big brother."

"But we shall hear you out. I suggest the Temple of Ayr," Palomydes said. "Or, what's left of it. Ryence's forces set fire to it the first day of the siege."

"That will do," I said.

THERE WERE A few smaller chapels within the Temple of Ayr, and so we chose the one facing east, still relatively whole and the least devastated by the fires. It stank of smoke and lingering incense, intensified by recent rains, but there were enough stone benches for all three of us, and Gareth had found some bread and cheese and apples to feed us.

I wrestled with what I should tell them, but tried to keep my body calm and fluid, my movements uncomplicated—that was what Hwyfar always did. You never could tell by her body language when she was perturbed; she kept all so guarded. Until recently. During our parley with Ryence, I was certain she was about to squirm out of her seat and under the table.

There was no sense in explaining what I'd endured on the Path. If I told them I had seen my mother, I risked too much. I had already lied by omission to Gareth, and now I would have to lie outright.

"When I returned to Withiel," I said slowly, measuring my words by adding a kind of singsong quality to the telling, "I intercepted one of Ryence's missives. I learned that they are expecting forces from Arthur within the day."

"What?" Palomydes looked stricken. "You should have told us sooner. Does this mean Arthur is playing both sides?"

"I was not sure what to believe after my quest." It was the first time I had used that word, and I felt strange using it, but it worked, for my companions gave me twin sober expressions. "And the way Ryence acted at court just now leads me to believe I am correct."

Gareth frowned down at the dirt-strewn ground. "It's a clever move, you have to admit. Avillion is not what it was, even with Leodegraunce in better health."

"We were sent here on a promise," said Palomydes, and I could tell he was getting angry. His sense of justice was always greater than all of us combined. He had not yet been dulled by the politics of Carelon. "She will be betrothed—we all know that."

"And you believe that?" Gareth said, and though his words made my chest ache, I did not argue with them. I needed them to believe in the precariousness of the situation. "The only knight she's spent any significant time with is Gawain, and he's spoken for already. Arthur is just hedging his bets. Avillion is no small jewel. And if Ryence can prove a more stable hand…"

"Does Hwyfar know?" Palomydes asked.

"She does not know of Arthur's troops," I said. "Leodegraunce has been given no indication of relief or aide. I have asked. Gareth, unless you have heard otherwise? Neither of them trust that Arthur will come through, and I cannot give them false hope."

Gareth shook his head miserably. "I hate diplomacy, brother. More and more every day."

Palomydes made a disgusted noise, then said a string of words in a language I did not recognize. I was not certain which of the languages he spoke it might have been in, but I needed little translation.

"You are his nephews, his blood," said Palomydes. "I do not understand how he would keep this from you—how you would only discover this through happenstance."

"He trusts us to do well by him," said Gareth firmly. "We are more than blood."

"I know it does not seem honorable, friend," I said to Palomydes. "I simply want you both aware. I do not want us to lose more lives than we need, nor risk more than we must. And I have a favor to ask of each of you before tomorrow, this is why I have asked you here. But first, I need you to tell me what you know of this champion of Prince Ryence."

By their exchanged look of discomfort, I knew my chances of winning tomorrow were growing dimmer by the moment.

"They call him Loholt the Bold." Gareth licked his lips. "He's not even twenty, but he's built like an aurochs. Some foster son of Ryence, so they say, reared on the finest food and best swordsmen Ys could find." He reached up to his forehead. "I can vouch for his speed and his power."

"That was from Loholt?" I could not imagine my brother falling in such a way to another.

"I could not outmaneuver him," said Gareth, voice straining with emotion. "Not even through the boiling rage I felt. I was a plaything to him. If Morien had not come to my aid, I would have been fatally wounded—and he nearly was, in his turn."

Palomydes put a comforting hand on Gareth's shoulder. "You fought well. Loholt is a champion, yes, but he is a man like any other. But Gawain—you have never seen a foe like this."

"You would not believe the foes I have seen," I said. "But I take your words to heart. I know my limitations well. I am no longer quick, I am no longer agile, but I do not relent. I do not falter."

"Stubbornness has always been your most endearing quality." Palomydes laughed.

"Surely this Loholt has a weakness you've observed." I could not imagine any knight, especially one so visible on the field of battle, could be without fault.

Gareth appeared to consider this a while, then finally said, "He drops his right shoulder slightly before he feints. And I think he's nearsighted. Not that it will help you much. But I noticed him squinting quite a bit while we were mounting our attacks."

"I shall take what I can," I said. "Now, to business. Gareth—I need you on the fastest horse we can spare, and I need you to get word to Arthur. I believe we have a chance without reinforcements, if I win. But if I do not, we will dig graves for me and for Avillion."

We agreed that Gareth would meet Arthur's forces with a message, informing them of the duel. I had no idea who was among them, nor their number, but surely, they would understand the precariousness of the situation and act. With the bulk of our forces locked inside Withiel, I needed someone with the capability to move under cover of night in silence.

He was more than happy to comply, and we agreed he ought to leave a few hours before first light.

We bid farewell to one another in the ruined gardens at the Temple of Ayr, and I watched Gareth walk away, wondering if I had senselessly sent him into danger. But here, I was his commander, his captain. And I needed information—there was none better among my knights.

Should Arthur's troops come to our aid, I would not need to duel Loholt at all. He, or his proxy, could intervene.

If there was no rescue, Gareth was meant to light a beacon.

No rescue meant I would probably die. And Avillion would fall with me.

Palomydes, though; I had a different request of him.

We stood side by side in the remnants of the gardens, two headless gods the only sign of its former glory. Even in winter, before the fire, it had been resplendent, making me feel a connection to a god I'd long ago cast aside.

I struggled to find the right words, but I could not contain the lies forever, and Palomydes was my greatest friend in the world. If I did not live, and if Avillion fell into ruin, Hwyfar needed protection. Not just from Arthur, but from herself. Some things I could not leave to my own brother. Some things, like my love for Drian, had been kept between me and my brother in battle.

"I know you love her, so let us begin there," said Palomydes, before I managed a full sentence.

I grasped for words, any words. But all I managed was: "Palomydes."

"You may have fooled your brother and the rest, but only because they respect you so much. I have traveled with you through the bowels of war. You came back changed, and so did she."

When I went to explain, he held up a hand.

"No," said that prince of distance lands. "No explanation. No excuses. I understand your impossible position. I, too, was a prince once. But unlike you, I was able to escape my bonds. I need no convincing, so long as you do not ask treason of me. And the more details I have, the closer it becomes to such a thing."

Was it treason? I did not think so, not so long as I could orchestrate it correctly. And there it was, the hinge of my survival: I had never played the game well. Mother had, Arthur had—even Gweyn had, in her way. I had relied, for years, on brawn. Now, I realized, I was doing no different. I had orders, yes—but I must interpret what I could between the lines on the parchment.

"Should I lose tomorrow, Princess Hwyfar will be in a precarious situation. She, like many women of Avillion, has powerful tendencies, and these are sometimes awoken by distress. I would like you to keep her from the duel by any means necessary. Her mother, Queen Tregerna, is in the lower levels of Withiel, with a small cadre of soldiers and prisoners. She will help you if you require."

Palomydes looked at me askance. "I do not think preventing Princess Hwyfar from doing *anything* is an easy task."

I laughed. "Oh, I am aware. But Queen Tregerna is a skilled herbalist, and I think Leodegraunce can be convinced as well. If she reveals the true extent of her abilities to Ryence, or even to Arthur's troops, they will understand her true threat. They may come down harder than we are prepared."

"Carelon is not safe for women of renown—especially those who are not well understood," Palomydes said softly.

"Should I die—"

"Gawain…"

"Should I die," I insisted, "she may require extra protection—from herself, from those who would use her. From Ryence, from Arthur. I would ask, if the situation presents itself—if Arthur requires it, and the moment of distress is at hand—you offer yourself as her husband."

"It would be my duty, and my honor."

My friend did not hesitate. He embraced me, holding me with all his strength. We stayed that way for a time, in silence, until he pulled away. There were tears in his dark eyes, and he was shaking his head.

"I feel a foreboding in my bones," said Palomydes. "I believe in Braetan, Gawain, I do. But I cannot help but see the edges crumbling. If Avillion can fall like this, if the well can be so poisoned, what next? I do not like the Christian priests skulking about Carelon; I do not like how closed the circles become at the table. And now, our own troops lingering like crows at the edge of a battle. That is not how brothers behave."

I took the dagger from my side, the one forged to destroy me, the one I had made my vow with to Hwyfar, and handed it to him. "Take this," I said. "If you cannot—" I hated to say the words, but I knew I had to say them. "If there is a moment you think she has become unsafe for herself, the dagger will prevent her from wreaking more havoc. Look to the eldest soldier among the Lyonesse guard for a sign. She alone understands."

"That is a heavy request," said Palomydes.

"A small blow, to wound, mind you," I clarified, wincing at the mere thought. "It was done to me." Holding up my hand, I showed him the scar in my palm. "She owes me a scar for a scar."

Palomydes nodded, taking the dagger. He paused, marveling at the strange craftsmanship. Then he gave me an impish smile. "You have not told me what happens if you *win*."

I sighed. "If I win, I get to go home to Carelon, and I fulfil my duty to Arthur and my mother and marry as they have planned. But Hwyfar is safe. And Avillion is safe. There is no happy ending for us, Palomydes. Some quests do not end well."

"It is a shame," he said, sliding the dagger into his belt. "I find you most deserving of one."

"I must report to the barracks in a few hours," I said, wearily. The best I had was a few hours rest. "You know the rules."

"Barbaric habits. But yes, I know. You must be under lock and key to prevent any magical intervention, any tonics or potions, any foul play, or information. I suppose they will send Ryence's champion in soon. He really is a beast of a man, Gawain."

I laughed. "They've said worse about me."

Palomydes sniffed the air, wiping at his eyes. "Go with peace, my brother. May Fate favor you. I will be your sword."

CHAPTER FIFTY-SIX

HWYFAR

"SURELY THERE IS some other way around this." I looked across at my mother that evening, my anger flaring, but she only stared back at me, grim and tired.

I had taken the afternoon to prepare myself, to rage, and mull about my room, before seeking out Ahès first. The anxiety over not being able to see Gawain ate at me, and I had to do something to keep myself occupied that did not include chasing after Ryence's retinue and tying their scrotums in knots.

Though I had made every effort, I could not reach Gawain. Part of me had hoped that through our bond I would repair what we had lost, but no amount of willing a connection worked. He was under guard, of course, by a few of Ryence's soldiers, to prevent him from escaping and avoiding the duel—Ryence's champion had arrived late that evening, as well, cloaked and under heavy guard.

I could think of no way to get to him.

So I took Ahès along with me to meet Queen Tregerna, and the three of us sat together in one of the dank outcroppings of the lower bailey, above the cells, to discuss the day's impending tragedy.

We had informed my father that there were soldiers of Lyonesse among our numbers, and he had consented to their presence, but my mother's identity was still secret to all but

Gawain; with all my father had to deal with, I did not think it wise to tell him. But I was glad she remained with us.

"Proud princes love nothing better than a good story," said Queen Tregerna, smoothing the sleeves of her leather armor.

Ahès sighed. "Prince Ryence saw the opportunity to best Gawain, and Gawain was wearing the armor of the Green Knight. I did not think for a moment he would recognize such an old symbol, but so he did."

"Gawain is going to die," I said, looking between my mother and the Skourr priestess. "I can't understand why he would ever consent to a thing like this, knowing he cannot win."

"Gawain is hopelessly in love. He believes he has a chance to save you, and Avillion, at one fell swoop," said Ahès softly. "He does it for you, and for you alone. You cannot be together, but he can give you this."

I looked over at her in shock, and my mother laughed that deep, bubbling laugh of hers. "You might have spent time among minstrels, my dear, but you have lost your talent for concealing such things," said Queen Tregerna. "Perhaps those who do not know you so well are convinced otherwise, but Skourr Ahès is no fool. The two of you burn as bright as twin stars together."

"I… I am…" I whispered, looking at Ahès's placid expression.

"You are human," said my mother.

"This is all madness," I said. The power within me felt coiled in on itself, like a snake. I wanted to scream, to weep—I would lose myself to it, soon enough, without proper training.

My mother reached out to take my hand. "It is madness, yes. But what is love, but shared madness?" Lifting up the cuff of my sleeve, she revealed the bracer there, brows rising. "And old, old magic."

I pulled my hand back. "So am I to sit by and watch?"

"If you wish to remain alive," said Ahès.

Well, we would all die. I hardly felt that was reason enough to avoid getting myself involved. "I could rain down ruin, I know I could. I can feel it in my bones. I could boil Ryence's larval champion alive with my rage."

"I know. And what do you think will happen then? Carelon prefers their witches well-behaved—and so does Avillion, come to think of it. If there is scheming, it happens in the shadows, and so it has always been," my mother said.

My face burned, like a child scolded. "I promised Arthur I would marry, in exchange for help from his knights. I can see no other way out of my promise, except for one. I can take the Vow of Passage."

"Oh, Hwyfar," said my mother, and there was true regret in her voice. "I forget, you know so little of the world of priestesses, though you hold their power. Skourr Ahès, perhaps you can better explain?"

Ahès's eyes reflected that terrible pity. "The Vow of Passage—it is only given to women, unmarried, who have not given themselves otherwise."

Gods, I had never once been shamed in my life for my behavior in the bedroom; and what I felt in that moment was not shame, exactly, but embarrassment at my ignorance. I had assumed that the Vow of Passage was for *any* priestess. But then I realized that Morgen must have been of marrying age, and Vyvian, too. They had chosen freedom over marriage, bound to it like a husband. Virgins.

My whole world spun a bit, and I had to lean against the stone wall. I had to tell Gawain.

I had no out.

I would *have* to marry.

"That isn't to say that they remain chaste," said Queen Tregerna, softly, like one might to a frightened horse. "But, even in Avillion, it is transactional. You are forfeiting your right to marry—marrying your discipline instead of marrying for value, for land and profit. Renouncing your dowry, donating it to the temple instead."

"I can't breathe," I said.

My mother's hands were cool on my forehead. "You can and you will. Hwyfar, you were named first among my daughters,

406

and you were honed to be a queen. Do not fail us now."

The edges of my sight prickled, but just before I thought I might go away again, as I had the night Gawain and I had been separated from our party, I saw a knight approaching us in a damask cloak of grey and blue, expression grim. I knew the face well and seeing him brought me comfort: my one-time arms tutor, Palomydes.

Breathe. Gweyn would have held my hand and reminded me of our practice. Gawain would have, too.

I felt my muscles loosen, my body shift around my nerves. I did not have to be a prisoner to my reactions. And I had no time for it.

"Your Highness," said Palomydes to me, bowing at the waist. "Skourr Ahès." He did not know the soldier beside me was the Queen of Lyonesse, and I had to forgive him for the slight.

The blush on Ahès's cheek was enough to draw my attention away from my spinning thoughts and beating heart. If I was not mistaken, she was rather taken with the foreign prince. Not that I blamed her.

"Palomydes," I said, forcing the most brilliant smile I could manage, even if it made my lips tremble. "To what do we owe this visit?"

"I have been sent as your personal guard through tomorrow's events," he said, always the courtier. "It is my great honor."

"I need friends more than I need guards," I said softly.

For the first time in many years, I realized how true that statement was. How quickly I had gained friends, and enemies. How I had spent years in Carelon and managed neither, really. I had lived above it all, detached from it all, in a fog of drink and tinctures and sex, but I had felt nothing.

Now I felt everything. Every heartbeat was agony.

My mother was eyeing Palomydes with no little skepticism. "The princess has plenty of soldiers of Lyonesse," she said to Palomydes. "I hardly think one of Carelon will make much of a difference."

"I am humbled in your presence and know there is much I should learn from your famed warriors," said Palomydes to my mother, the woman he did not know was the Queen of Lyonesse herself. His charm was so disarming. "But this is a most essential assignment. From the Prince of Orkney himself."

My heart lodged in my chest, and I scolded myself for such a reaction. Like a love-sick maid at her first spring festival.

"Oh, did he?" I asked, in a very terrible attempt to sound uninterested.

Palomydes dropped his voice low, leaning over to me. "If you have a moment, princess, I would have a word in private."

WE WERE NOT far from my alcove, and so that was where I brought Palomydes. A brazier burned nearby, casting wavering golden light into the small space.

"Gawain sent this," Palomydes said, as we slipped into the stairwell alcove and out of sight. It was a small scroll of parchment, along with a Pendragon ring, of all things.

I clutched the scroll to my chest, daring not to look at it. "Thank you, Palomydes."

"I am aware of the complications," he said in that soft, measured way. "I sensed it the first time you met, actually, when we arrived in the Great Hall. I have traveled all of Braetan with Gawain, and we have endured many hardships together. Though I am not his brother by blood, I am his brother in spirit."

We had made an oath, but now I saw our oath had burst from both of us. Our pain had cracked through.

"There is no way he can win this fight," I said, tears burning my eyes again. "Palomydes, how can he be so foolish?"

Palomydes laughed, a little bitter but mostly amused. "I do not think I have to tell you that it is in his nature. He has always taken up causes bigger than he, and that is a true effort. The only knight who ever bested him was Lanceloch du Lac, and he is the best Braetan has ever seen. Do not have so little faith in Gawain."

"I have every faith in him—but it's his reason that concerns me."

"I know. But this is his fight."

"This is *my* inheritance, *my* Isle. Gods' bowels, this isn't his fight, Palomydes."

I clearly shocked Palomydes with my language, but he kept his patience. "If you reveal yourself, as you are now, you risk a great deal. The world is not yet ready for who are. There is no saying what could happen."

"Forget about me. Do *you* think he can survive this?"

I stared him down, right in his eyes. I poured all my presence into that stare, tried to bore into his very soul, summon up the power of a queen, a priestess, a courtesan, a warrior.

"Ah, Your Highness," he groaned. "I hate this whole business. I am here to protect you."

"And how exactly do you propose to do that?"

"Gawain does not want you harmed."

"Gawain is an oaf who has pitiably little sense at times—especially when his honor is involved."

"You do know him well."

I rubbed at my temples. "I do not want to compromise his standing with Arthur, no matter my opinion of Braetan. That is his family. We both knew this would not end well, Palomydes. I had no hope of it. But it felt so inevitable." Gods, the misery would eat at me for the rest of my life.

"He knows you well, too," Palomydes said. "What is why he sent me and not Gareth. Gareth would not understand. The ties of blood are complicated. But I understand the inevitability of love, and the contradiction of duty."

"So he wants you here to ensure I do nothing rash."

Palomydes gave me a wry smile. "He would presume to do no such thing. Just that you do nothing *so* rash as to ruin your reputation, endanger yourself, and end up on the end of a gibbet."

* * *

I TOOK THE scroll to my tower, and alone, I began to read. Gawain's handwriting was offensively beautiful. I had assumed it would be angled and uncouth, but instead was as disciplined and ornate as a monk's.

Love,

This is not the ideal end, I know. But it will prevent more bloodshed either way. I have every hope that, even if I fail and my life is forfeit, the people of Avillion will not suffer more than they already have. A thousand years of peace, and now this... Arthur will not abandon you, even if Ryence triumphs. I have to keep that hope—we have one duel instead of a needless war.

Love, I am so tired of war. I could not live with myself knowing I could have prevented it. Nor knowing I could have given you more peace.

Perhaps it is selfish to think but, knowing that our days together were so few, knowing our future is, as we have always known, a future without each other—

You are my answer. My joy. My peace. My pain.

Your fury has carried us so far. I am in awe of you.

But perhaps now is time for you to yield. Not forever, but for a day. Or a few hours. There is power in that, too.

I will think of nothing but you if the end comes.

Your Gawain

The ring felt too heavy, even for its size. My body felt too heavy, my soul like it might fall out through my feet. And I wept, alone in my room, until my eyes were red and puffy and my face raw from it, as I had done my last night before leaving for Carelon.

I had planned to write to Gawain, to ask Palomydes to bring him a message, to tell him that I could not take the Vow of Passage. Yet now I understood that would not be fair. Gawain was right, in a strange way. Ever the tactician, he knew that his death or grave injury would prevent the needless deaths of many more people. More soldiers, of Avillion and Ys and Lyonesse. For they were, whether or not I liked to admit it, all my people.

Three strands, like the Braids of Una. I could not fight in Gawain's stead—not that I was incapable, only that the laws of the land prevented me.

I could be angry at him all I wanted. But the oaf was right.

Perhaps yielding was not weakness as I had once thought, but was instead surrender, that brought clarity—and with it, vision. For I had burned in sunstroke fury so long I was naught but cinders, and I could continue no longer in such a fashion—not for myself, and not for Gawain.

CHAPTER FIFTY-SEVEN

GAWAIN

MY TENT WAS spacious, though flanked by an unbroken succession of guards, and after an hour of pacing within, I finally found a comfortable spot on a bed they'd pulled from some remote corner of Withiel and fell asleep. What dreams I recalled were speckled with dim faces, impressions of emotion, but formless and meaningless.

Dawn had not yet streaked the horizon when I awoke in a cold sweat, thinking that Gareth had returned. Blinking, eyes blurry in the dark, I tried to make out the unfamiliar shapes around me, my brain slowly bringing them into focus.

Then I smelled a familiar aroma: fresh baked, seasoned bread, with that as-yet unidentified spice I had initially despised but now could not get enough of.

"They're still hot if you should find yourself hungry," Hwyfar said from her perch on the trunk by the back of the tent.

Heart hammering in my chest, I rushed out of bed and went to her, wrapping her up, crushing those damned Braids of Una between us, crumbs everywhere. How she had found her way in, I had no idea. I did not care. She was in my arms, smelling like ash soap and leather, and she just held onto me and said nothing as we breathed in and out, out and in, together.

Finally pulling away, I had to touch her face, to smooth her hair, to make sure she was real. So much had befallen us of late that felt beyond this world, I needed the reassurance.

"How did you get here?" I asked her, voice low as not to raise any alarm.

"Food delivery," she said simply. She leaned back, showing me her outfit. I could just make out the ensemble: with her short hair, her plain clothes, boots and a bit of a slouch, she indeed looked the part of a kitchen servant. The attending guards, not familiar with Withiel, and only intent on keeping me inside my tent, would have had no questions. "We won't have long."

I kissed her forehead, and she let me. "I should beg your forgiveness for this ridiculous duel. But it is not all pride."

"I know. And I can't hate you for it. I think I would do the same if I thought I had a chance to stop more fighting." She held up her hand, sporting the ring I had given her the night before on her thumb. "I had half a mind not to wear it, you know. Yet here, you have turned me sentimental."

"I'm glad you got the ring. Elayne gave it to me, but I thought you should have it."

Hwyfar stiffened, looking at the ring. "Elayne of Lyndesoires?"

"She gave it to me secretly. In a golden apple, of all things."

"Golden apples are the sign of Avillion," Hwyfar said softly. She was thinking very hard about something, worrying her bottom lip as she often did. I wanted to kiss her, wanted so much more. "Elayne told me she had a child, twenty years ago, before she went to Lyonesse with my mother. That my father helped her with the pregnancy, and that she gave the babe up—I don't suppose he lives here. I wonder if that's what she means. You don't think he's—"

"Arthur's?" The thought was strange to me. But he was the only Pendragon man who could have fathered a child of that age, the only one who would have had a ring such as this. "He would have to have been so young. And women do not often tempt him." I closed my hand around hers. "But I do not want to spend our last few minutes speaking of my uncle's bastards."

"No." Her touch, hands on my bare neck, was a healing balm,

soothing me in a way nothing had since we had been apart. "I came to tell you that you don't need to worry about my anger—about me exposing you, or us. I will not unleash my rage. I will stay in my tower; I will keep my distance."

I breathed into her hair, trying and failing to resist the pull between us. "You could have sent a note."

Her lips played along my jaw, finding the boundary between skin and scruff. "Ah, but then I could not do this," Hwyfar said. I felt her teeth nip at the edge of my mouth, and I gasped, feeling the want, bright and urgent at the center of me.

So, I kissed her as deeply as I could, drawing her to me by her waist, feeling the response in her. I wanted to remember every part of the kiss, each impression of her body against mine, each terrible moment of unresolved passion.

Gods above, Hwyfar met me with her own fire. Her wicked mouth, that tantalizing tongue. Agony, truly. And joy. And underneath it all, a stillness that I knew as the bedrock of our connection.

It was a farewell.

She pulled away. I clasped her wrist, feeling the bracer beneath my fingers, cool against my skin. She clasped her hand over mine. A warrior's departure.

Then, she was gone.

THE NEXT MORNING, I somehow had the presence of mind to request Bors and Lanval to assist me. I would wear the Green Knight's armor, which brought with it power and promise, but was a far cry from the attire they knew—but I needed them to help wrap and support my knee and shoulder. Bors had fought with me, and knew battleground work well enough to show Lanval some effective techniques, and though our supplies were low, by the end of their work, my leg was secured enough that I felt relatively confident it wouldn't buckle after a single blow. I could surely withstand at least three.

"Someone delivered a tabard, and there's a flag out there for you that matches already," Bors said, coming back from the flap of the tent. He looked at the package in his hands as if it might bight him. "There's a note as well."

He passed the parcel to me, and I recognized the Orkney blazon immediately: the unicorn on a green field, stitched in silk. A bit hastily done, perhaps, but far better than having to wear the hideous colors of Avillion. The note was written in a hasty, jagged script.

> *Gawain—Do not falter.*
> *Tregerna Rex*

Some queens were kings, I suppose, and some princesses, princes. That single sentence was not just a reminder, but a threat as well.

"You look as if you've beheld a ghast," said Lanval, when I kept staring at the note.

"Is it a *lemman* of yours?" Bors asked.

I crumpled up Queen Tregerna's note. "No, but a good reminder." Handing the tabard to Lanval, I said, "Help me get this on. Bors, bring me the axe and Galatyne."

Bors looked confused. "But your shield…"

Yes, I could use the shield. And most of my life I had fought with sword and shield together. There were many advantages to such an arrangement, especially in battle, and most certainly for a man of my stature. All I had heard from our informants had told me that Ryence's champion, Loholt the Bold, favored a Gallic rectangular shield. But I favored lighter armor already and needed nothing more to slow me down. A two-weapon advantage would be helpful, and since I could manage each with one hand where most would need two, I did not wish to advertise my weaknesses when I might instead overwhelm my foe, at least briefly.

"My shoulder is enough of a hindrance without a shield," I said, taking the longsword from Bors. "I know my limitations."

Lanval's expression was almost motherly. "Gawain, we have all been changed by our time away in the forest, but I think you most of all. You seem strangely calm."

There had been no sign of Gareth. I had lain awake after Hwyfar's visit, too restless to find sleep, hoping for news. What little hope I had in Arthur dwindled to a bitter disappointment. Hwyfar saw him for who he was, far better than I had. I should have listened to her. I was blinded by his kindness, his understanding of me. Even kindness can be a tool of the wicked.

The axe's handle felt warm in my hands, as it always did, the wood with a hint of green in the grain. "No matter the result, my friends, Avillion will not suffer more needless death. That is worth dying for, if it comes to it."

They fell silent, and the fire sputtered a bit. Outside, I could hear people shuffling in, horses and carts beginning their circling. Crows on the field. Crows with green eyes.

I thought of Ymelda, wherever she was. Perhaps this is what she was trying to show me all along. Perhaps this is why we had to break our bond. I did not want to share this with Hwyfar, this emptiness, this sense of inevitability. Losing my faculties had been hard enough, but coming upon my death in such a clear and final way—I was glad to keep this to myself. Lanval was right. I felt an overwhelming sense of peace now that I came closer to the end, even more now that I knew Hwyfar would not intervene.

Uther Pendragon, my grandfather, had not been so much older than I when he met his death. My mother, the few times she had spoken of him, had recalled him battered, injured, fallen in a battle he could not back down from. Perhaps we were not so different. My height and stature, she said, my bright green eyes, were all from him. I was a babe when he died. I do not think Uther ever saw me, ever even knew of me, born so far out in the desolate Orkneys. Had he expected me to claim Pendragon as my own? Did he pin his hopes on Arthur to build on his dream of a unified Braetan?

And my father... well, damn him to the cold ground. If we met on the other side of the Underworld, I would not know his face.

"I am as ready as I can be," I said to my friends, to Bors and to Lanval. "I suppose I have fought my life long for this."

THE WEATHER SHIFTED that morning as noon approached, the first hints of spring on the air, with deep notes of loamy earth and a touch of honeyed hives. The sun shone bright down on my face as I rode out on the field, upon the largest horse they could find, a slate grey charger with a black mane and a placid temperament I was told was called Hengreon. Which was well enough for the duel.

Unlike a tourney, a wartime duel was no game, no pleasant afternoon for spectators and love tokens. There was no joust, no accounting of points. They had cleared a small space for us, and drawn a chalk circle on a small rise in the land just below the main towers. Withiel was not poised for such theatrics, so the best view was up on the castle itself, or slightly down below where we would fight, where our tents had been. Even in the bailey one would get a better view. Ultimately, Loholt and I would be alone, with no easy assistance.

The horse was for show, not for fighting, but it gave me a good view of the crowd. I spied Prince Ryence and his courtiers, bright-faced and squinting in the sun, gold flashing on their chains, their rings, and the threads in their fine garments. They looked smug and comfortable, guarded by an array of knights and kept behind a wooden enclosure like honored spectators, their pennants flapping in the breeze.

Across from them sat King Leodegraunce beneath a canopy, away from the sun, wrapped in thick furs, and flanked by his priestesses—those who had been loyal—and as many knights as remained between us. Not so many, really. I had hoped to see Gareth among them, thinking perhaps there might be some misunderstanding between us, but he was not among their number. The rest were present, though, including Lionel stifling a yawn, likely having stayed up all night fretting and trying to plan alternate attacks in case of my inevitable failure or Ryence's treachery.

But I had read Ryence right. He really did mean for this to happen. The idea of his champion beating me was too good a chance to pass up. A pathetic victory, smudging Avillion's peaceful forces into oblivion, was not the kind of tale that made it into books. Defeating Gawain of Orkney, however—that would be remembered.

The crowd cheered, seeing me approach, and I raised my hand to greet them. As their champion, I was given the first entrance, and I took the moment to breathe it in: the perfect blue skies streaked with long white clouds, the brilliant green grass, the mottled castle wall hung with vines and lichen, and the faces of many beloved friends. I did not see Palomydes, nor did I see Hwyfar. If they looked on, it was far away, as I had hoped. And that was well enough. I could not bear the look on either of their faces.

A glance at the horizon showed me nothing: no sign from Arthur, no sign from Gareth. It would be me, and me alone.

Carefully, favoring my strong leg, I dismounted my horse, and took up my stance on the field, under the banner of Orkney. I no longer saw the unicorn as my father's symbol; it had never really been his, he had never known what it meant. No longer was it just mine, though. I knew it meant more, to Hwyfar, to Avillion. Reforged.

The horns blew again, and the crowd below parted, as Loholt the Bold rode forward on a white charger, his helmet streaming a long scarlet plume. He looked every bit a champion: golden armor gleaming, pristine tabard, brightly painted shield, standing tall with the surety of youth I knew I once possessed. I knew little of life in Ys. Perhaps Loholt had seen battle before this, where he had been thrown against barely protected priestesses and unprepared guards. I did not know. But from where I stood, I saw the pompousness of an untried soldier in the way he set himself, the angle of his head, the way he'd trained his horse to prance.

Still, he was strong. And limber. When he swung himself off the horse, it was with the grace of a man who knew no injuries, nor the pain of morning aches. All that equipment, and he might as well have been wearing training leathers for all the impediment it gave him.

I was still the taller, but Loholt was just as broad, and as he approached me, I was struck by his gait as he approached. He could snap firewood with his bare hands.

"Greetings, Sir Gawain," he said, his voice smooth and practiced. The sun was behind his head, obscuring his features. "It is my honor to meet you here today."

I was still puzzling him out when I replied: "Sir Loholt. May we bring honor to our people."

My opponent slid his shield down over his arm as the trumpets blew. From where I stood, I could not hear the exact words that King Leodegraunce cried out, but I understood them well enough. I had fought in duels before, though with lesser stakes.

I pulled out both my weapons and we began to move slowly around one another in a circle, Loholt's armor flashing into his face as he moved.

"Could they not find any proper armor to fit you, Orkney?" Loholt asked. "Or would that crippled leg not hold the weight of it on top of your gut?"

Certainly, I was used to words like this in the ring, but these felt more spiteful, somehow.

"You know as well as I do that this armor was earned. Unlike that sword of yours."

Loholt turned his sword over, letting me get a better look at it. I suppose it was a decent thing, to get a glance at the weapon that would take my life. I had fought in enough battles, pulled enough blades from dead bodies and skewered them into the living, to be able to tell such weapons apart in a heartbeat. But I knew its maker, for I carried one by the same hand. Caliburn had been forged by her, and so had Galatyne. Vyvian made a most specific impression on her weapons.

"This one, you could say," he said to me, voice dropping low, "is in the family."

And as I looked across to Loholt, and we circled, the light moved into his face, and I beheld my own gooseberry green eyes staring back at me with piercing menace.

No, Uther Pendragon's eyes.

Elayne told me she had a child, twenty years ago, before she went to Lyonesse with my mother.

CHAPTER FIFTY-EIGHT

HWYFAR

WE OBSERVED FROM my tower balcony as the first blows rained down on Gawain, through long gauzy curtains. Palomydes, Ahès, and I stood together, with a better view than any of the spectators below, watching the two warriors circle one another from on high, their banners flapping in the wind.

I had already put my armor on, instructing Ahès to help me, and to her credit, she did not ask any questions. Light as it was, a long dressing gown covered it well, and Palomydes could not detect it.

I had anticipated Gawain would at least put up a fight to start—knowing his pride, he would want to give a show. But something was wrong. As they turned in the ring, he went from offensive to purely defensive, allowing Loholt all the attacks, and simply blocking.

He was giving up.

"I don't understand," I said. "Palomydes, what is he doing?"

Palomydes leaned out the window beside me. "I cannot say. Never have I seen him behave in such a manner."

"He isn't even trying." I couldn't very well say that I had left the night before to visit Gawain, but I had no cause to think that he was planning to go straight to his death without *any* attempt at winning.

Even Ryence looked disgusted. He was pacing his little box, red-faced, shaking his fist. This wasn't even entertainment.

I could hear Bors bellowing for Gawain to move into a better position, see my father move uncomfortably in his chair. But they were all so far from me, I was useless.

When Loholt struck Gawain hard enough across the head to send him crashing down on his knees, with no retaliation at all, I had enough.

"Show me the dagger Gawain gave you, Palomydes," I said to the knight beside me, without looking at him.

"What?"

I turned to see his face, full of surprise. "The one Gawain gave you. To stop me from..." I screwed up my face in a close approximation of a madwoman and flexed my fingers like a dead corpse in the field. I had searched his room for the dagger, and not finding it, had known.

"How did you know? No, I would prefer you not answer." Palomydes pulled the dagger out from behind, where he'd hidden it in his cape.

"A most wise reply."

Palomydes paced nervously, worrying his hands together. "But Gawain's plan, Your Highness..."

"Yes, please, Palomydes, do regale me with the many tales of Gawain's renowned mental prowess. You have fought by his side for years, surely you can vouch for his measured, level-headed responses to dire situations."

Palomydes closed his mouth and said nothing more.

I continued. "In this situation, however, I do believe he was onto something. His instinct was correct. As furious as I was that he thought you capable of such an act."

Ahès inched closer, looking at the carefully wrought weapon. "This is quite an implement."

"Truly, it is. And my anger is an impediment in this situation. It is elemental. When Tregerna—under enchantment—impaled Gawain's hand, his strength was subdued. His rage. His anger. He was utterly impotent."

Ahès understood well before Palomydes. "His power."

"You think Gawain's strength is magical in nature?" Palomydes asked.

"I know it is," I said softly, watching the dull silver dagger in Palomydes' gloved hands. "Tell me, do you have any explanation otherwise?"

Below, the sound of axe against shield got our attention, and my heart stuttered in my chest. I had thought of this too late, lost in my own panic, despair. In all my fear, I had lost sight of what my mother, and even Ymelda, was trying to tell me all along: I had three pools of magic—Avillion, Ys, and Lyonesse. The fury? It was the same as Gawain's inheritance, elemental and emotional, down to the foundations of Withiel herself: Avillion. The blade of Ys would contract it, so long as it ran in my blood. It would force me to use what else I had.

Gawain was up again, back on the defensive, Galatyne lost in the grass, axe in both hands. But the young warrior was fresh as a new stallion. He was still hesitating. Gods damn the man.

Palomydes saw it too. "What is the matter with the man?"

"I do not know," I said, shaking my head. "But you need to pierce me with the dagger."

"My lady?" Palomydes' day was clearly tumbling toward a most terrible conclusion.

"It will force me away from using the magic of Avillion. Ahès will be here to ensure I do no harm otherwise. I mean to calm myself. But as I wear the armor of the Green Knight, I believe I will be more connected to Gawain once I am pierced. I will understand what is happening—I will be able to help him." I took a step closer to Palomydes.

Ahès frowned over at the knight. "If you do not have the courage to do it, then I shall."

I put my hand on the wooden railing of my balcony, just as we heard Gawain cry out in pain. I knew that sound: he had gone down on his bad knee. Again, not because he had been bested, but because he was not fighting as he should.

"Palomydes, now!"

*   *   *

MY WORLD EXPANDED, contracted, and then narrowed to long, pale strands of light and the span of air between Gawain and me. Where my armor touched my body, I could feel warmth and connection, the little tickling sensation I remembered as Gawain. And indeed, when I turned my eye inwards, I could see the remnants of our *carioz* again, drawn thin and ragged across the expanse, from the balcony and down to the sparring field.

I turned to see Ahès and Palomydes, and they did not move. Palomydes' face was drawn in pain as he still plunged the dagger into my hand, a fine spray of blood rising ever so slowly from the wound, and Ahès' resolute expression changing imperceptibly. All was washed of color, but I noticed their own auras of light, pinpricks and blossoms around them, dancing.

Pain was gone. Pain was Avillion. The pain of breaking waters before birth, of soil bursting open in springtime, of ice breaking through stone.

What brings you pain, Hwyfar?

It seemed I did not need my body; and time, that gift of Lyonesse, moved like clay beneath my hands. Gweyn had the answers all along. Truth was always the greatest pain. She knew. She had trained us.

What brings you peace, Hwyfar? Lyonesse was peace. The cup, a vessel. The bowl, empty and yielding, open.

What brings you joy, Hwyfar?

Ys, most corrupted. The shield, lost. The protector, safety. Connection. Now, visible again, wound like threads of silk.

I searched desperately for the long strands of *carioz* that once flowed from Gawain and me, and found that tiny, near-invisible strand still connecting us. It barely shimmered, but as I drew closer to it, it glowed stronger, catching in the sunlight.

Breathing in, calming myself, I began weaving between us. There was enough filament already in the armor, whatever the Green Knight had left for us, to give me a connection—the joy of life. For wasn't armor a kind of shield already? And the power of Lyonesse, of time itself, wrapped around me as I brought each iridescent fiber together. The filaments were fine, finer than spider silk, but I realized they were everywhere. Before, with the magic of Avillion swimming in my body, that restless elemental fury, I had not been able to see just how much of the threads existed in the world: *carioz* made up all the world. It was not Ys, or Avillion, or Lyonesse, but it flowed through and between, like a golden thread in a tapestry.

And I saw, too, that I had already begun the work. From my wrists, my bracer held strands that reached out toward Gawain; from Gawain's wrists, his bracer called out to mine.

Down and down the long line of bright thread I wove, like a great spider spirit, knitting and knotting, pulling myself closer to him with every turn of light in my fingers, leaving my body behind. Down from the balcony toward the sparring field, each blade of grass moving so slowly in the wind, until I was hovering over Gawain, just as Loholt's sword was beginning its slow arc down upon his head.

I could see what Gawain saw, then, tying off the last of our *carioz*, or whatever magic I was now making—praying to all the remaining gods and goddesses that it was not some false simulacrum like Ymelda had created.

But the sun was in my eyes, our eyes.

So I listened to Gawain.

And slowly, as I started to let go of time, and to sink into Gawain's mind, I could hear the words:

Son of Arthur.

CHAPTER FIFTY-NINE

GAWAIN

I COULD NOT kill Loholt—he was Arthur's bastard.

And I was ready to die rather than have my cousin's blood on my hands. I knew this was Ryence's doing. The Pendragon ring, it had been Arthur's.

Elayne could never have known this was my end, but now I was burdened with the truth before me: I would not die a kin-slayer.

Dying a coward in the eyes of those before me was better than that, even if it was not the end I wanted. Nor, really, even in my own measure of myself, the end I deserved.

Loholt loomed over me, the sun blazing behind him like Ayr himself, and I thought only of Hwyfar. Not of Arthur, nor of my brothers or mother. How strange, in that moment before darkness, that a woman I had truly known only a measure of scant days felt more real than anyone else in my life.

Get up, you idiot.

Then she was *there*, and I was breathing again, her presence rushing into me, just as Loholt's killing blow was descending upon me. Our *carioz*, or a power very like it, snapped into place, light and sound and feeling returning with resounding clarity, and her voice in my head:

I don't care whose bastard he is—I will not let you die like some sacrificial aurochs let out to slaughter. You said you would not falter.

My hand—the one that had been pierced with the dagger at Tregerna's court—cramped and stung, but my body felt reinvigorated. The blow that should have killed me, I blocked easily, rolling out of the way with the spryness I could have only dreamed of moments ago, my reflexes getting the better of me.

She was siphoning her strength into me.

There is no hope for this, Hwyfar, no matter how long I hold on. I won't kill Loholt, I told her.

I stood again, and my knee did not buckle, though I was a bit unsteady on my feet. My armor seemed to hum around me, pull me in tighter. It almost felt as if Hwyfar was in my arms, and I could smell the scent of her hair beneath my chin. I squared my stance.

Loholt staggered back a bit, giving a nervous laugh. He was not prepared for me to come back from such a terrible show.

"Just playing games with me, are we, Orkney?" Loholt asked.

The crowd was cheering now, blood thrumming in my ears. Hwyfar's presence was like a cool, deep stream, leading me along with pulsing clarity. There was no anger there, no fury, just clear, constant power. I could bend it to my will, and the well was deep.

I felt Hwyfar shimmer at the edge of my mind, her presence shifting.

Do not die a fool, Gawain. Fight.

Loholt lunged, a messy attack that I easily avoided, and he got his pretty sword stuck in the sod. In times of old I would have paraded around the ring while he pulled at his weapon, but instead, I picked up Galatyne and waited.

I had gotten under Loholt's skin, and he was tense and edgy now, stomping toward me, muttering words either incomprehensible or profane.

Yet, no matter what he tried, I was moving out of his way. I had already tired him out before, when I was on the defense. And in a way, I still was. Now, his shield was a hindrance—and yet, for all his training, he would not let it go. By the time he squared his stance again, I was already behind him, kicking him from behind, disarming him, confusing him.

There is not much time. Gawain.

I needed to tell her. While Loholt straightened his helmet, I took a moment to share what I had learned.

Hwyfar, I thought Arthur would come for me with additional forces. I thought it was possible—I'd heard it was. I sent Gareth to scout ahead. But he left me here. To die.

The look she would have given me.

You make your own tales, and you've never needed Arthur. This is your *story, Gawain. Teach Loholt like you would teach your own brothers a lesson. You need not kill him.*

I had not considered such a thing. He was not recognized as a bastard—perhaps I could treat him like family, then. *My love, you truly make me see the world in a better way. When this is done, I will find a way back to you—*

The regret from her raised a bitter taste in my mouth. *I wish I could give you a lifetime together; then I could break you of your loyalty to Arthur, but I cannot.* Her voice was weaker, more distant. *But I will give this to you, now, which he would never grant you.*

A surge of strength that followed ripped through me. My lungs felt ten times their size, my spine crackled, and my legs shivered with power, muscles tensing and quivering. The axe head glowed green, and I roared with it.

My world rushed into bright clarity, and the sun's very strength seemed to flow into me, from my head down. I was blazing with fury, and my weapons felt light as driftwood. My shoulder and knee no longer hurt; my back moved with limber grace, my ribs expanded freely.

As Loholt went to charge me, I twisted, and cracked him under the helmet with Galatyne's pommel, just as Hwyfar had done to me with the *graal* spear. Truly, it was the last thing he expected, so intent was he on that gleaming axe head, pulsing an unnatural green. And who was to blame him? I would have done the same thing.

Loholt's helmet flew off his head, and I felt his nose crack.

I kicked at his shield, which did not come free right away, but it threw him just off balance enough—like a well-trained soldier, he had a very rigid way of holding his shield—so I was able to then hook his other leg with mine and send him to the ground.

Looking down at Loholt the Bold, there was no doubting it now. He looked more like me at that age than my own brothers had, what with Elayne's pale features. Loholt's golden curls coupled with my own green eyes. Hard to say whose nose he had, though, given the blood. Arthur's, probably.

In a moment, I was stepping on his sword hand, axe to his throat.

"I believe we have some important conversations before us, my friend," I said to Loholt. "But for now, this duel is finished. Do you concede?"

Loholt turned his head, spat out a tooth, and said, "I concede."

I looked down at the crowd, expecting to see Prince Ryence's face screwed up in fear and fury, but instead, I saw him hastily climbing out of his box, scattering stools in his attempt to remove himself. The crowd was no longer paying attention. They were looking elsewhere—to the hills.

My heart sank. Had Arthur come? No, he couldn't be here. Not now.

I squinted, shielding my eyes, and I spied horses running across the fields, and flapping banners: an army on the way to defend Avillion.

But not the colors of Carelon. It was banners of Lyonesse that streamed behind these new forces: blue and argent on a field of black.

THE FORCES OF Lyonesse were led by Gareth and young Sir Tristan, the nephew of King Markus. Their herald told us that Queen Tregerna had sent word as soon as she'd learned of trouble, by way of two of her priestesses, in hopes her cousin would provide aid. It was a risky proposition, but one that proved fruitful.

There was little resistance from Ryence's men, least of all Loholt.

Breathlessly, Gareth told me of his adventures as I searched for Hwyfar. I could not see her. The window of her tower was shuttered.

In the harbor, Gareth had found, not Arthur's ships, but the ships from Lyonesse, though one of them was capsized. He had lost half a day working with the forces to save the horses and provisions, men and arms, and then rushed across half the length of the Isle to get to us. Tired though they were, their numbers were still far and above those of Prince Ryence's, and coupled with our own, far too many.

If Arthur had sent us any additional support, it was nowhere to be seen. Mother was wrong. Or she had meant to frighten me.

Growing, gnawing worry crawled at me as I tried to make my way back to the keep.

I insisted Loholt be brought to the infirmary for immediate treatment, and Gareth almost argued with me. Still sensing Hwyfar, albeit weakly, I tried not to worry, but measured my responses as swarms of priestesses and soldiers streamed out of the castle in celebration. The tide was impossible to push through, and everyone wanted to touch me, my armor, my axe, to thank me.

Their praise fell dully upon my ears.

King Leodegraunce issued a statement I barely heard, and then I was being escorted into the castle, as a few outbreaks of violence broke out here and again. "You are needed in the Great Hall," the king said to me.

Hwyfar... tell me how you fare.

She did not reply.

I could feel *carioz* again, a weaker version of what we once had, but blissfully, blessedly returned. If she could rebuild *carioz*, perhaps I could borrow her strength, her resolve, for I had so little left.

Once inside the castle, I found it disconcertingly quiet. My eyes took a moment to adjust, auras of rainbow light refracting at the edges of my vision, and my skin burned from my time in the sun and wind. People crowded in behind me, and stared as I walked past, at the weapons still on my back. I should put them away, I thought, and yet—

My knee buckled halfway to the Great Hall, and I had to use the axe handle to support myself. What strength I had been given drained away, exhaustion rolling in. Whispers everywhere. Eyes following me. A trickle of blood from my nose. I remembered just how many cracks to the head I'd had.

Bors met me at the double doors to the Great Hall, and helped me catch my breath, giving me a flagon of cider.

"You're going to need to prepare yourself for this," he said to me, handing me a small, embroidered handkerchief. I looked down at it and knew it well. It was one of Hwyfar's. How?

"Prepare?" I asked him.

But before he could answer, the doors swung inward, creaking against their ancient hinges.

And there, standing in the middle of the Great Hall of Withiel, was Arthur, King of all Braetan.

CHAPTER SIXTY

HWYFAR

I LOST MYSELF in the magic. I became a siphon, and a siphon only. Gawain did not know how to take from the stream. Though I knew he did not mean to, by the time I realized I was being drained of my own life, I could no longer reach him. My only defense—the magic of Avillion—was gone, trapped beneath the dagger's biting power. I needed pain, and anger, to pull away.

As I let myself drift away, I understood that death was a release from a future I did not want. I had never expected it to come like this, of course, never considered ending my life as an answer to my mounting dread. I was tired of being Hwyfar, and as I watched through Gawain's eyes, seeing the forces of Lyonesse streaming across the hills, the panic of Prince Ryence's soldiers, the relief in my father's eyes, I felt the call of peace.

Gweyn was waiting for me.

Gawain would be free to live his life without me, without wondering what our future could have been. That gave me a measure of joy, too. He could continue. Perhaps he would meet another like Drian, a love who would know him and help him forget.

Except just as I felt my spirit parting from me, a most unusual unfurling of myself, the dagger came out of my hand, and I rushed reluctantly back into my body.

My tower room was dark as night, wind whipping across my

432

face, and a lavender fog roiling out from a dim figure standing at the door.

I was sprawled on the floor, limbs weak as a newborn lamb's, bile streaming from my mouth, eyes bleary. Palomydes was in a defense stance, sword at the ready, and Ahès was prepared for battle, her staff kindling with pinkish-grey light, just above me.

"That is enough, Princess Hwyfar," said a voice I recognized, commanding and strong. "You gain nothing by sacrificing everything."

The fog parted, and the maelstrom began to calm.

Morgen le Fay strode into my room, dark purple robes billowing about her, the long gray braids she always wore rippling about her like snakes.

My vision swam, and in what felt like a heartbeat, the sorceress was beside me, holding up my chin to look me in the eyes. Her beauty was piercing in the way a rock face is lovely: hard, bold, weary. The concern, though, brought me closer to understanding just how dangerous my game had been.

"I could not let him die," I whispered to her, so softly I could barely hear the words myself. I no longer had the power to lie.

Morgen's brows knit with pity. She wiped the sweat from my brow. "You and I must speak, and soon. My sister informed me of your proclivities, as well as her fears you might dabble in such foolish, untrained magic. I convinced Arthur to send his best, but rather surreptitiously."

"He cannot know—Morgen—"

"Shh, he knows nothing beyond the threat to his favored nephew, and the true risk that befell Avillion. I fear his preoccupations with his wife's Christian priests have made him forget that Avillion was key to giving him Braetan," Morgen said to me softly. "But he is here. And he is asking to see you."

I gave a mad laugh, between a sob and a giggle, and held up a shaking, bloody hand. "I hardly think I am capable of standing before the king of all Braetan."

Morgan pulled something from her cloak. "Have you not heard? There has been a miracle. As Loholt the Bold fell upon the ground, defeated, all the apple trees on the island burst into bloom, and then fruited golden apples." She held out an apple to me, yellow as the noonday sun. "I am certain it will bring you all the strength you need."

CHAPTER SIXTY-ONE

GAWAIN

I DID NOT mean to fall into Arthur's arms, to sob like a child. Yet I did. Seeing him, standing there, the look of abject terror and worry on his face—I was once again barely fifteen, and he my cautious caretaker. He, the only adult who had never scolded me for who I was, for whom I loved, how I felt.

The sound of Arthur's own weeping echoed in the near empty Great Hall as we embraced.

Arthur held me away from him, hands on either side of my face, looking up into my eyes.

"I am so sorry, my boy. I'm so, so sorry," Arthur said. "I failed you. When it mattered, I failed you."

I had never heard Arthur say anything like it. And I had been through too much, learned too much, to argue with him.

I looked around the bare hall. The courtiers and knights were still celebrating out on the field. I did not recognize the scant few knights with us still but knew them as Arthur's. My knee pulsed with pain; my hand throbbed incessantly. I could hardly see out of my right eye from the beating I'd gotten at Loholt's hand.

All I could think to say was, "I did not falter."

"You were like Ayr reborn," Arthur said. "Imbued with power by the noonday sun. I have never seen anything like it, in all my days. Never before."

435

"Loholt was—"

"A stunning opponent, yes, of course." Arthur breathed out, looking at the glowing runes and symbols on my armor, clearly visible in the dim hall. "To say nothing of this! When Morgen told me she'd had a vision of you on a quest, I had no idea you were capable... well, given everything."

We were here, yet again.

"Yes. Given everything." Bitterness crawled back.

Arthur frowned, putting his hand on my shoulder. "It was a stunning show, my boy. Stunning. I can think of no better way to go out, in the tales. Better than I could have instructed the bards to tell it, even. And that's even before all this business with the Green Knight! You, alone, facing down an enemy of ancient, profane power. My goodness, it will be the talk of the kingdom."

"The Green Knight was no foe. And, besides, I had help," I said. "Princess Hwyfar, she..." Saying her name kindled a fire of alarm in my chest. Where *was* she? "And Queen Tregerna— there was a great spell, and—"

But I knew Arthur was no longer listening to me. I knew that vacant look on his face. It did not matter what I said.

The sounds of people gathering out in the antechamber rose and I could feel the impending press of expected performance. Arthur was here, and Arthur must make a show.

"We will have plenty of time to discuss on the journey home," he said to me, absently patting my arm. "But for now, we have to sort out all the politics of this business. When we ran into the forces from Lyonesse, I had to send home half our own soldiers to prevent us looking like fools, but now I'm going to have to make good with Prince Ryence. And then Leodegraunce has the gall to un-mad himself, and then lose his own *graal*. Honestly, it is impossible to keep up sometimes."

The great doors opened wide, and King Leodegraunce, flanked by his guards, Gareth, and Tristan, entered. Tristan had grown a foot since the last time I had seen him as a teenager in

Carelon; now he was a black-haired, keen-eyed man of twenty, his lion-emblazoned tabard a little loose on his lean body, but still cutting an impressive figure.

Arthur clapped me on the back. "Give us a big smile, Gawain. Square those shoulders. Wipe your face. They need to see a champion."

Then, to our right, where just the day before, Ryence had entered with his guard, came Palomydes, Ahès, and my aunt Morgen, of all people, and behind them, Hwyfar.

CHAPTER SIXTY-TWO

HWYFAR

THERE STOOD ARTHUR on the dais, as if he were king of Withiel and Avillion, draped in cloth of gold and fur, above Gawain. My *carioz* reached out to him, but I pulled it back. I could not risk the connection. I must have gone rigid as we entered, because Morgen put a comforting hand on my back and whispered, "Put on your best mask today."

"I told Arthur this was a matter for priestesses," she had said to me, as she helped me prepare. "By the look on his face, I might as well have told him it was a matter of our monthly blood."

Once, I would have been able to muster a smile, a cool, detached personality to go with it. But now, and especially after what had just happened, the effort was monumental. Morgen chose a dress of thick silk velvet damask for my arrival. It clung to my body in just the way that Hwyfar of old would have preferred and tucked my hair back into a coronet and wrapped with a pearl-studded veil. I wore elegant drops of amber at my throat, my ears, my wrists. Gone was the warrior, gone was my armor, and I felt hollow and alien in my own body, awakened from a dream.

How had I played the game for so long with such ease?

When my eyes met Gawain's, I suppose I knew the answer. I never had anything to fight for before. I never had anything to hide. I could play all the games, gamble my heart, risk myself time and again, because Arthur had taken all I had been made for. Hwyfar of old had no foundation, no history. I had holed myself up in Carelon and lived a fantasy of pleasure and artifice while men and women lived and died around me.

One of Gawain's bright eyes was swollen shut, but the look of relief on his face was enough to know he had been worried sick. He stood within arm's reach of Arthur, and my father flanked his other side. I saw, too, Sir Tristan, beside a handful of my mother's soldiers.

Someone had summoned minstrels. Prince Ryence was surrounded by knights, Erec at the command, all grim-faced.

Everyone carried branches of blooming, fruiting golden apple trees in their arms, blossoms in their hair. I could smell the kitchens already stoking the ovens, heady with bread and honey. Had we done this? Was our *carioz* more than one duel, more than our love? Golden apples.

"Hail King Arthur!"

"Hail Princess Hwyfar! Hail the Princess of Avillion!"

"Hail Sir Gawain!"

It went on for some time like in this manner, until I finally made it through the crowd, men and women falling at my feet, kissing the hem of my robes. Priestesses wept. I did not understand— nor did Morgen, for she offered me no explanation when I turned to her, but kept her red lips pressed tight.

I arrived at the dais, brushing apple blossoms from my face, to stand before Arthur, only because I had to.

Falling to my knees, I looked down at the homely stone of my own castle and awaited to hear the proclamation of Arthur.

"Arise, Princess Hwyfar," said King Arthur. "My sister and my friend."

Those words made my skin crawl. I was no sister to him, and certainly not his friend.

I rose, forcing myself to look only at Arthur, the man who had rejected me at a glance, keeping my back and shoulders straight as possible. *Look, people of Avillion,* I wanted to say, *your princess is of a height to this king. She does not shrink from him.*

And distantly, I heard in reply: *Aye, but I am still taller.*

Gawain.

"My lord—Your Majesty." I nearly choked out the words, so shocked to hear, to *feel* Gawain. "Thank you for coming to us in this time of need."

"It is not I who should be thanked, but you, and Sir Gawain, and the people of Lyonesse. I am told you performed a miracle here, as well," said King Arthur.

Morgen was the one who replied. "Indeed, she did. All of Avillion saw a vision of the princess this noon, rising on the hillside, a figure in the distance, championing the legion forward to victory."

"A mighty princess for a mighty age," said King Arthur, holding up his hands as the crowd cheered in reply. "And the earth itself celebrated in reply, bearing golden fruit!"

My father looked at me with kind, tired eyes. "A miracle for a new age. Healing and strength to the land."

Someone placed a garland of apple blossoms on my head.

A quick glance at Gawain informed me that he was just as taken aback as I was and trying very badly to hide it behind an excuse to rub at his eye. Had we been shielded from some great illusion?

The new tapestry of our tale was being woven before our eyes.

"Avillion is once again safe," King Arthur continued, conviction so strong in his voice that for a moment I even believed him. "Come, let us tend to our wounded, bring our traitors to justice, and broker new alliances toward peace. Never again shall this isle suffer such insidious assault. For soon Princess Hwyfar shall join herself in marriage to a lord of her choosing."

"No, she shall not, Your Majesty." Then a pause. "With all due respect."

My mother's voice rang through the room, and all eyes turned toward the back of the room.

I had been looking for my mother as I knew her: a steely woman in soldier's leathers, a mass of grey braids, and riding gear. But now, at the opposite end of the hall to Arthur, she was the very picture of a queen of old. She was draped in grey silk, embroidered with the lion's paw pattern she had favored during my childhood—taken, I was certain, from her own coffers in her room—a low belt around her waist of hammered silver set with jet. She had combed out her hair and twisted it behind her ears and at the base of her neck in intricate coils, wrapped with blue ribbon. On her head she wore a bright crown of black pearls. She still carried a spear.

My father/ gasped, and Sir Kahedin had to help keep him upright. "Gods, Tregerna…"

Sir Tristan fell to his knees, seeing his aunt, and then half the gathered forces did the same: this was their queen, returned at last, after all, thought lost for so long.

I knew what this meant. I knew what she was giving up for this.

"Queen Tregerna of Lyonesse," said King Arthur. To his credit, his smile did not falter. "We heard word of your perilous capture and blessed rescue—to God be the glory."

"I do not need welcoming in the halls of my friend King Leodegraunce, in the halls of my daughters," she said, walking toward the dais with a smooth, unconcerned stride. "And it is to my daughter Hwyfar and Sir Gawain that all the glory belongs, Your Majesty. No god of yours."

Arthur's smile faltered, just a hair. A strange flicker of hope kindled inside of me. He had not looked directly at me once during the entire proceeding. I was, as so many in his life, invisible.

"Of course," Arthur said, as Tregerna approached. "It is good to see you."

I could scarcely find room to breathe. What was she planning? I had given my word to Arthur. Now, he had cornered me.

"I realize, in her distress, Princess Hwyfar made a promise to consent to marriage in return for support against Ryence's forces," said my mother, her gaze fixed on Arthur's with the precision of a trained marksman. "But that was before I was freed. Before I claimed her as my heir. Which I do. Right now."

The murmurs through the hall, of shock and, to some degree, relief, gave me chills. Her kingdom was second largest to Arthur's, certainly greater than Avillion's. King Meliadus was a steadfast regent.

King Leodegraunce cleared his throat. "Avillion has contracted with Arthur to claim no heirs, in exchange for peace and protection. But through the dissolution of marriage, Queen Tregerna is correct. Hwyfar is the rightful heir to Lyonesse."

Arthur let out a strange laugh. "Well, certainly we can come together to some agreement. I expect Lyonesse, sooner or later, will see the benefit of a united Braetan."

"Will we?" Queen Tregerna looked about at the room, her forces clearly outnumbering the rest.

The room fell silent.

I watched Gawain, gently reaching toward him with *carioz*. This was the moment I had run from time and again, the dread too wide and too terrible, a hungry gulf of uncertainty. Again, faced with Arthur's judgement, unable to escape.

Gawain looked at me, resolute, green eyes blazing, and gave me a nearly imperceptible nod. Had I not spent days with him, learned to know the most intimate movements of his body, I never would have noticed it.

Then, clear as a bell in my mind, I heard Gawain's words.

Arthur cannot keep you to an agreement he himself never meant to uphold; I know he was prepared to side with Ryence if the tide turned.

Gawain leaned over to Arthur and whispered into his uncle's ear. And I understood that he spoke the same words I had just heard, but now to Arthur. Perhaps the greatest power Gawain ever wielded was in that whisper, at least in the long thread of my own fate.

The King could not bargain with me, not when we could expose his untoward dealings. Avillion was no threat while

King Leodegraunce was under the thumb of Ys. Now, he had Lyonesse behind him. And Gawain would not falter. What a pitiful place for Arthur to stand, fragile alliances hanging like spider silk, and him alone to decide.

Arthur sobered, the smug brightness of his expression dimming. Licked his lips. His eyes went to me, to my face. He saw me, at last. I looked back at him, and I blazed in fury, firm in my power and my love.

I dare you try and tell me who to wed.

His eyes shot wider. Let him hear my rage.

"Of course, Queen Tregerna, your wisdom focuses me. As Sir Gawain reminds me, the *graal* quest must take precedence for us," Arthur said at last. "Avillion is a most treasured country, and our peace with Lyonesse—especially in these turbulent times—is our utmost focus. I hereby release Princess Hwyfar of her debt to the crown. Tomorrow morning, we set sail for Carelon."

CHAPTER SIXTY-THREE

HWYFAR

Somewhere in the castle, Gawain was restless. I did not know his thoughts, but our connection let me understand this small whisper of him. Stretching out through *carioz*, I gave him what comfort I could, even though it stung me to do it. Tomorrow, he would be gone from my life, and I was left to my new freedom.

Freedom.

From an unwanted marriage, perhaps. But not an hour after Arthur had released me from my oath, Morgen had called for me.

It did not surprise me to see Anna Pendragon standing before the mirror, a shimmering reflection of her bodily self, but I had not anticipated Vyvian, the High Priestess and chief advisor to Arthur, to be present as well. A small, compact woman, with white hair shorn like a man's, she wore black robes that shimmered in the light of the hearth, and her dark eyes took me in as she leaned heavily on a knotted cane.

"Welcome, Princess Hwyfar," Vyvian said to me, holding out her broad hands. "We need to discuss a few things with you before we leave."

I glanced behind me as an unseen force pulled shut the heavy doors and the temperature in the room dropped. Fear mingled with a kind of awe. I felt magic here, sharp and strong, like flux upon the anvil.

"I have come; I am prepared," I said, folding my arms. I was taller than all of the women, but I felt insignificant in their combined strength; my powers reached out in response to their own prying—a strange response I had not anticipated.

"We have discussed your abilities," Morgen said, always the diplomat. "And we understand you have held the Spear."

Vyvian was Arthur's advisor and aunt; Morgen and Anna were his sisters. My trust had been my folly.

"I have held the Spear. I have wielded it. But it is now lost. I do not have it, if that is what you seek," I said. If Arthur meant to bully me into giving him information, he would not have it.

"Then you gave it to Elayne?" Vyvian asked. Her voice dropped lower, and she appeared nervous for a moment.

"Do you mean Elayne of Astolat?" I asked. "The bearer of the Cup? The mother of Loholt the Bold? She is gone far now, I am certain."

Morgen's eyes widened at this information, and I could not help but gloat a bit at this revelation. Let them know their precious Arthur was not infallible. I could not yet trust Morgen, not knowing her place in her brother's *graal* quest.

Vyvian closed her eyes, letting out a long breath. "Hwyfar, you have no mind how much relief that brings me." She sank forward on her cane and Morgen put her hand on her aunt's shoulder.

"It may seem difficult for you to understand, Hwyfar, but Arthur must not have the *graal*," Anna explained from her ghostly station by the mirror. "Though he seeks it, and seek it he must, he may never hold all three."

"We worried you might have kept it," Vyvian said, taking a step closer to me, peering up to take me in. "Now I understand: the power you showed at the duel—that was simply you. You healed the land—you gave your fury to Gawain."

I let her look at me, unashamed. "I made magic work for me. I wove my own tapestry. To save the one I love."

"Morgen distracted the crowd with a vision of you on the field," said Vyvian, nodding in Morgen's direction. "But the power from you could not go unnoticed across the Path, not to those with the Sight. I was awoken from a deep sleep to a vision of flames, and I came to you as fast as I was able."

"Gawain's fate could have been to die upon that field," said Anna, and try as she might, the strain in her voice was palpable. "And for that, I can never truly show you my gratitude. We knew the threads of his life twisted toward that end and did not believe it possible to stop it, though we tried."

Morgen drew closer to me. "Before Hwyfar, it was not possible. Perhaps we have all become too disciplined and missed the importance of the wildness of magic—how Avillion once was. When there was no difference between Ys and Lyonesse and Avillion."

"I wish to visit Modrun and learn from her," I said, and it was true. Relief washed over me as a part of my future came together, a glimmer of hope. "I do not wish to be a disciplined priestess."

"I would never expect that of you," Vyvian said, a warm smile on her face. "But there is much left for us to do. The Path connects us all, but there are forces at play more heinous and insidious than those you have encountered. We may need your assistance, if you are willing."

"Do you not fight for Arthur?" I asked. "Is he not your liege?"

"We fight for the people of the realm," Vyvian said simply. "And while the Pendragons do the same, we steer their ships. But when the people suffer, we may move the winds, change the currents, and uproot the banks as needed."

Anna held a finger to her lips. "But we are quiet. We bide our time. We wait. Patience is the game of women in the shadows."

"You may be the next queen of Lyonesse," said Vyvian. "You will unite the lost kingdom with Braetan, in peace if nothing more—your mother was my protégé, you know, and I am certain she will teach you even more than you have already learned."

Morgen pressed a key into my hands on a gold chain: the key to the storeroom where I had found my mother's armor. I had lost it.

"We will grant you one last night, under our protection. The moon is full, and Arthur will sleep deeply and without dreams. Find your love after the eleventh bell of the Grey Chapel."

"Why would you do this for me?" I had to ask. They knew the risk.

"You are not the first among us to love a forbidden man. Nor will you be the last. We cannot protect you from the future, but we can at least grant you this," Anna said softly.

UNDER THE BLUE light of the full moon, silver rays piercing the clouds and frosting the lake, I slipped through the castle like a ghost. Though I passed soldiers and guards, priestesses and courtiers, none saw me as I clutched the key.

Nervous as a maiden, my heart fluttering in my chest, I fumbled for the lock, trying to reach out with *carioz* to sense Gawain, but feeling only the vague impression of him nearby.

Then, soft, his voice. "Behold, my love."

He was standing in the shadows behind me, and I had not noticed.

I did not want to weep again, yet as he enveloped me, all words fled. He picked me up, kissing my neck, and held me close. If I had the sight I'd been given in the forest, I imagined we would be blazing together.

Setting me back on my feet, he pushed open the door to the storeroom and we slid into the space.

It had been transformed: a palette, food, a warm fire, coverlets and furs aplenty amidst thick silken pillows.

"Let me look at you," I said to him, running my hands over his face. I needed to remember him this way, to burn the moment into my memory. The swelling around his cheek and eye were still terrible, and I wondered if I was capable of—

"Don't even think on it." He grabbed my fingers and kissed them. "You nearly turned to ash on my account today once already."

Carioz. Still a glimmer.

"It must hurt."

"I always hurt."

I was still trembling, my heart and chest stinging with the knowledge of impending separation.

"Then we should sit," I said, gesturing to the mountain of soft pillows behind us.

"You will have to thank your mother for arranging this," Gawain said as I helped him down, and I realized—of course—he would be unaware of the circumstances. I had not considered telling him who I had spoken with before, but I had also not realized my mother was complicit. "I would have tried to find you on my own if she had not."

I sat facing Gawain, my legs over his, pulled close so we were nearly nose to nose.

"She had help," I said, not knowing how much to tell Gawain just yet. His mother and aunts knew him better than he thought, and I felt their protection around us still. "Thank you. For turning the tide."

Gawain gave me that puzzled, lovestruck look that always cut through me, knowing that he knew me, *felt* me, and saw me. "I did not falter, even when I thought I would. Arthur was here, but not for me. For the *graal*. But you, and your freedom, are more precious than a thousand *graals*."

"And your freedom?"

He leaned his forehead on mine. "I lived my life free until now. Perhaps it is my penance."

"You sound like Lanceloch du Lac," I teased, and he covered my mouth with a kiss before I could continue.

Ah, to feel his lips against mine, the press of his beard on my skin. I could live my whole life in our pleasure, and yet…

"Gawain," I pulled away.

"My love?"

"Tonight, I want only your arms around me, your voice in my ear, and your heartbeat beneath my hands."

He smiled. "It is my honor."

Now, it was his eyes that filled with tears. Not of rejection, or anger, but of understanding. Our *carioz* sang between us, painful and knowing and strong.

I desired him; I always desired him. But in this final night, before we would be parted forever, it was the comfort of our *carioz* that I desired alone. Then, perhaps, I would have the strength to watch him go, to be the princess that was expected, and to start to build a life for myself again in freedom.

"I won't give up," I said to him. "I will find a way back to you."

"I will never leave you, so you will never be lost."

Gawain pulled me close, and we sat together, talking late into the night, until traitorous time took him away.

CHAPTER SIXTY-FOUR

GAWAIN

AND SO, HWYFAR and I were parted, casualties of politics and family duty.

Carelon changed little upon my return, but it felt different. My own quarters seemed dull in comparison to the opulence of Lyndesoires and the wildness of Avillion, and no sooner had I arrived than my mother descended to discuss potential matches, detailing their various virtues and lands and pedigrees.

Loholt was invited to court, and Arthur was besotted with his performances in the joust. Lugh's Tournament would be soon, and I was hoping to be settled in somewhere by that time. I wanted to be spared the embarrassment of sitting in the stands while other men my age still competed. The longer I lived away from Hwyfar, the more pain I felt in my body, the more I was reminded of what little I could still do.

Though I asked, no letters arrived from Hwyfar. My aunt Morgen assured me she was safe and being looked after, that the rebuilding of Avillion would take time, and that I was better off focusing on my new life.

Each day, hope dwindled.

A few nights I lost myself to drink and darkness. Palomydes was not there to help me, as he was now at court in Lyonesse. When I looked for Gareth, I found he had gone to stay with Bedevere. Gaheris remained with Lanceloch at the Joyous Guard for the spring. I visited Gweyn's grave more often than I should, and spoke to her of her sister, and began to wonder if I had dreamed my adventures. Yet, whenever I was closest to that precipice of despair, I would feel a distant whisper of *carioz* and fight on another day, even when my knee hurt more than it had in years.

On the first of May, I was at last informed my marriage contract was done. Legally, the scrolls were signed: I was married by law to a woman named Dame Angharad Ragnell. She was the daughter of the elder Lady Ragnell, a prominent noble in the north, who owned a significant castle keep by Inglewood Forest. As for my wife, I was informed that she was a quiet woman who had no real interest in marriage whatsoever and had hoped for a life of spinsterhood. However, her scheming mother hoped at least for a suitable political alliance, if not children.

"You will have free rein to hunt, ride, and do whatever you like," my mother said to me, as I set out two weeks later. Arthur had not come to say farewell; since I had returned to Carelon, he had scarcely visited me at all, though the tales of my quest and adventures had spread so far and wide I could barely leave my apartments without hearing them.

And just as well. I had seen Arthur the man, Arthur the king, and Arthur the politician. But I had also challenged him, and he did not take kindly to such behavior. I could still love him. But I would never trust him. In a small way, I looked forward to leaving Carelon for a new life, even if it meant my retirement from court and the field. Life after Hwyfar was empty, anyway.

I took a small group with me up to Inglewood, mostly tradespeople and new knights, and was glad to see the land well maintained. The forest itself was nothing like Brocéliande, but denser and full of low-growing clusters of alder and hawthorn. Early spring violets carpeted the ground, and as we approached the road to the keep itself, called Thistlewood, clusters of daffodils trembled in the wind to welcome us.

Loath as I was to admit it, I could enjoy it here. Providing the Ragnell family was, as my mother insisted, an insular sort, I would keep my strength up in the woods and, if time permitted, find a way to get letters to Hwyfar, at least. I had to start somewhere. I could *feel her* all the time, an ache that never left me.

Though, in the back of my mind, the worry persisted that we would never find our way to each other. In that case, I resolved myself to being a good husband, as good as I could be, even if I could never love anyone in the way I loved Hwyfar. Because she, at least, was free. I had lived a lifetime without concern—now she could choose her path.

Thistlewood rose above us, a quaint keep covered in ivy, built in the style of the Joyous Guard: a large tower surrounded by a lower bailey, and a main house in the center. There was an orchard, an herb garden, even an archery field. I heard sheep in the distance, bells clanging. It smelled of fresh earth and sweet grass.

A shrunken old man met me at the door to the manor, and I dismissed my groom to tend to the horses.

Inside, the house was dark, but clean. It smelled old, though, like no one had been inside for a long time. I thought I caught a hint of rosemary on the air.

The old man took me through a narrow corridor to a wooden sitting room, beams almost black with age, the walls stained with ages of smoke, and hung with dingy tapestries. I was glad for the sturdy bench he gave me, and the hot spiced drink, a local specialty, plus a small nob of cheese.

I could hear movement throughout the house, creaking floorboards, and the occasional skittering. Crows outside the window chased one another.

No matter what this woman was like, I would be a friend, first. I could give her at least that. She would not want for food, or attention. I had plenty of money, what with my fortune from Orkney—to say nothing of my castle and servants, should I ever decide to take her there—so she could live in comfort. If she needed an education, I could give that to her as well. Perhaps she had a desire to get into the merchant trade or write poetry.

I had no idea. She could even have a lover. I could live with such a thing. They could even have a child, and I would claim them as my own.

I looked down into the clay cup in my hand, at the swirl of oil from the herbs. I could taste cloves, rosemary, and a bit of honey. It reminded me, painfully, of the honey of Avillion. The taste of it on Hwyfar's lips. The taste of her skin, the sounds of her pleasure... Gods, I would never stop aching for her, and part of me hoped I never would.

Sighing, I put down my cup and waited, staring into the fire.

A moment later, two robed figures appeared at the door. One was stooped, the other taller, but with a shock of grey hair. I stood, nearly hitting my head on the beams as I did so.

"My lady," I said, bowing. "I have come from Carelon. Gawain, of Orkney. Your husband."

I presumed the bent figure was my wife, and I gave her no judgement. But then, I realized, she was just doing so to walk through the doorway. For this place, like so many, was built for smaller folk than she.

For it was Hwyfar, princess of Avillion, and her mother, Queen Tregerna of Lyonesse.

CHAPTER SIXTY-FIVE

HWYFAR

I RUSHED INTO Gawain's arms, and he held me, kissed me, held me again. There were no words but tears, no sounds but sobbing and laughter, my mother joining in and handing us both kerchiefs, as the crows and wrens argued outside Thistlewood, and the fire popped merrily. I had never cried so many tears of joy, and never had felt such a sense of relief.

He had made the trip; we had managed the ruse. I had been holding my breath for weeks in hopes it would work, not risking communication with him for fear that Arthur's spies would intercept or interpret any possible messages.

My mother had brought the plan to me the night after Gawain left.

"My mother's people lived here," she'd explained. "And this is my land. I am Dame Ragnell. Well, I have the papers. And very good scribes. And I do own the land. Arthur may be keen enough to be rid of Gawain, especially after what he pulled in front of everyone, that with enough of a dowry—which of course we have—and a good story, far enough from Carelon, ours may be the most impressive proposal…"

And I suspect Tregerna had had words with Anna Pendragon and Morgen le Fay. I cannot say for certain. But like Anna, I am getting familiar with feeling disturbances on the filaments of the Path, the great web that connects us. I do not think that

Anna wished to be on the wrong side of Lyonesse, its magic, and the key to keeping Ys at bay—and unlocking the power within. And I had saved her son. Inadvertently, Gawain had left Arthur's exacting eye by giving me my freedom.

Breathlessly, we explained the story to Gawain. He had to sit down a few times. I noticed traces of grey in his hair that had not been there before, and how he hissed when he moved just so. I could never cure him of his pain, but I could help him—together, we could build him a life that suited him better.

"I must be in a dream," he said, holding my hands, looking up at me from the bench by the window.

"Dreams do not have briars stuck to the hems of their gowns," I said, gesturing to mine.

"Hwyfar, you are free," he said.

"Yes," I agreed. "I was free to make my own choice."

"But your work—you need to train with Modrun, and there is Lyonesse…"

"I can live in both places." I smoothed Gawain's hair, already grown past his ears. I longed to pull upon those curls soon. "I know the Path, remember? I am a daughter of Lyonesse, not just her heir."

I felt the threads of our *carioz* healing, winding together, tightening. This land, this bond, this promise; we would begin anew, and become more than we had ever considered.

"And you choose this?" He was trying so hard not to fall apart, his giant shoulders shaking. "You choose me?"

"Again and again and again," I said. "Until my last breath."

EPILOGUE

HWYFAR

A YEAR TO the day after we freed the Green Knight, we found our way to the Green Chapel, together. An oath to an ancient god was no small thing, and I felt full of both joy and a kind of sublime awe as we approached.

The journey was long, but the way was not so treacherous this time. We had expected more trials and tribulations, and had come prepared, but instead spent most of the journey discussing changes to Thistlewood we planned for the spring and reveling in lovemaking under the stars.

The Green Chapel was massive, built not of brick but ancient, petrified vines. This late in winter, the great sweeping lines of the building were glazed in ice. The arches were covered in crystalline winter flowers, and the Green Knight stood at the stoop, beside Modrun, Yvain, and his lion. They all wore green robes—the lion's mane was tied with silk ribbons—and beckoned us within.

"We have prepared a feast for you," said the Green Knight, their voice emanating from the very earth itself.

Gawain looked at me, and we both bowed, falling to our knees before the Green Knight, in recognition of their power, and in gratitude.

"We are honored," I said, gazing up at the beautiful scene before us. Snowflakes fell, each one downy and lazily swirling down to meet us.

Modrun came to me, helping me stand before embracing me. She gazed adoringly at Gawain, who gave her a guileless smile.

"You are all so beautifully attired," Gawain noticed, Melic the lion nuzzling his arm. "What is the occasion?"

The Green Knight laughed and said, "Why, the marriage of Sir Gawain and Lady Hwyfar, of course."

ACKNOWLEDGEMENTS

WHEN HWYFAR OF Avillion burst into her first scene in *Queen of None*, I knew immediately I needed to tell her story. Like a goddess of old, she stretched every passage she was in to its limits, insisting there was much more work on my behalf.

I couldn't make her simply a libertine; I could not walk away with merely Anna Pendragon's rather haughty—and admittedly curious—impressions of her. But nor did I want to compromise Hwyfar's rebellious nature, her sensuality, and her cleverness. She, as many women in similar situations throughout history, had very little agency, but unlike Anna, she did not hide in shadows: she cast a long one. As she says to Gawain: "I built my own legend." Yet for all her bluster, her fury, and her power, Hwyfar's tale is one of moving beyond trauma, to embrace vulnerability, and to let down one's guard long enough to allow love in.

When initially imagining this story, however, I did not set out to write a dual point of view novel. When Gawain and his knights arrive at Withiel, everything changed. My big red oaf of an Orkney, dim-witted as he may be, shoved his way into the narrative with his beard and his belly and his missing tooth, and showed me how much he'd grown in the ensuing years between *Queen of None* and *Queen of Fury*. I never meant Anna to be a fully reliable narrator, but through his eyes I saw just how much she missed about her own son: his own trauma, his pain, his struggles, and his capacity for love and goodness. For patriarchy and toxic chivalry does not just break women, but men, too. And it's a rare man who chooses to use his power to fight against that lumbering monster of progress and politics, even when it wears the face of those you love.

Theirs remains one of the most profound love stories I've ever written, and one that will stay with me as long as I live. But it also opened up Arthur's realm far beyond the walls of Carelon and set the stage for the next chapter. It's a bridge between the small world of Anna Pendragon and the immense world of Morgen le Fay.

To every woman who was underestimated because of her reputation: may you find your fury, your joy, and your peace.

To every man who felt he could not measure up to society's standards: may you find the strength, wisdom, and courage to make your own way.

To my husband, Michael, whose heart, gentleness, and kindness are reflected in Gawain's best moments.

To my dear Jennifer for walks in the woods, adventures in culinary lore, mutual love of tea and food, and a bond that defies words.

To E.J. Dawson, who read and critiqued this book and made it what it is today. Her encouragement made all the difference, especially when it seemed as if the story might never come to publication.

To my parents, who gave me a garden of art and music to grow up in where every story I've ever written began.

To my late Aunt Corinne, who sent me a volume of the tales of King Arthur and started this whole adventure.

To my sister, Llana, and our adventures in crystal hunting and making magic.

To all my writing buds, but in particular Paul Jessup and Jonathan Wood.

To Dino Hicks, official Knight.

To my in-laws, Mike and Caroline, who have brought us to the beach every year since I've been a part of this family. Much of this book was written in a little chair in the living room of the last rental we outgrew, the sounds of the ocean a constant counterpoint.

To David Thomas Moore and the whole editorial team at Solaris, who took on this adventure.

To my agent, Stacey Graham at 3 Seas Literary, for all the things.

To the Swedish folk band Garmarna: thank you for giving Hwyfar a voice in music. Those 1,000+ plays from the US during 2022 were all me.

And for anyone who has ever looked Fate in the face and said "No."

Natania Barron

ABOUT THE AUTHOR

Natania Barron is an award-winning fantasy author long preoccupied with mythology, monsters, and magic. Her often historically-inspired novels are filled with lush description and vibrant characters. Publications include her 2011 debut, *Pilgrim of the Sky*, as well as *These Marvelous Beasts*, a collection of novellas.

In 2020, Barron's *Queen of None* was hailed as "a captivating look at the intriguing figures in King Arthur's golden realm" by *Kirkus*, and won the Manly Wade Wellman award the following year.

Her shorter works have appeared in *Weird Tales*, EscapePod, and various anthologies, RPG, and game settings. In addition, she's also known for #ThreadTalk, which dives deep into the unseen, and often forgotten, world of fashion history.

Barron lives in North Carolina, USA, with her family and two dogs. When she's not writing, you can find her wandering the woods, tending her garden, and collecting rocks.

🐦 @nataniabarron
📷 @nataniabarron
♪ @nataniabooks
🌐 www.nataniabarron.com

FIND US ONLINE!

www.rebellionpublishing.com

/solarisbooks /solarisbks /solarisbooks

SIGN UP TO OUR NEWSLETTER!

rebellionpublishing.com/newsletter

YOUR REVIEWS MATTER!

Enjoy this book? Got something to say?

Leave a review on Amazon, GoodReads or with your
favourite bookseller and let the world know!